NOT ENOUGH FOREVER

A Novel By

Kathleen Haun

aventine press

Published by Aventine Press
55 East Emerson St.
Chula Vista CA 91911
www.aventinepress.com

ISBN: 978-1-955162-23-4

Library of Congress Control Number: 2023908055
Library of Congress Cataloging-in-Publication Data
Not Enough Forever / Kathleen Haun

NOTE TO THE READER

In this day and age, Google is a friend to a writer who includes historical references. One can ask odd questions like, "What does 'pinking a seam' mean?", or search for more information about a person, place or event mentioned in the book.

Because of this, I have sometimes not gone into quite as much detailed explanation as I have in my previous novels. *Sometimes* being the operative word here.

Friends may tease me that I live in the 1800's, but I very decidedly appreciate writing in the modern age of today.

Kathleen Haun, 2023

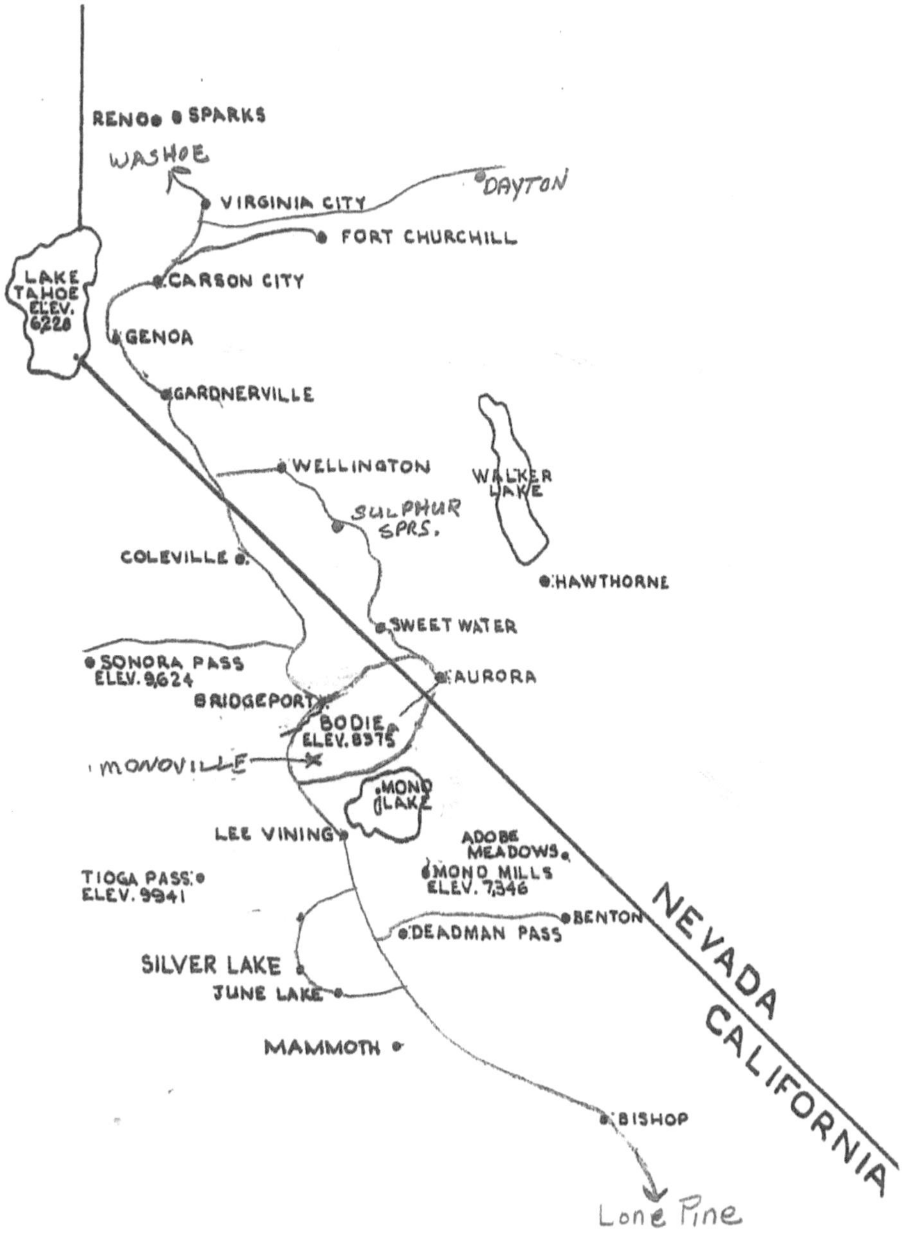
RENO
SPARKS
WASHOE
VIRGINIA CITY
DAYTON
FORT CHURCHILL
LAKE TAHOE ELEV. 6228
CARSON CITY
GENOA
GARDNERVILLE
WELLINGTON
WALKER LAKE
SULPHUR SPRS.
COLEVILLE
HAWTHORNE
SWEET WATER
SONORA PASS ELEV. 9,624
AURORA
BRIDGEPORT
BODIE ELEV. 8375
MONOVILLE
MONO LAKE
LEE VINING
ADOBE MEADOWS
MONO MILLS ELEV. 7,346
TIOGA PASS ELEV. 9941
BENTON
DEADMAN PASS
NEVADA
CALIFORNIA
SILVER LAKE
JUNE LAKE
MAMMOTH
BISHOP
Lone Pine

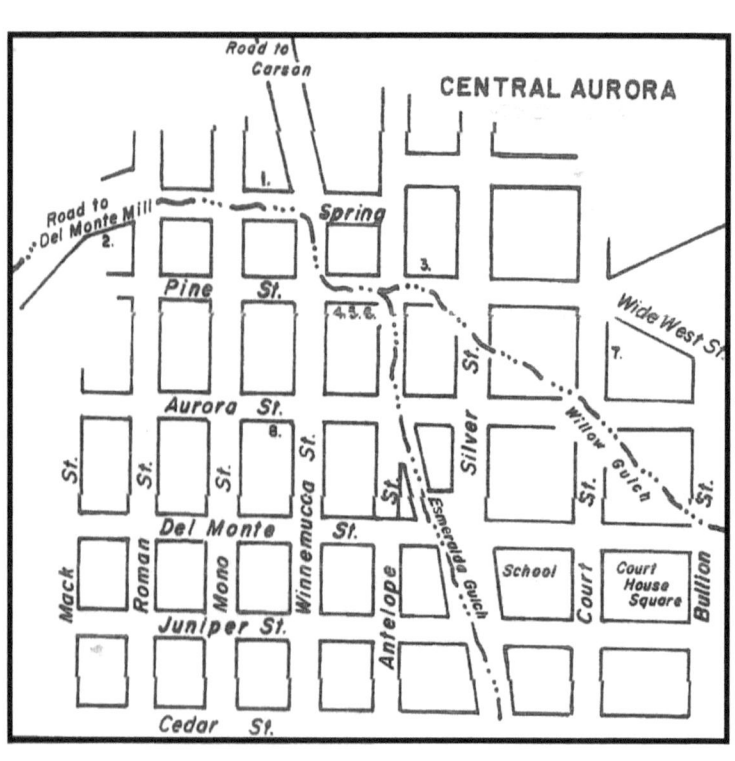

PREFACE

This novel is a work of historical fiction, with an accurate history of real places, events and customs in the 1860's and 1870's. It is filled with people who lived in the Eastern Sierra locations mentioned, along with the addition of fictional characters. The main fictional characters are Dolly, Robert, Jane, Lucy and Roger, all of whom were introduced in *Chasing the Dream, No Trees for Shade, Declining Fortunes*, and most recently in *Digging Deeper*.

People in the 1860's and '70's flocked to towns in the West for a number of reasons. Many wanted to leave behind the Civil War or its aftermath to just "settle down". Others wanted adventure, and to "make their fortune". Toward this end, people frequently moved from place to place. Sometimes they left a town because of rumors of a new discovery that could make their fortune if they were quick enough to get there before it played out. Some people wanted to shed themselves of their past without much caring where they went, as long as it was "far away". In the early mining camps of California and Nevada, this nomadic life was so common as to be considered normal. It is with these adventuresome and ever-hopeful transients in mind that I wrote this book.

Whether referring to a place or a person, "transient" should not be assumed to mean that value was absent. The people and mining camps of California and Nevada contributed mightily to the advancement of both states, as well as playing an important part in the country's history.

Considering the early era in which the action of this book takes place, it might be helpful to keep a few things in mind.

- *Lake Bigler* is now Lake Tahoe.

- *Up the hill* from the Carson Valley refers to the mining towns along Gold Canyon, which included Devil's Gate, American Flats, Silver City, Gold Hill, and Virginia City.
- *Piute* is the spelling used in the 1800's for what is now spelled *Paiute*.
- *Washo* is a tribal name; *Washoe* is the name of a town and a Nevada County.
- *Placers* are those areas where gold can be washed from gravel using rockers, long-toms, sluices and dredges that utilize water and gravity flow. Virginia City mines were *hard rock mines*, meaning they had to be drilled out, blown up using black powder, and developed through shafts and tunnels.
- *Tailings* are the left-over rock brought up from a mine when the ore is removed. It shows up in black and white photos of the era as huge white mounds east of town.
- *The rush* refers to the California gold rush of 1848 through the 1850's.
- A *duster* was a long, light cotton overcoat handed out by stage lines for travelers to wear over their clothing, especially when much of the trip was through dusty areas.
- An *excitement* was a term used to indicate a new gold or silver discovery, usually somewhere else.
- A *whip* was a common name for a talented stage driver, such as Hank Monk.
- A *lead* (pronounced leed) was a vein of gold that could be followed along its length, and could be anywhere from a foot wide to yards wide.
- The *Sanitary Fund* was a Civil War charitable fund to benefit wounded soldiers, a precursor to the Red Cross.
- *Snowshoes* were often what we now call skies, but occasionally also the flat, webbed item.
- *"The war"* was always a reference to the Civil War, also known as the War of Secession.
- *Two bits* = 25 cents. *One bit* = 12 ½ cents, but given in change for a quarter as 10 cents. Saloons were defined as either a "one-bit" or a "two-bit" house, depending on how much they charged for a drink or a cigar; but also denoting its general quality.
- *Parlor house* meant a high-class brothel, run by a madam overseeing a stable of "ladies". It might offer such amenities as meals, drinks, a piano player, and the security of a bouncer. At the lowest end, were

cribs; one or two room cabins housing a single prostitute, and often without a kitchen.

- *Mammoth Mountain* above Mammoth Lakes, California, was at one time called Pumice Mountain.
- A *coyote hole mine* is a shallow exploratory digging.

DEDICATION

This book is dedicated to those who have explored
the Eastern Sierra mining towns of California,
and wondered what it had been like
in the beginning.

CHAPTER 1

Placerville, California
Summer of 1875

What is a widow lady to do when her 17-year-old son runs away from home, leaving behind only a note saying he is going east over the Sierra Nevada to a mining camp called Aurora?

First, she yells at the sofa, picturing her son sitting on it, and then she reads again his note.

Mom: I need to be getting on with my life. You are attached to Placerville, but I want more. I want adventure in my life like you and Dad had in yours. I want to make my mark in the gambling halls of towns at the height of big things. I can deal any card game going, and can easily get hired on in their gambling halls. I'll write you as soon as I get to a town with outgoing mail, trying first Aurora on the border of California and Nevada. I know you will understand.

Your loving son, Roger

Each time Lucy Murphy read the note, she asked herself the same question. "What in the world makes him think I'd understand?" Nevertheless, each time she read Roger's words she was also a little more rational in her reaction. Because she did understand. She was no stranger to the longing for adventure in one's life. At seventeen, she had experienced more of it than most adults.

Lucy didn't doubt that her son could keep coin in his pocket, what with his skill with cards being so well-developed. She certainly wasn't one of those mothers who thought seventeen was still a child, being well-aware that men of that age ran ranches, served as law officers, and worked in mines. Many teenagers had even fought in the Civil War a decade earlier. Boys became men by seventeen, just as girls were often married women with children by that age. No, her primary concern was about the inherent dangers in the areas through which he would be traveling.

Lucy knew it would mean a big change to her life by going after him, since there was no question in her mind about doing just that. A number of things had to be completed first, however, and she was now house-clearing in preparation of her departure. As emotional a process as it was, her inherent honesty kept her from believing the fiction that she would ever return. The closest she came to such a thought was when she put into storage with a friend those things she refused to believe would be lost to her forever, like her precious rocking chair covered in petti point roses. "Someday," she promised herself, "I'll send for these things, even if right now I don't know where I'll be."

That done, she turned her attention to those things to be packed for the trip, including basic clothing, her best jewelry, money, and her derringer. She knew from experience how easily she could hide that on her person. Everything had to fit into saddlebags or be tied behind the saddle, for she was going to ride Diamond all the way. A wagon, or even a light rig, would only slow her down. If necessary to keep on the move, it would be easier to replace a horse than a wagon. It was a hard thought, especially considering how fond she was of this horse, purchased for her as a yearling eleven years earlier by her husband. But she reminded herself that this was no time to allow sentiment to blur her focus.

Besides, after a decade of being called "the widow Murphy", Lucy was ready to move on. She almost guiltily admitted to herself that she was looking forward to getting away from her controversial local reputation. Women were willing to pretend they didn't know that she dealt cards in the back room of a saloon, because one had to do whatever one could to survive. But they couldn't ignore her outspoken opinions on everything from women's suffrage to the idea of women serving on a jury, or the fact that she rode her horse astride. Having to keep silent about what she considered rational views, called silly notions by men and scandalous ideas by women, had given Lucy an unusual perspective as to why her son longed for new and unrestricted experiences.

The most difficult step was leaving her home, purchased with her late husband in 1862. Three years of joyful events had filled that house before Jim had left near the end of the Civil War to join the Nevada Volunteers. These men had assisted emigrants coming from the war-ravaged states as they neared the end of their difficult westward journey along the Humboldt River in what was then Nevada Territory. So many families had been in desperate need of assistance at that point, their supplies and fresh water almost depleted. Some wagon trains had to deal with Indian hostilities in the area, and even groups of white outlaws taking advantage of those families lagging behind.

For a long time after receiving news that Jim was missing and presumed dead, Lucy had held fast to hope. But after receiving word that his whereabouts were still unknown, coupled with the fact that she had not heard from him for months, she had reluctantly accepted that he was dead. She had also accepted entreaties from close friends to wear socially acceptable *widow's weeds*. Her compromise was to wear gray or dark purple dresses. Black would have been too final an admission. She had, however, refused to wear a bonnet with a veil, as was traditional during mourning, declaring that she wanted no filter between herself and the townspeople she knew so well. If she looked distressed or sad, they would just have to deal with it.

She couldn't explain to anyone why she didn't feel like a widow, but only that her husband was "away" somewhere. She assumed such a feeling would go away over time, but it had never changed. She had long ago stopped trying to understand it, just accepting the feeling as part of how she chose to cope with Jim no longer being in her life.

After a full morning of packing the last things to be stored, Lucy decided to take a break. However, still being in clearing-out mode, she sat on the sofa in the parlor with a box of letters on the table in front of her. These could not be put in storage, nor could they be taken with her. The two letters she had received from Jim were the only ones at the bottom of one of her saddlebags. She looked around at the crates of dishes, stacks of bedding, and boxes of books sitting on the few pieces of furniture that would remain with the house. Refusing a sudden urge to brood, she gave herself a mental shake and turned to the box of letters staring up at her as though daring her to read them once again.

Odd, she thought, that reading them would seem challenging now. Maybe it was because she knew to what memories they would lead. At the same time, thinking that maybe it was a good way to accept the past while preparing for the future, Lucy pulled the earliest dated letter from its yellowed, brittle envelope.

It had been thirteen years since she had last seen her best friend, Dolly Robbins, but a steady stream of correspondence had helped bridge the distance and keep alive their close ties. Having been an only child, Lucy had never known the concept of having a sister. Nor had the term *extended family* been ideated as yet. Nevertheless, the meaning of both was deeply felt, even if undefined.

Unlike Lucy's tall, slim outline and dark auburn hair, buxom and blonde Dolly had changed little from the vivacious girl that had been forced into a parlor house in order to survive during the rush. Fortunately, Dolly had caught the eye of the local blacksmith, and after their marriage, they had moved to Placerville. Lucy knew all of this because she had worked as the cook in that parlor house, back when she had been chasing her dreams of a happy life. A few of the letters were from Jane Leon, a woman with whom Lucy and especially Dolly had developed a close association. She had felt pressured to leave Placerville at the end of 1862, as had Dolly and Robert.

Lucy chuckled to think that she was about to get on a horse and follow much of the route her friends had traveled. No stranger to suddenly shifting her circumstances, she figured it had happened at least a dozen times in her 38 years, and always from necessity rather choice. Well, other than the decision to buy this house on Cedar Ravine in Placerville.

She remembered the day they had moved in; *they* being herself and her husband Jim, five-year-old Roger, and Freda. Dear Freda, happily married these last eleven years, after mothering first Lucy and then Roger. It was good that Freda now had a life of her own. Dear, beloved Jim, Lucy sighed to herself. Only when Freda had openly acknowledged Jim's death, had Lucy finally accepted it, mainly because she knew there was nothing short of death that would have kept him from her.

The years after Jim had left had not been easy ones, and she looked back on them now only because Dolly's letters reminded her of them. Money had been the biggest challenge. She had tried working as a cook in two restaurants, had dealt cards in the back room of dear old Goldie's saloon, and had even tutored students. Once, when Roger was twelve and things had gotten particularly difficult, she had been forced to cash in a few of the gold nuggets stashed in a small velvet pouch; a secret legacy left over from Lucy and Jim's adventures before they had married.

Eventually, she had been forced to sell the house and property. The new owner had fortunately not wanted to live there, and had allowed Lucy to rent the house for a very reasonable amount as long as he could stable his horses in the barn, to be cared for by Lucy and Roger. It was the remainder of the money from the sale of the house that would allow her to take this next step. She was determined not to use the last of the gold nuggets in the little velvet pouch.

Trying not to sigh, Lucy looked down at the letter lying on her lap. It was dated in the summer of 1863, although Dolly, Robert and Jane had left Placerville in the fall of 1862. More accurately, the three of them had fled from the town. But rather than digging deeper into that, Lucy put those unsettling events out of her mind.

She had worried at first, not having heard anything from her friends for so long. But heavy winter snows on the Placerville Road across the Sierra always delayed the mail. Besides, she knew her friends would be looking for a place where they could settle, something they might find more difficult than they had anticipated.

Lucy removed the padded cozy from the large, round tea pot on the silver tray before her, poured herself a cup of the hot liquid, and settled back to read again Dolly's first letter. It had been written in cramped handwriting on both sides of the paper, and edge to edge, in order that Dolly might preserve her stock of stationery. The first letter always made Lucy smile, as it was so typical of Dolly to start right in with no sentimental preamble, almost as though keeping a journal instead of writing a letter. It had obviously seen some rugged handling, with the letter having been started immediately upon the trio leaving Placerville, and additions made whenever possible. The smudges of soot and spatters of grease indicated that Dolly had done much of her writing at night by the light of a campfire.

September, 1862: *What a trek is the Placerville Road! It twists like a writhing snake, with us on its back and our covered wagon made to follow its torturous gyrations no matter what. East of Placerville we took the toll road around Peavine Ridge opened just last year, then left the old road at 12 Mile House. We are following the ridge and slopes on the south side of the American River, and will cross over it further east and then keep going the rest of the way on the north side of the river.*

(Later) *We travel either on the right edge of the road with a perilous drop-off to the churning river far below, or pushed up against the side of a mountain wall that towers above. When a lighter wagon or rig comes up behind us going at a greater clip, it just depends on our placement on the road as to which way we move to let it pass, as the drivers are seldom willing to slow down without a lot of violent threats and oaths. We don't have to worry about a long train of mules pulling a heavily loaded freight wagon when heading toward us. We can hear the tinkling of the bells on the animal's collars even when they are still around a bend in the road.*

From the beginning of our journey, we have been caught up in a crush of humanity the likes of which I could never have imagined. At first there were with us only those who had come through Placerville; a flow I was used to seeing that was made up of supply wagons and mule trains. But we now have with us smaller wagons, men on horseback, and a surprising number of those on foot. Much of this comes in from side roads and trails. I crane my neck to see how far down these trails I can see, but it is not very far because of the rise of the road coming up through the trees. Where does Swan's Road, Henry's Road or Sugar Log Flat lead? I will never know, but I will always wonder.

Everyone on the road stops to pay the tolls at a surprising number of stations along the route, even those on foot who are charged two bits to continue. But there is usually good water at these places, and some make available help to repair a wagon or doctor an animal. Still, the tolls are beginning to add up. One man was heard to complain that he was running low on money, but had to go forward because to turn around meant paying the same tolls on the way back.

We passed tiny hamlets with names followed by Flats, House, Junction, Hall, Tavern, or Ranch. Some were identified by a single possessive name such as Moore's, Yarnell's, or Osgood's. Some were little more than a wooden shack, while others like Berry's had corrals and sheds next to a two-story inn with a general eating room downstairs and sleeping cots in the big room upstairs.

We came to Berry's Tavern after traveling about 45 miles, much of it a steep upward grade. Some people are calling the tavern and station "Straw-berry", because of Mr. Berry's reputation for trying to feed teams straw instead of hay, along with his renown as a bit of a bombast.

Some of those traveling on foot look upon our wagon with envy. However, seeing a woman on each side of Robert, they are not antagonistic about it. Some push a wheelbarrow and others pull small carts. One man doing this had rigged a harness for himself, as though he was a mule, and indeed when he tried to pass someone, he brayed similar to a mule. As people laughed, he would grin and laugh with them, but I noticed that they all let him pass.

So much noise! Men seem to enjoy shouting to one another when out of doors, especially teamsters whose animals must absorb their complaints. Sometimes, after walking and talking together for some while, men will form small groups, both for company and for protection. These groups seem to have more spirit, and walk more quickly than those men who are determined to stay aloof and alone.

It is interesting to think that most of those on the road around us are traveling to one singular point on the map; the Comstock mines. Some are not, of course, but I hear little talk of anything other than the wealth each hopes to find in Gold Canyon. One man we invited to share in our night's coffee did scoff at that. Instead, he said he was going to Monoville in California. Another man was carrying seed and planned to farm south of Genoa just the other side of the mountain. Yet another wagon was loaded with general merchandise for a store the man is going to start in Dayton, unless his wagon breaks down somewhere before that. If it does, he plans to sell his wares as well as his wagon and team, and continue on foot, as then he'll not be in such a hurry.

October, 1862: As we continue on, the traffic on the road is of such a congestion that it fair takes my breath away, but possibly that is also from the amount of dust raised by it. Even with the cold nights and a day with light drizzle, there is somehow always dust in the air.

The diversity of those around us is most interesting. There are many freight wagons loaded with mining equipment and food supplies, some bearing such heavy loads that it takes over a dozen mules or horses to move it along. Those on horseback and on foot all carry bundles of provisions, a rifle and no doubt a knife concealed in a boot. Often, they have a shovel or pick slung across their back, especially if they have done some prospecting in the past and are familiar with the exorbitant cost of tools in new mining areas. Long lines of pack mules seem to be with us most of the time, carrying loads of such weight and bulk that my heart goes out to the poor beasts.

Herders push along cattle or sheep that scatter between those traveling on the road. Then, with the help of herd dogs, they bunch together again when there is room for them to do so. Bellows, bleats, brays and neighs echo off the canyon walls along with the shouts, whistles, and imaginative swearing of harassed male voices. This morning we passed a man walking along with a pack on his back while playing a squeeze box and singing at the top of his lungs. It all melded together into a caterwauling that kept us and our horses ever alert.

And yet all of this is nothing compared to how it was two years ago when word came of silver on the Comstock, far more valuable than the pale gold being dug out of mucky blue mud. Evidently, the gold being pale and the blue of the mud should have alerted the prospectors to the presence of silver, but it took some while for them to figure it out.

Even though we three travelers hover this side of our thirtieth birthday, we feel like senior citizens of the road. It is an enthusiastic, energetic youth that moves along with us. There are, of course, a few men starting to show some gray, but if their bodies are a little more limited, their eagerness is no less than the youths that pass by them with a condescending grin. They receive a grin back from those whose years have gained for them a wisdom about mining that these young pups have yet to learn.

We have stopped for the night at a good toll station. It charged us the same as all the others, which for us means 50 cents for horses and a wagon. This does drain our purse of coins, but it also means that the section of road for which we are paying is being maintained. It is especially nice when we are one of the first over the road after it has been dragged or watered. If the road is <u>not</u> in decent condition, the negligent toll keeper may find himself facing a gun by a man refusing to pay.

But know this. Every way-station has been set up with only men in mind. Therefore, we camp nearby among the trees and boulders, but make use of the food supplied in the station that Robert brings out to Jane and me. If there is no station, we eat from our own provisions, and in this way, we do not run out of food. On a more delicate if not practical subject, after once using a privy at such a station, Jane and I now use our chamber pot within the wagon's cover *while guarded by the other one of us. The contents are dumped in pits along the way that have been dug out for this purpose. Robert does it for us so we don't have to discommode the men using the pits directly with their backs to the road.*

This magnificent road was first surveyed and cleared by John Calhoun Johnson of Placerville back in 1852, and I wonder if it will ever become a route more major than it is now. Hard to imagine, but what if it was wider and the roadbed groomed in such a way as to make it less vulnerable to the ruts of rain run-off. For that to happen, of course, it will take a lot of black powder and a lot of men with shovels to widen this particular narrow ribbon of road. But nothing can stop the crush of winter avalanches.

*(**Later**) We decided to turn off south before Hope Valley, first stopping for supplies at Carey's Mills, which has had a post office since 1858. Daniel Woodford, in the area since '49, has an inn and way station here. Some think the area should be called Woodford's, since Mr. Woodford provided a remount station for the Pony Express, the riders coming in by way of Echo Summit and along the eastern edge of Lake Bigler. Robert says that there are suggestions abounding for a name change of the lake, since former California Governor John Bigler is a secessionist with strong Confederate ties. Dr. Henry DeGroot of the U.S. Dept. of the Interior said last year that it should be called "Tahoe", which is a Washo name for "water in a high place". Of course, others have offered up names, so it will be interesting to see if any of them become permanent.*

I am glad that we have sufficient supplies as we head south to Markleeville, as the rumors of it are unclear. But I have learned that if I can't be certain of what we will have in the future, I do know what we have right now, and can therefore feel thankful today.

I had the most interesting conversation with Jane the other day while Robert had a beer at a tavern. As I watched him walk away, I realized that she was watching me. "Jane?"

"I was just thinking about how much you adore Robert. But you love others, too."

"Of course, I do. Like you and Lucy."

"But that's different." Of course, she was right, but she had something more specific in mind. "With our female friends there's an element of trust."

"I trust Robert!"

"But not like you trust Lucy." When I nodded reluctantly, Jane smiled kindly. "I think men fear close female friendships. That's why they so often

ridicule them, or try to characterize them as something not nice. They sense that they can't compete with two people who understand one another to a depth and degree they can't begin to grasp." I couldn't argue with her, and when I told Robert about our conversation later to see his reaction, I was surprised that he didn't argue the point.

The fall colors surround us as the nights turn crisp. The road to Markleeville, which was carved out by the men from Murphy's Diggins, was about as basic as a road can be. Then, at a toll bridge that crossed the Carson River, we entered tiny Markleeville, founded only last year by Jacob Marklee. He thought he could take advantage of the traffic from the silver mining at Silver Mountain City, up on what some call the Ebbetts Pass area. He recorded a land claim of 160 acres in Douglas County, Nevada Territory, not realizing his land was in California. We were told that he is a man of quick temper, and we saw this in our short stay. But he was accommodating, and Robert thought him generous. We stayed only long enough to buy rice and beans while listening to him several times declaring that he was expecting a post office there sometime in the next year, which is a great sign of progress for any village.

After departing, we traveled through forests and meadows, on what had originally been Indian hunting trails following animal migration routes. Only a few wagons have traveled it before us, I think, although there is a mine working north of the road that supplies copper sulfate to the Comstock for the processing of silver. The road carried us southeast through the lower hills of the Sierra, past a marshy area, around rocky outcroppings and past a few cliff walls crumbling onto the narrow road. Most of the way, we were traveling at the bottom of a trough of hills that rose on either side of us.

It was sometimes a steep but short pull up, and a long gradual descent past that. But always the road was narrow in those spots where we wondered what we would do if we encountered a large freight wagon. Fortunately, the one time that did occur, it was at a point where we could pull over onto a level strip of land. The freighters passed silently and we too remained quiet, all in an effort not to spook our horses or their mules. The roadbed switched between hard and rocky, to soft with sand.

It was that last that almost did us in. At one point our back right wheel suddenly sunk into a pit of sand, causing the whole wagon to stop. Although we stared somewhat stupidly at it for several minutes, not surprisingly it did not budge. We had a good laugh at ourselves and Robert got out his shovel, pulling *out much of the sand forward of the wheel. He then lay a piece of canvas along the slope, tucking it under the wheel as much as he could. With Jane pulling on the halter of the lead horse, and Robert and I with our shoulders to the back of the wagon, it pulled forward just enough to be free of the hole. We rested but a moment before proceeding, being a lot more mindful of the terrain. When it looked like there could be spots much the same, I would drive the wagon while Robert walked ahead with a stout stick to test the ground. In this way we avoided a repeat of this incidence, but travel was tense and slow going.*

We stopped for a long rest in a grassy area, where the horses could graze and drink from a small stream. It was so pleasant that we were sorry to leave, not knowing what lay ahead of us and the uncertainty wearing on our nerves. After a night of rest, we continued our journey on numerous downhill sections around huge boulders, finally coming out on a well-traveled road leading to the California towns to the south.

Lucy stopped to consider, based on all that she now knew. If they had gone north to Nevada, how differently might their lives have turned out? How much stress and travail would have been avoided? On the other hand, maybe the challenges that followed had helped to mature them into the people of character they became.

We eventually followed a rushing, boulder-strewn flow of water through a pass that Lt. Walker once traveled. It was an incredibly beautiful area, with rock walls on either side of the canyon trail, and with dense forest beyond. It led us to a large hot spring on what is becoming a major freighting route. It is not far from what someone told us was under construction as the Sonora and Mono Wagon Road over the Sierra. It has always been just a steep and winding trail best for pack animals, even if occasionally a wagon would manage to get over it.

The improved road was started last year and will allow for travel between Sonora in Tuolumne County on the western side of the Sierra to the mining towns of the Eastern Sierra, except when the first snows close it for the winter. It will follow the course of the Stanislaus River beginning about 30 miles east of Sonora where a stage station will be developed, and it will pass along the ridges on the south side of the Stanislaus until it reaches the high, sweeping meadows where a prospector named Frank Pickel is now raising cattle. There, it will cross over the river and follow a small tributary to the crest of the Sierra, where the road will drop steeply down the eastern scarp to Leavitt Meadows where Hiram Leavitt is setting up a station. From there the road will more easily travel through meadows and low ridges to the point where we camped at the hot springs. This is how it was described to us by the station keeper, Sam Fales, who charged us a reasonable toll for continuing, and nothing for one of the best cups of coffee I had tasted in weeks.

This connection between the southern California mines on the other side of the mountain, the Eastern Sierra mines, and those of Nevada Territory, should be of great benefit for many. But with so few routes over the Sierra, I fear it will always be a challenge for freighters. Some people half-jokingly say that there may someday be a major route from Southern California that will travel north and south all along the eastern half of the state, possibly utilizing the Cajon Pass far south in Indian territory, and coming up through a narrow but deep valley between the Sierra and Inyo ranges. Somewhere in that valley, it is said there spreads an ancient lake. But that is the territory of the Piute and Shoshone, and there is some fighting between them and the few settlers coming into that region, so such a route seems doubtful.

The water at the hot spring was boiling, with a cool, running stream nearby. We were told that Fremont had passed through this area back in 1844, although then it had been just an Indian trail. The state of the wagon road seems in places not much more than that now, but most of it caused us no problem. We camped at the hot springs overnight and well into the morning, pushing on south until we reached a small hamlet called Big Meadows.

This inviting place is normally composed of acre upon acre of long green grass cut by dozens of meandering streams, and filled with grazing cattle. But at this time of year, it has turned a rich, golden brown, and only a few cattle are present. We learned later that the majority had been herded to a range in Nevada Territory free of the deep snow that this region will soon be seeing. The mornings are already frosty, with a daytime invigorating chill even in the sun.

What little of a town there is, resides on the eastern side of the Walker River, which I now realize must have been the rushing body of water we followed part of the way here. Surrounded by the curve of low hills in the distance, the area feels much like traveling through a huge bowl left behind by giants. It is in these hills where they have established sawbills. The American Hotel houses the only saloon, and the wood of it already looks old. There is also a blacksmith on the road leading up the river canyon, a butcher shop, and a store being built *by A. F. Bryant, who has a ranch east of the village in a wide, low-lying area. Not surprisingly, the town has an assayer for those stout-of-heart men working nearby placers.*

When we arrived, a number of freight wagons were scattered along the riverbanks, the teamsters resting from their efforts of hauling goods to destinations north and south. Their campfires burned sagebrush, mixing its pungent odor with the smell of frying bacon and the tobacco of pipes and cigars. Lanterns and candles shone through the windows of the few buildings, making us feel welcomed and happy to be once again part of a community, such as it is.

We have set up our camp at what Robert considers a respectful distance from the freighters, but we can still hear their good-natured bickering, bartering of supplies, and ribald jokes that Jane an I pretend not to hear. I long for the freedom that would allow me to laugh with the same abandon that these men take for granted. But just like the freighters, Jane and I wrestled tonight with a pot of beans over a fire wanting to lay down in a wind so strong that it whips the canvas of our wagon.

This little hamlet has been established near a bridge of wood and pounded-earth that allows wagons to cross the river, although to one side of it is a worn path where herds of cattle and other loose stock have often crossed. We have been welcomed by several of the local townsmen, because Robert gave them some good advice about how to help a valuable but sick horse. I especially like George Byron Day who everyone calls "By" Day, and who is currently in business hauling hay at $100 a ton, along with lumber, to the mining camp of Aurora.

We were visited by Mr. Day our first evening, and he described to us this trip he makes while the harvesting weather lasts. It's a day's trip there of about fifteen miles, traveling east where he must cross a high ridge as flat as a table. This leads to the crossing of a difficult and rough creek about thirteen miles slightly northeast of Big Meadows, then up a creek some are calling Bodey Creek, which leads to Esmeralda Gulch. This leads into the town of Aurora, about which Mr. Day talked with great enthusiasm.

Although we have had a few other men visit our camp, we have seen no women, although I assume there must be a few somewhere. But if so, I would have expected them to have welcomed the opportunity to talk to any women passing through.

After the rigors of getting over the mountain, we are happy to be able to rest in this wide, lush meadow and enjoy the company of the friendly folks who live here. I am even happy to share it with grazing cattle and sheep that will feed the townspeople through the winter. There is also present a number of well cared for oxen, used to haul logs to the saw mills.

Several ranches are being built in the surrounding meadows, some growing hay and others more involved with the herds. Some of these ranchers also own sawmills in the hills. But the town portion has little to recommend it at present, although it serves quite well the needs of those here, as well as the freighters passing through.

I watched the blacksmith putting shoes on an ox belonging to one of the freighters who had hauled supplies here from Genoa. Oxen are not willing to lift a leg like a horse, so they use a gallows frame to lift them off the ground while the blacksmith works quickly. The freighter left the next day, hoping to return with one more load before the snows hit the passes over the mountain. This is a crucial decision for these stalwart teamsters, as the wrong decision can lead to disaster. Still, that last trip means not only money for them, but crucial supplies for towns soon to be under deep snow.

Those living here talk constantly about their big plans for the area, and the sound of nails being hammered into new construction begins at dawn. I picked up one of the square nails made here by the blacksmith and put it in my purse for good luck. I hope the town is successful, as I quickly grew fond of these hardy men. It was because of their generosity that we were able to stock the wagon, wash clothes, and most importantly, rest and graze our horses. But after four days of this, we have decided to move further south. Someone told Robert there is still a need for men at Mono City, also called Monoville. This had been our goal, so we were heartened.

<u>October, 1862</u>:: *It is late afternoon, and I have a few minutes to write you. We have stopped about six miles south of Big Meadows at a small mining camp on Brown's Creek, some calling it Dog Creek, the headwaters being up on Dunderberg Mountain. The camp consists of several small cabins and a store. Not much beyond that, and therefore the reason it is called the commonly derogatory name of Dogtown. Most of those who had been prospecting in this area have left for Monoville, but there is a man by the name of Cord Norst still here. He and his friendly Indian wife, Mary, have not lost faith in the area's potential. When they accumulate enough gold dust, they take it to Big Meadows to have it assayed and turned into supplies. Mary told me that some* men are calling the Big Meadows area Bridgeport because of its narrow bridge over the East Walker River.

Also here at Dog Creek, there are a few prospectors who live in tents and rough shacks in what some consider only a temporary camp, along with a white man with a Chinese wife. The small wooden and stone store is run by a kindly French woman and her husband. She seems to have some doctoring ability, as she treated a grease burn on my hand so that the pain disappeared more quickly than I had expected. We paid good money for a small bag of tea and a brick of sugar, and were happy to have it. There are so few things to enjoy while living out of a wagon, but a good pot of tea is one I hold dear. We stayed only one night, and then early the next morning continued our journey south for another eleven miles.

Monoville After a long day spent getting here, we discover that most of the miners have moved on to what they call the "Aurora excitement". We were not surprised when we remembered what Mr. Day had said about that town.

To get here, the horses pulled us up to the top of rolling hills and then loped down the other side, to be faced with yet another uphill climb. From the top of some of the hills we could look down into deep gorges filled with trees turning bright yellow and orange, mixed with some still green. It was a sharp reminder that the whole area is not brown scrub, but that enough water accumulates in these ravines to allow for stands of trees to grow. I imagine there were at one time many more than the two stands we saw, the rest dwindling because of the area's need for timber to build and wood to burn in stoves.

There is not much left of the town of Monoville, other than a large number of deserted buildings. There are also vacant lots where once stood a building, it having been hauled off to Aurora, or dismantled for firewood. However, at its peak only two years ago there were close to forty buildings, and even a two-story hotel. They say twenty-two of the buildings were saloons. But there were also such civilized businesses as butcher shops and a bakery, several laundries, restaurants, a post office, livery and blacksmith, a lawyer who also prospected, and even a doctor's office and a ten-pin bowling alley.

The greatest difficulty for the area at the beginning was the absence of water, since the placers were located in dry gulches amid huge granite boulders. Water was only available in town in the spring after the snow melt, and the rest of the time it had to be hauled in from the river miles away. But never doubt the tenacity of men when it comes to the finding of gold.

They built a 14-mile water ditch from Vaughn's Creek by the river, at a cost of $75,000, with 200 men to do it. They had to whipsaw 40,000 feet of lumber to line the ditch and make a large flume. It only took them four months, but the winter of '60 into '61 sent most of them away to avoid the snows in the area that were as deep as twenty-five feet. The snow in the men's new ditch didn't melt until late July of '61, when the water company began selling the water at twenty-five cents an inch.

To think of all this effort, all the trees cut down for the wood used, and now the area is practically a ghost town after such a short time. They may have ridden here on horses, but they were carried along by waves of faith. Then, when success didn't happen quickly enough, they discovered how thin was that faith. Motivated by rumors of greater wealth in Aurora, most have moved on to that excitement. I have to wonder, how long will they be satisfied there?

So here I sit on a bench outside the last Monoville store while Robert finishes off a well-deserved beer in the saloon across the way. I look around me at what is mostly just a single street of buildings consisting of a store, several saloons, an assay office, and one of the larger hotels of the past now serving as a rough sort of boarding house. The men on the streets are also rough looking, and neither Jane nor I are comfortable here. She in fact is at the other end of the bench reading a book discarded by some man who left it on the bench.

The men who pass by are watching us, as they do whenever we are outside the wagon, and although most seem polite enough, Robert does not like the way some leer at us. I, on the other hand, do not see anything but a wistful kind of appreciation in their eyes. And maybe the fleeting memory of someone once dearly loved now far away, left behind until fortune might smile upon the man walking past us.

(**Later**): At the point of my previous writing, I saw a man go into the assayer's office, and leaving Jane on the bench where she was enjoying her book, I went inside. They seemed exceedingly pleased to have an interested audience, especially a woman who has developed well the artifice of looking at a man with worshipful adoration.

The assayer, a respected man in any mining town, was in this instance old enough to have some gray strands in his short beard. His soft black hat was gray with dust, as is most everything here, and a long canvas apron covered his red shirt. He said he was going to do an acid test on the bit of ore brought in by the miner to check it for silver content.

After grinding the sample down to practically a powder, it was placed in a horn, which in this case was an ox horn cut in half along its length. The lighter particles were then washed out, as they certainly will not contain anything of value. What was left at the bottom was what was described as "sulphurets and other metallic matter". This was then washed from the horn into what they called a matrass, which is a flask made of annealed glass, with a narrow neck and a broad, flat bottom so that it must sit upright.

The assayer then poured in a quantity of nitric acid, covering what still looked like grains of rock. He then held the flask over a small lamp's flame until it began to boil. At this point sharp fumes escaped that were at first red in color, but then turned white. After the contents had cooled and settled, the liquid in the bottom was poured into a vial of clear glass and a few drops of salt solution added. The contents of the glass tube at once assumed a milky hue, beginning at the top and then gradually descending to the bottom of the vial. The milky matter formed was rather thick and clung together in little strands. This white material is chloride of silver.

The assayer held the tube up to the sunlight coming in the window for several minutes, and the chloride took on a rich purple color that was beautiful to behold. The two men grinned, and the miner yelped with joy. I told the man congratulations, assuming that his sample must have contained the silver for which he had been hoping.

But the assayer was not done. The thick liquid was placed in a small hole dug out of a piece of charcoal. He then took the flame of a candle and gently blew this over the thick solution in the hole until it was smelted, and thus produced a little button of pure silver. The miner yelped even louder upon seeing this, as it was proof of what was in his claim. Having shared this moment of joy, I can finally understand some of what these men experience, as watching all of this was as captivating as any stage show I have ever seen. And I now know why they refer to a new area of discovery as "the next excitement".

November, 1862: As we sat around our campfire last night, an older man was invited to join us. Robert had met him earlier that day in the saloon and had thought he would be an interesting guest for Jane and me. Mr. Machin was elected to the California State Assembly from Mono last year, and has a law practice here. He says his hobby is observing human nature, and as a consequence he has many a tale to tell about this small remnant camp, mostly *from its beginning in '59. He says the last year has "coughed up nary an excitement". However, as he tells it, there was once as many as 1,000 men here, whereas now there are only about 150. Many left after the deep snow on May 25, tired of the cold and wind, and lured away by tales of rich finds in Aurora. Besides, the post office had closed in April.*

Mr. Machin has a wonderful sense of humor, and laughed when telling us of a time when he and some friends were prospecting in the Owens River Valley. They were robbed by Indians. The Indians were not interested in harming them, simply taking their guns and horses so that they had to walk all the way back to Monoville. He said it was a great adventure, and his wistful smile gave evidence of that.

He had given Jane several curious looks before asking her if she was a single lady. She informed him that she was a widow, and his interest sharpened. She is after all an attractive woman with her dark hair and nice figure, even with her normally wary expression that can harden in a flash. Which it did at that moment.

He turned away from Jane, it being obvious that her guard was up, and launched into more about the camp. I asked about the presence of women. He told us that for most of its existence, it had "three females" permanently living there. "First, there was a colored lady from Visalia who did cooking, sewing and other types of things miners didn't have time or inclination to do. She's greatly missed. One man's wife was here for a short while before she went off with another man. But she decided to leave him behind before winter set in, and in the spring of '61, to everyone's amusement, she returned to her original Monoville husband."

When he finished a hearty laugh, Mr. Machin continued. "Until recently, we had here a gal named Kit Carson. She's the daughter of the famous explorer, and her real name is Adaline Carson. She came to California with her father, along with her new husband, a fur trapper named Louis Simmons. When he deserted her, she married George Stiles, I think the name was. She left Monoville back in '60, and there were rumors of her demise, but I recently saw her in Aurora. Then there was Cherokee Liz, a 300-pound woman of quick temper and masculine vocabulary." He glanced at Robert and winked, then said nothing more about this lady.

"Returning to the subject of the Owens River Valley," Robert told him, "a man at one of the stops we made said there's some heavy fighting going on there between the Piutes and the settlers."

"Oh, yes. But winter is coming, and that means the Indians will settle down. The Indian agents will give them food and blankets, and suggest they go onto a reservation and become farmers. Of course, the Piutes think anyone who suggests such a thing are either afraid of them or just stupid. The Piute men are hunters, and their women harvest. That's why they got so upset when cattlemen and miners started coming into the area. Thinking of themselves as fine warriors, though, they decided to object. On the other hand, when the Army comes to stop the fighting, the Piutes will head for the hills. Soldiers might be willing to die in battle, but the Indians aren't. Of course, when spring comes, they'll start fighting again. The settlers are pretty fed up with what they consider this winter coddling of the enemy."

"What do you think will happen, then?"

"Well, if the Indians could organize all their individual bands into one big unit, they'd probably win. But they don't know how to do that, so eventually they'll have to make treaties and learn to stick to 'em. Either that, or they'll be wiped out."

I didn't like the cavalier shrug he made at that point, so I made the comment that it was hard to imagine those first wagons back in the '50's getting over the Sierra to continue west. I was thinking about how difficult it was even now on the Placerville Road that we had traveled. He told us how he had come here over the Sierra on foot with pack mules, following the Sonora Pass trail, the one that ends near the hot springs where we had rested.

Mr. Machin said he had seen some signs of wagons having followed that route years before, and had marveled at the idea that wagons had ever attempted to cross there. He said these desperate travelers had been forced to get their wagons up and down steep escarpments using ropes with block and tackle anchored to trees or strung around boulders. He saw the scars of rope cuts in some of the largest pine trees. But he also saw the skeletons of oxen and horses, and the weathered remains of several wagons.

His face gave nothing away of his feelings, but his voice was low and strained. "It's still a route so difficult that if left too late in the year, even pack trains can get lost in the white-out of a sudden snow storm. A friend of mine experienced that just last year. With the snow so deep, his mules hadn't been able to eat any of the vegetation, so he fed them flapjacks. When he ran out of supplies, both he and the mules ate the boiled leather of harnesses. The mules had started in on the tails of their fellows just before he was able to get them down the mountain."

I shuddered at the thought of such hardship and suffering, and really didn't want to hear more. I was relieved when we were joined at our fire by Billy Milliken, one of the first to arrive in Monoville. He has a two-story building, part saloon and gambling hall, with a lodging house upstairs.

"Yep, this has been a grand place," our new friend proudly exclaimed. "With a chop stand inside, during the peak of the prospecting, I collected so much gold dust from customers in payment that I had to keep a barrel under the counter to hold it." He shook his head and managed a crooked smile. "A small strongbox is sufficient now." He shook his head again, without the hint of a smile. "But I feel a bit safer, too. Back at the peak, I was always armed with a pistol, a knife, and sometimes a shotgun nearby. A sidearm and a good throwing knife is enough now."

When Jane squeaked with alarm, Mr. Milliken looked at her kindly. "It's the way of these wild places, ma'am. Dick Vining and his friends were real handy with a gun. Another was Tat Tatman who hailed from Missouri and had represented Mariposa County, on the other side of the mountain, in the Assembly of 1857. He was a big guy, and was known for juggling a 16-inch bowie knife with ease."

He heard me mumble to Robert, "Interesting people here."

Mr. Milliken nodded, having evidently missed my note of sarcasm. "Yes, ma'am! Why, we even had Josh Talbot here for a while. He'd served as an officer in the Navy, and had been an officer in the Mexican Army when they subdued the natives of Yucatan. He even fitted out an expedition to explore and prospect along the Amazon River." He paused to take a swig of something from a silver flask he produced from a pocket of his coat, putting it back without offering it to either of the other men. "What a great talker ole Josh was! He was a writer, too, and after the summer of '59, he went to Genoa and worked on the Territorial Enterprise *newspaper there."*

Mr. Machin nodded. "The writer Dan DeQuille came to the camp back in '59, too. He was gathering up stories that he's published in that paper. He now works in Virginia City. But like so many who moved on, they just missed the big excitement of '60. Men came in by way of Keysville and the South Fork of the Kern River, some with cattle and hogs to sell here. Teamsters from Visalia brought in loads of flour, bacon, beans, rice, tools, whisky, stoves and cigars. One guy came from Keysville by way of the Owens River in thirteen days. He made the trip several times, so we could put in orders for things we needed."

He looked off into the distance and seemed quite happy with whatever memory he was recalling.

I noticed that Robert was very quiet as the men talked about the rough element they had known, not as eager to hear more of their exploits as I was. It was a mild observation on my part, and I meant to ask him about it later. For some reason that I cannot explain, I still have not.

Mr. Machin looked suddenly somber as he continued. "The winter of '59 was a bad one. It started snowing in the middle of November and soon there was five feet of snow covering everything." He suddenly looked sad. "A friend of mine, William Bodey, froze to death that winter. He made it not far away to the southeast. They named a creek after him. At the same time, a couple of men left Monoville for supplies at Genoa in Nevada Territory, 90 miles to the northwest, and actually made it back with food roped down on sleds. It was all that saved our lives that winter. When it arrived, some of us were beginning to ponder what the Donner Party had been forced to do to survive."

No explanation of this event was necessary, as everyone had read about it in the newspapers or been told about it. I thought of the barren hills around us, with few trees and only seasonal streams, nor even an artesian spring, and yet a view of a huge body of undrinkable water at the vast Mono Lake just down the hill. What water Monoville had available was still brought in by way of the flume built earlier, or hauled by wagons up from the creeks flowing into the lake.

Jane suddenly retired to the wagon. I remained by the fire, huddled by Robert's side with a single blanket around us as the night air settled in. We offered our two visitors the last of the coffee in the pot and Robert brought up something he had heard someone mention. We were given the full story, and it made me wish I too had retired to the wagon.

A man simply referred to as Farnsworth rode into Monoville with a mark on the leggings portion of his tall boot where a bullet had grazed him. He said he and his prospecting partner had been set upon by Indians, and his partner, Mr. Hume, had been killed. Sure enough, a party of miners came into camp shortly after and said they had found the body of a man, on an island at the Owens River crossing and had buried his remains. All, that is, except his head, which was missing.

"Now," Mr. Milliken said, "everyone found this odd, since the Indians in that area have always been peaceable. Lee Vining pointed out that the area of

Farnsworth's leggings, where the bullet had grazed him, showed powder burns. This meant he had been shot at very close range, or had done it himself."

Farnsworth was put under guard and a group of nine men from the town went out to the area where all this had taken place. They went to an Indian camp near the discovery of the body and talked to the tribal chief, and together they exhumed the body where it had been buried by the discoverers. They then held a form of inquest. One of the Indians had seen two white men camped about three miles further north, and eventually they found the exact spot. When they removed some uprooted bushes, they discovered that the area was covered in blood. The missing head was found with a hatchet wound on the right side, as though a right-handed man had come up behind the murdered man.

Two men were immediately sent back to town with orders to put Farnsworth in irons, there being no jail available. But before they could get there, Farnsworth escaped in the confusion of a snowstorm. They searched the area, but never found him. Eventually, they found out that Hume and Farnsworth had met and partnered up in San Francisco, where Farnsworth saw that Hume had a valuable gold watch and $700 in gold with him.

Mr. Milliken's frown was fierce. "People think that all of us who have come west have turned into greedy heathens, unconcerned with laws and an orderly society. But just because we don't have some fancy courthouse doesn't mean we're not interested in justice. Even in the early years, we had lawyers here. And as a whole, we adhered to the basic rules that underly any society gathered together, whether we were a reader of the Bible or just someone who likes fairness. We all agreed that you don't take from another what isn't yours, and you don't take someone's life or what they need to keep that life together, like his water, his horse or his gun. And we all agreed that a fair fight to protect yourself is not the same as murder, like we figured Farnsworth did."

Robert lowered his voice. "Someone told me that Hume's head was kept here, pickled in a barrel of brine."

The only response was a crooked smirk and a shake of the head. Robert chose not to ask anything further about that, and I sure wasn't about to.

Instead, Robert asked about the search for what some call a lost mine in the area of what is called Pumice Mountain. Mr. Milliken gave a sharp snort. "Oh, that. Yeah, a Dr. Randall came here from San Francisco in the spring of '61, looking for an outcropping of red cement rock that was supposed to be embedded with gold. I saw the samples that had been given him by a patient. They were good."

"Didn't he have a map?"

"Yeah, but it was rough. The main thing it said was that Pumice Mountain would be visible from the ledge. Hell, that's easy to do from hundreds of places. The damn mountain stands out, the way it swoops down and all. The doctor hired some men here to go with him. This year he did the same thing, hiring Gin Whiteman as foreman of the group. But word had leaked out and there were men swarming the Pumice Mountain area. Doubt it'll ever be found."

I mentioned the small camp on Dog Creek that we had passed through after leaving Big Meadows. Mr. Milliken said that it had been a fairly robust little camp until one of the miners there had made the first discovery at Monoville. Then most of the men had left Dogtown. Of course, most of those men have now moved on to Aurora from Monoville. I laughed and said I wondered where those men might go next after Aurora played out. But the men didn't laugh, only nodding their heads in that knowing manner of men who have seen much of the hardest parts of life.

This transient lifestyle is normal for these men, as I suppose it is for us right now. But we are traveling only to look for a place that offers a stable future before we put down roots. We, at least, will not settle for this nomadic way of life.

CHAPTER 2

1862 – 1863

The next letter picked up by Lucy was of particular interest to her, in part because it was written from Roger's present location.

November, 1862: We are now in Aurora. The road here was narrow, rock-strewn, and rutted from recent rains, and we moved over it very slowly. This gave us the opportunity to view the magnificence of Mono Lake to our right before heading northeast on a wagon road that cut through mile after mile of desert scrub.

Just like the rivers here that are closer to creek-size than the wide expanses such as the Mississippi, Mono Lake is unlike any lake I have ever seen. When standing on its shore, it is difficult to grasp how huge this incredibly salty body is, as the far shore is beyond the horizon of sight. There was enough wind to create white-caps on the lake's dark surface that lapped the shore as tiny foamy waves, while above were puffy gray clouds we worried might bring rain. It was a breath-taking vista that made one feel an insignificant creature within the realm of its ominous beauty. Hundreds of small sea birds bobbed with unconcern between the waves, and I longed to know what they were.

At last we were passing between St. Mary's Hill to our right and Mt. Hicks to our left, where we crossed Esmeralda Gulch on a narrow, rickety bridge. We were facing the original site of the diggings at Aurora. This, thank goodness, is not where the town has been set up. For that, we turned north with the big Esmeralda gulch (more like a small canyon) to our right. After several minutes on a well-used road, we entered the town on Antelope Street.

The gulch splits the town, moving up Silver Street, cutting over to Antelope and up to Pine, where it swings over and up Winnemucca Street to Spring before continuing its path west. There is another, smaller gulch that enters the town from the east and cuts across to join the big gulch. A number of plank bridges allow for crossing these gulches; an easy feat if not wearing long skirts. But this was never meant to be a place for women. That women have arrived here at all is more grudgingly accepted than welcomed, and then only because we serve men's needs.

We are surrounded by sloping hills that cannot be dignified by being called mountains, but they give definition to the town like parenthesis around a worded phrase. At one time they were dressed by a sparse covering of Pinion pine, but now most of that has been cut down for fuel, much to the anger of the Piutes who are used to harvesting the pine nuts from them every autumn.

Of one thing Jane and I became immediately aware, and that is that women here can only be a spectator in a man's world. But what a world it is!

Strength the men have, of course, but also cleverness and inventive imagination. Whatever challenge confronts them, they find a way to master it. If a tool would better perform a task, they create it. If shelter is needed, they build it, even if it is only an extension of a natural cave in the side of a deep gulch. If the ore needs to be milled, they make use of an arrastra while building a big mill. These are not talkers, but doers. And because this is the type of man who has settled here, there is now a real town in Esmeralda Gulch that will someday become a nice little city.

Three years old this August, the town began with three hunters named Hicks, Corey and Braly. They found an ore body that amazed them, and having recently read a popular new book called "The Hunchback of Notre Dame", they named the area the "Esmeralda Mining District" after the book's heroine. Of course, such news cannot be kept a secret and men who have not found instant success in Monoville, Virginia City or elsewhere, are rushing to this site. It has transitioned from a camp to a village to a town in a matter of months. And now it is filled with huge freight wagons hauling in hay, lumber, machinery, and all kinds of food. Some of this comes from the Big Meadows area, some from Carson, and some more recently from as far away as the north end of the Owens River Valley. Fish from streams and gull eggs from Mono Lake are brought here, too.

The wide meadow not too far from the original discovery site was the perfect place for a town, allowing room for the buildings to be laid out on a grid of streets. With a cemetery conveniently situated to the north of town, and mills far enough away in the hills to keep much of their noise from the ears of the citizens, it is more welcoming than I had expected.

The mines here are considered shallow by those who know of such things. The gold is not easy to extract, being embedded in hard rock. This means that men must sink shafts and extend tunnels along the leads. There is no washing away of sand in rushing streams here, as was done in the California gold country. No, here they must crush the rock, process the particles with mercury that will attract the gold (called a composite), apply heat to that and only then see the gold or silver that remains. This is only after the ore vein is opened up, often by black powder explosions that rock the earth beneath our feet and that fills the air in town with choking dust when the wind is in our direction.

All of this requires a great deal of money. They must build the mills that can process the ore once it is found, for why find it if you cannot break it down and release the gold? The money to do all of this comes from investors who buy capital stock issued through the new San Francisco Stock and Exchange Board.

Robert has found work here at one of the livery stables, as the mules and horses that haul the ore from the mines to the mills must be shod often. I think he was hired only because he made it clear to the owner that he didn't want to be a miner, and therefore unlikely to up and leave suddenly.

Jane and I have set up what can only loosely be called housekeeping in two rooms of a low-rent rooming house. But at least it has no wheels beneath it, and the roof does not leak. Jane has not been feeling well, so I have made her rest. I don't remember her as particularly fragile when we all lived in Placerville, but the travel has left her weak and given to headaches. It means I am forced to go out alone each day to gather our food, and do our laundry in a tub on the back porch.

A small communal kitchen allows me to prepare our meals, which is made up mostly of soups, stews and bread. While the bread bakes, I heat the irons on the hot stove top so I can iron our clothes. This way, I don't waste the wood. Only when I can scrounge a few eggs or a bit of meat does a meal change much. Potatoes and carrots seem to be plentiful, so we shouldn't have to worry about scurvy. But to be safe, I bought a bottle of lemon syrup and we drink a glass of lemon-laced water several times a week.

The first morning here, I looked out from our room on the second floor of the boarding house and scanned the barren hills, thinking it a very lonely spot indeed. But then I spotted a stubby old pinion pine on a hill, and wondered how on earth it had escaped the hatchet. Now, each morning when I awake, I look out and say good morning to it, and I feel like I'm greeting a friend that has survived hardships such as we have. Silly it may be, but I find comfort in it. I think that living here, I will need every bit of comfort that I can generate for myself, as there is certainly nothing gentle or lovely here.

Robert took pity on me and my days of routine labor, and rented a rig to bring me out to see where the first men here lived. This is hilly territory and everything of importance is located either along a gulch or at the foot of a high hill. Having traveled so long in a wagon, I have an appreciation of shelter, as the elements can be severe. To escape them here, the earliest miners had to dig into the steep, high sides of the gulches. They next extended walls beyond the caves with rock stacked without mortar, which blocked them from strong winds. Using sticks tied together, they created a lattice floor that raised them above the ground, upon which they stacked straw and rawhides for their beds. They had to do this because the first winter was harsh, with the ground seeping water from the hill. Even the sourdough starter for their bread would freeze until placed outside in a shaft of sunlight. Only cavemen or local Indians have ever lived as primitively.

Some with a cynical view of life might say that these early miners throughout the West had another choice, if it hadn't been for their lust for gold. However, in their search for wealth, as with so many men even now seeking their fortune, they created towns. And also new mining inventions and methods. Some of these towns will remain and even grow, although many more will wither away and become desiccated remnants of hoped-for promise.

Besides the buildings disassembled in Monoville and brought here, there are brick buildings going up. Limestone is readily available here, so with the high heat of the pinion pine, men have turned it into lime for mortar between bricks.

Which makes this a good point to report that this morning I looked out the window and immediately realized that something was amiss. My old pinion pine was gone. Someone must have cut it down. I stood transfixed, bereft and feeling suddenly drained of hope. I sat on the edge of the bed and wept, glad that Jane was still in her room and Robert gone to work. In that moment, flooding through me was a loneliness I never imagined I could feel. I was consumed by the full realization of the loss of all I had held so dear, left behind on the other side of the mountain. Especially you.

*No one was ever my champion as you were, with never a hint of judgment.
I never told you, but I often worried that something would happen to you and
I would lose you from my life, such a thought bringing tears to my eyes. And
now here we are so very many miles of travel from one another. And I don't
know who to blame for this circumstance. Probably no one, but it feels like
there should be. Thankfully, the butter and egg man pulled up out front, and
wanting to get a good share of butter for our larder, I pulled myself together. As
I have so often heard you say, "Oh, well, needs must."*

*The post office opened here in September of '61, shortly after Congress carved
out Nevada Territory from the western portion of Utah Territory. This means
that I can easily get this letter off to you. The eagerly awaited mail stage arrives
every other evening, sometimes at almost midnight. Someone always cries out
"stage acomin'", so Robert gets in line for any mail that might be coming to us,
as we have a mail box and that gets handed out before "general delivery" mail.
He seldom comes back with anything, but maybe now we will occasionally
get a letter from you if we stay here for very long. We did get a note from Mr.
Milliken in Monoville, and it was such a great event that we sat together in our
tiny parlor as Robert read it to us. It was a note about nothing in particular,
but was oh so welcome. As you will see from the post mark on this envelope, it
is not stamped as from Aurora, but rather says "Esmeralda, N.T.", since that is
the county of the Nevada Territory in which we reside.*

Lucy sat back and thought of all Dolly had been through in her life.
Dolly had assumed that life in Placerville as a married woman would give her
permanent respectability, but she had enjoyed such a secure future for only
three years. Then in early 1862, Dolly had sent Lucy an urgent summons
that had culminated in Lucy and her family moving to Placerville. But
because of what took place that summer, Dolly and Robert, along with
their friend Jane Leon, had been forced to leave that town. And, therefore,
all the letters from Dolly that had followed. Although Lucy had enjoyed
the company of many other women, none of them had known the depth
of her as had Dolly. With Dolly gone, Lucy had relied on her husband for
much of the comfort of close companionship. But as Jane had pointed out
to Dolly, it just wasn't the same.

Roger had been a boy of seven when his father had left. By late 1864,
after three years of war, many men were seeking relief to their conscience

because they had stayed in the West instead of fighting in major battles. When Lucy and Roger had finally accepted that Jim was not going to return, Roger had taken on the role of a man much too early in his life.

Although they had each developed a social set of their own, Lucy and Roger had always been there for each other. More than most mothers and sons, they had shared their lives without judgment, determined to be accepting of choices not always ones they themselves would have preferred. After Roger turned 16, he had worked in the saloons and gambling halls, the owners willingly claiming him to be nineteen to conform to the law. With Lucy also occasionally dealing cards, it gave the two of them needed income as well as mutual understanding.

Lucy looked down at Dolly's letters and poured another cup of tea before focusing on the next one. It was a good way to avoid recalling too many memories of Jim rooted in the past.

__November, 1862__: I have not mentioned the cemetery north of town, composed of a couple dozen graves and dotted with small scrubby trees. Iron and wooden fences surround many of the graves. A few of them have a headstone, but most are marked only by a slab of wood crudely carved with a name and a death date. A couple have only a wooden cross without a name on it. Some died by what they call a natural death, which means illness or accident, while about a dozen are from what is referred to here as "violence or otherwise". I have been hesitant to ask what "otherwise" means.

But while I cannot grieve for those at the cemetery because I never knew them, I do grieve for my old way of life. Remember our rides into the hills when we dared to ride astride? And our many conversations over pots of tea and baked goods? It was so cozy. Nothing here can be called cozy.

This morning as I look around at the thirsty brown hills, dusty buildings creaking in the wind, rutted roads slimed with mud, and tired horses with their heads hanging, I wonder why it is so cold. It should be hot. This is a place that should always be hot; where women sit in rocking chairs while fanning themselves with paper fans, where men run the back of their forearms across sweaty brows, or plunge their faces into a water trough like the horses do their soft muzzles.

Instead, I am burrowed into my heaviest coat, sitting up in bed with the weight of the blankets holding me in place, and the clay warming-jug at my feet now cool. I am dreading when I have to get up to start supper. God, how I hate this place! I said that to Jane the other day and she said nothing, simply staring at me with eyes that offered no argument. Yet neither one of us will ever say that to Robert, even though there are times when I think he would agree. I feel that allowing myself to have a good cry, I would feel better. But I refuse to give in to it. I must remain strong for Robert and Jane.

We have been saving our money to see us through the winter here, which I can tell is not going to be an easy time. With the mountain roads so torn up by wagon wheels, and then frozen over, and then covered by deep snows, the town's mail and supplies will be crucially impacted. In fact, this will probably be my last letter to you until spring, as snows are predicted soon. May you have a beautiful Christmas. My thoughts will be with you there, along with so many wonderful memories. Give my best regards to my old friends, or at least those who will admit to remembering me fondly. But for sure give a big hug to Roger.

Lucy remembered that it had indeed been a wonderful Christmas that December of 1862, the first in their new home. Jim had given her a silver-backed hair brush, and he had helped Roger give her a photo in a silver frame. The photograph was of Jim and Lucy, taken on their wedding day by a Jamestown photographer immediately after the ceremony. They had been forced to sit absolutely still for a long time, and so they were told not to smile. Regardless, they at least did look very pleased with themselves. Although remembering the wedding night that had followed brought a lump to Lucy's throat, it also brought a sense of gratitude that such a man had been in her life. Then she smiled, adding the thought, "And how fortunate for him that such a woman had been in *his* life."

Lucy decided to take a break, putting more kitchen things into crates while clearing away a welter of emotions. The house looked smaller now that it was emptied out, most of the furniture given away or sold. Within each space where once sat a chair, there was a memory of when it had been there with Jim or Roger in it. Suddenly, she realized that the sooner she left, the better off she would be. It was time for a new life, with new friends and new experiences. The past had become a burden, and she needed relief from it. If Roger didn't want her with him, she would find a town of her own choosing and make a life there. As this sense of resolve embraced her, so did a greater sense of peace. Nevertheless, she found herself late that night reading more of Dolly's letters by the light of a coal oil lamp.

Aurora, *March, 1863*: *The winter snow and cold seems to be lessening somewhat, but it is still very much with us. In spite of that, men get about almost as much as in the summer. But they have tall boots, not skirts that drag in the wet of snow and mud.*

Disputes over mining claims, however, are not seasonal and seem to occur year-round. And sometimes they don't end well. A couple of years ago, a local named David Webber argued with another by the name of Wilson over who had the right to a lot here in the town. I don't know what led up to Wilson killing Mr. Webber, but he did. And then last year a miner named Gebhart was trying to defend his claim up on Last Chance Hill and a man named Gossland shot him. Not long after that, three armed men took over the Monitor claim, threatening Sam Clemens who now writes for the newspaper in Virginia City, and his partners. Mr. Clemens and his friends chose not to pursue the subject, and so escaped unharmed. But this is the type of thing that happens here all the time.

And just last month Ed McGrath killed Tom McLaughlin in a dispute over a mining claim. So I guess it is no wonder Aurora has garnered a reputation for violence far greater than other towns of the Eastern Sierra.

Aurora, *April, 1863*: *The snow has mostly melted and mail is once again on the move. It was a long, cold winter with snow occasionally at such depths that only Robert ventured out, and then only with snowshoes. Jane and I would stand in the doorway of the boarding house's upstairs balcony on the best of days, watching the activity down on the street. It was like watching a stage show, and I think it is the only way we kept our sanity.*

We share the kitchen with three other occupants of the boarding house, but being men, they seldom use the stove. Clever Jane worked out an arrangement with two of them in exchange for their keeping the stack of wood next to the stove piled high. In return, Jane and I keep them supplied with fresh bread and other baked goods, as well as soups and stews. I don't know where they get the wood that they bring us, and I'm afraid to ask. I'm just thankful that I don't have to find it or chop it. Or nag at Robert to do it.

But even with this supply of wood for cooking and heating, I will not soon forget the unremitting stiffness of my hands from the cold while attempting to cook breakfasts, the grasping of a knife taking great effort even though I had just held my hands near the wood box of the stove. Dough rolled out on the table was always stiff even mid-day, although I must say the biscuits were always nice and flakey. When Robert would come in from work outside, it would feel to him cozy and warm, but my lips would often be too stiff with cold for a proper kiss. At night, there never seemed to be enough blankets, although we had so many that their weight made it difficult to move.

My point is not to complain, but to make it clear why I am determined that we will not spend another winter here. Robert does not disagree with me.

We have had more violence lately, although in one form or another it doesn't really ever disappear. We have a newspaper now, the Aurora Times, so we learn of events we might otherwise have missed.

A Chinese man recently stabbed McKint, a miner working at Winters Mill, and a man Robert knew and liked. He lingered a week before dying, and with the Oriental having disappeared, that was the end of that except for a nice funeral well-attended. But then a few days later, John Donovan stabbed Dick McGuire. They had been enemies for some time, Robert said, although few seem to know why. But neither of them were especially upstanding citizens and belonged to rival groups. Robert was playing billiards with Mr. McGuire in the Pony Saloon at the time that Donovan came in, pulled out his knife and pushed it into McGuire.

I expected that Robert might have a difficult time sleeping that night, but other than a shake of his head after telling me about the incident, he seems to be taking it in his stride. Has he become so adjusted to the specter of death around us that he feels nothing more than resigned acceptance? Or is he not wanting me to see how much it upsets him? It is probably some of both. Maybe because Donovan and McGuire were known to have threatened one another, the Justice of the Peace ruled it justifiable homicide.

Although every man carries a knife, and many a gun tucked into a coat pocket or the waistband of their pants, it is usually the gun that is pulled out. Nevertheless, there are more misses than bullets that find their mark. But when we hear the shots ring out, we never know if it will be reported that someone we know is injured or dead. Or in jail for doing the shooting. I find it odd that although Robert keeps a knife in his boot, and hunts with a rifle, he refuses to carry a hand gun in a pocket.

He is right now out at a meeting of the Union Club, a group of men who are ardent supporters of the Union Army in this war that seems to never end. With paper money having declined in value, only coin is given out after gold is weighed by the assayer. Workers at the big mills are paid with company scrip, which most businesses accept. But few gamblers will take it. The newspaper says the credit of the Federal Government is being upheld by trade, manufacturing, exports, and by heavy taxes on imports as well as domestic products, and just about anything that can be taxed. But I suppose there is no such thing as having a war on the cheap.

It was reported at the last meeting Robert attended that the Confederacy has been weakened by the Union's rigorous blockade, by the various interruptions of southern industry, the loss of whole or parts of States, and by the Federal control of the Mississippi and its great tributaries. At the beginning of this month, we heard that the Confederacy's General Jackson lost his life from wounds suffered at the battle at Chancellorsville. Still, Lee and Stuart were able to force the Federals back to the Rappahannock River. And so it goes, one side forward and then back. I do care about the war, but there is so much of a pressing nature right here in our lives, and the fighting seems so very far away.

Speaking of war battles, the carnage of them is never spoken about by women. We have enough carnage in our own lives it seems. I am not the only woman of the town who has had to patch up their husband upon his return home from a night out with his friends. Although I am not about to join the Temperance League, several times I have come close to at least being able to sympathize with them. Yes, that's what I said. Several times.

Certain ones of the dozens of saloons are especially known for their rowdy reputations, but don't ask me why one saloon might tend in that direction more than another. Robert told me, as he left one morning, that he would be home right after he got off work. But when some of the lads with whom he works all chided him for not agreeing to go with them "for just one drink", he felt he couldn't refuse. He didn't get home until midnight, by which time Jane and I were frantic. The next day I fumed and fussed as I fed him breakfast. Jane stayed in bed all morning with an upset stomach.

However, when the fussing on my part and the excuses on his part ran their course, we fell into a good conversation. He admitted to me that his father had been a weekend drunk, as some call it, and Robert has always been afraid of that pattern becoming his own. I told him it would be a matter of choice for him, since he had never been much of a drinker and so had proved he was not a slave to it. This logic seemed to cheer him considerably.

I then asked him, "What do you think would happen to Jane and me if you were killed?"

He stared in surprise. "I guess you would go back to Placerville."

"How? From November to May the passes are closed. What money we have would have to sustain us until the following summer, and with that gone, how would we support ourselves until we could afford the stage fare? We have no room to rent out, and no kitchen in which we could bake things to sell. We might take in laundry and do a little sewing, but that would barely be enough to feed and house us. We could wait tables, but few businesses allow women to do that."

"You've thought about this, haven't you?"

"Robert, when men who are our only support don't come home when they're supposed to, all women think about this."

Neither of us dared bring up the obvious, which was my returning to "the business" in a brothel. Which, of course, is something Jane claims she would never do. But she has never had to face the choice between that and starving to death.

I left Robert to ponder our conversation, which has not been renewed. However, he has not again stayed out so late.

At a recent Union meeting, a large man introduced himself to Robert. When Robert asked what the man did, he said, "I'm a miner." A man overhearing this laughed as he walked over to them. He then explained to Robert that the man was one of the wealthiest of the large mine owners. They had all laughed at the understatement, but I didn't find it so amusing. It was a statement played for effect, and was therefore actually rather condescending.

Later, after Robert had left for work, I got to thinking that I actually know very little about Robert's past. His comment about his father's drinking was a revelation to me. My past is an open book; my first marriage that ended in my husband's sudden, accidental death the day after I got out of bed after losing my baby due to his beating of me, my time spent in a Nevada City brothel where I met you back when you were for a short time the cook there, and of course, all about my unfortunate family.

So there is nothing about me that he does not know, or at least very little. I don't think he has purposely hidden anything from me, but I do begin to wonder why I know so little about his life before we met in Nevada City. I take that back. He has briefly mentioned men he knew in Sierra City and Downieville. These towns are well over 100 miles to the north of Placerville, but were very active camps during the rush.

As was done last year, Aurora celebrated May Day with a picnic out on a hillside near town. I was tired of looking down upon the life around me from the balcony of the boarding house, and was eager to be part of it again. Jane chose to bake for it, but not to attend. The celebration was one of the few where women were not only invited, but could actually participate, even if it was just to bring food and organize games.

Wooden arbors for shade were fitted up with chairs that sat upon carpets laid over the sand. Wagons hauled to the area boxes of plates and utensils, baskets filled with fried chicken and other good things that were laid out along with iced tubs of bottled beer. Heaven knows there is right now plenty of ice in the sheds cut from the creeks and packed in straw.

One of the few young girls here was crowned Queen of May, and she recited a poem "To the American Flag", as had her friend Hattie Green when she had the same honor the previous year. Mrs. Garesche once again sang "Charming May", and everyone applauded politely, unable to generate more enthusiasm than that. Her voice is not exactly theater quality, but her courage is commendable.

Then, in the evening, there was a grand ball, with everyone wearing their finest clothes. Robert and I danced until our feet ached, drank punch and ate cake wonderfully made by someone else, and had a gay old time. It was, overall, a day I will not soon forget. The most significant entertainment we regularly enjoy is listening to the playing of the brass band on Sunday afternoons, or watching the members of the Deluge Bucket Company No. 1, our fire unit, on parade through town.

During one such parade while Robert was at work, I was invited to join a couple on the upstairs balcony of the three-story brick Exchange Hotel. I declined at first, finding heights a little difficult, and the narrow balcony not having a railing around the edge. But I gave in and climbed through one of the tall, arched windows, stepping over the raised sill to get out onto the balcony. It was crowded with couples, the men standing against the wall behind the seated ladies. There was an empty chair near the end and I took it quickly, finding the height not so disturbing while seated.

One of the men standing behind me was evidently upset about something, and although he was talking to the man next to him in a low voice, I could hear him describing why he was angry with someone who he felt had done him wrong. He spoke for several minutes with a vituperative splendor that was quite *amazing, while oblivious of the women who could easily hear him, although politely pretending they didn't. He seldom repeated himself, expressing a wide-ranging vocabulary of swear words that I found fascinating. The only other woman I was sure could hear him was next to me. Her lips began merely pursed, but ended up folded in upon themselves until they completely disappeared. Oh, it was such good fun, and I had the most difficult time not laughing.*

Robert invited a friend to supper the other day. William Hoyt came from Placerville this March, so you can imagine how excited Jane and I were to talk with him. Fortunately, he was not aware of the Placerville sensation in which we were embroiled last summer. He now works in one of the mines while building himself a nice little cabin that he constructs around himself while he lives there, although the only day he gets much done is on Sundays. He hopes soon to have enough money that he can buy lumber to put in a floor, having just finished a stone fireplace. This is typical of the men who come here planning to stay awhile.

I have joined a sewing circle run by Mrs. Hutchinson, a formidable lady who has set herself up as a leader among the married ladies of the town. She is kind, if not somewhat domineering, but she has a beautiful hand at embroidery and I have learned much from her. She also heads our efforts to raise money to equip the hose wagon with a new canvas fire hose. The men even held a parade one evening to honor us. This sounds more impressive than it is, since the fire brigade loves any excuse for a parade.

A Sanitary Fund has been set up to benefit the war effort, and two silver bars, each valued at about $2,200 have been sent back East in support of the Union cause.

When initially receiving this letter, Lucy had been surprised that Dolly had not asked about the effects on Placerville of the drought so prevalent in California at that time in '63. Thousands of cattle, sheep and horses had been dying from lack of water, along with agriculture of all kinds. But Aurora was located in an arid landscape to begin with, and had been focused on its own survival and prosperity. Lucy thought again that it was probably Roger's memory of Aurora as it had been when Dolly was there that had lured him to that area. When he turned fourteen, Lucy had let him read the letters sent from Dolly. Aurora was far different now in 1875, Lucy reminded herself, and probably not for the better.

Lucy sighed deeply and picked up another letter. This one was from Robert to Jim at a time when Jim was just beginning to think seriously about taking up the offer to help at a way station near the Humboldt Sink in Nevada Territory.

Dear Jim,   *May, 1863*

Hope this finds you doing well, and the other gamblers doing less well because of you. Ha – ha! I have found work here in Aurora more easily than I thought I would. I met a young blacksmith by the name of Wilson Butler, and he talked his boss into hiring me. Wilson is a nice fella with a high forehead, thin short hair, and a square chin beard several inches long.

Wilson's father, Daniel, is in his 50's, but has nevertheless gone east with his youngest son Elijah to fight in the war. They had been in Bodey, a tiny camp west of here in California, with Wilson's sister, Elizabeth Kernohan, who is married to a Bodey miner. A spinster sister, Marietta, lives elsewhere but is thinking of coming to Bodey as well. Wilson's brother, Ben, moved from Aurora to Bodey earlier this year, and Wilson is now thinking of doing the same. There is another family there, one member being a friend of Wilson and Ben by the name of Roger Horner, but he has left recently to join the war from his family home in Wisconsin.

Frankly, I don't know why anyone would want to live in Bodey. Billy O'Hara, a black man with great dignity and good humor who used to live here, now runs the Empire Mine's boarding house there. He talks up the town of Bodey to anyone who will listen. All in all, there are only about 50 people living and working there. With so few buildings, it can barely be called a town.

But here, we have hundreds of residents saluting daily the American flag atop the town's 50-foot liberty pole. We are seeing flush times, with building going on steadily, both in town and up on the hills where large brick stamp mills are going up. James Stark, a famous stage actor, is even building a 60-stamp mill as he embraces the mining culture. I'm not sure, but it may have been through his efforts that this March the town built a small theater, where children perform, maiden ladies read poems and instruct young people on proper comportment at dances, and the school teacher teaches reading to those who can't. A couple of times a company of professional actors visited us with a traveling play that included a magic act and a singer. We have become a refined little town, with only a fist fight, knifing or shooting a couple times a week now. (Dolly says I have become a little too fond of sarcasm lately.)

As people arrive, they are finding it difficult to find lodgings, and it's not unusual to find a dozen cots and bedrolls crowded together in rooms meant for one or two. But the streets are even more crowded, with pack trains and wagons bringing in mining tools and machinery, as well as food (a good portion of which is liquor), hay, and merchandise for the stores. We recently even received several billiard tables for the gambling halls and the best saloons. We have 40 now, off-set I guess you could say, by the fact that we also have two churches and a schoolhouse. With all of this traffic, crossing one of the muddy and busy main streets through town is a daily gamble. It is especially difficult for the women.

Lucy took a short break from the letters, thinking fondly of Robert and how wonderful he had always been to Dolly. The people in Placerville, although not unhappy to have Dolly and Jane leave, had deeply regretted losing Robert from their midst. It was a thought that brought a deep sigh from Lucy as she remembered all that had happened back in 1862, when her weeks of digging deeper had uncovered strange and tragic events. She returned to the sofa and picked up another letter from Dolly.

August, 1863, Aurora: *I find the names of places here of an interesting mix. The hills are given colorful names, such as "Last Chance", expressing the attitude of many a miner toward their stay here. But many are named after the important men who discovered the area, like Mt. Hicks. And, of course, there's the more obvious names of Aurora Hill and Silver Hill. Then there are the directional names like "5 Mile House" station to the north, while to the south will be found "5 Mile Spring", both indicating how far they are from the great hub of the area, Aurora.*

Out of the estimated 5,000 people here, there are only about 250 women, half of which I think are prostitutes, and about 80 children. There is also, as in most towns, a small Chinese district. Mostly, they run laundries, but they are not welcomed as miners. Piutes come to town to sell fish from the streams or gull eggs from Mono Lake, and sometimes to stage a colorful demonstration of one of their tribal dances. I always enjoy this, as I feel like I'm getting to know an interesting culture a little better. But there is something disturbing about seeing white men tossing coins at the dancers when they finish. Of course, I dare not express this to anyone. Robert has warned me that such criticism could bring down unnecessary wrath upon us and make employment for him almost impossible. And it is, after all, money the Piutes need.

Maybe it is because I am overly tired by the heat, dust and noise after almost a year here. I thought we would not be staying here much longer, but I now wonder. Of course, I have not spoken of this with Robert, as he likes his job at the livery, the Real Del Monte Mill, and odd jobs that he does for ladies whose husbands are too busy to complete them. I am also fed up with the degree of violence fostered by too much drink and too much masculine competitive spirit. As for general lawlessness, we have recently experienced much of that as well. Most of it consists of fights in saloons or drunks waylaid in an alley, or maybe a short brawl in the street over some alleged slight. Thankfully, little of it draws much blood.

The stages that haul bullion to Carson or over the mountain to Placerville and Sacramento are one of the main targets of real danger. A popular stage driver here is a man I only know by the name of "Dutch Jake". He got tired of being held up, even with a shot-gun wielding messenger riding next to him. Jake knew his bosses were holding back on firing him only because he had such a good reputation for honesty, but his vanity had been pricked and he was wanting to get even with the hold-up artists. As soon as he found out that he was to haul a large consignment of gold, he asked that no guard go with him, and after explaining his plan to his bosses, they agreed.

Jake is an ace hand at handling mules, and he had several cantankerous, wild mules still in training that were only partially broken to pulling a stage. Nevertheless, these were the ones he hitched to the stage while the bullion was loaded on board. Sure enough, once on the road Jake was accosted by masked riders. As soon as the robbers stopped the stage and approached with guns drawn, Jake triggered a hidden shot gun. The mules exploded more violently than the gun. The robber holding one of the bridles was thrown into the brush and the other was trampled. Jake continued on with the chest full of bullion, and returned to town with a reputation that he wasn't someone to mess with. As for the mules, they were okay except that the lead mules both had their inside ears clipped by a piece of shot from Jake's gun.

You may be smiling at this, but of a more serious upheaval is the court case pending between the Real Del Monte and the Pond Mining Company. Each is high up on Last Chance Hill, and each is claiming ownership of a rich vein that runs between them. With few rules about such things, claims are usually *held with a degree of force, and the two entities are doing just that. Both sides have hired gangs of men to hold physical possession of the area while the Nevada courts prepare to rule.*

But it is the men hired by the Pond that have caused so much concern among the general population. They have hired John Daly, a known gunfighter in his mid-twenties, with a reputation for killing anyone who gets in his way. The men with him are referred to as the Daly Gang, and are at least as ruthless as their leader. I must admit that he is a handsome man, and even exudes considerable charm when he passes a lady. However, there is a hardness in his eyes that makes my skin go cold whenever he looks at me in what I can only call a speculative way. Who better than me, with my past experience with men, to correctly interpret what he has on his mind? I don't dare tell Robert about this in case he decides he needs to flaunt his masculinity by challenging an insult to my honor, which after all has not really been insulted.

The Daly Gang now lives in a small house on a hillside looking down on the town, and therefore anyone approaching them is clearly visible. It is now accepted practice to be away from the saloons by midnight, when Daly and his gang like to begin their drinking of the best whiskey while playing cards until just before dawn, at which time they go home and to bed. One messenger who dared to disturb their slumbers before noon now walks with a limp.

Most of Daly's men live with a popular soiled dove, such as Three-Fingered Jack McDowell who lives with Nellie Sears. She is a relative of a Daly friend who was shot and killed while stealing a horse at Johnson's Station on the Walker River some months ago. John Daly has promised revenge for that. These girls, favored as they are, still are not permitted to enter the saloons with the men, any more than any townswoman. Such is the custom in most of the mining towns, unless as here, they deal cards in one of the finer gambling halls. I say this by way of background, since I am the last woman in town who would ever pass judgment on those in the profession.

Do not envision Daly's men as rough looking thugs in dirty denim. No, these are well-paid men who wear the best suits, regularly visit the barber and the bath house, smoke small black cigars, and eat steaks at the finest restaurants. And every one of them wears their gun holster tied down to their leg. All in all, a very intimidating group of men. Several townsmen set to testify on behalf of the Real Del Monte found out they were marked men and sold up their claims before leaving town during the night. The president of the Real Del Monte, when he found out he too was a target of the gang, moved to a more secure house at the same time that he hired a bodyguard. An attorney for the Real Del Monte also goes everywhere with a well-heeled bodyguard.

September, 1863: *Our entertainment this past week consisted of a fight between a badger and a bobcat on the main street, a shotgun duel between a doctor and the editor of the local newspaper, and being part of a crowd watching teens throw pieces of brick at a house next to the Sazarac Saloon. This last ended quickly when gunfire chased away the hoodlums. This petty crime, coupled with the looming threat of the Daly Gang (called by the Aurora Times "the barbarian sway"), gives little to recommend this town as the capitol of Washoe.*

As it turns out, back in '62 when we were in Placerville recovering from the exceptional winter floods of '61, the Washoe Star Dramatic Troupe came from Carson to Aurora's little theater. They presented Dan DeQuille's comedy, Ingomar, known to be popular elsewhere in the territory.

I found out that when John Stark, the actor turned miner, first arrived here, his wife Sarah was with him. They were accompanied by actor friend, Jimmy Griffith. It wasn't long before the wife returned to San Francisco, leaving behind the man she called "Mr. Quartz-Struck Stark". Now that he has built a mill and is doing fairly well, I wonder if his wife will return to him. Robert, who has met the man, says Stark conveys the impression that his wife will always prefer a big city like San Francisco over our humble, and quite violent, village. She is, after all, a stage actress of some repute. Last November, Mr. Stark went to San Francisco for a short time, and everyone there thought his temporary insanity about mining had left him. But he only visited his wife, and returned here with mining supplies.

As for Jimmy, he stayed to help Mr. Stark for a few months, but quickly came to the conclusion that he was more suited to San Francisco theatricals and returned to that city. Frankly, I think his wife had the right idea.

October, 1863: *We continue to be well, but I do not always feel particularly safe. Still, Aurora continues to put in its bid to be the capitol of Washoe. The Bulletin newspaper recently noted that, "Aurora is certainly a beautiful town, and the surrounding country exceedingly romantic as well as rich in mineral and agricultural resources. What a great pity that such a country should be* *thus 'submerged'. Are there any ladies in Aurora? We presume not — a few importations of this kind might tend to dissipate the darkness of the barbarism."*

Well, really! Of course we ladies are here! And in many ways, we do try to elevate the general society. But a bake sale to raise money for books and slates for the schoolhouse, or a picnic to celebrate a holiday, or sewing circles among ourselves, cannot overcome the threatening tendencies in the turbulent sea of men through which we swim as minnows. To even hint that the presence of women can dissipate the barbarism of thugs and ruffians is to attach to us a magical influence that is not only unrealistic but unfair.

Out walking one day, Jane and I heard a commotion down a side street and stopped to investigate as part of a gathering crowd. We saw on the street a pile of men's legs, arms and heads mixed in with sticks, bottles and rocks. Scattered here and there were splashes of blood to add a bit of color. But although they wielded such basic weapons along with much shouting and cursing, there was not one gun in evidence. It lasted but a few minutes, and ended quite suddenly. After everyone stood up and sorted themselves out, each simply walked away in different states of damage.

Jane laughed as we walked away. "They can walk, so it'll be forgotten by tonight when they'll probably share a few drinks."

"Maybe." I had seen the ugly looks on some of their faces as they glanced back over their shoulders at the others departing. And I was correct. One of them stabbed another of them later that day. But since the man did not die, and did not press charges, it was considered an accident. Only then did everyone involved in the melee get on with their lives.

We had an election on September 2, and most of the men living here voted. Of course, none of the women went with them. There's a lot I could say about that! The men went to the Aurora Armory to cast ballots for officers for <u>Esmeralda</u> County, Nevada Territory. Then, amid much joking and laughter, they trooped over to the police station and cast votes for officers for <u>Mono</u> County, California, since the border was still unresolved. At the same time, surveyors were working to define the border. On September 23 we learned that we are definitely situated in Nevada Territory by a few miles.

<u>October 30, 1863</u>: *I ran into Mrs. Gorman while out shopping the other day and we got to talking. I invited her to join me for pie and coffee, and we settled down in a restaurant. Robert had told me something of what her husband had* been involved in recently, and of course the newspaper had commented on it. But hearing the conclusion from her made it all the more satisfying.

Her husband and John Campbell had several times got themselves caught up in various arguments. It came to a head recently when her husband lost his temper and approached Campbell in a saloon, with a revolver pulled from his pocket. But instead of using his gun, Mr. Gorman surprised everyone by reaching out with his hand to slap Campbell across the face before walking out of the saloon. Campbell took an unusual tack and sent Gorman a note, in which he challenged him to a duel.

Mrs. Gorman reminded her husband that duels are against the law, and he seemed to give in to her argument. However, being a man of uncertain temperament, Gorman sent a friend to tell Campbell that he'd meet him at Clayton's ranch outside of town, where they should walk 13 paces from each other with a gun in one hand and a knife in the other. Well, the upshot of this was that after a good-sized crowd showed up, so did Sheriff Francis. Everyone reluctantly returned to Aurora. After a lot of drinking and grumbling, someone came up with the bright idea of taking the show across the state line into California, being that it's so close.

At this point in her recitation, Mrs. Gorman sat back in her chair and gave me a look of disgust. "When I got wind of that, I was totally fed up with my husband. The good-for-nothing was making a fool of himself. Not that I minded so much about that, but I don't need him dying and leaving me without his income. So, I got on a friend's horse and rode out to where they were meeting. I stopped the horse between the two men just as they were turning to face one another. I shouted at them to stop the nonsense and get along home like reasonable adults." She said even the crowd seemed chastised, and everyone immediately returned to town.

Robert says nothing more has been said between the men, and frankly I think Gorman and Campbell are probably glad that it's over, with themselves both alive.

When I praised Mrs. Gorman for her bravery, she shrugged and said, "Desperate action for a desperate situation."

Later, I thought of all the brave women who have walked beside a wagon crossing the country, who keep up homes on prairies and protect them when their men are off somewhere, who plow fields and milk cows, and after all of that have a hot meal on the table each night while caring for children. But *we're too fragile or stupid to cast a vote, sit on a jury, or run for public office.*

I posed these thoughts to Mrs. Gorman and she laughed with agreement. I then made the rash comment that Robert seldom carried a gun and I was sure he would never enter into a duel.

Her response followed a derisive snort. "Honey, never feel confident of any man. They'll always let you down."

"Robert may sometimes let me down in small ways, but he has the best of intentions."

"Yeah, well, they have a habit of forgetting those." She shrugged eloquently. "But don't worry. They always have a good excuse." And she issued forth a long, guttural cackle.

I am haunted by a single question: What must happen in a woman's life to make her so cynical?

CHAPTER 3

1863 - 1864

<u>*November, 1863*</u>: *The worst thing has happened during the town's election for City Marshal. There were a lot of men running for the job, and then the thug Daly put up one of his men for the job. The citizens spread out their votes among far too many reputable candidates who sought the position, so that Daly's man garnered the most votes. He immediately set up John Daly as his Deputy Marshal! As a consequence, hardened crooks and thugs have been appointed as policemen, and every day we must suffer seeing Daly and his men swagger through town with badges on their lapels.*

These thieves and killers now collect license fees and pocket the money, rather than it going into the general fund for its intended purpose. General licentiousness has increased, with drunkenness and gambling. Prostitution is blatantly exhibited night <u>and</u> day, rather than just under cover of darkness as in the past. But is the population upset by all this? No! The general attitude seems to be that as long as the thugs don't interfere with peaceable citizens, the killing of one another of the criminal element is of no concern. You see, John Daly recently killed one of his own gang members, and some citizens have voiced their pleasure at this.

George Lloyd has always been acknowledged as one of the worst of the gang. Back in Sacramento in late '61, he and John Daly even got into quite a bloody fight with one another. But before John left Sacramento, they declared they were over their feud. George then got into several gun fights where he killed a man, although he was acquitted. Still, he evidently felt it best to leave Sacramento, whereby he joined his old pal here. It has been rumored that George is one of the few men tough enough to challenge Daly for the gang's leadership. Whether or not this is what happened on the night of October 24, while in the saloon of the Del Monte Exchange, the two contentious friends got into an argument that escalated into a gun fight. Some say George Lloyd was the 11th man killed by John Daly, who of course has not been charged.

The trial opened this month between the Real Del Monte and the Pond mills over who has access to the wealth of ore in the lead. The trial was still unresolved when the Esmeralda County court session ended, so it has been moved to the court in Carson City with a new jury impaneled.

Lucy remembered well her anxiety after receiving that letter from Dolly. Although somewhat reluctant to answer her questions about how wild a place Aurora could be, men there in Placerville had nevertheless told her the truth. Jim had tried to reassure her, but it had helped little. After Jim had left Placerville to join the Nevada Volunteers at the Humboldt River, Lucy's general sense of anxiety about Dolly had only increased.

Knowing that Jim was heading in that general direction had not helped. She and Freda had tried valiantly to hide their worry, but Roger had been too observant and intelligent a boy not to understand. The two women had often been awakened by Roger's nightmares, taking turns staying the rest of the night in the big easy chair in his room. To blot out that disturbing memory, Lucy reached for another letter.

December 26, 1863: *It has been quite a holiday season! Early in the month we women turned out, with the assistance of some men from the Esmeralda Rifles, to dedicate a new military hall. We put up flags and bunting, emblems, paintings, and even mirrors. The men added arms and such like belonging to the company. That night we attended a formal ball there, where everyone was courteous and congenial. There were about 60 of us ladies, decked out in our best dresses that we had all agreed to trim in red, white and blue lace and ribbons. The paper described us as having "mingled as gracefully as sylphs in the mazy dance". Ha! The music was furnished by the Aurora band, and they did a very commendable job, too. The men of the Esmeralda Rifles were so pleased that the affair had not been marred by violence, that they paraded through the streets the next day with their brass band "discoursing sweet music among the silver laden hills", as the newspaper put it.*

Then day before yesterday, two companies of Aurora firemen, dressed in their red flannel shirts, held a dance that turned out to be quite a good time. This was a good thing, because the fire engine they had ordered for the town had not arrived as planned, and several buildings burned down during the week prior.

In a few days we are going to be visited by performances of "the Wizard of the East and the World-renowned Wizard and Ventriloquist". The performance will be held at Preble and Devore's Hall, a dollar for adults and 50 cents for children. The town is abuzz with excitement.

At the same time, men are still talking about the Indian removal to Fort Tejon on the other side of the mountain. They were the Piutes and Shoshone who had surrendered at the fort in Independence in the Owens River Valley. It is said that about 50 have straggled back to their homeland in the Valley. Because there have been only a few scattered incidents of hostilities, settlers are feeling it a safe place to bring more of their cattle to escape the drought. Miners and settlers are arriving there in increasing numbers, inhabiting more of the land still occupied by Piute and Shoshone tribes. I find the whole subject disturbing, and think there will inevitably be more fighting. But I am hesitant to broach the subject to anyone, not knowing how my ideas will be received coming from a woman.

<u>January, 1864</u>: New Years was celebrated here with loud gunfire, fireworks, and of course, much drinking. But it was done without too much injury to others, maybe because it was too cold to spend much time outdoors lurking in alleys. But at least there is no deep snow, like last winter. My hopes of leaving have nevertheless been put on hold.

On January 10, possibly because the second trial ended in a hung jury, the Real Del Monte and the Pond management came to an agreement out of court. It was decided that the vein belonged to the Real Del Monte. While all of this was taking place, John Daly killed his next victim, a man who had killed two friends of his. Again, bad man killing bad man, and no one in town seemed to care. "Seemed" is the operative word.

When John Daly returned to Aurora from Carson after the settlement of the lawsuit, he discovered that in his absence Aurora had elected a new marshal, Daniel H. Pine. And the Police Department had also been scoured clean of the Daly gang. Daly was not a happy man, swearing retribution and many other nasty things, but with his power no longer backed up by the Pond management, and without connection to the law, he was no longer a person of great influence. With his power gone, so was the people's fear that he once engendered so easily. Although we hoped this would allow us to see the back of him, he has decided to stay in Aurora.

February 1, 1864: *Being a Monday, after we finished the laundry today, I went into town to do some food shopping. While at the market I ran into William Johnson of the Walker River Station. He has come to town to sell the potatoes that he grows, as well as to get supplies for his return. He had other produce too, and I purchased much of it directly from him. The others in the boarding house gave me coin so I could do this, since Jane and I do most of the cooking. Our landlady is away much of the time with her family.*

Bill has been bringing produce to the town for the last couple of years, and the miners no longer experience scurvy as they did in the first years here. So he has become a well-liked friend of many. Life at the station had always been uneventful for Bill and his wife, until a year ago when his hired hand, John Rogers, shot down James Sears for stealing a horse. Sears was the brother of the soiled dove I told you about who is a favorite of the Daly gang.

Later *Robert just got home and informed me that he ran into Bill Johnson at the Merchant's Exchange Saloon, on the corner of Pine and Winnemucca. The two of them got into conversation while playing billiards, and Robert has invited Bill to dinner tomorrow night. Jane and I are looking forward to it, and are planning the menu with a ridiculous amount of excitement.*

Robert also said that when he left to come home, one of Daly's men seemed to be getting friendly with Mr. Johnson, buying him drinks. Robert felt there was something queer about that, but Mr. Johnson rebuffed his suggestion that they leave together right away. Few men will turn down free drinks.

February 2, 1864: *Bill Johnson has been found brutally murdered. Evidently, when the Merchant's Saloon closed at two this morning, Mr. Johnson and the man who had gotten so friendly with him, left together to go to Porter's Saloon on Antelope Street. There, Daly and most of his gang were waiting for poor Bill Johnson. Bill, too drunk to be alert to what was happening, went inside and let them buy him a drink. When he staggered out of the saloon to head to his hotel,* *one of the men smashed a gun butt into his skull and Daly shot him through the head. Victim number 13 now lay dead, and James Sears has evidently been avenged. But this was not enough for the blood lust that had been raised among these horrid men, now also drunk, so William Buckley pulled out his knife and severed Bill's jugular vein.*

The next day when all this was revealed to the town, the citizens' lackadaisical attitude about the gang finally disappeared. If villains want to kill each other, everyone thought "so what"? But when they start killing innocent people, especially friends of the town, that is thankfully too much to bear for everyone here!

Coroner John Moore is now holding an inquest over the body, while a large crowd gathers outside his office.

__Evening__ Sam Vance, one of the Daly gang who was called to testify before the Coroner, was shot in the groin as he moved through the crowd to get to the Coroner's office. The police have taken Vance, as well as his assailant, to the jail under armed guard.

This violence has finally ignited the anger of the townspeople, and 400 citizens have met in Armory Hall in the Wingate Building to form a "Citizens' Safety Committee". During the rush we called it a "601 Committee". By any name, it is a vigilance committee gathered together to see that justice is carried out in accord with the law. The commander of one of Aurora's two militia companies has been chosen as First Officer. The men now have control of their own guns, as well as 40 rifles belonging to the militia.

__Feb. 3:__ So much has happened since last I wrote. One of the witnesses who had been present during what happened to Bill Johnson tried to leave town before he could be forced to testify. He was forcefully brought back. He reluctantly told what happened, detailing the ruthlessness of Daly, Buckley, Three-Fingered Jack and a man he called "Massey" Masterson. He also said that the only reason he left town was because Buckley had threatened him if he didn't. Other witnesses came forth, too, but it was only because of the presence of the "Safety Committee" that they had the courage to speak up.

Daly, Three-Fingered Jack, Massey, and two men called Irish Tom Carberry and Pliney Gardiner were finally arrested. Vance was already in custody, recovering from his wound. On February 5, Robert took his rifle and joined a posse that went to Adobe Meadows to capture Bill Buckley, as he had left town and was seen to be heading toward Mono Lake. As it turns out, Buckley walked clear around the lake, ending up at Lee Vining's old cabin. Robert said that Buckley wouldn't have been spotted out in the sagebrush by the posse if it hadn't been for a barking dog who spotted him.

While all of this was taking place, Mrs. Johnson arrived for Mr. Johnson's funeral, and a large group of us followed his coffin out to the cemetery. A newspaper reporter from the Sacramento Daily Union was present and called it the largest procession ever seen in this town. As the minister spoke, Mrs. Johnson looked so alone and confused, and my heart near broke for her. I moved to her side and put my arm around her shoulders as her husband's coffin was lowered into the ground on ropes. I could feel her trembling with repressed emotion. After a few kind words said over him, Jane and I took the new widow to our rooms. We plied her with hot tea and cake before she had to leave on the stage to return home.

All the streets are now closed off by the Safety Committee, numbering close to 600 men. Although Robert is not part of the Committee, but he lingers among their gathering. I want him home safe and out of the way of whatever might follow, but my pleadings to him are of no avail. He explained that the Committee is convinced that if the killers go to trial, they will somehow be let off by gang members intimidating witnesses.

Feb. 8: After much discussion among the angry and resolute Committee members, Robert said last night that they have come to one unanimous decision. So today the Committee has rushed the jail and over-powered Deputy Sheriff Demming and Marshal Pine, although with little resistance, Robert said. They then took possession of the prisoners. All the mines, mills and businesses throughout the town have closed.

Feb. 9: Early this morning Daly, Buckley, McDowell and Masterson were sentenced by the Committee, and the main sound all morning has been the hammering of nails. A "gang gallows" now stands in front of Armory Hall, allowing all the killers to hang together. And they say 5,000 people are gathering around to watch the proceedings. Governor Nye in Nevada, having been telegraphed what was happening, has demanded that nothing take place. He has also ordered a hundred troops at Fort Churchill to be in readiness, and *he is now headed for Aurora. Of course, I recoil from this, but having lived each day with the fear of the Daly gang's unremitting brutality, I have to admit that part of me hopes Mr. Nye will be too late arriving.*

__Evening__ At noon today the guards formed a square of men with their backs to the scaffold, their fixed bayonets pointing out at the crowd. Robert was there, but at the edge of the crowd. While Jane remained in her room, I went out onto the balcony of our boardinghouse to stand with the others who live here. I was the only woman with them, but none of them objected, so focused were they on what was happening below us on the street.

All four prisoners mounted steps to the platform as though they were merely out for a sociable stroll. Daly accepted a drink of brandy, said something nasty to one of the Safety Committee standing near him with a rifle, and while his hands were free, took from his pocket a bunch of silver dollars that he threw out into the crowd. Once his hands were tied behind his back, he raised his voice and announced that although he and Buckley were guilty, the other two up there with him were not. Buckley pretty much said the same thing before dictating a letter to his brother in San Francisco, after which he told the Pond representative to "give the money owed me to my dear mother".

This wasn't enough drama in an already shocking event. As they came to tie John McDowell's hands behind him, he pulled a derringer from his pocket. So much for the security measures of the committee! He put it to his breast and pulled the trigger, but it failed to fire and he threw it down. "The son of a bitch of a pistol has fooled me!" He then again declared himself innocent, and as such threatened to haunt forever those responsible for his hanging.

James "Massey" Masterson seemed unconcerned about any of what was happening around him and simply said, "Gentlemen, I am innocent." There was some laughter among those in the mainly silent crowd. He might not have participated in Johnson's killing, but he was by no means an innocent man. But no jeers were called out at him, and the crowd settled down to watch.

None of these protestations of innocence changed anyone's mind. Their hands were tied behind their backs so they couldn't reach up to the rope, and their ankles were tied together so they would fall straight down. Their eyes were covered with bandanas, and the nooses were put around their necks. It was half past one when a small signal cannon went off behind the gallows, and the rope was cut holding the nooses in place. All four men fell through the trap doors beneath their feet. Only after dark were their friends allowed to cut them down.

I left the veranda feeling ill and disoriented by a shock I was surprised I felt. Robert had told me to stay inside with Jane, but I knew when he had said it that I would not obey him. I paid the price with nightmares the next two nights. Jane saw how shaken I was, but said nothing, only bringing me a cup of very sweet tea. She had been frightened for months at the presence of the Daly gang, their antics and escapades regularly reported in the newspapers, and she was relieved that it was over. Well, so were we all, and this relief quickly overcame any repugnance at the method by which it was obtained.

Now, with the Daly gang a memory no one speaks of, more commonplace situations take place. For one, my friend Mrs. Lake continues to attract unwelcome attention from Charley Wheaton, who has evidently fallen in love with her, or whatever feeling he calls it. She, of course, finds him scary and unpleasant, especially as he is 55 years old and she is only in her twenties.

Her husband, Bill, is a bookkeeper here in town and of a refined nature, while Wheaton is an uncouth ruffian. She has even received love letters from him, which she immediately casts into the fire. She says he at least does not use objectionable language, but he has changed from simple declarations of admiration to hinting that he believes spirits have willed her to him body and soul. It has her frightened and her husband furious, and mutual friends are trying to reason with Wheaton. I told her to save his letters as evidence against him, just in case they are needed for some reason. She said she couldn't imagine what that might be, but I know better the reactions of men, and her husband will only stand so much. To be sure she didn't ignore me, I took two of the threatening letters with me when I left.

February 17: Governor Nye arrived soon after the Daly gang hangings and met with the executive council of the Safety Committee. Robert told me that the governor listened attentively to their explanations, especially about the evidence that had been gathered by the Coroner's Jury. Afterwards, he told them to return all the military arms to the armory, and close the saloons at 9 PM. The most chastisement they received from him was when he warned them not to do it again or he would put the town under martial law. He and his men then stayed through the weekend, but seeing that everything in the town had returned to normal, he left for Carson.

However, things are <u>not</u> as before. The Committee has felt its power and is not ready to let go of it. Squads of them have delivered orders of banishment to particular men known to be violent and unmindful of the law. The town's newspaper supports this and has set up the rallying cry of "Hemp for assassins, and for outlaws, banishment." Several men have left before being given "a ticket to leave", including gamblers of dubious honesty and thieves of many types. But where have they gone? Have towns like Carson, Dayton, and Virginia City seen their arrival?

Lucy remembered that this still had not been the end of the whole affair and searched for the next letter that addressed the topic.

April, 1864: *Late last month the brother of Massey Masterson arrived in town to settle Massey's estate with the Pond people. He threatened some of the vigilantes he held responsible for his brother's death, although Robert said it seemed to be somewhat a hollow threat just to let off steam. When the Committee told him to leave town, he brashly decided to stand up to them. With the firing of their signal cannon to alert the whole of the Committee, in less than half an hour there were four companies of vigilantes assembled on Silver Street. The sheriff told the brother that he could have protection in the jail, but he wouldn't guarantee that he could hold him against the Committee if they decided to break into the jail, as they had done to get at his brother. The brother saw reason and soon was on the next stage out of town. Such is the power of the people here.*

But now the town has had enough of the Committee, and a group of 50 citizens have written to the governor. The Aurora Times *has written that, "The danger of a bloody collision between the officers of the law and the Committee, which threatens hourly to come about, is by no means a pleasant subject to contemplate." However, before Mr. Nye could call out the troops at Fort Churchill, our sheriff wired him that the Committee had officially disbanded and that no more disturbance was expected.*

Remember Sam Vance, the Daly gang member who ended up with a groin wound on his way to testify? Well, he was finally fit enough to stand trial in the district court here. The judge wouldn't let anyone off the jury just because they were familiar with the case. I mean, who around here isn't? A packed courtroom listened to eloquent speeches made by Sam Vance's attorney as well as the prosecution. After half an hour, the jury brought in a verdict of "not guilty", and the judge admonished Mr. Vance to lead a better life in the future.

I wouldn't hold my breath for that to happen, but Vance was soon on a stage out of town, headed for Virginia City. Poor, unfortunate Virginia City. Whether there, or some other town in the future, it's a safe bet that he will end his days with a bullet in his chest from the gun of someone even tougher than he thinks he is.

I said the same to Robert. He said nothing in response, but I swear he turned pale and a small bead of sweat appeared on his forehead. I guess all this violence has begun to affect him, as it has so much of the population here.

Sometimes I think it isn't the violence that upsets me as much as it is the prevalent casual attitude toward it. Two men recently decided to have an organized fist fight, meeting just outside of town with a good number of men trailing after them. They called it a "rough and tumble" affair, which means all bets off as to civil behavior. With one of the combatants much larger than the other, side bets were mostly on the big guy. But just as they squared off, the smaller man suddenly leaped in with a blow to the jaw that landed his large opponent on the ground and unconscious.

As the winner walked away, several people saw him drop a stone from his hand, which caused some few to object to the outcome. But as was explained in the newspaper, "Hitting with the stone is the 'rough' part, and knocking him down is the 'tumble' part." I have heard no comment about how the large man faired after that, and it seems no one cares. He was, after all, the loser. And I sigh inwardly!

However, I assume he is still alive, which cannot be said of Mr. Montgomery, who died of head injuries up on Last Chance Hill after a brutal fight with another miner, Mr. Conner. Since Conner declared it was "self-defense", the case against him was dismissed.

Robert was walking home with a friend the other night when a man jumped out from an alley and grabbed Robert's friend. He put a gun to his head after shoving Robert aside so hard that he fell into the street almost under the wheels of a passing wagon. Then the attacking man stopped and took a better look at the man who was locked in the crook of his arm. "Oh, hell, you're not... Sorry." But as he walked away, he couldn't let it go at that, and had to add a comment to prove how tough he is. "It's a good thing you're not him, or I would have sent you home on short notice."

Robert took his friend into the Wide West Saloon and they calmed themselves over a couple of drinks. When others there were told what had happened, Robert said that most responded with laughter. Men!!

Later *It is now official. We are in Esmeralda County, Nevada Territory. Bridgeport is in Mono County, California. The court records from here were loaded onto wagons and brought to the Hasslet brothers' ranch out on the road to Bodey, and will remain there until a county seat can be determined.*

"Ah, yes, here it is." Lucy reached for the letter that had brought her great relief, and that had been written over a number of days.

April 18, 1864: *We finally all sat down together and discussed the subject of where we should go to be away from here. We all desire a town with a degree of settlement to it. Jane and I voted for some place where the violence was less than what we have had to accept here in Aurora. Robert informed us that this might mean a town whose livelihood was not dependent on mining. We decided that Bridgeport might fulfill this need, because of its many sawmills. We certainly enjoyed the short time we spent there, and we figured it must have grown some by now.*

Two days later we headed out on the Bodey and Aurora Road, with our old wagon full of our things. I suppose the alacrity with which we were able to pack shows how lightly we had settled ourselves into Aurora. Or maybe it just shows how eager we were to leave.

Although I was certainly not unhappy as we left Aurora, I looked back on it as we passed the cemetery and felt a fondness for all that it was trying to be. Like any town, there is the positive and the negative. The main example for us was that although Robert was making good money, it was a toss-up between the winters or the violence as to which was most wretched.

As for the route we took, the northern route to Carson seemed so long, with only primitive way-stations along the route that serve the stages. Therefore, we traveled toward Bodey in such a way that we passed the Bodey Ranch of the Hasslet brothers, Ben and John. We stayed only long enough to water the horses and join them for a cup of coffee. It is here that they cut the long grass of their meadow, hauling it to Aurora and Bodey, getting a good price for it.

The brothers recently ordered a sign for their ranch to hang over the wooden arched entrance just off the road. Bob Howland, the Aurora sign maker, was told to paint the name of "Bodey Ranch" on it. However, Mr. Howland thought the spelling as given him not pleasing to the eye, so he spelled it "Bodie". The brothers shrug this off as of no account, and hang it proudly. They said more than once that they sure weren't going to pay for another sign.

Ten miles west of Aurora we entered what I suppose can now be called "Bodie", more hamlet than a recognizable town. The name refers to the man who was one of the first to discover rich quartz in the area. William Bodey died in a snow storm before receiving the reward of his discovery, and was the friend of Mr. Machin mentioned to us back in Monoville. There are about twenty buildings in Bodie, some of wood and some of adobe, and even a few tents, with mine openings scattered over the hills that look down on them.

This growth is evidently due to several good mines consolidating. The New Mexico Shaft is said to be very rich and the shaft has been opened to 80 feet with the vein 6 feet wide. Tunnels from this shaft are also being run into the company's other promising veins. The mill to process this we passed on the road six miles before reaching the village itself, but no doubt more will soon be constructed.

Those who earlier discovered this area are either dead or have gone on to Virginia City, swept up in the Washoe fever that followed upon the Ophir Mine's rich discoveries. Now, that and other mines are located along what is being called the Comstock Lode.

But some few dozen indomitable and ever-hopeful souls have stayed on to work the Bodie diggings, most of which are coyote holes with large winch housings knocked together and perched over the holes in order to raise and lower men and buckets. The largest production we saw was at the San Antonio Mine, where there is a crude horse whim hauling out the ore. It has a shack protecting the mine entrance, and a pulley arrangement to lower and raise the workers. It must be yielding fairly well, as the wagons leaving the hill for the mill are so heavy that it takes six large mules to pull them.

When Lucy turned the page, she was reminded that Robert had added some pages to the letter, mostly for Jim's benefit, being unaware that he had left Placerville.

So, Jim, on our way through Bodie, I took the time to contact Wilson Butler to say hello. He doesn't miss Aurora at all. He introduced me to Billy

O'Hara, a tall black man with an ingratiating smile and a strong handshake. I had not met him when he lived in Aurora, and I immediately liked him. I can understand how he has been able to talk a number of people into staying in Bodie longer than they might otherwise have done. The Empire Boarding House is not much more than a large cabin, but the bar is well supplied and the food not too bad. There are two rows of cots upstairs for those who need them. I took one of these, leaving the wagon for the women.

The town is located along Bodie Creek that runs north and south. It has about two dozen dwellings, and is surrounded by sagebrush and bunchgrass. There is not one tree for shade. With three saloons, it's considered a bachelor paradise.

There is one good road that comes in through meadows and low hills from Aurora, and a freighter's toll road down to Dogtown and on to the Bridgeport Valley. Someone said there is a rough road west over the hills, but appropriate only for pack trains. Streets are being surveyed and building lots marked out as "choice lots" for homes, promoted in newspapers near and far. They simply don't mention that these lots have not been surveyed.

Other than Elizabeth Kernohan and her little girl, there is only one other woman in town. I left Dolly and Jane at the boarding house after breakfast, ready to step out for a walk. I <u>almost</u> laughed at the expression on their faces when they were told of the scarcity of females. But being married longer than a minute, I knew better and just walked away.

Wilson introduced me to Robert Kernohan. He didn't stay to visit. Unlike Wilson, Billy and the other men I met, I found him cold and not very welcoming. But he seemed to have something on his mind, and I shouldn't judge him on so brief a meeting.

Had an interesting talk with Wilson. "We'd have more development going on here if we could get more investors interested. With all the excitement at Virginia City and Aurora over the last year or two, they've gotten all the attention. Why would miners want to work here if they can get better jobs there? But you just wait. When those mines begin to decline, we'll pick up here."

"You guys had several mines merge last year, didn't you?"

"Oh, yeah," he nodded. "They formed the Bodie Bluff Consolidated Mining Company. Leland Stanford, the governor of California, was made president of the company. They offered over 11,000 shares of stock worth a

little over one million dollars. This year, we've formed the Empire Company of New York with 18,000 shares worth about ten million dollars. It holds the rights to several mill sites, tunnel rights and some buildings for offices that are going up. But unlike most mining companies, the Empire prohibits those damn assessment charges to the stockholders that other companies demand from time to time."

Lucy skipped the rest of Wilson's glowing expectations for the town. It's history since then had been a cycle of small mining discoveries followed by quick abandonment. The town had not totally emptied, even so, but other than Billy O'Hara, the Butler clan and a few others, Lucy had been told that it remained mainly an area of hope for some and disappointment for even more. Robert had mentioned that he saw its potential, but also that he thought great success was destined only for those who had the financial backing of San Francisco wealth. Dolly's description of that day had been vastly different, and had made Lucy smile when she first read it. It did so again now.

While Robert was being shown the glories of Bodie, Jane and I wandered through its two merchandise stores. That didn't take up much time! We then seated ourselves on a dusty bench outside the barber shop. I assure you, we were not thinking about the town's future, or the richness of mining strikes. We were fearing that Wilson's enthusiasm might rub off on Robert.

We did, however, have a few minutes of enjoyment when a young woman approached us carrying a child of two years. Looking at her, it occurred to me that this woman with the square jaw, deep-set eyes and no-nonsense mouth, was just the type of sturdy woman who could not only endure but thrive in a town like Bodie. Her hair was long and parted in the middle, held back by a simple ribbon tied at the top. Like us, she knew better than to wear a fussy bonnet that could be ripped off by sudden gusts of wind.

"You must excuse me," she told us with a warm and welcoming smile, "but it's been so long since I've talked to women from ... well, anywhere else." Her laugh was full of mirth and self-mockery. Her child was adorable as she clutched her mother's skirt and peeked up at us.

"We understand perfectly," I told her. "I'm Dolly Robbins and this is Jane Leon. My husband is taking a tour of the town. We're on our way through from Aurora."

"I'm Elizabeth Kernohan, and this is Helen Anne. We live on Browne Street by the spring at the west end of it, not far from the Homestake Mine. Where are you headed?"

Jane and I exchanged a look. "We're not sure yet. We think our next stop will be Big Meadows."

"Well, from a purely selfish perspective, I wish you'd stay here. It doesn't look like much right now, but I'm convinced that someday it'll be a thriving town. It'll just take a couple of really good strikes."

"I'm sure you're right, but after our time in Aurora, we're desiring somewhere that's been settled for some time."

Elizabeth nodded with resignation. "Oh, I do see your point. But that means you'll probably not be satisfied with Bridgeport, even with its delightful setting. If you go on to Carson, you'll probably be much happier."

After discussing the previous winter's hardships shared by us all, and which was the Kernohan family's first one there, Elizabeth talked about the small vegetable garden just planted by her husband. We told her a little about Aurora, mostly about the shops there, and not mentioning the violence. Elizabeth expressed eager anticipation of a day's outing there to shop. We then parted company, somewhat reluctantly on the young mother's part.

I watched her move down the street past the few buildings of wood already showing weathering by strong winds and harsh winters. I felt a sudden gripping of anxiety in my stomach. My mind reeled as I wondered, 'How on earth can I ever live in such a place?' Our eastward view was that of hills covered in small mines, shacks, and a web of narrow, well-worn paths leading from one to another. The only other things up there were huge piles of wood, a mule barn, and two large boarding houses that I knew would be filled with rows of cots. And a kitchen with food of dubious quality. Beyond the hills, and encircling the town, was nothing more than mile upon mile of sagebrush. Even with a lovely blue sky overhead, its brightness merely accentuated the lack of anything attractive below it.

In all fairness, there was definitely a certain moodiness enshrouding the place that I still find hard to define. Does determined expectation have such vibrancy that it can radiate out until it becomes an atmosphere that simmers in the air along with the heady fragrance of warming sage? I had the haunting feeling that there was something waiting here just beyond my mind's ability to define it, and that if I could only bring the picture of it into focus, that it would be more spectacular and more exciting than my imagination could foresee. But then I heard the crunch of gravel underfoot as Robert joined us, and I was brought back to reality with an unwelcomed thump.

Robert sat on the end of the bench and beat the dust from his pant legs before taking a long swig from his canteen. Jane and I remained silent as he extolled the many virtues and great potential of the town. He ended his dissertation with, "Interesting place."

I could stand it no longer. "Are we staying here, then?"

Robert looked at me aghast. "God, no! There's no opportunity for us here. I'm not a miner, and they already have two blacksmiths." He then noticed the strained look on our faces. "Hey, I'd never make a decision like that without discussing it with both of you."

As I felt my heart beat more gently, I told him, "Some men wouldn't consider the women in their lives before making such a decision."

Jane grunted. "Most men wouldn't."

I think Robert was surprised at our jaundiced view of men in general, but he nevertheless said nothing more about it.

April 30, 1864: We finally arrived in Bridgeport, setting up camp just east of the log and rock-cribbed bridge. Oh, the green glory of the surrounding meadows! I had forgotten how lush an area could be after our time stuck out in the dry desert. There is a little snow still on the mountains wrapped around the town, although not as much as in most years. The meadows are only just starting to show green grass, but there is at least the promise of more. Many of the trees are putting on new leaves, the lime green of their freshness glittering in the sun. When a big black and white magpie flew through my first view of the meadows, I was tempted toward tears of joy and relief.

All of this is hard to believe, however, considering the extent of the drought throughout California. The pastures are full of cattle and sheep brought here by ranchers in desperate need of grazing for their animals. There are also a number of oxen used at the sawmills that mix in well with the cattle. When the haying season begins, this activity should help with the local economy, as the hay can be sold at good prices in Aurora and even Bodie, as well as north into Carson City. But at the same time, water in the rivers is low and there is less residual snow on the mountains than is desired by the ranchers. Robinson Creek is low because Mr. Tinkum has kept water back for use at his sawmill. Many are not happy about that. (Lovely fresh gossip at last.)

The buildings and businesses are still mostly on the east side of the bridge. But because so many sawmills are up and running now, houses and shops are being built on the west side, and going up at a rapid rate. The sound of hammering is never absent, going on until it is too dark to see whether it is an iron nail or a thumb nail about to be struck by the hammer.

I focus now on such mundane and humble things taking place, hoping to leave behind the lingering memory of the base cruelty and barbarism that we experienced in Aurora. I relayed to you much of it, but there was so much more that I did not write about. I think one of the last straws, as they say, was the day I left the merchandise store and had to step over the body of a man stabbed while I was inside, and who was now lying on the edge of the sidewalk. Since no man moved aside to let me pass easily, it was either lift my skirts and step over the victim's lifeless form, or step down into a sea of mud in the street where a stream of the man's blood was pooling. I stepped over the dead man's legs as I clenched my jaw. I looked back and saw the men grinning at me, mocking my obvious disgust. And I felt a flash of intense anger. I walked up to the one most amused and said, "Shame on you! What would your mother think of your behavior?" That sobered them all!

A deputy walked up with another man and they knelt down beside the body, one casually pronouncing, "Yup, he's dead alright." I didn't wait to find out what had happened, but simply hurried home. Robert found me at the table trying hard not to weep in a fit of frustration. Having told Jane what had happened, she too was not looking very happy.

Now, every bright Bridgeport morning I look out onto pastures that are a little greener than the day before, and I find unpleasant memories a little more distant and my spirits elevated. Even Jane appears more motivated to be out and about, and each day she goes for long walks.

She has introduced herself to a number of women and this has helped to bring us into their society. One of my favorites is Mrs. Day, whose family has been here from almost the beginning. Her husband, George Byron Day that the men call "By" Day, is the friendly, outgoing man we met when passing through on our way to Aurora. He greeted Robert like an old friend and has been very helpful in finding him work.

Big Meadows, recently called Bridgeport Valley, started on the east side of the narrow river with the basics of store, blacksmith and saloon, a few rude cabins, and Kingsley's Inn. Everything was built to serve their immediate need of survival in the middle of a huge, lush meadow surrounded by tree covered mountains. Freighters quickly found the village a welcoming oasis of civilization. And because of their friendliness and generosity, the citizens here have avoided trouble with tribes in the area.

The new buildings on the west side of the bridge are substantial and have a New England feel to them, as they are painted blue and white. Most of the homes and corrals are surrounded, not by picket fences, but by slab fences, the boards running horizontally between posts. It gives everything a look of permanency so lacking in all of the other places we have been. So far, we have experienced only infant towns, and although a little matured after five years of growth and prosperity, this town feels different. I hope it means that it will last well into the future, as its setting is so very special.

After traveling for days from Aurora with nothing more than a wagon and a tent for shelter, our arrival here has been joyful indeed. All the people we have met have been wonderful to us, hoping that we will stay. They recognize that Robert has skills that would be a good addition to the area.

They held a dance at the end of last month to celebrate the moving of the official books into the County office now that Bridgeport is the County Seat of Mono County. There were even about fifteen couples from Aurora. This bodes well for a lively and growing community.

I might add that Jane and I are two of a very small number of women seen on the streets. This being easily understandable of a mining town, I had expected a greater number of us here. In fact, so few women as young as myself are here that I have become adjusted to the furtive stares of the locals and the open leers of freighters. But even they are not as bold as when in Aurora, although enough to make me a little uncomfortable. Nevertheless, if Jane or myself happen to catch the eye of any man, they always show the greatest courtesy to us as they tip their hat, or at least dip their head before looking away. I think they realize that they are in a more refined town than some they visit.

Lucy had often wondered how comfortable Dolly and Jane were with such scrutiny. It was understandable, of course, because many miners stuck in small, isolated camps had not seen a respectable young woman in many months. And Dolly was blonde, buxom, and pretty. Men might have appeared to be bachelors, and even acted like it on occasion, but many of them were married with a family left behind somewhere far away. In any case, it was a rare man who failed to make a strict distinction between a good woman, and one not so good.

Ever since men had arrived in California for the rush back in the 1850's, they had faced the dilemma of whether or not to send for their families. Those wives who didn't join a wagon train and head west, or come by ship around the horn, stayed where they had rooted security. Some men claimed they would send for family after they made a big strike. When that didn't happen, they had to choose between admitting failure and returning home, or remaining in the West with its free-wheeling life style. For those thinking their new way of life was preferable to their old one, they simply faded into the West, leaving future generations of family to wonder what happened to their ancestor.

Having been on a wagon train crossing the country to California from New York in the mid-1850's, Lucy sat back and let her memories flow where they might. Eventually, however, she leaned forward and picked up the next letter from Dolly.

**May, 1864:** _We have rented a small one-room shack on the western edge of town, owned by a foreman at one of the sawmills. Until recently it was the home of three men who have moved on. It took quite a bit of airing out and scrubbing before we could get rid of the smell of them._

We immediately built two small bedrooms onto the back, which is delightful for warm weather, but we will need much caulking before colder weather arrives. We are left with one barely acceptable common room with a table and four chairs that sits in front of a decent stone fireplace. The fourth chair is just in case someone comes to visit. If there is ever more than one person visiting, one of us will have to stand, at least until we can purchase or make more. There are four low tree stumps outside the front door that we use in the evenings after supper while the house cools. It is pleasant, and in this way, we have met several people as they pass and accept our invitation to sit and visit.

The small sheet iron stove, with a barely adequate fire box, has two eyes. We are very grateful for this, as in this way we can heat water in the iron kettle on one while a one-pot meal cooks on the other, and we don't have to use up our firewood so quickly. Believe me when I tell you that we find in this something for which we are actually grateful. Maybe we wouldn't be if we hadn't spent so much time on the road cooking over campfires of dry scrub. In comparison, *this small house and small stove is an elegant way of life. Still, I am looking forward to getting a larger stove when one is available.*

I keep emphasizing the word "small", don't I? Well, that's because everything is small, until we can build on or move elsewhere. I obtained a roll of muslin, cut some lengths, tinted it all in a bowl of strong tea, and have draped the lengths of it across a nail in each corner of our four windows. With the addition of a rag rug next to each straw-mattress bed, and a larger one under the table, it begins to look very homey. These rugs were sold to us by two local women who make and sell them to help support their family during the winter.

These delightful ladies showed us how to bake in our heavy iron kettle atop the stove, since it has no oven. Jane made a cake that turned out just right. So I decided to make one for these women in appreciation for their friendship. It had a somewhat tough crust on the outside, but it was nice and moist inside and very good in flavor. Still, it prompted a review of instructions from the most tactful of them.

Robert is working as casual labor anywhere he can find work. He is also helping to dig ditches to spread the water that arises in the spring so it doesn't flood the meadows or the town. Right now, he is working on draining the water into the marsh just south of the bridge. Soon he will be hiring on where needed to help with the haying. Ranchers help one another while the women cook for them, one ranch after another until it is all done. Jane and I are looking forward to this. Robert comes home exhausted and hungry every day, with only Sunday off. He does, however, still find time to visit the saloon owned by Jim Booth, one of his new friends. Robert is fond of only one beer, but the place has a billiard table that he likes very much.

So tired was he the other night that I almost didn't ask him to help us put up a sturdier clothesline. I'm glad I did, because the weight of all our clothes was causing quite a sag in the ropes of the old one we inherited. Laundry is difficult enough without that.

Lucy could testify to that. Even if one had a good mangle to help wring out the clothes on the side of the rinse water tub, it was still a backbreaking chore done every Monday. Why Monday? Because for those who bathed only on Saturday nights to be fresh for church on Sunday, Monday became the day to boil work clothes worn for several days. Linens were washed separately, and women's *delicates* separate from that. So at least three loads of wash, each soaped and rubbed on a wash board, wrung out by hand or mangle, rinsed in clear water (with or without starch), wrung out again, and then hung on a clothesline to dry. That was Monday. Tuesday was for ironing everything; a series of heavy flat irons of various sizes and shapes heated on a stove top. And it was done no matter what the temperature outside, with hot winds blowing in summer and ice covering the clothes in winter. So, one either was shaking off dust or ice crystals before bringing everything inside. Lucy closed her eyes and sighed, "Unless there's a laundry in town and one has the money to pay them." Lucy left that woefully commonplace subject behind and returned to Dolly's letter.

We are accumulating a nice savings dedicated to "our home", as we call it. It means that in a month or two we can decide whether to stay in this house or build a nice new one. Or even possibly move on to somewhere else.

I have discovered that back in July of '62, when we were all so wrapped up in the drama of our lives in Placerville, that there was much happening across the country. I'm not saying that we were unaware of the continuing war, but you will no doubt agree that it was not our primary focus.

You probably realize by now that President Lincoln signed into law the Pacific Railway Act, authorizing construction of the First Transcontinental Railroad. Robert says that Congress has been discussing this possibility since 1856. It will be built here in the west by the Western Pacific Railroad Company and the Central Pacific Railroad Company of California. The Union Pacific will build west from the Missouri River towns in Nebraska and Iowa, to meet the one being built eastward from the Oakland Long Wharf in San Francisco that will extend to Sacramento before heading east. Since most of the fighting is to the south of the Union Pacific work, men think it can go on without interference from the war.

Robert is more interested in the fact that last year the government formed what they call the Bureau of Internal Revenue that will help fund the war. The Bureau will collect taxes, and levy excise taxes on most items consumed and traded in the U.S. The act also introduces what is referred to as a progressive tax, with the intent of raising millions of dollars for the Union. I suppose this will mean that the price of goods will be increased, and most of us feel that the cost of coal oil and animal feed, two of the basics of life, are already expensive enough.

May 20, 1864: *I think we will be moving on from here after the haying, probably north to Carson City in Nevada Territory. We hear it is a larger, more settled place. Someone said that if we go there, we should stay at the Ormsby House Hotel on Carson Street. So far, because of the work Robert has done in Aurora and here, he has been able to support us. This means that we have not had to use much of the money from the sale of the Placerville house and livery. Frankly, I am more concerned about the odd people with whom we come in contact. But maybe that is just a hold-over from our time in Aurora.*

Robert has gone along with a wagon taking a load of cut lumber to Virginia City, a trip of four days travel from Bridgeport. Being so well-muscled, he often helps make deliveries from the sawmills, because he can unload a wagon so quickly. He will be gone about two weeks I would think. Before he left, I told him I would be expecting a detailed description of Virginia city. They say it is a very wild place, although I am told a number of good women do live there.

Jane and I are spending this time while Robert is gone, being busy with productive endeavors. We are almost done with white-washing the exterior of the add-on portion of the cabin. We have baked several loaves of bread, as well as another cake, which we again shared with the ladies who made our rugs. They enjoy coming to our little house right now. There is an odd relaxation when one knows there is no possibility of a man entering at any moment, which of course shifts all attention to him and his needs.

Yesterday we laundered bed linens using our landlord's big tubs, while airing out the straw mattresses that we lugged out into the sunshine. Today we put down the largest of the tubs in front of the stove and heated enough water that we could both bathe and wash our hair with unusual thoroughness, using scented soaps brought from Placerville, tucked away for "someday special". Oh, how luxuriously special it was!

CHAPTER 4

1864

Lucy smiled as she picked up the letter that arrived next, this one from Robert to Jim.

(Sunday, May 29, 1864 Bridgeport) I hope you are keeping well. I came home from Virginia City to find that the ladies have been very busy. They are right now making apple butter from last year's fruit, given them by a neighbor. Being a slow Sunday for me, I thought you might like to hear of my trip to Virginia City by way of Carson.

Mr. Warren, a local man, is a Mormon who refused to return to Salt Lake City in '57 when the church bid all Mormons in the area to do that. So I knew he wouldn't be drunk much of the time, something you can't always count on with freighters. Not that it seems to hinder their ability to do their job. We camped out until we reached Carson, where we spent one night at the St. George Hotel. Bridgeport has nothing so fine.

On the way to Virginia City the next day, we stopped at a small town on the Carson River called Empire, a milling town only a few miles east of Carson. We traveled there slowly with our heavy load, carrying not only lumber but also some iron tools. The Daily Accommodation stage easily passed us soon after we started out. It was carrying mail, and would move on from Empire to Virginia City and the towns between.

Billy Wilson, the owner of the stage line, is a grand fellow and has an office in Carson City's Ormsby House and in Virginia City at the International Hotel. He leaves Carson at 9 AM and is ready to start his return at 2:30 PM,

*stopping again at Gold Hill and Silver City as he rolls down Gold Canyon,
with a quick stop in Empire. Five hours each way, with all those stops and
changes of teams, means he's pretty tired once home again. But it's only a 12-
hour day, after all, which is a typical work day for many people. With a union
backing the miners, their shifts down in the mines are only eight hours.*

*Empire is barely more than one long, wide street, fairly well packed down
and not too many mud holes. This one street is lined with one-story wooden
buildings with modified false fronts above their entrances, with only a couple of
buildings of brick. Nearby is the Mexican Mill, similar in layout to the other
mills going up along the river to service the mines up canyon.*

*From a distance, a mill makes an uneven skyline of roofs over what looks like
a jumble of sheds, each having its own purpose in the milling of ore. These sheds
appear pushed together and pegged in place by tall, black smokestacks. Trestles
and ramps and loading docks, as well as huge water wheels on the river side, are
stuck around the edges. A dozen of these line the river, and more are planned.*

*They have been using what is referred to as the Washoe Pan process, utilizing
steam and mercury after grinding the ore down to a sand-like consistency. It
sure is better than just using crude arrastras. Will finish this later.*

Lucy sat back and looked at the last page of that letter. Robert had not
after all finished it. Some little time later his letter had been put into an
envelope along with a few pages written by Jane. Because of the length of
Jane's letter, Lucy concluded that Robert's few pages had cost her an extra
ten cents in postage.

Lucy had received only one previous letter from Jane, a woman with
whom she had developed an unexpected friendship back in the summer of
1862, when the upheaval among their friends had occurred in Placerville.
Poor Jane had felt she had no alternative but to leave with Dolly and
Robert. Lucy shook her head and picked up Jane's letter.

My dearest friend,   *Genoa, Nevada, June, 1864*
*I am well aware that it has been a year since I last wrote you, and for
that I apologize. But I know that Dolly writes you often, and that you are
consequently well aware of our progress through various mining camps of both
California and Nevada. Even Robert has taken to occasionally relating to you
details of his adventures. But I have no adventures to relate.*

I am a tag-along on another's adventure, and for much of our time in Aurora I was not well. Nothing serious, just a general malaise along with various aches and pains. Interestingly, whenever there was something in which I could participate, the pain seemed to disappear. Inevitably, however, it always returned, although I have felt much stronger since we arrived in Bridgeport.

From the beginning, I enjoyed our time in the meadows. If there had been something of a productive nature that I could have done, I might have considered staying there. Yes, even with Dolly and Robert moving on. The ladies we met were wonderfully friendly, and I enjoyed several times partaking of time spent with them while working on large quilts. And they often had bazaars where they raised funds for various town projects. I helped to organize them, and once I even sold candy in a booth set up under a large cottonwood tree. Yes, I liked it there very much. But the work Robert did was very hard, and the town did not need another blacksmith.

We are now in Genoa, once known as Mormon Station, and I also like it here. But after only a small taste of this town, I think we will soon be moving on to Carson City. I can tell from the way Robert talks about Carson with enthusiasm, even after being there only once for a short time. I think, for him, it means more opportunity.

Genoa is a small village, situated on the west side of the Carson River. Immediately up against the town on its western edge, is the looming Sierra covered in scattered stands of trees and cut with deep ravines. Spreading out to the east are Carson Valley meadows turned into pastures, the river winding through it lined with willows and reeds. The town is therefore backed by the forested foothills of the Sierra (although showing much recent cutting), and fronted by a productive agricultural loveliness. Genoa acts as a trading post, with a sawmill and a grist mill, and a very fine dairy. No one goes hungry here.

Although small, Genoa (pronounced Gen-O-a) is not isolated in its location, as Carson is only several hours away. The earliest of the settled Nevada towns, Genoa was eleven years ago just a trading post in a marshy area. The rich grass was available to arriving emigrant wagon trains from the East, giving them a rare opportunity to rest and feed their teams. Then the Mormons came and soon there was a fort with a blacksmith shop and large corrals for livestock. This was followed by small, wooden houses to accommodate the growing population, much of it made up of travelers who decided to stay here rather than attempt the dangerous climb over the Sierra.

The Overland Emigrant Trail passes through the middle of town, and still sees a lot of travelers. Only two years ago this was Mormon Station, Utah Territory, but in 1856 when the area was surveyed, the name was changed to Genoa. There is still a fort here, more of a large two-story log cabin than what one usually thinks of when hearing the word "fort", although there is a fenced yard of vertical-placed logs out back of it. The cabin is also made of logs set vertically, with horizontal boards across the high front, and one small window toward the peak indicating a partial second story.

The roofs of the other buildings in Genoa are also sharply peaked, as I am told the snow gets deep here in winter, what with it being right at the foot of the Sierra. I just stopped a moment to wonder why I am going into so much detail, when we are not going to be living here. It's just so charming a town. And truth be told, I wish we were staying.

We are putting up at the Union Hotel across from the fort, with the McLean Blacksmith Shop on one side of it and the telegraph office on the other. Stages arrive and depart from the hotel twice a day, and I enjoy watching the passengers while sitting on the front porch. Although our accommodations are nice, two-dollars a day for the three of us, even with breakfast included, seems expensive to me. But Robert seems not to mind.

He has had several small jobs here, mostly of a general handyman type, but it seems that he spends most of his time drinking at Hansen's Saloon, where he gathers local gossip. He says it is information that he needs to determine if we stay here or go elsewhere, but I think it is the society of other men that really draws him there. I cannot blame him for that.

Dolly and I wander through the town or go in the opposite direction of the saloon to the Jacobs Brothers' shop. There is little for us ladies there, being mostly general merchandise related to farming and housekeeping. But the brothers are popular gentlemen and we overhear an array of interesting conversations.

The brothers have evidently offered two of the lots they own on the corner of Fifth and Main to the County Commission for the building of a courthouse. They have also donated lots for the building of a Masonic Lodge. I could tell by the way men greeted them that they are considered important men of the community. It is because of the steady development and availability to travelers that the town has had telegraph lines from Placerville since 1858, something that Carson didn't get until a year later.

(June 25) Yesterday Robert found work in a blacksmith shop that makes farm equipment, which is needed as the marsh is drained and planted with grains. Dolly was given permission to use the hotel's kitchen to make fruit-filled hand pies, which the hotel buys from her and resells at a small profit. I have been crocheting summer shawls for months, and decided to sell them to John Childs, the owner of the lovely brick dry goods store. He sold them all right away, although he kept one back to give to his wife.

Mrs. Childs was delighted with it and sought me out at the hotel, inviting Dolly and me for a visit at her house. During our visit, she told us of a woman named Eilley Bowers, who right now is in Europe with her husband, Sandy. What made Mrs. Bowers so interesting to our neighbor was the fact that at one time Mrs. Bowers was nothing more than a laundress who boarded miners in Gold Hill, and who took stock in mines in trade for money owed her. Then she married Sandy and merged her mining ownership with his, creating a mine that has become fabulously productive.

Mrs. Bowers had property up by Washoe Lake, left her by her first husband, an obedient Mormon who went back to Salt Lake City when called. Evidently, Eilley didn't want to go back. Instead, she divorced him, which tells us much about the strong-minded Mrs. Bowers. When the money began rolling in from their mines, Eilley and Sandy decided to build a large house on her property near Washoe Lake, designed to be similar to some of the great houses of Scotland, which is her homeland.

Mr. Neely is the architect, having lived in Placerville when we did. He was first a lawyer and then a politician who became California's fourth governor when he was only 30 years old. You may recall that he became mired in some dubious actions all through the 1850's, changing his party affiliation and unable to control the San Francisco vigilante committee. But at least he understood what was asked of him by Mrs. Bowers in the building of her dream home.

Mrs. Childs said the big house is built of stone, with rich wood accents and big windows surrounding the two-story mansion on both floors. Just imagine so much glass shipped here!! She said the whole thing cost close to $200,000! With the foreign treasures they are shipping back home from their European trip, can you imagine the total cost of that place? Dolly is especially taken with the story, and longs to see the house. To me, it sounds a silliness and a waste.

(July 1, 1864) I was correct in my supposition that we would be moving on from Genoa. We are now situated in Carson City, and we all seem to feel that it is a most settled sort of place. There is work here for Robert of several types, although right now he is working as a blacksmith at a livery stable. He seems quite content with the work, and is spending a little less time in the saloons than he did in Genoa. He has even been asked to join a local lodge.

We are only three miles west of a growing number of mills along the Carson River, and several hours from the mouth of Gold Canyon. That means Carson is a supply town of considerable stature, as it is surrounded by truck farms growing all kinds of produce, as well as dairy farms.

I cannot help but think of the emigrants of the late 1850's, and some even now who follow the old route. After surviving their trek along the Humboldt River and crossing the 40 Mile Desert, they reach Ragtown and its meager assistance. Of course, they have also reached the waters of the Carson River. But how glorious it must be for them to finally reach Carson and all there is on offer here.   *Jane*

Lucy thought how much she treasured the few letters she had received from Jane. It allowed her to better understand Jane's later decisions. But she quickly put aside those disturbing events and found one of the next letters she had received from Dolly.

July, 1864: The men are all abuzz about the actress Adah Menkin coming to Carson and Virginia City in a matter of weeks. She is to act in the play where she is scantily clad. Interestingly, many of us women want to see the infamous play. Why should we be denied such a theatrical experience?

In the meantime, Robert and I did something amazing of our own. We went to a going-away party at the home of Mr. and Mrs. Sandy Bowers near Washoe Lake. Sandy, as everyone calls him, although his real name is Lemuel, is returning to Gold Hill and their small residence there for a few weeks to oversee their mining interests. The deepening depression throughout the country right now is adversely affecting the Comstock mines. Robert says the mines seem to be holding steady, but at the same time he reminds me that all mines must eventually run out. But the silver from the Comstock mines plays a big part in the country's economy during this war, so any hint of a downturn causes much concern here and in the East.

But none of this was on display at the party given this weekend. How were we so fortunate to receive an invitation? Sandy Bowers was in Carson on business and was introduced to Robert by the owner of the stage line. Robert and Mr. Bowers got to talking about horses and how they can be shod in such a way to fix foot and leg problems, and Mr. Bowers was very impressed with some of Robert's ideas. As he left the saloon, he invited Robert to "bring your missus" and come to a party Mrs. Bowers was planning. Knowing how thrilling this would be for me, he readily accepted.

Robert even managed to include Jane in our invitation, but she declined to come with us. It was very generous of her to let us have such a formal occasion for just Robert and me. On the other hand, Jane has been showing low energy lately and I don't think would have endured well the long trip north and back. Being just the two of us, we rented a shiny black buggy and packed it with blankets, food and our formal clothes. By leaving very early in the morning, we were able to get to the party by the evening, even with a stop to change clothes. We planned it so that after the party we could camp that night in a secluded spot just off the road near a stream, described to Robert by one of his friends. That way, we figured there would be plenty of water and even grass for the two horses. The second night we planned to stay at the home of some friends just a few hours north of Carson.

But as plans so often do, things changed as we left for home after the party. A light rain began to fall; just enough that we could not put our blankets on the ground. We remained in the buggy, thankful that we had brought storm curtains for the sides of the it "just in case". Bundled together under blankets, we listened to rain drops lightly tap on the leather top and the breeze rustle the leaves on the trees around us. The only thing that did not change was the rushing of the creek nearby, and the occasional snort of our horses tethered under the cover of a large tree where they had no problem falling asleep. We, however, could not sleep, so we talked about our experiences that night, the men and the women having been parted from one another for most of the evening.

Of one thing we agreed right off, and that was the realization that we will never again be entertained among such magnificence or fed with such extravagance. Frankly, I'm fine with that. A bowl of soup and a cup of hot coffee would have gone down very nicely as we sat there in the damp, chill air. Instead, we had cheese, crackers, and an apple with our water, and were grateful.

Robert had encouraged me to buy a new dress, but I didn't get carried away. The skirt was fashionably full without hoops, and the neckline just as fashionably low-cut, but it was the burgundy color that made the satin glow. Even so, I was dressed more simply than many of the ladies at the party. A few matched the Eastern fashion of hoops and crinolines holding out their skirts, making movement sometimes precarious when near a table. I refuse to conform to such ridiculous custom.

The two-story house is so large that it can be seen from quite a distance. Out front of it is a grass lawn somehow maintained in this arid country, and it surrounds a fountain lined with Spanish tiles, the sound of the water hitting the tiles creating a rhythmic, musical cadence. But, oh, the house! On every side, tall plate glass windows look out over a railed balcony that skirts the house. Each window's glass, frame and velvet curtains with lace shears cost over $1,200.

There is a flat roof above a mansard edge where small windows can be seen, no doubt giving light to the attic. In the middle of the flat roof is a round gazebo, from which a tall pole rises up to carry our national flag with its 35 stars, making the house look more like a government building than someone's home. As we entered, I noticed that the transom over the front door is etched in great detail, its prisms tossing back an eye-catching sparkle from the dozens of candles and kerosene lamps.

The house admirably blends Georgian Revival and Italianate styles of architecture. My, don't I sound like I know what I'm talking about?! To me it was just a square, two-story mansion made of quarried granite that was built by stonecutters brought all the way from Scotland.

The house couldn't sit any closer to the mountain. Someday the slope above may be covered with the growth of new pines and other trees, but now it is mostly bare. Only a dozen uncut trees stand, surrounded by bare earth and littered with downed trees stripped of their branches. No doubt they will soon be cut up for burning in the kitchen stove or fireplaces. Yet there are a few seedlings that for now are of no interest to loggers. Hopefully, someday they may be large enough to shelter their own seedlings.

When we pulled up in front of the grand mansion, a liveryman took our horse and buggy away, and immediately another rig pulled up to take its place. A man in a black suit and white gloves politely invited us to ascend the wide flight of steps to the porch, where another servant similarly dressed gestured *for us to enter through the large front door into a narrow, long reception area. Here our wraps were taken from us and whisked off to someplace out of sight. I will say now that upon leaving, all of this was reversed, and without our having to hunt out our wraps.*

We walked upon rugs imported from some foreign realm as we passed a huge, gilt-framed mirror over a marble table, with its twin on the opposite wall. Both of these had once been in a Venetian palace and cost $3,000. The price of the furnishings has not been kept a secret, by the way. Before turning to our left into the parlor, we tried to ignore our curiosity at seeing a steep flight of stairs leading up to the second floor as it hugged the righthand wall.

Robert later explained to me that upstairs are the elegant bedroom suites for Sandy, Eilley and their daughter Persia, a toddler who remained out of sight with her nurse. One upstairs room has been set aside for a billiard room, where Robert and a few other men enjoyed a quick game and a shot of Sandy's bourbon.

The parlor was a magnificent room. I immediately noticed that around the edge of the ceilings ran a plaster-of-Paris frieze sculpted in place. I later learned it was done by artisans brought from Scotland. They also created the large plaster medallions on the ceilings above the crystal chandeliers. Just thinking about men up on a scaffold working on these made my neck ache! The lights showed off well the red flocked wallpaper that covered the walls in every direction, as well as the red velvet drapes. Robert chuckled, murmuring under his breath something about a French whorehouse. I moved away from him before he could more loudly repeat himself.

We were told proudly that the silver hinges and door knobs throughout the house were hammered from the silver taken from the Bowers mine and fashioned by a San Francisco silversmith.

We quickly realized that the parlor was full of people meeting up with those they already knew. Since this did not apply to us, we wandered through the room admiring the furnishings so grand that I could never have imagined such opulence. At the same time, parts of it seemed misplaced, and certainly there was nothing that invited one to sit and relax with a cup of tea.

At the head of the room in a deep window was a raised platform upon which was a large velvet and gilt chair embossed with golden fleur-de-lis, much like I have seen in drawings of royal personages. Seated upon it was Eilley Bowers, dressed in shining blue satin, diamonds at her neck and wrists, and showing a fondness for feathered fans. She greeted everyone as though she was the sovereign queen allowing the peasants into the castle for a rare treat, which I suppose in a way was true. After all, the men who call themselves the Washoe Boys, who worked alongside Sandy in the mines, have on celebratory occasions referred to Eilley as the Queen of Washoe.

Her smile was not at all standoffish, but warm and kindly. She was obviously in high spirits, happy to see those she knew, and even those she did not. She has certainly come a long way from her days in a boarding house in Gold Canyon when her pork, beans and batter biscuit meals were considered a grand thing. Many there that night who are now well-off had at one time been in dour circumstances, and could no doubt appreciate the difference between eating then, and dining now.

Lucy stopped to think about all she knew about the early years when Eilley and Sandy had met. Back then in Gold Canyon, as Eilley had served the miners, she had patiently listened to them complain about the gooey blue stuff that clogged the riffles of their rockers. They had wanted gold and had to grope through the thick blue stuff to get it. And when they did dig out the gold, it was lighter in color than any they had seen before. At a time when gold dust was $14 to $15 an ounce in Placerville, this gold was assaying at only $11 an ounce. Only later would they learn that such gold was a clue to the "blue stuff" being silver, worth more than gold. Lucy chuckled and went back to Dolly's letter.

To be honest, I cannot state that Mrs. Bowers is a great beauty. Character is obvious upon her features, and a determined glint is in her eyes, but she is short, with a square face, sleepy eyes and a straight slit of a mouth that seldom fully smiles. Her dark hair that night was artfully swept back from her face so that the diamonds in her ears could be easily seen, and indeed I almost stared at them. Still, I couldn't help feel a little sorry for her; an odd feeling, I know, considering the abundance that surrounds her.

As she put out her hand for Robert to accept with a brief grasp of her fingertips, I sensed a puppy-like quality of wanting to please and be acknowledged for the effort. I commented on the beauty of the house and she gave me the only truly bright smile I saw from her. To admire her house was to admire her. And once again I was filled with a sense of pity for her that I dared not allow her to see, so I curtsied and walked away toward the dining room.

Sandy is cut from different cloth altogether. He is tall, with a high forehead, eyes that bore into you as though wondering if he should trust you or not, and a closely cropped beard that hides a small mouth. He looks like what he is; a miner who struck it rich and still isn't as comfortable in a fancy suit as he is in miner's denim and flannel. But he has a kind and ingratiating smile, and I could see why Robert had immediately liked him. Yes, Eilley and Sandy have come a long way from when she cooked "for the boys" in the mines, even doing their laundry and darning their socks. She was mother and sister to them, and not a one lacked great respect for her.

Now she sat in her fancy parlor surrounded by paintings of desert and mountain scenes in frames covered with gold gilt. Keeping them company were rich tapestries from ancient European estates. Rugs throughout came from Spain in compatible colors and were scattered over the dark plank floors under groupings of satin-covered sofas and chairs.

I counted four fireplaces of marble in the rooms we visited, shipped from overseas during their European trip. Tall crystal or carved wooden candelabras stood on the ends of the mantels, the candles in them adding warm light to the rooms. Servants replaced the candles as they burned low. Large marble urns planted with tropical plants lined the walls and filled a glass conservatory along with other plants. There, among marble statues, were canaries warbling in brass cages. Strangest of all, chained to a perch was a scarlet macaw that occasionally let out a loud squawk to make itself known.

Most of the rooms led one into the other through wide arched openings. Off the large parlor was a smoking room for the men, and even more popular, a long dining room with a mahogany table down the middle that was laid out with all kinds of food. Fish in aspic, pheasant on a bed of greens, a whole roasted pig, lamb cutlets, and a side of beef being carved and served in portions requested by the diner. Bowls of salad, whole little potatoes drenched in butter and herbs, glazed carrots, creamed peas, pickled beets, and more. The desert table was piled with small cakes on glass pedestals, custard tarts, nut and berry pies, crystalized fruits, and even ices shaved and drenched in liquors. A whole table was set aside for iced bottles of champagne and the saucer glasses in which to serve it. This was a very popular area all evening. Oh, how I (and several of the other ladies) wanted to see into the kitchen!

One woman stated that she had been in there once. She spoke of a long, rectangular black stove that had been specially made in San Francisco. She said there were several ice boxes (they have their own ice shed out back), a huge walk-in pantry, and open shelving filled with glassware and white china pieces, with copper pots hanging from overhead racks.

I overheard a woman telling another that ahead of the couple leaving for their European tour, a massive oak chest had been filled with bars of bullion from their mine in Gold Canyon. It was put on a special Wells Fargo stage headed to San Francisco, with armed guards aboard to protect it from mountain bandits. In San Francisco, Shreve & Co., the well-known silversmiths, converted the silver into a magnificent dinner service.

When they set sail for England, the silver service was in the chest, a gift meant for Queen Victoria of England, one queen meeting another. One of the guests told Robert that they did just this, in exchange for some sprigs of ivy cut from one of the walls of the Queen's castle, and which are now growing up the side of the house.

Now, this story was denied by some of the women with whom I talked. They said the couple never got in to see the Queen. After all, since Albert's death in '61, the grief-stricken Queen seldom meets with the public. Some people also say that the ivy was taken without permission. Sandy, however, never mentioned the silver service to the men that night, instead talking about the fine hogs he had seen in England, along with wonderful sheep in Spain, and the cattle he had envied around Rome.

At this point, I had formed a very clear picture of our host and hostess. Sandy is a man who knows who he is and is happy with that, and is capable of enjoying his wealth. Eilley is a woman who is trying to live down the poverty and struggles of her past, and who will probably never be completely satisfied with all she has. Still, I hope that one day she learns to value her admirable character and many talents more than her plate glass windows and fancy rugs.

The party continued, more around us than with us. At least that's the way I felt. At one point, Robert and I met up, and both of us desiring some fresh air, we wandered out back of the house. There we found a large concrete pool meant, we were told, for swimming. It was filled with hot water piped in from a nearby thermal spring, which water gushed forth from the mouths of silver-headed mountain lions at the edge. It was set up so that the water could be emptied into a nearby stream.

It was while we were admiring this, that a man Robert had met in Carson came outside with his wife. While Robert talked with Harold Levi, Mrs. Levi and I walked over to some chairs and gave our feet a rest.

"Did you see the mahogany piano forte?" She sighed with a combination of pride and envy, and I hid a smile.

"With all that's on display," I commented, "I'm sorry that we won't be seeing their daughter."

"Oh, well, they're very protective of her, you know." Mrs. Levi leaned a little closer. "There's much speculation about her. No one knows her origins, you see. Eilley, whom I know slightly, gave birth to a son in the summer of '60, but he died two months later. The next summer she gave birth to a girl who lived only three months. Poor Eilley was just devastated. I think that's when she concentrated her attentions onto this house, in an effort to somehow make up for losing what was in actuality more important to her. And then they return from Europe with this child!"

"Did they adopt her from an orphanage?"

"One rumor is that the girl was born on shipboard to a woman with no husband. Another rumor is that the mother was unwed and died during the delivery. I have no idea why either rumor has gotten around, but as you say, they may just have adopted her from an agency. I find it puzzling that amid so much talk, neither Eilley nor Sandy have offered to tell the truth of the matter. And, of course, no one is so coarse as to ask."

Uncomfortable with such a private subject, I diverted the conversation into a discussion of the new mills being built along the Carson River. Mrs. Levi has a brother who works at one of them, so she was happy to discuss this. I then mentioned the camels I hoped to see that carry salt from the Columbus Salt Marsh in Esmeralda County to the mines at Dayton and Virginia City.

"Oh, yes, it's quite a sight. They're housed at Dayton, you know." She pursed her lips and declared, "The men who drive them are heartless." She actually gritted her teeth as she shook her head in anger. "The poor animals' padded feet aren't meant for the sharp rocks that lead up through Six Mile Canyon into Virginia City."

"I've heard a lot about that canyon."

"It's a nice buggy ride now, on its way down to Dayton. Of course, it's been torn up by prospectors, but there are still a number of small trees along the creek that runs through it. And bushes are already covering abandoned mining sites. Most of the trees are the ones that aren't good for lumber, of course, but still, they're green and so little east of Virginia City is. I was surprised to find it a true canyon, with steep-sided rock walls in places that narrow the passage through."

"And it's through this that the camels come into town?"

"Yes. They sometimes leave a trail of blood on the rocks. But they have to be brought into town at night that back way, because the horses and mules go crazy at the sight and smell of them. When the salt packs are removed, the camels head straight up Mt. Davidson where the earth is soft and they can fold their legs beneath them and look out over the vast expanse of desert below."

"It's almost as though they're dreaming of their desert homeland."

Mrs. Levi looked at me and smiled. "That's exactly what I thought. And please call me Ann." After a moment of silence between us, she spoke hesitantly. "Might I call upon you some time? It would be nice to have a friend in Carson with whom I feel so comfortable."

I returned her smile, as well as the spirit of her comment. "I think that would indeed be very nice. I'll look forward to it. And I'm Dolly." I reached into my beaded purse and pulled out a small tablet and pencil, writing down my name and address. That way, it is up to her to call upon me first, although I did add that I know a café that serves the most wonderful pies.

Once we were all back inside, Mr. and Mrs. Levi headed toward the reception room in preparation for leaving, while Robert and I entered the library. The shelves were ceiling high and filled with books bound in red, green, blue and gold leather. A stunning display indeed, but they had been bought "by the yard" and shipped here, then unloaded onto the shelves for display. They will probably never be read, at least by the current occupants. Sandy, after all, cannot read.

A servant approached us and invited Robert to join the men in the smoking room for a nightcap. He then informed me that the ladies were assembling in the dining room for coffee. This was a most tactful way to let everyone know that the evening was winding down and we should all think about our departures. But while Robert followed the servant, I didn't want any more refreshment so I ducked out a side door by the conservatory to stand on the side porch. The fresh mountain air and the lessening of the noise within was a great relief. As I walked along the porch toward the back of the house, I discovered another woman who had the same idea. I excused myself and started to turn around, but she arrested my movement.

"Oh, please, don't let me deter you from enjoying this wonderful air. If you're not determined to have it all to yourself, I would very much enjoy your company."

I walked to her side and stood looking out over small new trees and shrubs in a garden approaching the steep hillside behind the house. We introduced ourselves by our first names only, an unusual occurrence, but acknowledging identity while at the same time holding onto the mystique of sharing anonymously a moment of intimacy. Sheila and I stood silently for several minutes, simply breathing in the cool air, both of us having had enough of the constant social interactions of the past several hours. She was a petite, dark-haired woman about my same age, but with the calm and dignity of one much older.

I was thinking of introducing myself in more detail in case she too lived in Carson, when something interfered. Above us on the second-floor balcony that gave a ceiling to us below, we could hear the entrance of a man and woman, his footfall heavy and hers light. We remained silent, as we had just seen Eilley and Sandy downstairs and so realized that whoever they were, they must have snuck upstairs through one of the bedrooms to the balcony. The woman's first words, not to mention her tone of voice, was one of desperation.

"Oh, Lionel, I was so hoping that you would be here."

"Of course. I knew you would be here with your damn husband, but I was hoping to catch at least a brief moment alone with you." There was a long pause followed by the woman's loud sigh.

"I'm happy now," the woman said, "even if this is all that we can share tonight."

"As soon as I saw how drunk your worthless swine of a husband was becoming, I knew the chance was upon me to get you alone."

"I can't stay out here long, though. We should use this moment as an opportunity to arrange our next meeting."

"I want it to be for more than just a few words or an innocent luncheon."

"Oh, yes!"

"Maybe we can manage it when the lodge meets next week. He'll be there and no one will comment if I'm not. I do sometimes miss a meeting, what with my business being what it is."

The couple muttered a few indistinct words to one another and then reentered the house. My new friend and I looked at one another with raised brows and then broke out in very unladylike giggles. We hurriedly collected ourselves before also retreating into the house. We parted with a nod and a smile as I went into the dining room for a quick cup of coffee.

Soon after, in the reception room as we donned our wraps, I looked round for Sheila, but didn't see her. However, once outside, as our buggy moved away we passed the one carrying Sheila and her husband. We waved to one another and smiled with what must have looked like conspiratorial mirth, because Robert questioned the exchange. I told him I would tell him later, although I'm not sure that I will, not wanting to be accused of eavesdropping. Or maybe I just don't want to lose the lingering mystique of the moment whenever I recall it.

Driving away from the mansion felt like slowly waking from a lovely dream, the memory of it persisting even while the real world slowly came back into focus. And now, several days later, it is as though I have read a fairytale book that began, "Once upon a time...".

Lucy remembered that the next letter from Dolly had not been as light in its tone. It was as though Aurora never left a person, even after they moved away. Whether by newspapers or letters from friends, the saga of life in Aurora was broadcast far and wide. Maybe, Lucy concluded, it was the exciting, even grotesque nature of the stories told about it, that attracted those men in pursuit of adventure, including Roger.

July 15, 1864 *Remember my telling you about a duel in Aurora between a friend's husband and John Campbell? The story took a new turn last month, and I have just heard word of it from my friend, Mrs. Gorman herself. Campbell once again turned belligerent after imbibing too freely at the Del Monte Exchange Saloon, where he got into an argument with Mr. Parlin, a large and powerful miner. Mr. Campbell had worked hard to acquire property as well as interest in several mines, and I think he had fostered some jealousy among those less fortunate.*

In any case, at some point both men pulled their guns and bullets flew. Both of their shots missed. But before another shot could ring out, Parlin grabbed Campbell and hit him over the head with the butt of his gun, splitting his scalp open. Even so, Campbell refused to go down and tried to fire his gun. The revolver's cylinder jammed and so the two men fought with their fists until Parlin backed Campbell over a barrel and fired twice, hitting Campbell in the side and stomach. Finally, the men around them stepped in and stopped the action, although even with all of his wounds, Campbell still wanted to fight. Instead, he was taken to the doctor's office where he died four hours later. Parlin turned himself in to the sheriff, after which the coroner's jury found he had acted in self-defense. Mrs. Gorman says she can at last cease worrying about the feud with her husband starting up again with Campbell.

Lucy picked up the second letter she had received from Jane. It was quite confidential in its tone, and had been somewhat worrying to Lucy when she had first read it.

(Sunday, July 17, 1864) I am only now able to be alone to write you. Dolly and Robert go to church on Sundays, something I seldom do any more. I still feel some guilt about what happened when we were all in Placerville in '62. Sitting in church somehow makes it worse. I do not much like the feeling of being judged, although I am quite aware that it is me who is doing the judging. My staying home also gives Dolly and Robert a break from me, and frankly, me from them. We live so much together, and they so generously do not want to leave me alone. Little do they realize that it is something I enjoy. I suppose I could tell them that outright, but I don't know how to cushion the telling of it so that it is received well.

You see, I have come to realize that being alone is not the same as being lonely. However, to those who are happily yoked to another person, it's difficult for them to realize that. I simply find the daily routine of our days increasingly irksome. Dolly is a wonderful cook, and she enjoys it. But so do I. At the same time, Dolly considers it her kitchen, and sets in to prepare the meals without usually consulting with me. I therefore simply assist most of the time. On Sunday mornings, however, while they are out at church and the meal they take afterwards, I can at least bake desserts that last us for several days. And I can feel productive.

I am sorry if I seem to be whining a bit, but I am tired of holding back my tears, and find that "talking to you" in this manner helps to dissipate that urge that is fed by simple frustration. I have to smile at that. We women hold our heads up high with dignity while grieving losses, suppressing complaints of illness so as not to upset our loved ones, and swallowing our anger at men's stupid decisions. But given enough frustration, coupled with a feeling of powerlessness, we then shed tears. Men have little patience with this phenomenon, as they don't understand it. They seem to think that if they can define a problem, they can then somehow fix it, not realizing that's not possible when the problem is an emotional one.

By the way, Dolly never refers to Mrs. Helms, the oh-so-controversial woman we once knew in Placerville. I think she has put that part of her life behind her, the same as she did her time as a soiled dove in Nevada City back during the gold rush. I imagine even you and Dolly never refer to that time, although that is when you first met. Someday I hope to know all that went on back then, when she married Robert after you evidently left that town so abruptly with Jim trailing after you. Now, that about sums up what I have pieced together over the years. But I know it is none of my business, and so of course I have never queried Dolly about it.

Lucy couldn't hide a smirk as she said out loud, "And, indeed, you shall never know." With that satisfaction admitted, Lucy finished Jane's unusually revealing letter, only too aware that women seldom were so open about their inner-most feelings. Maybe, Lucy thought, it had been a matter of the miles between them, alleviating the need for Jane to deal with eyes upon her while so openly discussing her feelings.

So, Lucy, I have made a decision. The next time Robert talks of going to Virginia City, I am going to insist that he take Dolly and me with him. We will not be denied the opportunity to see that great town.

I have made a new friend outside the circle of acquaintances that Dolly and I share. I met her after a service at the Presbyterian Church, which I had wandered into while out for a long walk one Sunday morning. My friend's name is Mollie Clemens and she is the wife of Orion Clemons, the Territorial Secretary. They have recently moved into a charming house they built on the corner of Spear and Division streets. Their happiness would be complete if it were not for the passing of their only child, eight year old Jennie, who had been a student of Miss Clapp's Sierra Seminary. She passed away the first day of February from meningitis brought on by spotted fever. They buried her at Wright's Cemetery.

Her passing has been hard on the family, and not made easier by the reaction of Orion's brother, Sam Clemens, also known at the Territorial Enterprise as Mark Twain. He has been lashing out in print at the undertaker, Samuel Wright, who is a well-known local carpenter. He is right now the only undertaker, and he also owns the cemetery. Mr. Clemens accused Mr. Wright of extortion of the grieving by charging them prices that are exorbitant. But it has all settled down now, and everyone attributes Mr. Clemons's rage to the intensity of his grief over the loss of his favored niece.

I think Mollie likes me because I will let her talk, or not, as the fancy takes her. I sit in her parlor and drink her tea, heating more water for the pot as needed, as though her kitchen was my own. One day, we baked a cake together, and she seemed to enjoy that. She is a rather masculine looking woman, although she dresses well, if not plainly. She wears her hair in the current fashion of parted in the middle and swept back, with its abundant length held by a ribbon. At rest, her long face is off-set by a prominent nose and a strong jaw. But when she smiles or talks of Jennie, every aspect of her softens and she exudes a warmth that shows the real woman she is, and the friend I have come to appreciate. The only other time I have seen Mollie soften so much is when she talks about her husband's accomplishments.

She is fresh in my mind because I ran into her yesterday and took her to lunch. Her sadness hangs over her like a transparent veil. She told me, "But so many people are feeling the loss of children." She made it sound as though having such an intensity of feeling was a sin. My response to that was strong. "Their grief is there's. It has nothing to do with yours and shouldn't be compared. Grief is too personal for that. Would you try to compare a blueberry to a melon?"

She managed a smile at that, and our conversation turned to things more general. We even shared some few bits of harmless gossip, a sure sign of a woman returning to at least a semblance of normality.

CHAPTER 5

1864 - 1865

There was more about recipes, as well as a description of a dress Jane was sewing, but Lucy skimmed through that to the end of the letter. She then picked up Dolly's letter written a month after the one from Jane.

__Carson, August, 1864__: Carson City! A civilized place at last. This time we may have found our permanent home, as there is much industry here, and Robert is once again thinking of setting up a livery stable much as he had in Placerville. But I am beginning to realize that there is about my husband a curiosity for what he calls "other places". I never saw this in him before, but I see it now. With Carson being the hub of so many of these other places, I am hoping that short trips to see them will suffice for him.

He is also enjoying the company of men met in the saloons. He spends more time in them than ever he used to do, even when in Aurora. Maybe it's because these men here are of a better class, with less tendency for random violence, and just hard working family men.

He tells me that one of the most popular of the stage drivers, Hank Monk, spends a good deal of his time in the saloons, and has wonderful tales to tell of his trips over the Sierra. He drives the stages at a fast clip, and considering that the mountain roads are narrow, with nothing between the stage and a sheer drop-off. We traveled his main route, the Placerville Road, and once was enough. Robert and some of the other men often have to carry Mr. Monk out to his stage because he's too drunk to walk. But evidently, once the reins are in his hands, he knows just what to do. Passengers awaiting their trip with him, having seen him drinking, don't seem to mind. They toss back the last of their drinks, cash in their chips or gulp the last of their meal, and run to get inside the coach before it leaves without them.

What is Carson like? Its core is a large central plaza that is acres of open space, most of it surrounded by a slab rail fence knee-high to a tall man. This is framed by wide streets, and on three sides by buildings of wood and a few two-story of brick, all of which overlook the plaza, huddled together as though seeking comfort. These include some of the first houses built here, shops old and new (market, bakery, hardware, dry goods, and a periodical and tobacco shop). There are also law offices, and the assay office in the Harris Building.

This bastion of civilization was very welcome, as all around it was a vast plain of dry, heartless scrub of no value to anyone. Dust seemed to be the main import and export, seldom damped by water wagons, and even less by the weather.

The plaza itself, disgracefully full of weeds around the edges, is used mostly by freighters to set up overnight camps. However, the town also uses it for charity bazaars, livestock sales, the gathering of parades before starting out through town, and for military honors — all of which we have enjoyed since arriving here.

To establish Carson as a place attractive for settlement, there is a schoolhouse, a church and even a small theater, along with several surprisingly nice restaurants. And, of course, there are a large number of saloons and gambling halls. Oh, and the Express Stage Line that carries Wells, Fargo & Co.'s express and the mail into California and over to Aurora. So you see how civilized and developed we are!

Upon arrival, we stayed at the Ormsby House on the corner of Carson and Second streets, so we saw much of the traffic through town. Robert quickly became friends with Mr. Gibson and Mr. Vance, the proprietors of the hotel. His very public association with them has allowed us to quickly fit into general society.

There are several streets of houses around the outer part of town beyond the business district. Some of the houses are two-story, and most have large front porches where people can escape the heat of the kitchen in the evenings. We hope to obtain one of these houses, several of which are for rent. Many of the houses are on lots given away in the earliest of times, simply in exchange for the promise that the lots would be built on. Interestingly, on the west side of town, there is a large oval race track with bleachers ready to receive spectators. When viewers' interest in the event wanes, they can look beyond the arena to the beauty of the Sierra in the distance.

Carson City has progressed as much as a town can that is only four years old and now in Nevada Territory. It is expected that Nevada will become a state soon, and serious men say that when that happens, Carson will become the capitol. If so, there are plans for a domed building of locally quarried sandstone to be built right where the plaza is now, necessitating a traveler to go around it, meaning Mosser Street to the north of it and Second Street on the south of it.

The main street through the grid of straight cross-streets composing the town is King Street. If one continues west on that street, it will take you all the way to Lake Bigler through King's Canyon. Some of the people here are particularly eager to change the name of the lake, since as I mentioned before, Governor Bigler is such a southern sympathizer.

The lake area is indeed a very beautiful place. Its dark blue water is surrounded by old growth forests, much of which has been harvested for use at mining towns. But it is also a sacred place to the Washo Indians. First called Lake Bonpland by Fremont, and as it still is on some maps printed in France, the local tribes refer to it as Tahoe, which means something like "big waters in a high place". There is a sawmill at a tiny hamlet on the eastern shore called Glenbrook, reached through King's Canyon Road to Spooner Summit. How do I know this? I went there on the stage with two other women.

The stage charges 50 cents round trip, and that includes, at least for men, a stop at the springs for a bath. It is all the way a steep and winding road that only brave women eager to escape summer heat will travel a second time. I doubt I will be one of them. Robert and some friends have been there, with of course a stop just as they left town at the brewery on the corner of King and Division Streets.

When men talk of the future of the town, they get quite animated. They talk of railroads, sawmills, a courthouse, parks, three-story buildings of brick, and even a U.S. Mint someday. They also talk about Abe Curry's Warm Springs Hotel east of town used as the prison, and which will soon be next to a large territorial prison now under construction using stone quarried on-site, and with Mr. Curry as its first warden.

Back in '57, Abe Curry purchased the Eagle Valley Ranch here and, not liking the way the area was being developed, decided to start a town of his own.

I have met the clean-shaven Mr. Curry twice, and I find him a stern, rather cold man. He has what I consider mean, deep-set eyes, and a hard, square jaw accenting a tight mouth. He should make a good warden. He and his partners, Green, Musser, and Proctor, attempted to lay out a townsite. I'm not sure what prompted it, but they sold out to Major William Ormsby a year later, and he did develop a proper town that included his merchandise store. He also decided to call the town Carson City, in honor of his friend, the explorer Kit Carson.

It is obvious that citizens here desire Carson to be the central-most prosperous place in the whole of the area. But all of this depends on Nevada shedding its status as a territory and becoming a state. In the meantime, they have not forgotten Mr. B. L. King, who along with his daughter, started a way-station here in 1852, and thus started the whole thing.

That it is a more settled place now, expected to last well into the future, is proved by the number of churches already established. The Presbyterian Church is just finishing construction, but already completed is St. Peter's Episcopal on the corner of Telegraph and Division Streets. Many of the ladies from these churches help to maintain Treadway Park, a popular picnic area, by planting flowers there each spring.

Oh, yes, I think we will like living here very much. For here, there is a female society in which Jane and I can participate. And people talk of things other than mine productivity, the amount of water being pumped from a shaft, mining stock values and swindles, and miners' health problems.

Lucy thought back over the last fifteen years. So much had happened to Dolly that had been of a life-changing nature, as well as to herself, Jim and Roger. When she had begun receiving letters from Dolly, Jim would wait patiently to see if Lucy would pass him the letter, or just read to him those parts she considered not too personal. Lucy had been protective of Dolly from the time they had first met in Nevada City, during the rush back in the '50's. Therefore, she read to Jim mostly descriptions of places and events, but none of Dolly's feelings about anything. And Roger heard only about the travel and places; and maybe a few exciting events.

Dear Roger, she sighed, now just about to turn eighteen. He had become a professional gambler like his father, a foregone conclusion from the time he had been four. With long fingers and an odd genius of ability, he had been able to handle cards better than most adults by the time he was five. He had always had an independent nature, reaching out to his father's cards almost before he could hold a spoon. Roger's fondest memory was when his father had let him, just seven years old, join a real game with adults. He had won 3 out of 4 hands. To his great delight, he had known by the men's reaction that they had not "let him win".

The note Roger had left Lucy had said he was heading to Aurora in Nevada. Lucy recalled the letters Dolly had sent from Aurora, and fought an involuntary shudder. Of course, what Dolly had described had occurred a dozen years earlier, so Lucy sat and pondered what that town might be like now. Surely it was smaller, what with much of the mining a thing of the past. Did Roger assume it had grown into a major center of activity? Would he be disappointed at what he would find there? Lucy recalled her conversations about Aurora that she'd had with men in Placerville, and she was not comforted.

The next letter in the stack had been from Robert to Jim. Whether Robert had not yet received Lucy's letter informing them that Jim had left home, or they simply never received it, she was not sure. Mail delivery was not always dependable, especially during winter, times of flood, or during local conflicts.

(*September, 1864*) *Hello, Jim. I thought you might like to hear from good ole Robert for a change. I'm stuck for the night in a tiny town on the Carson River, a few miles east of Carson. A new friend of mine, the foreman of the Carson & Tahoe Lumber Fluming Company up at Glenbrook on Lake Bigler, accepted a commission to haul supplies to Dayton, with a stop on the way at Empire City, where I am now. Mr. Terry needed help with the heavy load, and I can always use the extra money, so I volunteered to go with him. Life in Carson is more expensive than I anticipated. Empire is near a number of mills along the Carson River that process ore brought to them by mines up canyon and any outlying mine.*

Part of the time on our way here we were on a fairly good road, one regularly traveled by the hundreds of people on their way to Gold Canyon towns, Virginia City or Dayton. About two miles out from Carson, I could smell sulphur and was told it was from some boiling hot springs nearby. Not long after that we veered off to our right onto a road that was much rougher, as it was rutted by the heavy iron wheels of ore wagons. It was a dry, dusty stretch through sand

and sagebrush as we moved up some rising hills toward the Carson River. With the sprawling buildings of the Mexican Mill within sight, we knew we were close to our destination because we could smell the river.

(**Later**) *We have completed the delivery of our load of wood and tools. We had a surprisingly good supper at a chop stand in one of the saloons, hosted by Ed Dorsey, superintendent of the Mexican Mill. He has a nice house on the edge of town that I know Dolly would envy. I also had one very strong drink at the saloon, just to be friendly. But not being in the mood to get drunk or lose money at the tables, I have retired to a rented cot in the corner of a sea of them in the Kinney Hotel. The second floor is just an open common room of what will be a very crowded space of tired workers after the evening shift-change at the mills.*

Although referred to as Empire City now, the town is more often referred to as Dutch Nick's, or even as Dutch Hotel, which is on some of the older maps. It was started a few years ago by Nicholaus Ambrose. The main street is only about three-quarters of a mile long, but has all that is needed by way of market, saloon, barber and bath house, blacksmith and livery, several rooming houses, and a scattering of homes. It developed from the way-station Nick established here in the early '50's in aid of the emigrants passing through the area, with a saloon and store, as well as a log cabin he called a hotel. Even that much was no doubt a welcome sight for those bedraggled travelers.

As rough a place as it is now, back in the '50's it was much worse. Even the soiled doves avoided the area. Mr. Dorsey told me that in September of '57, two merchants bringing supplies to Nick were waylaid by Indians, and one of the merchants was killed in the confrontation. But there is little violent death here now. On the other hand, back in '61 a man named Juan Gonzales was poisoned by another man out of revenge for something.

Oddly, some people refer to the town as Seaport Town because the Carson River overflows its banks most years, sometimes right into the town, what with it being so close to the river. That may be why their cemetery, which the locals refer to as Hillside Cemetery, is up on a hill above the town. I hiked up to this lonely place before retiring tonight, walking to the back of it through overgrown weeds and sand dotted with ground squirrel holes. There were several wooden crosses with names burned onto them, a few more permanent headboards with names neatly painted, and even one with a simple iron railing around the grave.

There was no grave marker inside the railing, just two little wooden crosses, and I wonder if this belongs to Mr. and Mrs. Ambrose's first children. They were twins, Mary and Charles; Mary dying soon after birth in '58 and Charles in the winter of '61. It took only a few moments to reach the back of the cemetery, being so small, but from there I could look out past the town and the river to the green, sweeping plain they call the Carson River Valley. It was a view that should bring peace to those visiting this small burying ground.

There are a number of lumber and quartz mills along a six mile stretch of river here, with more being planned. As we passed the Mexican Mill, I could see long lines of wagons loaded with ore waiting to be unloaded. Back in the summer of '61 there was a quartz mill just above here built by Atchinson and Harrington that had 16 stamps. And to think, the Mexican Mill now has 44 stamps. This is proof of how much mining is being done up the hill in Gold Canyon.

The population back then, for the whole area, was just under 300. Now there are about 700 souls working here. Enough population that in October of '61, the legislature for the Nevada Territory set the boundaries of the Third District for Congressional representation to be within Eagle Valley, Carson City and Empire City, and I guess a few other places nearby.

*(**Later**) While at the saloon earlier, I met three carpenters boarding at this hotel, George Lynch, John Mahoney and a man who only went by his last name, Tyler. Between them I learned that Nick's wife Rebecca was the first white woman to settle for a short time in Virginia City. They have several children, those that have survived their early years; Martin aged three years, Lizzie aged almost two, Lena still a wee infant, and I am told Mrs. Ambrose is expecting again. Nick was one of the first to the area of Six Mile Canyon that included Peter O'Riley, Pat McLaughlin and "Old Virginny", who gave his name to the big town on Mt. Davidson.*

Nick had been among those who had left Johntown to move into the canyon, since his customers were moving in that direction. He set up a big tent to house a saloon and boarding house, collecting $14 a week for blankets he provided, although the men had to sleep on them out in the sagebrush. The liquor he served them was the famous "tarantula juice" still talked about here.

Nick is now in charge of what by comparison is a refined little town, although Empire City is a town of mostly men. Out of the 700 or so people here, I could count on one hand the number of good women I have seen, with only a scattering of children. And yes, of course, I've seen a few of the other kind of woman, but they are not as conspicuous as in some places. I am told that a new family has arrived only this week and more are expected. With the growing number of mills along the river, there are good jobs available for those who are not distracted by thinking their fortune lies with finding the mother lode.

(**Later**) It was to the lumber mill that we brought most of our wagon load. The timber is cut around Lake Bigler, and then brought here down flumes to the Carson River so it can be floated downstream right to the mill that perches on the river bank. The mill produces fuel wood, as well as tall posts for supports in the underground mines. Most coveted is the lumber for building.

It's somewhat unusual to have lumber mills and quartz mills so close together, but with the river allowing for steam and water power, I guess not so unusual here. The water wheels are huge, the biggest I've ever heard of.

(**Later**) After our one night in Empire, we moved on to Dayton, although Mr. Terry calls it Chinatown because there were once large numbers of Chinese brought here to work. It is the final resting place of Old Virginny (James Fennimore or James Finney, depending on who you talk to). It's a small town. Lots of short streets, corrals, big wooden barns painted red, and stone storage sheds.

Back in the early '50's, there wasn't anything at Dayton other than Spafford Hall's place, a tiny but busy way station. But in '54, Spafford sold out to James McMarlin, who of course renamed it McMarlin's Station. The next year the Mormons brought some fifty Chinese here from California to help dig a ditch to divert the waters of the Carson River into Gold Canyon. Where there's mining, there needs to be water somewhere nearby.

After the ditch was done, the Chinese stayed on to mine, although in a limited way because of the restrictive rules of the mine owners and Miner's Union. Their camp became known as Chinatown, or Johntown (after the derogatory name of John that whites attach to the Chinese men). But it was also known as Mineral Rapids and Nevada City until 1861 when Mr. Day surveyed the townsite and named the town Dayton. They proudly claim to be the first place in Nevada to have had a dance, a marriage, and a divorce.

(Later) *I have to admit to some anxiety as we passed up Gold Canyon and through the crowded station at Devil's Gate, an austere and unfriendly area set up at the squeeze of a narrow pass with two high side walls of rock. Besides a blacksmith, there is a shack set up where the freighters can buy drinks and food for themselves and their teams, make repairs, and if smart, avoid the low-class card sharps who hang about. We paid our toll and continued up Gold Canyon, passing through the congestion of shacks at American Flats and past many coyote hole mines along the way.*

The names of the mines are posted on raw boards, written in tar, whitewash or even dried mud if new. Names such as "Future Hell", "Wild Cat", "Hell a Roaring", "Hog Pit", and so forth. Some crude, some humorous, all bold. We dropped off a barrel at a small store before continuing to Silver City, Gold Hill, and all the tumbled-together clumps of shacks between them. We passed the grave of Ethan Allen Grosch whose marker declares "Son of Reverend A. B. Grosch, Born at Reading, Pennsylvania, Died Jan. 28, 1857". I suppose in the far future people will wonder who this man might have been, but those who know say a silent "thank you" and tip their hat before moving on. For he is now acknowledged as one of two brothers who first realized the "awful blue stuff" the gold seekers were complaining about was silver.

Thankfully, we stopped at the tiny bar of the Old Stone Hotel for a quick beer and a pickled egg. It was cool and inviting, and I regretted having to leave. These little towns along the canyon merge one into another as a continuous irruption of hardworking men. Some are wielding picks and shovels, and others pushing wheelbarrows from mine openings overhung with winches. Some of the bigger openings use mules to haul out small wagons loaded with chunks of ore. Most of this is then put onto a huge ore wagon pulled by long lines of mules or horses. These passed us as they rolled down the winding road to the mills that we had left behind on the Carson River.

We traveled along with those wagons that were returning empty, soon to be filled again with whatever ore had been taken out while they had been delivering their last load. The colorful shouts of the teamsters merged with the sounds of hammering on new construction, along with the clanks, thuds and rattling associated with the mines, all filling the air without ceasing, while the brays and whinnies of dozens of teams acted as a background chorus. The men who crowded outside saloons, assay offices, restaurants, and markets, added their loud voices in their efforts to be heard. And yet, amid all of this, I knew there were men sleeping soundly in boarding houses.

These canyon towns have nothing in common other than their efforts to find wealth. The men here are not interested in putting down roots or providing for a future townsite. They build only what is needed to support their efforts, and when the men become dissatisfied, they move on. If any of these towns survive into the far future, it will be a miracle.

I asked Mr. Terry what it had been like back at the beginning of the mining excitement, before even this much rudimentary refinement was present. He stroked his beard and smiled in a way that can only be called wistful.

"For starters, it wasn't silver back in '58 that drove everyone to break their backs searching. It was gold. We grumbled and swore at the blue mud that clogged our rockers. One time a Mexican who'd worked mines in Sonora saw me and some others throwing buckets of the blue stuff off to the side. He told us we were throwing away $2 to get $1. We didn't pay any attention. Didn't even question him, like we should've. We didn't know until '59 about the blue stuff being silver.

"Back then we were wrapped in the stupid superiority of youth. The future was something to scoff at. We only wanted enough gold to buy a wild time at Spafford Hall's place. There we could gamble and drink the god-awful, boozy concoction we called tarantula juice. We swore it was what kept away the scorpions, coyotes, and wild cats at night. And made the tarantulas sick if they bit us. 'Cause we threw down our blankets out in the sage brush at night. Best sleep I've ever had."

He laughed loud enough to cover the braying of his mules and spat onto the ground. "The ancient water that brought the gold and silver to the area had long since drained away, leaving no grass that would've enriched the ground for agriculture. Typically, those are the things you need for a mining town, water and animal feed. We did have a few springs and lots of alkaline bunch grass. There was a creek in Six Mile Canyon, but none up hill on Sun Mountain. All supplies had to be freighted in. We ate at Eilley Orrum's, where we were served the best pork and beans around. Or we spent the evening at Chinatown, where we were met with smiling girls and the juice. By midnight, wherever we were, desert dust would be gone from our throats and gold dust from our pockets, and we'd stumble to our night's rest. The next day would be much the same."

"Must have gotten monotonous after awhile."

"Naw!" He drew the back of his hand across his beard, and for a split second I could see his mouth, and it was smiling. "On Saturday nights we'd *go up to the second floor of Spafford Hall's at eight o'clock where a yellow-backed fiddle would strike up a lively tune. Ole Spafford would climb up on a raised platform at the end of the hall and yell out 'Take your partners for the French-four.'" He laughed in that raucous way of his that hinted of wonderful memories he cared not to put into words. "There weren't many females there. Eilley, of course. And Laura Ellis, who had a ranch at Chinatown, and who also served meals to the miners. A few of the soiled doves that knew how to dance would join in. A few times we even took a turn with Princess Sarah, daughter of old Chief Winnemucca. Yep, those were the days."*

He shook his head and turned quiet for the next half hour. I too slipped into memories of my early youth. I concluded that I was lucky to have survived those years, and sure am grateful for what I have in the present. But my friend seemed despondent with his memories, at least until we reached our destination and he encountered men he knew who welcomed him. And who bought us drinks at the nearest saloon.

*(**October, 1864**) As I set out to walk through Virginia city, I was surprised to find it less than what I had expected. Everything I had been told about it was reminiscent of wild and untamed abandon, and that was certainly true at night. But during the day I could see that it's mainly a sea of shanties near the mines, with the business section along "C" Street and a few nice houses further up the hill. The mine owners and superintendents have the best ones.*

There are, as in all mining towns, boarding houses throughout the town filled with rows of cots where shift workers take turns sleeping. An unusual but short rain storm turned the dust to mud and made travel on the steep and slippery streets leading downhill to the mines difficult to navigate. There, we were greeted by giant piles of cast-off tailings, ponds full of dirty water pumped up from shafts, and huge mill complexes with white steam billowing up from tall, black smokestacks. The small mines might be somewhat reduced, the owners fearing that "borrasca" will soon replace "bonanza", but the assay offices still have enough business that one of the assayers was eating beef steak for breakfast at the table next to mine.

It's no wonder that in a town like this there are few good women. Many of the females I did see were not shy, especially about making it clear what they did for a living. One old dear, bent over with hard years and wearing a ratty shawl and limp bonnet, was soliciting handouts. Few people failed to give her a dime, just like I did. A man pulled me aside and told me that she had a pension from her late husband and had no need of handouts. But I figure any old woman who would be willing to compromise her dignity in such a way must need the money.

There are some families here, with more arriving all the time, and there's even a small school for their children at the north end of town. And because of the danger in the mines, there is an orphanage in a small house run by the newly arrived Daughters of Charity for those children left on their own. But they also board children by the day for those single parents who must work long hours. The sisters are planning another fundraising fair for this December, as they need funds for more construction and these events raise a lot of money.

It is the arrival of the families, and the need for the businesses that support them, that is driving the building of a growing business district on "C" Street, along with homes on all streets.

The red-light district is at the bottom of the hill on central "D" Street. But there are also regular businesses and homes there, too, on the north and south ends of the long street. Wagons of planed lumber arrive daily to supply the constant construction of buildings, although it's often quickly sold right from the back of the wagon, if it's not targeted for a specific delivery. With stacks of bricks nearby, scaffolding embraces many of the buildings going up, giving the place a sense of permanency unseen in most mining towns. The general design seems to be a mix of Victorian excess and Western high-fronted illusion. So if another bonanza occurs, all will certainly be in readiness to meet the town's needs. I find it interesting that all of this takes place in the face of what is considered a period of financial down-turn for the country.

Lucy smiled at that, knowing as she did that the second hoped for bonanza had occurred just two years before in '73. It was still going on, but for how long, she couldn't help but wonder. She returned her attention to Robert's letter.

We delivered our load of tools at the California Pan Mill on the eastern edge of town. It's surrounded by huge ore dumps that look like honey-colored sand dunes, and the area certainly looked very busy to me. If all the activity I saw takes place in a borrasca, during bonanza times it must be an almost overwhelmingly exciting place.

Before returning to the wagon and our bedrolls as the night came on, we retired to the newly opened Boston Saloon on north "B" Street for a quick drink. The owner, Bill Brown, I think named his saloon Boston because that city is representative of freedom and liberty, and so it is sometimes used as a symbol by the abolitionist movement, and Bill is a black man. He is also a very savvy businessman. I say this because he has installed a recently patented gaslight system that will reduce leaks from the older, smelly system in most saloons. Of great good humor, Bill is very popular with his mix of customers. His place is one of the few that serves wine in stemmed glasses, appreciated by those from the South who sip wine and smoke red clay pipes instead of the more usual white clay. He recently hosted a group of men where he served a whole roasted hog's head as the centerpiece of their supper.

We sat at a small table, and I watched an older black lady at the far end of the bar smoking a pipe while asking for a glass of ginger water. When she saw me watching her, she frowned, but when I smiled and nodded my head in greeting, she also smiled before turning her attention to the drink being placed before her. She then moved to a table to join a game of dominoes just beginning.

As we leaned against the bar in the narrow establishment, we could not escape the town's constant voice. Stamps thump day and night, the steam hoists sigh loudly as they deliver men into the depths of the mines, whistles shriek to announce various things, bull-whackers and muleskinners shout their loud oaths at protesting beasts, and street vendors shout out extravagant claims about their wares. Meanwhile, we could feel the vibrations through the soles of our boots from the subterranean blasts beneath our feet, taking place somewhere in the maze of tunnels below the town. After a day's effort to be heard in all this, I'm not surprised that wives often remind their man to lower his voice after coming home.

We moved on to another saloon and ended up sharing a drink with Joe Goodman and Dennis McCarthy, owners of The Enterprise newspaper since '61. They were in their early twenties when they purchased the paper, and it quickly rose to respected popularity and profit. Ambition here in the West starts early in life, boosted by raw courage and the confidence to match it. Such young men have definite goals in mind, and they are determined to achieve them, not just try their hand at them.

Lucy stopped to reflect, then smiled. What Robert had of course not mentioned in his letter, but that Dolly had relayed as a point of discrete humor, was that while at the mill Robert had been visited by an urge to answer the call of nature more than would just wet the ground. He was shown to a small tent-like structure enclosing a two-foot wooden plank with a hole cut in the middle and supported by stacks of bricks on the ends. Beneath the board's hole was a small bucket, and near at hand a stack of old newspapers. The user was expected to take the bucket out to a large pit in the back, and then use a nearby shovel to toss in an ample number of scoops of dirt. The bucket was then returned to the lean-to. Knowing how private a man Robert was, Lucy had laughed out loud upon reading this. Not for the first time, however, she simply thought to herself, "Well, needs must."

Before leaving Virginia City, we were introduced to the man first called "Pancake", but who is now more often referred to as <u>*Mr.*</u> *Comstock. After watching him cavort in a saloon, I made the rash comment that he seemed to have had too much to drink. Mr. Goodman responded that even when sober, his behavior was not always of a rational nature. But evidently the mine owners are unconcerned about Mr. Comstock's reputation now adays, since other than a few scattered mines, what people so often refer to as "the Comstock" is really just the Ophir Mine and those near it on the rich lead, and some few in Gold Canyon. A while back, "Ole Pancake" sold most of his ownership in mines for far less than their value.*

It seemed that no matter which saloon we visited, there were always a number of newspaper reporters, editors, or type-setters leaning on the bar. They have a capacity for liquor that is unequaled by most men, no doubt built up by long practice. Probably not good for them, but their stories that are not fit for print make them such great fun that no one seems to care.

It hadn't been long before Lucy had received another letter from Robert. She had enjoyed his letters because they covered a much wider field of experience than either Jane or Dolly would be allowed.

*(**November, 1864**) Dolly and Jane are off visiting Carson's shops, and I am home with a head cold, having been confined to my bed by my caring nurses. So I thought I would tell you of an interesting interaction I had yesterday.*

One of the reporters for *The Enterprise* has for some time been a man with a luxurious mustache, curly hair, and deep, penetrating eyes by the name of Sam Clemens. I am well acquainted with his brother Orion Clemens, who was appointed Secretary of the Nevada Territory back in '61. Orion has the same deep-set eyes and curly hair, but the lower half of his face is covered in facial hair and he has a quiet, powerful demeanor. His wife Mollie is a friend of Jane's, I believe.

Orion once told me that his brother has, in the past, written his witty reporting under the name of "Josh", but has now changed his name to Mark Twain while writing for the newspaper. Brother Clemens was recently in a saloon here on a stop-over for a stage trip to San Francisco. It seems he has been banished from Virginia City for writing too many hoax type articles about those in that city, as well as those here in the Carson area, including some very angry women. His sense of humor being on the dark side of practical jokes, he sometimes goes a bit too far.

When I discovered who my drinking companion was, I introduced myself as a friend of Orion's and he held out his hand. "Call me Sam." It was then that I noticed his long neck, and thought to myself that it was good that he had plenty, considering how often he sticks it out with his verbal challenges. That's the type of thing, you see, that he might say in one of his joshing type articles.

When he discovered that I knew his history, and why he had been banished from Virginia City, he opened up to me in a surprising manner. I must say, however, that the intensity of his gaze sometimes made me want to look away for a relief from it. You see, he feels that people here have lost their sense of humor when he throws out his outlandish jests and even insults, which he sees as so absurd that they should be laughed at. Unfortunately, not everyone realizes that his so-called reports are absurd jests, so that the target of them is put in an embarrassing position and forced to defend themselves.

Over the last month or so he has been very much involved in helping to collect money for the Sanitary Fund, that esteemed and worthwhile endeavor that supports the welfare of those fighting in the war. Because of that effort, many were set to forgive him his tactless pranks. But he evidently couldn't resist a devilish urge to publish a claim that Carson ladies had diverted some of this charitable money into what he claimed was their "Miscegenation Society". Well, of course, there is no such thing here, or I dare say, anywhere else. The ladies, however, created an uproar, not finding it humorous at all. He told me *he had known this was not a good thing to publish and had actually set the article aside. But someone at the newspaper saw it and put it in.*

Before this, he had published a hoax article about a rival editor, who he claimed as a friend. Nevertheless, it did not go over well. For one who is so eager to claim inexcusable things about others in the name of humor, when he was roundly criticized by Mr. Laird of the Virginia Union, Sam became enraged and challenged him to a duel. This, as you know, is illegal. Sentiment having turned against Sam, once a respected editor of The Enterprise, friends urged him to immediately vacate Virginia City. Consequently, my meeting up with him over a beer in Carson.

He talked in a slow, drawling way, and yet he covered the terrain of his thoughts with words that precisely painted the images he wanted me to see. I wanted him to continue talking for as long as I could pin him to the bar. He spoke of his problems in a general way, and I think he took my silent nodding as agreement with his opinion that he had been unfairly treated.

Still, he was resigned, and even not that much blaming anyone but himself for going too far in what he had done. He had assumed people would simply put what he said into the same category as when he referenced the forests along the Carson River near Empire City, everyone knowing there was no such thing there. He told me that he now intends to write for San Francisco's Morning Call. There are also two literary journals there, the Golden Era and the Californian, in which he will publish his creative efforts.

Sam spent the remainder of his time with me talking about what it had been like being a political reporter at the first Constitutional Convention for Nevada here in Carson City last year. He said that his reporting back then had been serious and he had claimed the respect of his fellow reporters, as well as a growing amount of the public. There was real regret in his voice as he spoke about that.

Lucy stopped at this point, taking a few moments to recall that six months later Mr. Twain had also left San Francisco after writing articles exposing that city's police corruption. He had fled to the mining areas around Sonora and Angel's Camp on the western slope of the Sierra, and a year later had published his humorous story about the "Jumping Frog". Its popularity had swept across the country, and he had suddenly become a famous personality. He had then traveled extensively, and had found his voice on the lecture circuit talking about those travels. He had even returned for a visit to Virginia City in 1868, where his speaking engagements had been wildly popular. It was said of him now in 1875 that he was writing a novel about a wild young boy on the Mississippi River. She looked back down to Robert's letter.

When Sam found out that I had lived and worked in Aurora, it was as though we were suddenly long-time buddies, as I suppose everyone feels who has survived Aurora. I already knew that he had come to Nevada in 1861 with his brother, appointed Secretary of the Nevada Territory, with himself acting as his brother's secretary. He said he hadn't been sorry to leave Missouri. He had feared being forced by the Confederates to pilot gun boats down the Mississippi River. Besides, he had always wanted to see the West. He commented that someday he should write a book about his trip west with his brother, and his time in Aurora, and maybe even in Virginia City. He just wasn't sure anyone would find it all that interesting. He thinks a good title would be "Roughing It".

Throughout his time in Aurora, Sam had been writing letters to Virginia City's Territorial Enterprise *paper and signing them "Josh". In them, he described the life of a miner, but added a good deal of humor to them, too. The editor, my new acquaintance, Joe Goodman, had printed them. Sam couldn't hide his pleasure in stating that to me. In July of '62, he had been offered the job of editor. He was eager to explain to me that he had experience as a printer, so knew how to set type, and do other newspaper work. He proudly boasted that he had always been a voracious reader of classics, history and the Bible, so was an excellent speller.*

Unfortunately, the stagecoach driver came in and announced that repairs to the stage had been completed, and they had to be underway. I shook Sam's hand and wished him the best in his future endeavors. What an interesting man. One can't help but wonder what his future might be with so many interesting tales to tell.

Lucy, knowing how popular Mr. Twain had become, wondered what Robert now thought of that conversation. And how many times must he have repeated it to others?

November, 1864: *I'm so pleased that Robert wrote to you, Lucy, although it's probably the last one he will write. I'm grumbling because it seems he spends more and more time in the local saloons with the men he meets. Of course, where else can they congregate for short periods? There, they can swap their stories. And believe me when I say that they all have them, whether based on what happened to them or that which happened to others that they now claim for themselves.*

When Hank Monk, the local stage driver who works for "Doc" Benton, is there with them, they usually spend even more time drinking. Robert only drinks beer, but while he used to nurse one or maybe two for the whole of an evening, he now often drinks enough to cause him to walk unsteadily when arriving home. It's nothing compared to the reputation of Mr. Monk. Men laugh about how they sometimes have to carry him out to his stage when the passengers are ready to leave. But he has never had an accident. With dismissive impatience, Robert informed me that Mr. Monk doesn't need his legs under him when driving the stage.

Jane once saw Mr. Monk eating alone in a café and studied him while finishing her meal. When I commented that I wondered why he drank so much, she said, "Maybe because he can't cry." I asked her what she had seen in his face to make her say that. She simply shrugged, and left me wondering.

I had written to my friend Mrs. Lake in Aurora as soon as we arrived here, in order that she might know where we are. I was delighted to hear from her yesterday. She informed me that Mr. Wheaton's romantic pursuit of her has never ceased, and that finally his delusions became unbearable. A friend told Billy Lake that Mr. Wheaton's "spirits" had directed him to kill Billy and then force Mrs. Lake to marry him.

Billy Lake went out the next night and confronted Wheaton on Pine Street in front of the Wide West Saloon. Billy wasted no time taking Wheaton out with the double-barreled shotgun he was carrying. Sheriff Francis arrested him, of course, but the next day the coroner's jury set him free with a verdict of justifiable homicide. My friend is, of course, relieved that her ordeal with Charley Wheaton is over, but she still feels unsettled by the whole thing. I wrote and assured her that if she needs time away from Aurora, that she can always come and stay a few days here with us.

The other day as I sat on a bench on the sidewalk in the middle of town, resting from my morning shopping, I watched a Chinese gentleman walking down the sidewalk. With his shuffling feet, stoic face, and long braid reaching to his waist, I thought him such a colorful gentleman. His demure wife was with him, wearing a colorful silk dress and walking a little behind him. When they reached a small group of men standing in their way, the couple moved as one into the muddy street in order to continue their journey, only returning to the sidewalk when well past the men. They gave no sign of inner turmoil, just acceptance and obedience. They regained the sidewalk next to a woman not unlike myself; in other words, white and well-dressed. She gave the Chinese couple a look of disdain and impatience, and hurried past.

Do not assume the men had not seen the Chinese couple, because they had. I on the other hand, when standing up and walking the same course as the couple, was given passage as the group opened up to let me through. And when passing the woman, I was given a nod of acknowledgement. None of this surprised me, but the anger that suddenly welled up within me did. It took me some time to figure out why.

Having lived in the California gold rush towns of Nevada City and Placerville for so long, I have come to think of people, as well, people. Not where they are born, or what color their skin may be, or what language they speak. I see the world as a collection of people, with the same responsibilities of family and making a living. Robert says the Chinese are willing to work for lower wages, and are very industrious, which creates the fear that they will be hired over others. Which could impact the economy.

He didn't like my response. "So because they're determined to provide for their families, and aren't lazy, it's considered acceptable to treat them badly?"

"They're also associated with the opium trade."

"Yes, and which substance many a man and woman who is not Chinese partakes of."

He only shook his head and retreated behind his newspaper.

I am not unaware of the differences between cultures, but why should we denigrate those differences instead of finding them interesting and trying to learn more about them? I would love to sit down with that Chinese couple, or one from Scotland or Ireland, or a freed person from the South for that matter, and learn about their histories. What might I learn that would improve my life or that I could use to help others? I will never know, because my doing such a thing would cause such sensor that Robert's success in this town would be compromised.

And I laugh. Why? Because as I reread that last paragraph, it felt as though I was listening to you. And, although it is difficult for me to admit, those are the views my mother might have had on the subject.

We had a wonderful entertainer come to our town last month. His name was Steve Massett, a regular visitor to San Francisco ever since the rush back in '49. He delivered his famous "Drifting About" lecture. He has traveled extensively, and he described his adventures with wonderful humor and a dash of ludicrous perspective. He told of odd happenings with a quiet dignity, as though he has no idea why everyone before him is laughing uproariously. But he is also a very good mimic and delivered clever imitations of other actors and famous people. Oh, we had such a delightful time, and especially loved his concept of an English tourist visiting America for the first time!

Then, a week after that we had the Blaisdell Troupe, the Swiss bell ringers, performing with 239 bells weighting 5 to 12 pounds each, and accompanied by a violin, a flute, a cornet and a clarinet. The most loved by the men was a petite little gal called Clara Jenkins, who was a fine singer. Some of the miners tossed silver half-dollars onto the stage, which she quickly scooped up before dancing off stage right.

Someone threw a few greenbacks onto the stage, and the offender was booed by his brethren. When someone tossed a wad of territorial scrip, worth about 30 cents on the dollar, the man was pounced upon. When he wiggled free, he ran from the theater. I noticed, however, that little Clara left nothing on the stage floor.

December, 1864: *The most awful thing has happened! I ran into a man who had visited me several times when I was in Nevada City. He recognized me even while staggering out of a saloon, and he called out, "Hey, there's my favorite gal! Remember me? Ole Hal?" I recognized him, of course, but I pretended that I didn't by looking around me as though trying to figure out to whom he was talking. I continued to walk on as quickly as my skirts and an appearance of dignity would allow, but he continued down the sidewalk after me. I slipped into a merchandise store and then out the back of it, and therefore lost him. But, oh Lucy, why must my past haunt me? What will I do if I come upon him when he isn't drunk?*

But the incident had not gone unnoticed. Robert had been approaching from the opposite direction and had immediately realized what was happening. He explained this to Lucy in a letter that Dolly never knew he sent. In it, Robert revealed what he had done.

"Well, hello, Hal." As Robert had greeted the man, he gave him a hearty slap on the back. "Remember me? I worked at the livery in Nevada City back during the rush?"

"Oh, um, yeah, right." There had been a small glimmer of recognition as he struggled to recall who this old acquaintance might be.

"We need to celebrate." Robert had then led Hal into a small, one-bit house where he knew the bartender. He plunked Hal down in a chair at the back end of the narrow saloon and told him, "I'll go get our drinks." He then told the bartender to pour out two whiskeys, one a triple and the other a single mixed with water. With double the coin before him on the counter, his friend readily did as requested.

Returning to the table, Robert gave Hal the strong drink and watched as he gulped it down. In Virginia City, this callous treatment of hard liquor was considered impolite drinking behavior. Waiting for Hal's drink to take effect, Robert ignored several hostile glances in Hal's direction from men nearby. "So, what are you doing in Carson City?"

"Here on business. Filing a claim. Leaving this afternoon on the stage to Virginia City."

"Oh, that's nice. Where's your claim?"

Hal had presented a sly, lopsided grimace, the alcohol beginning to hit him. "Now, thas somethin' I'm not about to tell. But is up on mountain."

"Lots of small mines up there on Mt. Davidson. Do you have to go up far?"

"Oh, yeah, real far." He put a finger to his lips. "Shhh!"

Hearing the stage pass the saloon on its way to let off passengers and take on new ones, Robert noticed that Hal's eyes weren't focusing well. He picked up the man's small valise and led a now docile Hal from the building and to the stage depot. It was then that Robert had realized that behind the stage to Virginia City was a stage heading to Placerville, clear on the other side of the Sierra.

Robert quickly purchased a one-way ticket and handed it to the driver as he shoved Hal into the Placerville coach. He figured that by the time Hal sobered up enough to realize he was on the wrong stage, he would be so busy trying to get back to Virginia City that he would forget about

Dolly. And if ever confronted by Hal, who he doubted would remember their meeting, Robert could always say he thought the stage was going to Virginia City. All this had rushed through Robert's mind, more as a desperate idea than any cogent plan.

Robert had watched the stage until even the dust it raised was gone. Then, with a stab of guilt that was still less than his self-satisfaction, he had gone home to tell Dolly what he had done. Her relief had been beyond expression. Although that night she did find a way to express her gratitude in a manner that made Robert even happier about what he had done to ole Hal.

Lucy, almost against her will, was drawn to the opening paragraph of a letter written in the summer of 1865.

July, 1865: *I know I have not written for quite some time. I did receive your letter detailing the reaction of Placerville and vicinity to the death of President Lincoln. We too were broken-hearted, and sometimes when I think of it, so soon after the end of the war, I feel tears waiting to fall. In fact, it wasn't an unusual sight to see rough miners and freighters doing just that when we first heard. The grief was honest, open, and respected. We have gone from a town covered in red, white and blue bunting in celebration of the war's end, to a town draped in black, both people and buildings. Any man who speaks out against the fallen president is immediately jumped on, and is lucky if only forced to leave town. It is a summer we will never forget.*

The subject of the war, even after ten years, was still a raw wound for the country. Men argued over the details of famous battles and what "could have been done instead", while women avoided the topic altogether when visiting. It was considered an improper subject for feminine society, some women going so far as to declare an inability to understand "such things". Lucy had found this out the hard way when she had tried to bring up the subject of Reconstruction at a luncheon with four other women. Shutting out the memory of their unpleasant reaction to her broaching of the subject, Lucy jumped ahead to Dolly's next letter.

August, 1865: *I have not told you about a woman I have met here in Carson City, a very kind lady, but a sad one. She is often referred to by other women as* *"the widow Ganby". Sara Ganby and I have spent time together over lunches occasionally, and she has taught me to make a braided bread that is not only decorative, but also quite tasty. In spending time together, since she lives only a block away, I have come to find out a little of her background.*

She came here from Philadelphia with her husband. He was an experienced miner there, and having heard about Comstock wealth, he felt it would be a simple matter for him to find gold for himself. But, as so many have discovered, it was much more difficult than he expected. She said he was killed in a mining accident. She gave no details, and of course, I did not pry.

Well, after getting to know me and a little of my background, she decided to open up to me yesterday. It seems that her husband is not dead after all. He stole a few handfuls of ore from the freighting company he signed on with, and they had him arrested. He is now serving a fifteen-year sentence at the prison next to the Warm Springs Hotel. It is a new, and I must say, very imposing prison next to the hotel. It is constructed of part wood and part stone from a nearby quarry, using prisoner labor. Last year, shortly before we became a state, the territorial legislature purchased Mr. Curry's one-story hotel, along with 20 acres of his land, and appointed him the warden of what was being built next to his hotel.

Now that Sara has me in her confidence about her husband, with no one else knowing, she feels free to talk about him. I won't go into details about his past, which has always been a bit sketchy, even to her it seems. I have come to the conclusion, however, that whatever he has done that might be frowned upon by the law, Sara has built up a list of justifications for his actions. Still, she misses him terribly. She is only allowed to visit him on rare occasions and after much complicated arrangement. And always with a guard in the room. The other day she explained what it is like for her, and I don't think I'll ever hear of a prisoner's family again without thinking of her.

"It's like a death," she told me, "but one unacknowledged or able to be publicly grieved. Like any respectable widow, I can claim he's not in my life, that I can't talk to him or share with him, or hold him. But he isn't dead, there has been no ceremony with prayers, and there's no gravesite to visit. I feel foolish wearing black, so I don't. Still, I sometimes feel that I'm drowning in grief. But I must keep my feelings to myself, and say nothing to even those closest to me. Because, you see, they think I'm a widow of long standing. So, I just get on with my life while unsure if I'll ever hold my beloved again. My very much alive beloved."

Lucy couldn't immediately lay her hands on the later letters where Dolly continued Sara Ganby's story, and descriptions of their many times together, but it had developed into a cherished and much enjoyed friendship for the two women. As for the prison, in 1867 there had been a fire that destroyed the building. It was rebuilt, again by prison labor, somewhat larger and slightly more comfortable for its inmates. However, in 1870 a good portion of that building was destroyed in another fire. This time when it was rebuilt, of course by prison labor, it was built entirely of quarried stone that would last beyond the life of its use as a prison, which use would end 146 years later.

It was thought to be one of the most secure facilities in the country, being a large, two-story stone building with arched double doors through which a prison wagon could pass, along with guard towers built out from the second floor like bulging eyeballs. In Dolly's time, it was thought to be so secure that Lieutenant Governor Frank Denver, who had become the warden, could live with his wife and young daughter in a small apartment on the first floor. Bob Dedman, a life term prisoner, had served as their loyal servant. It took some hunting among the later letters, but Lucy finally found the one she wanted.

__September, 1870__: My friend Sara Ganby brought me a basket of cookies a few weeks ago when she heard that Robert was out of town. I think she prefers my company when there is no possibility that we will be interrupted, since the only time I see her is when Robert is away. Either that, or she has something against Robert. Maybe it's husbands, being that hers is still in prison. She has tried for his release several times, but none of her efforts have been successful. Of course, she also likes Jane, but I've noticed that she comes by when she sees Jane on the street.

When I expressed curiosity as to what it must be like for Mr. Ganby, she looked past me to the window and the view beyond. "They know not the time of day unless outside, when they can see from the sun the approximate time. Inside, they don't know, until the next event takes place. They're roused from their slumbers at six in the morning, then eat breakfast at 6:30 before going out to break rock at the quarry or rake the grounds or sweep out the cells. They have a substantial mid-day meal when the sun is high, and a light supper late afternoon. They are allowed an hour of socializing in the room where they eat, but it is heavily guarded and with the least raised voice among them, everyone is rushed back to their cells. Of course, some guards are more lenient than others. But they must be in bed at a certain time, after which all lanterns in the corridors are extinguished. But never can they say it is ten after, or a quarter to. Nothing so exact as that. Just another day that matches the one just past, and another after that to follow, and another after that.

"Once a month he's allowed to receive a letter from me, and I have never missed one. Then, recently, a man befriended by my beloved and who had served his time, came to me with a sealed envelope. In it was a long and detailed letter from my husband." She smiled almost shyly. "My husband. Oh, the sound of that! How blessed it will be someday, to be able to introduce him as that, to claim him as that, to lay with him at night as that."

How badly I wanted to ask her what was so "detailed" about that sealed letter. But, of course, that isn't something one does.

CHAPTER 6

1865 - 1875

Lucy turned to the first page of a later letter to review exactly what Dolly had said next about Mrs. Ganby, that most enigmatic of Carson City women.

September 15, 1871: *Sara Ganby has left town. No one seems to have known that she was leaving, or can guess where she has gone. Neither can I, although I think some people suspect that I do, because I was the only woman Sara spent any time with in the days just before her disappearance. They say she used to be quite sociable, but gradually withdrew from all town functions and even visiting with other women.*

Lucy then skipped ahead to the letter that followed that one.

October, 1871: *The most extraordinary thing has happened. You probably already know about it, since it has been in the newspapers everywhere, but in case you haven't heard, on September 17, there was a prison break. Twenty-nine men escaped. Their crimes range through train robbery, murder and thefts of various kinds. And worst of all, they broke into the armory and took 3 Henry rifles, several double-barreled shot guns and a number of pistols, and almost 3,000 rounds of ammunition. While escaping, they killed Matt Pixley, the young proprietor of the Warm Springs Hotel, as he fired at them through a window. They also seriously wounded several of the guards who tried to stop them.*

Twenty-two prisoners, some wounded and carried by those who were not, headed east over the high ridge just beyond the prison, then turned south. Two went on south near Carson, and five headed northeast across the railroad tracks between the mills at Empire and Carson City. A few chose other routes, and disappeared into the wastelands of the desert. General Batterman at Virginia City brought 27 National Guardsmen to the search, and Lt. Lyman came with 15 men from the Emmet Guard. From Genoa came Deputy Sheriff Lewis and 6 men, joined by Storey County Deputy Sheriff Tom Harkin and 11 men. Sheriff Swift and Sheriff Atkinson of Storey County, along with Chief of Police George Downey, Detective Ben Lackey, and an Indian guide joined the search.

Over the next few weeks, the six prisoners heading south killed three people, one of them a young U.S. Mail Clerk whose body they tried to burn in a fire. The oldest of these prisoners is 37 and the youngest only 18.

Some were recaptured and a few died of their wounds soon after escaping. Three got as far south as the Owens River Valley where two were taken by a vigilance group outside of Bishop Creek and hanged at a nearby cabin after a quick trial. The youngest of those who escaped was with them and was taken to the nearest jail. On October 5, because Bob Dedman had risked his life to protect Warden Denver and his family, the servant prisoner was pardoned. Some of those recaptured were brought to Aurora where the sheriff and his deputy were offered $500 if they would leave the jail for a few minutes. They refused. On October 12, the youngest prisoner, having been at Camp Independence in the Owens River Valley, was returned to the Nevada Prison. Meanwhile, on the 13th, one of the wounded guards died. On the 14th, the coroner's jury claimed that the 29 convicts were all responsible for the guard's death.

Lucy remembered what a splash all of this had made in newspapers, at least throughout the West. She also recalled that by the middle of November, 18 of the 29 escaped convicts had been recaptured, two had been hanged by vigilantes, and nine had still been at large. Eighteen convicts had been indicted for the murder of guard Isaacs, and arraigned for the murder of the postal messenger. On November 28, the jury had found all 18 not guilty, after testimony showed that most of the shooting had been done by prisoner Jones, who was still at large, and prisoner Morton who had been strung up outside Bishop. Lucy recalled that the young man, 19 by the time of his return to prison, had his case appealed by his father on grounds that he hadn't received a fair trial. He won his appeal with the Nevada Supreme Court, and left the prison in 1873.

In a letter sent in the spring of 1872, Dolly wrote:

Well, Lucy, I must confess to something. Among those who were not recaptured was a man the locals say was a Bob Ganby. When a marshal asked me if I'd heard from Sara after she left here, I of course told him the truth that I had not. But I do think Sara met her husband at some place stipulated in that sealed letter she received, and which I did not mention to the marshal. After all, the escape had been carefully planned by the prisoners for some time. She probably had suitcases packed in her home, and that's why she always came to my house to visit. And also why she was seen leaving town late one afternoon driving her buckboard with whatever was in back under tarps. After that, she was seen no more. I resist questioning the lawfulness or ethics of her decision, or mine. I only hope they make for themselves a life of righteousness that amends their transgressions. But still, I will miss her friendship.

Then, *in the* summer of 1873, Dolly wrote:

I suppose one can say that the final chapter of the prison escape back in '71 is the controversy that has arisen from it. Since it took place, people have been critical of the way the prison has been run, with Frank Denver in charge. A new Legislature repealed the warden position from that of the Lieutenant Governor, and gave it to a newly appointed warden, Pressley Hyman. Even so, Mr. Denver refused to quit. So, in March, Governor Bradley had to send troops in to force Mr. Denver to leave. It was all very undignified of him, and unsettling to the community.

Lucy, sitting on her sofa in 1875, reminded herself that all of that had taken place only a few years earlier. The bulk of Dolly's letters had been received in the 1860's, with only a few over the last several years. Circumstances can change so much over time, sometimes gradually and sometimes more quickly than one would choose.

With so much about Virginia City reported regularly in newspapers, Lucy had developed a curiosity about it. Especially considering that the papers eagerly reported whatever was sensational. Lucy searched through the stack of letters until she found the one she wanted.

Virginia City, Summer, 1865*: Robert finally gave in to the pleadings of Jane and myself and took us in a buggy to Virginia City. We were delighted by the small herds of goats grazing on the hillsides leading into town. They can be milked, and survive on the rocky hillsides where cows cannot. A good number of chicken coops can be seen behind businesses and homes. After all, when a hen ceases to produce eggs, it can be served up as a chicken dinner. And its feathers used in a quilt or pillow.*

We stayed at the Virginia House on the corner of B Street and Sutton. It is a nice, clean little place. Jane insisted that she have a small room next to ours that is usually meant for children, even paying for it herself out of her savings.

Today, Robert went off to drink at the Union Saloon on the ground floor of the Hanak Building. Jane and I talked him into escorting us as far as the B Street entrance to the International Hotel, so we could have luncheon while he "visited" with men at the saloon. Oh, Lucy, what a grand establishment the International is!

It is on the corner of C Street and Union, and backs up all the way to B Street, where we entered into a large parlor. It's all dark wood and red plush carpets, with gas fed chandeliers and wall sconces lighting it all. (The gas works are further down the hill on Union between L and M Streets.) Velvet chairs and sofas make up small seating areas, which we passed on our way to the dining room. This is a truly elegant room, 40 feet wide the same as the entrance, but also 40 feet deep, and with 16-foot ceilings, which meant more lighting from chandeliers the size of wagon wheels. This light is cast down upon the twinkling crystal and silver that dresses the tables, which are covered in exquisitely white cloths.

It was for us more elegance than we could almost tolerate. When we glanced at one another as we were seated in the dining room, we had to fight back giggles, like young girls at their first outing into adulthood. Our friendly waiter told us with great pride that they have a cooking range capable of preparing meals for hundreds of guests that was specially made at a cost of almost $2,000. Imagine!! After serving us, and seeing how delighted we were with everything, our waiter confided that until recently a Mr. Winn had been the hotel keeper, but had fallen out with the owners, Bateman and Paul. Mr. Paul even brought suit against Mr. Winn and won the case.

So now Mr. Bateman and Mr. Paul are completely in charge of everything, and they are adding a large area of rooms to the north, over the Haas &

Company's building. It will mean that the hotel can accommodate 140 guests. He told us quite confidentially that the owners are talking to Mr. L. P. O'Connor, a popular man of the town, about taking over the management of the hotel. When our chatty waiter walked away, we grinned at one another, enjoying knowledge we felt privileged to have; although we have since realized that many people know of it.

The first International Hotel here was merely a large one-story cabin of whipsawed lumber cut at Six-Mile Canyon east of here. From March of '60 until '62, it was all that was available other than the Virginia House. But then the current brick palace was added to the town, with its three stories of tall, arched windows and extensive iron work fronting onto C Street. Uphill to the back on B Street there is now a 4-story addition, where we entered. Out front on C Street, taking up a good portion of the first floor, is a tobacco shop, a stationery shop, a dry goods store, and a clothing store for men. But the dry good store sells fabric, which the growing number of women here appreciate.

After we finished our meal, we climbed up the stairs to the roof, which is surrounded by what they think of as a three-foot tall brick firewall. We scoffed at such an idea, while standing beneath a forty-foot flag pole with the stars and stripes flapping in the breeze under a sky of white clouds against a blue sky. But our attention was quickly caught by the view. We looked out over the town's many buildings that were stair-stepped below us, past the mines, and past the yellow piles of cast-offs from those mines. Beyond that are the canyons, blocked by a series of hills, each line of them cast in a different shade of blue, like waves upon the sea rolling towards those of us marooned on the shore.

Poor Robert had to listen to our descriptions and impressions that night at supper while in the simple café close to our tiny hotel. Even the next morning, while Robert tried to read a copy of The Territorial Enterprise, we added little details to our previous evening's recital. He was wonderfully tolerant of us. Either that, or he simply tuned us out while focused on the newspaper, and his obvious hangover.

After breakfast the third day of our stay in Virginia City, Robert escorted us out for a visit at the orphanage and boarding school of the Daughters of Charity. They do such a wonderful work, not only taking in those children who have been made an orphan because their parents have both died, but also all children who need schooling. When the sisters arrived last year, they were given a room at St. Mary's Church, but they and 12 children soon found a better place. It is only a single room building, but they have fixed it up as sleeping areas and a classroom. There are now 25 people living with the sisters. All the children receive a basic education, and the girls receive instruction in sewing, since every woman is expected to have that skill. After all, it is something useful in a home setting, but also as a respectable means of support for an unmarried woman. Not long after I left home as a girl, I got a beginner's job over-casting inside seams of dresses too nice to just have the seams pinked. I was about to graduate to binding seams when my employer went out of business.

Anyway, those who board with the Daughters of Charity pay about $4 a month for the privilege, and those who attend just the school pay $2 to $4, as they can afford. The sisters want to expand, but simply don't have the money for it. They are applying to the State to help them build an orphanage.

These are not cloistered women, and never have been. They have accepted the mission of helping in wild, untamed places here in the West as members of the St. Vincent de Paul mission, and I can think of no better place for that than Virginia City.

During the school session, we were given permission to sit at the back of the group of children, whose first language is French or Spanish, were learning how to read English. Robert and I were quickly bored, but Jane watched the whole proceeding with a rapt attention I had never seen from her before. Upon observing her more closely, I noticed that her eyes were misty and her face glowed not unlike a picture I once saw of a Madonna. It was with difficulty that we got her out of the room, and even out of the building.

Throughout the night I could hear Jane pacing in her room. Then, the next morning while Robert and I enjoyed breakfast at a café, Jane insisted that she was going for a walk and would meet us back at the cafe for luncheon.

Robert and I entertained ourselves by visiting what few shops there are that a woman might enjoy, and we even sat on a sidewalk bench simply watching people pass while we ate through a bag of candy purchased at a bakery. We returned to the hotel just as Jane also returned. Robert suggested we retire to a new cafe over on C Street, about which he had heard good things. After we were seated, Robert stared at the extensive menu like it was a naughty novel, but I couldn't take my eyes from Jane. She was unusually radiant, and more animated than I had ever seen her.

Unable to resist any longer, I asked, "Jane, has something happened that we don't know about?"

She put down the menu she was holding and folded her hands on it. "I have been accepted as a teacher by the sisters at the orphanage."

Robert immediately transferred his attention from the menu to Jane, staring at her, as did I. "What? What do you mean?"

She blushed as she looked up at us. "You may not know it, but I speak Spanish well, and passable French. Being in that room with those children yesterday made me feel as though I have a purpose in life after all. There are actually children who need me. And the Sisters can certainly use the help. They were especially happy to hear that I would pay for a room somewhere and didn't expect them to house me." She put a hand over mine and squeezed it. "I can't tag along with you two for the rest of my life."

"But, Jane..." I began.

"No. Please don't try to talk me out of this. I've thought it through very thoroughly."

Robert, ever practical and with an ability to take the long view of things, smiled at her. "Well, I think it's a noble thing you've decided. And if at some point you decide it isn't for you after all, we'll be somewhere in the region and you can always come back to us."

I leaned toward her, fighting the temptation to become emotional. "Of course. We'll stay in touch, and I look forward to your sharing your adventures with us." But I knew as I said it that this was much more than a simple adventure to Jane. It was to her as much a calling as any nun has ever claimed. The Sisters (they are not actually nuns), have given her this opportunity in recognition of the fact that the demand for their school is growing.

After we ate, we put Jane's things into the rig and drove her to a lodging house where she had rented a room. No grass growing under her feet even about that! What more of her things we have at home, Robert will bring to her on his next trip to Virginia City.

I now understand why, ever since we came over the mountain, Jane has been somewhat depressed in spirit. She was without purpose, and fearful that she would never have anything to do that really matters. So, if ever she does decide that she no longer wants to do this teaching, I think it will be a very long time into the future.

Lucy put the letter down and walked out onto the porch of the house she would soon be leaving. "The future," she thought. "What about my future?" Leaving the house meant leaving behind those things that constantly reminded her of a thousand little moments shared with Jim and Roger. What flooded her thoughts right then were those times with Jim, although more years had been spent there with just Roger. Maybe it was reading again Dolly's letters. Although Dolly and Robert had moved often before settling in Carson City, it was still "they" that had done so. Dolly always had Robert.

Lucy was a practical woman with a lifetime of wisdom gained from challenges, tragedies and exciting adventures. She knew that if she stayed in Placerville, hugging her memories while missing her son, she would stay that person for the rest of her life. And there was just too much life left to live for that to be the substance of it. There had to be challenges and adventures out there somewhere, and she was determined to find them. Returning to the parlor, Lucy flipped through a few of Dolly's letters to the one she wanted.

October, 1865: Robert has gone off to Virginia City for a few days with a friend, this time riding horses instead of in a wagon hauling supplies. There is some kind of theater entertainment that they want to see. They will be staying up canyon between the two towns at the old stone hotel now called the Vessey House. I think it should be called the Gold Hill Hotel, but what do I know?

It is the first time he has been away that I will not have Jane here with me. I never realized how lonely that would be. We did, however, receive a note from her and it seems that she has settled into her new life with surprising ease, and not so surprising satisfaction.

Being alone and on my own has given me pause to question what my life is to be, now that we have settled here in Carson City. I have given up on the idea that I will ever conceive. I know I am capable of that, since during my first marriage I was with child, and would probably have carried it to term if it had not been for the beating I took from my brute of a husband. The doctor at the time, not willing to admit why I lost the baby, nevertheless told me he saw no reason why I should not find myself expecting again at some point. So I don't know why it has not happened for Robert and me.

Lucy took a moment to roll her eyes and sigh deeply. "And of course," she informed the empty room around her, "it couldn't possibly be because of Robert. No, it's always assumed to be the woman's doing." She turned the page of the letter and reread the interesting part that came next.

With Robert gone to Virginia City, Mary Jensen asked me to accompany her on the stage to Dayton to see her elderly mother. She told me her mother is a fragile, vulnerable old lady and Mary is needing to make a decision about her mother coming to live here in Carson with herself and her husband, or not. Well, let me tell you now that the mother is one tough old lady who makes no bones about the fact that she doesn't like her son-in-law. Nor does she intend to leave her home right there in Dayton, no matter how much others might worry about her welfare. She had the habit of saying these things to me in a loud voice that was obviously meant for her daughter to hear.

But that came later. Our stage left Carson, traveling at a good clip with the Carson River to our right, past Copper Canyon, Spring Valley, and Spafford Hall's old place. The closer we got to our destination, the hillier became the terrain, and the more the stage would rock. Not so good for the stomach! We passed roads leading down to small mills on the river, roads so rutted they can only be navigated by experienced freighters driving huge wagons pulled by jerk lines of brave mules. Brave because they have to cross over a number of narrow bridges spanning ravines. There were many of these rigs lined up, waiting to unload into rock-lined chutes at the road-ends. In this way the ore can slide down from the back of a wagon at its closest approach, down to the mill below.

The river is low right now because of so little summer rain, so the water wheels are not functioning properly. One has to remember that the historic flooding of '61 into '62 actually changed the course of the old river, which has contributed to several of the mills shutting down. The bad economy and the lessening of rich ore from the mines hasn't helped. The miners call it "the borrasca", which is the opposite of "bonanza".

The mills are impressive, noisy places. Over the last few years the ore from mines in Gold Canyon, and sometimes even from Virginia City, have been processed in the Dayton District. They run day and night, Sundays the only day off. They are driven by over-shot water wheels from six feet to twice that in diameter, the water carried in ditches as wide as 30 feet and some 2,000 feet long. The workers brag that the size of the dams along the river, built of stone, are twenty feet thick at the base and ten at the top. The ultimate brag is about the yield, from 20% to 40%, some mills using both modern iron stamps and older arrastras. Considering all the chemicals such as mercury used in these mills, and how much of it leaches back into the river, I wonder if it's a good idea to eat fish from its waters. Finally, we passed over a network of rutted roads coming off the entrance to Gold Canyon, like threads of a spider's web spreading out to the mills between Empire and Dayton.

I was surprised to see farms around Dayton. As the need for food increases, these farms take more water from the river for irrigation. This causes conflicts with the mill men. Some mornings a farmer or rancher will wake up to find that their diversions from the river have been destroyed during the night. Many lawsuits have arisen from such conflicts, creating work for attorneys, as well as Justice of the Peace, John Reynolds.

As we entered Dayton, we could see the small cabins housing the waning population of Chinese. When the silver mines up canyon were discovered, they went there for better work at the mines. Of course, few mines would hire them for mining, but there's so much support work needed in a camp that they supplied important services. In fact, much of the Dayton population left, taking with them the lumber of their houses in order to start again up canyon.

Those Chinese who stayed in Dayton settled into what is now known as the Johntown area. They are not the only ones singled out for ridicule in order to fuel some people's need to feel superior. Beaner, Wop, Mick, and Dago are some of the least disgusting of the terms tossed around as a normal part of men's language, even by those being called one of those names. Since I, a mere woman, cannot speak up against it, I can at least be thankful that I have never heard such from Robert.

As we approached the town, I could see from a rise in the road all that was spread before me. Just then, Mrs. Jensen said, "It's going to grow into a considerable town someday."

I thought it had a ways to go, considering the number of empty and abandoned buildings, but I said nothing. Still, even lacking size, it has what might be considered pioneer charm. Mainly, it seems to say, "I'm trying to be all things to all people." It has for some years served the mills along the river, lent aid to emigrant trains on the Overland Route, and acted as a remount station for carriers of the mail. It maintains a post office of its own, and continues to supply emigrants and its citizens. At the most recent legislative session of the Assembly, the right to construct a railroad was granted. Thus, soon there will be a Dayton to Gold Hill route that will continue on to Carson.

There were ten hotels in which we could have stayed, but Mrs. Jensen took us to Union House, as it has a bakery and saloon connected with it. Turns out, she enjoys a brandy before bedtime. I took advantage of the bakery in the morning just as loaves of bread were coming out of the ovens. We slathered thick slices with apple butter for our breakfast. On our trip over the Sierra, Jane and I found that baked goods, when available at stations, were often of dubious quality. But heated over a camp fire and spread with apple butter brought along by Jane, it often sufficed as a meal.

Union House on Main near River Street should not be confused with the Union Hotel on Main near the Sutro Mill. Ours was run by Mr. Lanzac, and the other is run by a Mrs. Ham. When Mrs. Jensen told me this, I got the distinct impression that she was hinting at something important. To me, it hardly mattered, as all hotels are residences for those millhands who work at those mills within a few miles of Dayton.

We ate at the Dallam Restaurant near the hotel, the cook being Oliver Farnsworth and a friend of Mrs. Jensen's husband. Mrs. Jensen's mother refused to go with us. Something about Mr. Dallam that had earned her disapproval. She's from "the East", she informed me with a sniff of superiority. It was an attitude I had seen before. On their journey into the West, many of those from big eastern cities leave ox chains, trunks and stoves dumped along the trail, but they arrive with their prejudices and stubborn attitudes firmly in place. Most men, because of what they experience after arriving here, soften such attitudes at least to some degree. The older women seem to be less willing.

Those who first arrived in Dayton were the hardy souls who had made it across the Forty Mile Desert, and then after a short rest at Ragtown, endured the Ten Mile Desert between there and Dutch Nick's Station (and the founder of Empire City). Those who stayed in Dayton set up businesses that supplied those who were moving on toward the Sierra. Such generosity is at the heart of all the towns that have lasted, but were at some point expected to vanish.

When Dayton men moved up-canon in '59 at the start of the Comstock surge, the town almost dissolved into the desert. Mrs. Jensen's mother remembered the early years with unusual clarity, and much pride. "Left in Dayton were Joe Keller and Isaac Cohen who had a trading house, mill owner Mr. Nall and his family across from Mr. Keller, the Smith family nearby, and Wood's Butcher Shop that Mr. Wood sold to Bill Johnson. There was also Mr. DeGroot's store on Main near River Street, and some miners in a small frame house east of Keller's.

Morris Epstein opened a store out near Rose's Ditch. Of course, even after some of these men moved on, we still had a blacksmith. There were also about 30 Chinese west of the Old Log Store living in huts made of stone, mud and tule, since the wood of their earlier cabins had been taken for building up-canyon. But we rebounded over time."

We spent some time visiting in Mr. Mason's store on Main near Pike Street, where he sells stationery along with patent medicines and paint. I was able to stock up on some very nice stationery, upon which I am now writing.

Why on earth, do you ask, am I telling you all this? Because I am impressed with this hamlet in the middle of desert scrub, river mills, and farms. It is a completely masculine domain, with only a few women and children. Even so, Miss Mary White is the schoolteacher, and boards on the west side of Second Street near Tyler Street. People brag that a school is being planned out on Shady Lane, using wood and quarried stone or brick. Many of the men who recently arrived here to open businesses brought with them their families. Of course, the women have more in common with pioneers than the fashionable Easterners when it comes to their clothes, even with Carson City twelve miles away. But that is a buggy ride of several hours over rough and sandy roads, with the need to stable the horse while shopping, and the need to be back before dark or pay for an overnight stay. They are certainly looking forward to the railroad!

On our way back home, the stage had a problem with something, so after a slow pull up to Empire City, I was able to see the town Robert had talked about. It isn't much of one, really, noisy with the sounds of the mills and a population of men in grubby overalls. The barkeep at the Kinney Hotel, Mr. Bickford, was obliging to Mrs. Jensen and myself, along with the three men with us on their way to Carson. We were told to wait in the bar, where Mr. Bickford gave us coffee and asked if we wanted it "laced". I actually said, "Yes, please, with a little sugar," at which he nodded. But when I added, "And a little of your best whisky", he grinned. Mary said, "Coffee straight." But she smiled when she said it, so Mr. Bickford knew he wasn't dealing with a couple of prissy females.

The butcher, who boards at the hotel, came in and ordered a beer and two pickled eggs from the big glass jar on the bar. He noticed us at our small table in the corner, and after downing the eggs much as he would pills, he approached our table. His overalls were wet at the bottom almost to his knees, and his red shirt was in great need of washing. He removed his soft cap, blood-stained from much handling while working, and gave us a friendly nod.

"*Good afternoon, ladies. I'm Joshua Brunner, the butcher in the shop next door. Maybe you'd like to stop by before continuing your journey to Carson. Since you've been made to wait, I would be happy to give you a nice discount on some lamb chops.*"

"*Thank you,*" Mary told him. "*That's very kind of you. We'll be sure to stop by.*"

He put his hat back on, stopped to deliver the same message to our fellow travelers at the table across the room, as well as four mill workers just arriving for breakfast. As soon as he walked out, a woman seemed to appear out of nowhere, although I think it was from the back room. She stepped up to our table and said, "*I wouldn't touch those chops if I was you. They're probably about to turn and he's soaked 'em in vinegar to freshen 'em.*"

We just stared at her, unable to decide what to say. Mary finally found her voice. "*Beg pardon?*"

"*I'm Mrs. William Bueke. We live out in a cabin close to the Merrimac Mill.*"

We invited her to sit with us, as it was easy to see how eager she was to talk to other women. She was a small, hatchet-faced woman with prominent cheek bones, a small pointed nose and chin to match, and brows that tented over piercing grey eyes. Her mouth was her only soft feature, although it seemed to be puckered with either disdain or impatience most of the time. Thinking of the hard, masculine place she inhabits, I found compassion for her, if not a little understanding of why she had, beyond her appearance, no softness in her nature.

After all, the only men she comes in regular contact with are those with titles such as amalgamator, feeder, or millwright. For the rest, they are teamsters, carpenters, machinists, masons, and blacksmiths. Sam Ripley, owner of the one clothing and grocery store, is probably the only man other than husbands who takes time out to talk to the local women.

The cook at the hotel, Tom Griffith, came in and informed us that the stage wouldn't be leaving for another hour and asked if he could bring us some food. We accepted gratefully. When Mary asked his prices, he said it was "*on the stage owner*".

I told him to bring us, including Mrs. Bueke, whatever he had on hand that he thought we might like, as long as it wasn't too spicey. He laughed and returned with bowls of beef stew with potatoes, onions and carrots in a rich gravy. He also brought us a loaf of warm bread he cut for us at the table. I think it was the best stew I've ever eaten, and if I remember Empire City for nothing else, it will be that.

I got bored with the conversation between Mary and Mrs. Bueke about some mutual acquaintance, so I wandered into the kitchen. Mrs. Bickford was filling the order for the four hungry millworkers just off their shift. I offered to help by covering the biscuits fresh from the oven with a cloth, and wiping down the work table in the center of the kitchen. She was frying bacon and eggs in the biggest cast iron skillet I have ever seen. On one half of it were eight eggs frying and on the other half a pile of crisping bacon. Every so often she tilted the pan so the grease from the bacon washed over the eggs, cooking the whites but leaving the yokes a sunny yellow. She thanked me for my help, and then with practiced grace and efficiency, she scooped two eggs each onto four plates, along with a small pile of bacon and two biscuits. With three plates along the length of her left arm and one in her right hand, she left the kitchen at a brisk pace. The millworkers stopped drinking their coffee to grin with pleasure as they watched their food approach.

Mr. Bickford, working behind the bar, looked up with a smile as I walked up to him and thanked him for his kindness. I told him that Mrs. Jensen and I wanted to show our appreciation, and handed him a fifty-cent piece. Before he could respond, I turned and joined Mary and Mrs. Bueke by the door.

We stretched our legs by walking through the town, less than a mile long. Hills surrounding the town are covered in sagebrush, greasewood and salt grass, which brought to us ripe smells along with that of the low river. I was glad to see that a few trees had been left to grow in the town, as it gave it a less industrial feel. To reach the other side of the river, a wooden bridge had been built at a narrowing, and several small boys were pitching stones into the swiftly moving water. Beyond the Main Street businesses, we could see a few houses, with wood lots at each end of town full of wood cut for domestic use. We didn't have time to visit the cemetery on the hill that Robert had described to me, but I had seen enough of Empire by the time we saw the stage driver climb atop the coach. We hurriedly said our farewells to Mrs. Bueke while she showed undisguised regret, and arrived at the stage just ahead of the men traveling with us. We arrived home just as darkness descended.

I have taken it upon myself to join a lady's group that comes together from time to time to make simple quilts for the less fortunate. What I like most is *that while our fingers are active, so are our mouths. We talk about events in our lives, our travels from different parts of the country, and even how some of the ladies have come to this country from another one. Oh, of course, there is local gossip, but it is seldom unkind.*

I find it refreshing and comforting that none of the ladies know of my background before Robert and I married. I was, however, quite the sensation when I opened up to tell them about what happened last summer to you and me there in Placerville. One of them had read an article about it in a newspaper brought here from over the mountain, and to find out that I had been in the center of it was very exciting for them. Not a one of them was judgmental, and all think me a martyr and you quite the brave lady detective.

This week, when I informed the ladies that my husband was away in Gold Hill and Virginia City, they all looked over at Mrs. Strong. She is a widow lady of a rather retiring nature, and who had been one of the first to begin our charitable group. She looked up at them, catching them out, and when the other ladies blushed, she laughed out loud.

"Oh, my dears," she chuckled, "you mustn't treat me as though it happened yesterday. I'm quite recovered from it, and I have adjusted my life very nicely here in Carson."

Upon seeing my puzzlement as I looked from one woman to another, Mrs. Strong told me, "You mentioned Gold Hill and that reminded everyone of an incident that happened there a few years back." One of the women, sparing Mrs. Strong the ordeal of describing what had happened, proceeded to explain.

To reduce it down from the scores of details, along with interjected asides by everyone there, and even Mrs. Strong's vaguely related particulars, I will tell you in my own words what occurred. One of the mines caught fire, and not even all that deep down. But it was a hot fire, started probably from a candle dropped onto something highly flammable.

The fire was not long in burning before enough water was poured down to extinguish the worst of it so that the cage could be lowered. They waited above and called down, and rang the bell several times to announce that the cage was down. But no one got on it. It had been a small crew, and they had all perished. After a week of cooling, men could finally go down and retrieve the bodies, one of which had been Mr. Strong. None had been burned, but had been overcome by the fumes and heat.

When the women finished speaking, Mrs. Strong looked a bit drawn, but she quickly recovered and suggested that we break for tea and sandwiches. It was a welcome suggestion, as I think we were all a little shaken by the imagery of what had taken place not that long ago. And possibly because such a thing could so easily take place again.

Two letters in Robert's handwriting had fallen on the floor and Lucy picked them up reluctantly. Not so much because of their content, but because they had been written at a difficult time for her. They had arrived when it had been too long since she had heard from Jim, and she was fearing that something bad had happened to him. The dates of Robert's letters were out of order, and she had to bring her mind back to the year Dolly and Robert had arrived in Carson City. The letter had been meant for herself and Jim.

*(**October 30, 1864**) Many of Carson's citizens took a break on the 12ᵗʰ from their daily work and attended a unique entertainment brought to us by a man billing himself as Martin the Wizard. The hall was not full, but those of us present gave him a rousing reception to make up for it. Our local newspaper gave it a good review before "respectable audiences", but then added a facetious remark: "Respectable in what respect? – in intelligence, behavior or numbers?"*

His sarcasm aside, we here do enjoy theatricals, concerts, magicians, or even a nice rowdy speech. Then too, Virginia City men seem more willing to throw coins onto the stage than we do here. Dolly reminds me often that men have more reasons to gather together than women do. She also reminds me that no subject is off the table for men. Recently we had a big meeting where we backed the Union in support of its war effort. We did much singing of "John Brown", visited several fraternal organizations in their various halls, and gathered in saloons to toast the Union's successes on the battlefield.

However, all of this is nothing compared to the excitement recently caused by a young lady calling herself Cassimer. She's really just Emily Jordan. She came to Virginia City at Maguire's Opera House, and wagon loads of men went forth from Carson the morning of her performance in order to be assured of a seat to see her that night in the play Mazeppa, made famous by the scantily clad Adah Menken. I rented a horse so I could get there early and get a good seat inside. Those last to arrive had to settle for a seat in the adjoining hay yard where they can only hear what's going on inside.

She did a fine job, but her performance was almost cancelled because of the anti-Union political demonstrations all along the Lode. A Copperhead gathering had brought together about 1,700 "rag-tag and bobtail crawlers" (as the newspaper called them) parading with sagebrush brooms and torches. Meanwhile, over on Gold Hill at the Grand Union Meeting, people gathered for what was called an intellectual treat by way of a lecture by Miss Stanton, who spoke to a packed audience. So packed was it, in fact, that the floor gave way and fell five feet, causing a lot of confusion. Thankfully, there were no injuries.

By the time Miss Jordan had given something like six performances of Mazeppa, everyone was pretty well stuffed full from dining on her talents, although when she first arrived no one complained about her skimpy attire worn in the play. All that performing must have been taxing for her too, because by the end of them she was exhibiting a slight head cold. After she left town, one of the papers quipped, "Having been outrageously Mazeppa-ed by the fair Emily, the Territorial Enterprise precipitates its ire upon the lady's airy 'nothing to wear' impersonation of the character, and appeals to her, in the name of God, to blow her nose! Know, oh persecuted Emily, though it may be easier to show legs than ability, that an actress may 'catch a Tartar', as well as a cold by so doing. Accept our handkerchief—and a petticoat. Be modest and you won't be pen-pecked."

*(**November 20, 1864**) Well, Jim, I expect that you and Lucy have been celebrating the election just past, and are happy as we are that Mr. Lincoln has won his second term. Nevada has also celebrated, but maybe more than most because it followed what we were doing to achieve statehood on October 31 ahead of the election. It cost us over $3,000 to telegraph our proposed state constitution from Virginia City to Washington, D.C., but it was worth it, to say the least. Our statehood hinged on our state constitution getting there so that the STATE of Nevada's votes would help pass the 13th Amendment.*

Money was gathered among the citizens, after which young Frank Bell sat down at his telegraph and began sending out the proposed constitution. It was taken down in long-hand at the recipient station next in the line, and then telegraphed on to the next, with that one taking it down and passing it on. I wish I could shake the hand of each of those fine men. Then, finally, on the last day of October, we received the anxiously awaited response that began, "Let it be known that I, Abraham Lincoln," and ended with, "proclaim that the said State of Nevada is admitted into the Union."

I rode into Virginia City just as a man came running out of the telegraph office, shouting, "We're in, we're in." Other shouts began as I tied my horse to a post outside the Union Saloon next to the International Hotel. People were rushing into the streets, leaving groceries on counters, antes on poker tables, beers on bars, and meals turning cold in restaurants. The streets had no traffic because all wagons stopped where they were, suddenly surrounded by a milling crowd of exuberant people. Company D fired a grand national salute of 35 guns as well as one extra for our new 36th state. The cheering went on for an hour to one degree or another, with people finally returning to their previous pursuits. But the celebrating continued in all the Gold Canyon towns into the next day.

With the election a week away on November 8th, talk quickly turned to that. The newspapers got busy and asked questions like, "Are the Union men ready?" And challenging people with, "Anyone wishing to bet that Abraham Lincoln will not carry the new state can be accommodated to the extent of $500 by calling at this office." Whether that was to place a bet against him, or be throttled if they tried to do so, I'm not sure.

People like Miss Stanton, Dr. Bien and Col. Summer presented lectures atop boxes set up in the streets, sang new words to old patriotic tunes, and newspapers printed diatribes of opinion. Parades were everywhere almost every day, dances were held, Union men held rousing meetings, bonfires lit the sky each night, and of course flags were waived all over town as men cheered themselves hoarse.

Then came the day of voting. I was told that at Silver City a Confederate flag was nailed to the floor at the polling place so that everyone entering had to walk on it in order to place their vote. In Virginia City, the Metropolitan Band hung the names of President Lincoln and Vice-President Johnson on their wagon and played soul-stirring songs as they rolled throughout the town. It was quite a day.

(April, 1865) Can you believe, Jim, that Congress has had to pass a third Pacific Railroad bill of long-term loans, incentives and land grants? And all to supplement the cost of constructing the two railroads as the Central Pacific and the Union Pacific move ever closer toward one another. This building of a railroad has been going on for four years now, and there are a lot of people debating the value of such a gamble.

Lucy searched ahead to another letter she remembered from Robert. Despite Dolly's reservations about Robert continuing to communicate on his own, he did do so throughout the 1860's, although this one was something different.

(Summer, 1867) My God, we're thankful that this past winter is over. They say there were 44 snow storms in the Sierra. I believe it, since much of it fell on us. I hear even Placerville got its fair share as well. It sure put a crimp in the progress of the railroad being cut through the rock over the mountain, but evidently not completely stopping the work. They say that 20 Chinese workers were killed in a single snow slide, and they still haven't found their bodies.

At one point, even the Central Pacific's huge snowplow, pushed by ten locomotives, couldn't clear the track. It took over 2,000 men with picks and shovels to move the frozen drifts so they could clear a 15 mile path to get food and other supplies through on ox-pulled sleds. This, however, almost didn't work, as more snow fell too fast. Oxen foundered with exhaustion, many of them abandoned where they stood, left to freeze to death in the snow. Some say this is a reasonable sacrifice when considering how many hundreds of oxen, horses and mules have died pulling wagons across the country over the last twenty years. The trains will put an end to that. But that's about numbers and, as Dolly pointed out, not taking into consideration the animals' suffering.

Thousands of men have done incredible work getting over and through the Sierra, building trestles over canyons, bridges over ravines, and retaining walls to hold back rock slides. All of this while they cut away mountainsides, the debris used to fill in canyons. At the same time, they drove tunnels through solid granite with nothing more than picks and shovels, and occasionally black powder. These men also had to be fed, housed and paid, and all out where bears and mountain lions roamed if they hadn't been scared off by the activity. And let's not forget that the elevations where they were working were at 7,000 feet much of the time, which they were not used to at all. Nor were they used to having to deal with snow drifts in July.

Collis Huntington and Charles Crocker have backed this railroad enterprise, the success of which they must have doubted at least once during this winter. Projected costs back in the beginning of construction ran upwards of $150,000 each mile for the 100 miles over the mountain to the Nevada border. But it has been even more costly. Finally, what lay ahead of that push over the mountain *was the flat terrain of desert. For the railroad workers, it was a transition from winter's frozen hell to summer's searing hell, and a new way to die.*

With her forthcoming trip across the mountain so much on her mind, Lucy's thought turned to all the various groups that over time had persevered and suffered just to get over the Sierra; fur trappers, wagon trains, mule lines, ore wagons, freighters, and lastly, the railroad. And all of them, Lucy thought, probably could have been helped by tribal people if *they* had not been perceived as an enemy. Taking a moment to consider, Lucy shook her head as she wondered to which "they" that statement could apply.

She remembered newspapers saying that the energetic and determined Charles Crocker had moved the Central Pacific's construction along "no matter what". If something blocked his way, he cut it down, tunneled through it, blasted it apart, or built a bridge over it. When Crocker could no longer get enough local men to stick with the building, he brought in Chinese men from San Francisco and outlying mining areas. They were so efficient and hard-working that Crocker hired labor contractors to go to China and bring back thousands of young men from the Canton region, indentured and supervised by Chinese bosses who ruled them with iron fists.

Eventually, Crocker had 6,000 men he called "celestials" on his payroll, but when even this was deemed too few to get the job done, he hired 2,500 Irish immigrants. The *New York Tribune* described this polyglot bunch of workers as "a great army laying siege to Nature in her strongest citadel ... shoveling, wheeling, carting, drilling, and blasting earth and rock."

In early 1867 Crocker began using a new blasting oil called nitroglycerin. It was highly dangerous to work with, but it was eight times as powerful as black powder. Nevertheless, it only doubled the way through the hard granite mountains to two feet a day. In November of '67, Crocker went back to using black powder, sending in to the crews as many as 500 kegs each day. By the summer of '68 there were over 15,000 men clearing tunnels and grading the way for the track-layers following them down the eastern slope of the Sierra.

While snow continued to slowly melt around them, snow sheds were being built over new track to protect it from avalanches, eventually consuming 65 million feet of timber. Ahead of them, out in the Nevada desert along the Humboldt River, thousands of men were laying track, while surveyors worked ahead of them toward Utah. It was reported that Huntington, no slacker when it came to pursuing a goal, had sent a telegram to Crocker saying, 'Work on as though Heaven was before you and Hell was behind you.'

Lucy remembered the celebrating that took place in Placerville, like all the other towns in the West, when the telegram came on May 10, 1869, that 690 miles east of Sacramento and 1,086 miles from Omaha, Nebraska, the Central Pacific had met up with the Union Pacific at its eastern terminus in Promontory, Utah. Laborers in overalls mingled with railroad dignitaries in tall silk hats, and were photographed by newspaper men from California and the eastern states. The reporters called it the wedding of the rails, giving the event the symbolic magnitude that some likened to the landing of the Pilgrims at Plymouth Rock.

The San Francisco bankers and investors were the most pleased, as they expected their city to be the transfer point to the eastern states of trade coming from the Orient. But that was also the year the Suez Canal opened. Far eastern shipping bound for Europe used that passage rather than San Francisco and the transcontinental railroad. It was not the only miscalculation of the railroad's impact on Western society.

The railroad's presence meant that factories in the east, as well as towns along the railroad's route, could ship to California and other western states many goods at lesser cost than the same items available locally. Crops from the East could arrive fresh, along with manufactured goods and clothing. The result was that west coast businesses closed or were forced to consolidate with those once considered competitors, while commercial rents dropped. In general, real estate prices fell with a thump.

At the same time, Crocker no longer needed some 12,000 Chinese workers. Many made their way to Sacramento and San Francisco, although some ventured into towns like Virginia City and other mining communities. But wherever they went, they were willing to work for wages scoffed at by those referred to as Anglos, which at that time included Mexicans and "other nationalities".

Once the railroad across the country was completed, people in the East who were still enamored by all they had heard of the abundance in golden California, got on a train and came west. However, they quickly realized that there were too few jobs and no easy gold obtainable as they had imagined. In the first four years of the railroad's existence, at least 140,000 people made this journey. This resulted in a lot of disappointed and angry unemployed people, since the railroad, largely paid for by the government, had been promoted as something that would bring greater prosperity to everyone.

People were not unaware that Huntington, Crocker and their cronies had become immensely wealthy. This was similar to the wealth gained by the owners of the big mines on the Comstock, while those who worked for them made $4 to $6 a day, which nevertheless was considered a good wage.

People throughout the West talked about who they could blame for the tightened economy, but came up with no answer. The state government? For a while the president of the railroad resided in the California governor's mansion. That was looked at with suspicion. The County and City people? They had been financially dependent on income from railroad bonds and Comstock prosperity. The State's Supreme Court? Its chief justice had for a time been the legal counsel to the railroad, but he had just been doing what he had been paid to do.

In the end, most people agreed on one thing: greed, manipulation of the government, and probably a lot of misleading promises had been made by the railroad titans. But what could "the people" do about it, except make the best of each day as they always had?

Of course, if you owned a farm or orchard, you could now ship your produce quickly to Eastern purchasers. That was good. And if you could make something unique that was wanted in the east, and which could stand the trip, there were new markets opened up to you. If you were a businessman, you might be able to expand your business into the east. And you could now safely visit your relatives, or send for them to join you in the West. That too was good.

And now, Lucy thought, after all that, if the terminus wasn't so far away, she could take the train across the mountain into Nevada. But it wouldn't serve her purpose, for she needed to be well south of Carson City. Lucy sat back and thought of all that had happened to Dolly and Robert as the 1870's had begun.

In 1871, Dolly had written that tension had settled into her relationship with Robert, and she didn't know why. They had recently purchased a house, and although the payments to the bank were substantial, it was nothing they couldn't afford. Robert had a good partnership in a blacksmith and livery stable in the center of town, and with the town growing, it was doing very well.

June, 1871: So, Lucy, I really can't see what I have done to cause Robert's short temper, and frankly I'm beginning to think it has nothing to do with me. But short-tempered he is. He snaps at me easily, and is most of the time preoccupied. It seemed to start when some of his friends formed a posse and asked him to join them. They were going towards Pyramid Lake in search of someone who had escaped from the prison at Fort Churchill.

I was in the other room when they asked him, and I swear he was set to go with them until one of the men said a rifle wasn't good enough and Robert needed to wear his side arm. Robert said he didn't have one, and after the man offered to loan him one, Robert said he wouldn't carry it. The men were polite, but I could tell they were puzzled, and maybe a little irritated. They did finally accept his refusal, with surprising good will I thought, and they left immediately.

I went into the parlor where Robert had settled with a newspaper. I ignored that he was holding it up like a shield. "I don't understand, my dear. You had a rifle in the wagon all the way here."

"That's different. I won't carry a handgun."

"But..."

"Don't ask me again!"

He walked out of the house, returning very late and reeking of beer. He fell into bed, only partially undressed, and snored through the night. But he also called out several times from what I assume were nightmares. Just before dawn he got up and sat in the parlor, staring out the one window through which one can see the street. I got up, pulled on a wrapper, and went into the kitchen to make coffee. By the time I got the fire up, and the coffee grounds settled, I felt I had given him plenty of time to gather his thoughts. I took him a steaming mug and sat on the sofa next to him, silently sipping my own cup of the strong brew.

It was some time before he spoke, his voice low and not taking his eyes from the window. His first words came in a rush. "You've been very good about never asking me about my past before we met in Nevada City during the rush."

As surprised as I was at his words, I answered him calmly. "I guess I just don't care about that. I know who you are by the way you treat me and others. That's all that matters."

He turned to me with eyes pleading for understanding. "I wish so much that was true. You've always assumed that it was your past that must be hidden from society, because of your time in a parlor house. But it's even more important that I keep mine hidden." I didn't know how to respond to that, so I said nothing. "Do you remember during the rush, when a young woman was hanged?"

"In Downieville? Yes, of course I remember."

"Her name was Josefa, but since then people refer to her as Juanita."

Dolly didn't have to relate the details of that story to Lucy, knowing that she would remember it. The version of the story heard by Lucy and Dolly had been that Juanita had been a woman of reputed loose morals who had lived in the 1851 California gold rush town of Downieville on the Yuba River. That was where Juanita made a bad mistake the day following a rowdy July 4. She was brash, outspoken and living with a gambler named Jose without the societal blessing of wedlock. But along with being considered a loose woman, she also had two other "flaws" that set her apart. She was Mexican, and if not exactly beautiful, she was at least striking in appearance. Consequently, some men interpreted this to mean she was "fair game", and deserving of little respect.

A man in the town called Cannon was known as a loud-mouthed bully who played by his own rules. He respected no man, and certainly no woman like Juanita. He had gotten drunk the night of July 4, and had been staggering home with some friends when he fell against the door to Jose's tiny cabin, breaking it. The next day Jose asked for compensation and when Cannon refused, Juanita flew into a rage that attracted a crowd to watch the spectacle. Juanita retreated to the cabin, but Cannon called her a whore as he banged on the cabin door. She opened it with a knife in her hand, and stabbed him in the chest.

He died, and Juanita and Jose got a quick trial and an even quicker conviction by a judge who had accurately read the temperament of the crowd of half-drunk miners. He didn't accept her plea of self-defense, claiming as did many others, that this up-start woman had over-reacted. A couple of men tried to plead on her behalf, but they were threatened by the crowd to the point that they backed off.

The local doctor, Dr. Cyrus Aiken, came forward and said she was expecting, but no one believed him. After two other doctors disagreed, the leaders of the crowd made it clear that there was enough rope to hang the doctor as well, so he too backed off. At which point it was clear that the over-excited crowd had decided Juanita must hang for her crime. The judge agreed. It didn't help that she freely admitted to what she had done. The judge did, however, decide that Jose was not guilty of anything, although it was made clear to him that he should think seriously about leaving town as quickly as possible.

So they placed Juanita on a plank at the edge of the Jersey Bridge over the Yuba River that flowed through the town, the plank lashed to the base of the bridge with ropes. Another hung down from a high cross beam. After they placed a loop of this rope over Juanita's head, they let her have her last words. Before they tied her hands behind her back, she made sure the rope was beneath her long black hair for a quick snap. Looking around at the hundreds of men standing on either side of the bridge, along the river banks, and up on the hills around the town, she called out a saucy farewell. A signal came from the judge and with the fall of their axes, two men simultaneously cut the ropes holding down the plank.

Some said she bravely jumped before the axes cut the ropes, but that was accepted as fodder for good story-telling. Over time, it became clear that the number of men who claimed to have cut one of the ropes was more than could have fit onto the bridge, but so goes legends. Of course, when the townsmen sobered up the next day, there were murmurs of regret, but most of it was for the fact that they knew the incident would color the town's reputation for a long time. They had no idea how long. History has a very long memory.

When newspapers in the region found out what had happened, they roundly condemned the event. The *Sacramento Times and Transcript* wrote:

"*The violent proceedings of an indignant and excited mob, led on by the enemies of the unfortunate woman, are a blot upon the history of the state. Had she committed a crime of really heinous character, a real American would have revolted at such a course as was pursued towards this friendless and unprotected foreigner. We had hoped that the story was fabricated. As it is, the perpetrators have shamed themselves and their race.*"

Juanita's lover did leave the town that day, and no one knows what happened to Jose after that. Ironically, Juanita and Cannon were buried side by side in the old graveyard behind the town's little theater. However, in the early 1870's the bodies were re-interred elsewhere when the area by the theater became available for mining.

Lucy had heard it said by old men there in Placerville that Juanita's skull had been removed at the time of the disinterment, and that it was being used as part of an initiation ceremony by some men's secret society. But no one would swear to that.

CHAPTER 7

1875 - 1876

Lucy poured herself a glass of water before returning her attention to Dolly's letter from the summer of 1871. She remembered her initial reaction to reading about Robert's reference to Juanita's infamous gold rush hanging. Lucy had, at the time of the hanging, been a young girl and not too far from the actual event. Surprised that she felt some of the same emotional disturbance as she had back then, she returned to Dolly's letter.

My response to Robert was, "What about Juanita?"

Robert started to turn to me, but instead looked away toward the window and the busy street beyond. "I was there. I was one of the men who voted her fate."

I was stunned, and it showed. "Oh, Robert!"

"I was a different person back then."

"In what way?"

"I drank pretty heavily. I carried a gun at all times. I used it often. At first it was to defend myself, just like everyone else did. Then some punk stepped out from an alley eager for a drawdown. I survived. He didn't. Men knew then that I was fast. Word spread to the other camps along the Yuba. That's all it took for toughs out to prove themselves, to come hunt for me. They found out the hard way that I was as fast as I was reputed to be. But I didn't want a reputation and I didn't like killing.

"After I'd see them lying there dead or dying, there was always that first hit of incredible relief that it wasn't me. Then another feeling would follow. I still

can't come to terms with that thrilling rush of triumph. Where does a feeling like that come from in someone who always thought of himself as a decent person? That's when I would be almost overcome with soul-crushing despair. It never felt okay to do that to another human being. I admit that I felt less bad for the bullies whose cruelty I'd witnessed. Still, I hated being praised for my courage." He coughed out a bark of derision. "Courage, be damned! It took no courage to pull the trigger. Just enough self-protection as justification."

"Is that when you left that area?"

"Yes. I wanted no man to seek me out so he could brag that he'd taken me down. I just wanted to be someone unnoticeable. So I became a simple blacksmith in Nevada City known for never wearing a gun. I loved working with poor dumb beasts. They didn't challenged me, or admired me. They endured being shod the same as I endured my memories, stoically and with resignation. And then I met you. You gave me a shy glance, and for the first time in years I felt the warmth of goodness well up in me. And I realized there really was such a thing as salvation."

Knowing I am far from deserving sainthood, I ignored the compliment. "Why didn't you ever tell me any of this?"

"I wouldn't now, except that it's become necessary."

"Why?"

"Because I ran into a man when we were in Aurora who I knew back then. I could tell when he saw me that he was trying to place me, but he wasn't sure where that had been."

"Is that why we left Aurora so suddenly? It wasn't just because we wanted to avoid another winter?"

"That was part of it, of course. But, yes, I wanted to get away before he figured out where he'd known me."

I realized he was still having difficulty meeting my eyes. "There's more, isn't there?"

"Yes." He sighed deeply. "I saw him in Gold Hill recently. He's in Virginia City, working for one of the bigger mines. And this time, he knew where he'd seen me before."

"But Downieville was so long ago," I protested.

I mean, Lucy, it was! Lots of us did things we're not proud of back during the rush, but most people accept whatever it was because of the desperation of the times. But Robert's Downieville acquaintance was sharp, and figured Robert wouldn't want the details of his past known.

"George wants money. That's his name, George Mull. I told him I didn't have much money, that I'd spent most of it buying this house. He said I should sell the house and give him the money from the sale."

"No!"

"I've put him off by saying that it'll take me awhile to find a buyer in this market. He said he'd wait."

I sat deep in thought for several minutes. "Does this have something to do with why you joined the Nevada Volunteers?"

"Yes. He's a member."

"I don't understand. Doesn't that put you in greater contact with him?"

"Yes, but it also makes it easier to learn more about him."

I started to question the logic of this, but he got up and left the house, saying, "I'll be back later."

When Lucy had first read this, it had occurred to her that being in with the Volunteers might give Robert opportunities to be alone with the man while out on maneuvers. Where accidents sometimes happen. What actually did occur was stranger than that.

Lucy had begun reading only those parts of Dolly's letters that moved her forward to the present. She was less interested in the history of the area now, and more interested in what had been of greater impact to her friends. At the same time that Robert was dealing with the demons of his past there in Carson City in the early '70's, Jane was in Virginia City having problems of her own, as Dolly related to Lucy.

August, 1871: *Jane recently wrote to me with the news that she has met and agreed to marry a nice man who works there in Virginia City. So Robert and I went to see her last week, an adventure in and of itself. The stage stopped in Gold Hill and we transferred to the train while it took on water and passengers. After winding through the hills, past mines and their mounds of tailings, and passing through a number of narrow, dark railroad tunnels, we finally arrived at the station in Virginia City.*

A line of men with buggies met the train and we hired one of them to take us up the steep streets into the heart of town. Some of these men used to be freighters who had to find a different career after the train connected Carson to Virginia City. In fact, all town streets are not as full of wagons now. Of course, wagons are used locally, but seldom seen are the long strings of mules pulling huge wagons up the hill. Now the train brings the heavy mining equipment, barrels of supplies, and household necessities like stoves.

There is a much slower pace in Virginia City altogether. Reality has settled in after the excitement of the bonanza times as a worsening economy has replaced it. But major mines are still paying well, and even several of the small ones, creating enough reason for businesses and families to stay. Maybe not as many as a decade ago, but enough of them for those who still firmly believe that another bonanza will embrace the area. Of course, they dare not predict when.

It had been several months since I'd seen Jane, and Robert said he wanted to purchase some tanned leather from a man he knows who does a nice job of such things. The day we arrived we had plans for a fancy dinner at the International Hotel, being treated by Robert's friend Albert Hanak, who owns the building next door to the hotel. For some reason, the men have hit it off, having met through Barney Clark, who runs the Union Saloon on the ground floor of Mr. Hanak's building.

By the time we got to Virginia City, we had to head straight to the hotel's dining room. In our effort not to be discourteously late to meet up with Mr. Hanak, we didn't even stop to check into our hotel. However, after a sumptuous meal, we immediately did that. When I woke up in the morning, Robert had already left, leaving me a note saying he would meet me back at the room at one o'clock. I ate a small bit of breakfast and then headed straight for Jane's boarding house.

We greeted one another with enthusiasm. After several minutes of general talk, I gently inquired about her fiancé. After describing the friends who introduced them to one another at a small dinner party, she said, "My late husband was not a very good man, as I'm sure you remember. I was without affection for a very long time. Then he died. I think I had begun to think of myself as unlovable. When my fiancé gives me little compliments, I sometimes feel as though he must be talking about someone else. If there's love back of his words, I find there's only striving to believe on my part. But I do feel great affection for him. And gratitude that he's favoring me."

"Is that enough?"

"For now. I'm sure I'll feel more later because George is a fine man. So kind and generous. He works at the Ophir Mine's stable."

"George?"

"Yes, George Mull. He's looking to find us a house, as he thought he might be coming into some unexpected money from a relative."

I was dumbfounded, and covered it by shamming a coughing fit. By the time she had fetched me a glass of water from the pitcher on the dresser, I had gathered myself together. I quickly broached the subject of her life in Virginia City over the last several months while teaching. But inevitably we returned to her relationship. She asked if I would stand up with her when they set the date for the wedding. I, of course, had to accept.

I returned to the hotel at one o'clock as Robert had requested in his note, but he didn't show up. I ate a quick meal at a small cafe, and then hurried to the Ophir Mine's stable area, which was quite a walk. On the way, I purchased carrots at a market to feed to the horses at the stable as an excuse for being there. I came in at the back of the main stable, and after scanning the shadows and seeing that the big double doors at the front were closed, I concluded that no one was inside. Also, by the time I had finished feeding the carrots to three nearby horses, I was realizing that I had acted on an ill-considered impulse.

Thinking through what I had planned to do, I was suddenly overcome by a dread of finding myself face to face with Mr. Mull. He was a man I didn't know and who would think me interfering at best, and more likely an intolerable busy-body. Realizing I could cause irreparable harm to my relationship with Jane, not to mention whatever arrangement Mull and Robert had made, I picked up my skirts and practically fled from the barn and back into town.

What Dolly had missed seeing was Robert standing at the front of the barn in deep shadow. Unable to think clearly, he looked down at the heavy item in his hand, wondering what to do with it. It was an old iron wrench used for removing wheel hubs, and it seemed heavier by the minute. He vaguely wondered why he didn't just drop it, as bits of rust had left red deposits on his palm. Yet he simply looked at it as though surprised to see that it was in his hand. His eyes shifted to the stall to his right. A man lay on the thin layer of straw; a man he knew. It reminded him of years previously when a man had been found in his Placerville livery. This one was also dead. It was the man who had recognized him, George Mull.

Robert dropped the wrench in a water barrel on the far side of the stable, rinsing his hands in the water. He then dragged the body out to lay beside a wagon in the middle of the floor waiting for repair. He wiped some of the man's still wet blood on the iron and wooden hub of the wheel, then again rinsed his hands in the barrel. He quickly set a rickety folding ladder next to the fallen man, and made sure the body looked as though it could have fallen where it lay. He checked the stall and took up the few pieces of straw with blood on them, washed them in the barrel and distributed them among the stalls that looked the next to be mucked out.

Dolly's next letter had explained to Lucy what had occurred the following morning just at dawn when Dolly had raced to respond to a knocking on the door of their hotel room. She had been up all night worrying, wondering why Robert had not returned. But it was not Robert at the door.

Jane stood there with tears streaming down her face. "Oh, Dolly, George is dead!"

"What in the world happened?"

"George was such a dear man."

"Yes, yes, but what happened?" Dolly's first thought had been, "Fate can't be so cruel to Jane, and at the same time arrange things so conveniently for me and Robert."

Dolly had fought to keep her breathing even as she led Jane to the sofa in the corner of the hotel room. She sat next to her, resting an arm around her friend's shoulders. Jane took a deep breath before trying to talk. "He was found in the barn belonging to the mine he works for. They think he fell off a ladder and hit his head on the hub of a wagon wheel. There were some buckets and coils of rope and other things hanging from the ceiling they think he was trying to reach. They're assembling a coroner's jury, but the sheriff said that's what they'll probably conclude."

"You don't sound convinced."

She twisted the sodden handkerchief in her hands. "I guess I just can't accept that he's gone."

"Did you see him in the stable? Where he was lying, I mean."

"Of course not!"

There was a snap to Jane's words that was more than mere rebuke, but Dolly didn't immediately register on that. Dolly had known that Jane wouldn't have been allowed such a thing, but it was a way to lead into what she wanted to convey to Jane. "Might that be why you can't make sense of it? After all, you're just going by what others have described."

"Yes. Yes, I suppose you're right." She picked at the fringe of her shawl. "I guess I just never thought he could be that clumsy."

"Accidents happen all the time, though. I'm just sorry it happened to someone you cared for."

"Oh, Dolly, I wasn't madly in love with him." She shrugged and blew her nose with finality. "But it was a chance for a respectable life again, and he seemed to have enough money to keep us. I hadn't told you, but better trained teachers than I am recently replaced me at the school."

"Why didn't you tell me this earlier?"

"I didn't want you to think I was going to need you and Robert to shelter me again."

"Oh, Jane, that wouldn't be sheltering. That would be welcoming home a member of the family."

Jane leaned into the protective warmth of Dolly's arms as they closed around her. Resting her head on Dolly's shoulder, Jane exhaled all the anxiety and fear built up since the day she had left her teaching position.

Dolly debated whether or not to say anything about George's blackmailing tendencies. However, Robert arrived home and Dolly's relief washed away such an urge. After the women explained what had happened, Jane left. Robert mumbled something about taking a long walk, needing to be alone to think, and ignored Dolly's dismay at his leaving again so soon after arriving. He didn't return until well after midnight, but Dolly asked for no explanation, instead pretending to be asleep.

The next morning, she simply proceeded to make their breakfast, even though the effort to say nothing about the night before inhibited her effort to swallow. The subject had still not been raised by that night, nor by the next morning when Robert left to witness the proceedings of the Coroner's jury. It reached the decision expected of them of accidental death.

Robert returned to their hotel room to tell Dolly what had taken place. Women had not been allowed inside, although it was assumed that no self-respecting woman would want to be there. Dolly took Robert to the café she liked best for an afternoon meal, after which they walked much of the length of "C" Street. They stopped at a few shops, but purchased nothing. Throughout, Robert was obviously preoccupied and Dolly was becoming even more obviously irritated with him. It ended with them back at the hotel not speaking to one another.

As they finished their afternoon coffee at the small table in their room, Robert leaned back in his chair and looked directly at his wife. "Dolly, one of the deputies said that when he entered the front of the barn, he thought he smelled perfume in the air. But when the big front doors were opened, the breeze blew it away and the others who arrived thought him fanciful. But its left the impression with some that there had been a woman there very recently."

"Nothing too peculiar about that, surely. Besides, it was an accidental fall that killed him, right?"

"That's what they concluded."

"Interesting, though, that you tied together the smell of perfume and his death."

Robert looked at her for a long moment. "I saw you leaving at the back, just as I came in through the small side door at the front."

Dolly stared back, and then laughed. He hadn't expected that, and he showed his shock. "Oh, Robert, I'd hoped to keep that from you. I felt such a fool. I wanted to see this man that could be such a villain, and yet capture Jane's heart. Although I now realize it was not a love match after all. More a thing of security for her, and who knows what for him."

"What happened when you saw him?"

"But I didn't. I suddenly realized it had been a stupid thing to do, to come there, and I ..."

"You didn't come up to the front of the barn?"

"No. I stayed at the back near where I'd entered." Realization hit her. "Oh, my goodness! If I had, I might have been the one to find him lying there next to the coach." The look on her husband's face was not one she could easily interpret. "If you saw me leaving, why didn't you call out to me?"

His words came in a rush. "I thought maybe you'd come there to talk to him and things got out of control. And that you'd hit him with an old wrench."

"A wrench? No one has mentioned anything that would indicate he had been struck."

Robert cleared his throat, swallowed hard, and told her how he had moved the body and set up the scene. When he finished, Dolly said, "But that means someone killed him, possibly in anger."

"Yes." He hesitated a moment. "I too smelled the perfume mentioned by the deputy. It wasn't yours, I realize now, but having just seen you, that didn't occur to me then."

Robert rose from his chair and walked around the table, kneeling beside Dolly. He wrapped his arms around her and laid his head on her chest, holding fast to what he loved more than anything or anyone else in the world. Dolly cradled his head against the comfort of her breast, trusting herself to speak only after several minutes. "We need to meet Jane at the International Hotel for supper. We did invite her, after all."

The food was, as always at that hotel, one of unusual high quality, especially the dessert. Half-way through the meal, Robert became very quiet, letting the ladies chat between themselves. But their conversation was stilted and broken by long pauses. With the dishes cleared and the last of their coffee still before them, Robert finally spoke up.

"Jane, I must say the perfume you're wearing is very nice."

Dolly's eyes widened and she turned slowly toward Jane, who was smiling with pleasure. "Yes, it is. One of the merchandise stores just got in a new shipment of items, and a bottle of this was included, meant for the owner's wife. But she didn't like it, and since I was present when it was unpacked and I admired it, she just gave it to me."

Dolly murmured, "So no one else in town is wearing that scent?"

"No." Jane smiled shyly. "It makes me feel so special."

"Oh, Jane." Dolly closed her eyes and sighed.

Jane was obviously puzzled. "What's the matter?"

Robert lowered his voice to a degree the two women were surprised he could accomplish. "I smelled that scent recently. In the stable where George was killed. In fact, just after he was killed."

The color drained from Jane's face, and she stared at him as though she had never seen him before. "You couldn't have."

"But I did." He explained to her his misunderstanding because he had seen Dolly, and what he had done to the scene of the crime.

Jane dropped her eyes down to her lap where her hands were tightly folded. "You did all that because you thought Dolly had killed him. Now that you think I did it, what are you going to do?"

Robert leaned forward, almost laying on the table. "Jane, I committed a crime by what I did. I can't say anything. But to protect you as much as myself."

"Really?" She looked up at him with wonder.

"Of course. You're family, for God's sake!"

Jane tried hard to control the quivering in her chin, but it took her several minutes. She then told them, "Yes, I hit him." She looked up to fix on Robert's eyes. "But I didn't mean to kill him. Actually, I don't think I did."

Dolly took one of Jane's hands in hers. "What happened? You had agreed to marry him."

"Yes, I had. But he never wanted to discuss setting a date. I went to the stable just as I knew his shift was ending. I came in through the small side door and found him alone, just closing up. I told him that I insisted on him setting a date." She looked at Dolly and whispered, "After all, I'd allowed him to... Well, never mind that. He told me not to nag him, and if I was going to be that way, maybe it was a mistake for us to be married at all. I was shocked at his attitude and demanded to know if there was some reason why he didn't want to set a date. He turned on me and shouted, 'Because I'm already married.'"

Robert shook his head and muttered outraged oaths while Dolly asked, "Did he explain why he had asked you to marry him, then?"

"No."

His jaw tight with ill-concealed anger, Robert murmured, "Probably just so she'd... The bastard!"

"How did you respond?" Dolly asked. "Or do we already know?"

"There was a big wrench on the floor just outside the empty stall where he was standing. I'd almost tripped on it. I turned and picked it up, then swung around to threaten him with it, so he'd know how angry I was. I didn't realize he'd moved closer and was within range of the swing of my arm as I stood and turned. He fell down onto the straw, but then started to get up, swearing curses at me. I dropped the wrench and ran, expecting him to show up at my room in a rage to hurt me. When half an hour passed, I then feared the sheriff would come to arrest me. Instead, my landlady heard about him being found dead and came to me with the news. But she said he'd fallen from a ladder."

"And then you came to me."

"Oh, my tears were real. I was so full of guilt. I thought I'd hurt him and yet he'd tried to climb a ladder, but fell off because of his wounded head. Oh, I didn't know what to think. I just wanted to be with someone who cared about me."

Dolly put her hand on Jane's arm and looked across at Robert. He caught her look and shook his head. "I need to think about this. You two go back to the hotel. Jane can spend the night on the sofa in our room. I'll be with you later."

It was after midnight when Robert got to the hotel. He quietly undressed and climbed into bed. Knowing that Dolly was awake, he simply squeezed her hand reassuringly before turning onto his side to fall into a deep sleep. And because he was able to do that, Dolly knew he had come to a decision with which he was satisfied. Consequently, she too was soon asleep. Trust allowed for that.

Lucy knew only too well what had come next for Robert, Dolly and Jane. It was all explained in the next letter she had received from Dolly.

**July, 1872**: My dearest friend, I am only too aware that I have not written this past winter. In part, because of the inability of mail to get across the mountain, but also because so much has been happening.

Although the coroner's jury judged George Mull's death an accident, that didn't stop tongues from wagging. The deputy, first on the scene, continued to declare that he'd smelled perfume as he entered, and that it meant to him that a woman had been inside either before or just after George's death. When the wrench was found at the bottom of the water barrel, the coroner said it fit the break in George's skull better than the hub of a wheel. Worse yet, more than one person has been heard to comment that even a woman could kill a man with such an implement. It was a tense time, waiting for someone to step up to say they had seen Jane or myself at the stable around that time.

People began giving Jane odd looks, since she had been engaged to marry him. Whenever some woman would bring up the subject, I always made sure to say how happy a couple they had been, and how devastated Jane was to have lost her chance at marriage. That, at least, any woman understands.

Whether or not the women passed my words on to their husbands, I don't know. But the topic is seldom raised, especially now that everyone is busy getting on with summer activities. The cold of winter seems to be a season when people find time to brood about injustices and complain about the hardships of life. But it has all led to our making a decision of some magnitude. We have *sold the house to a new arrival, a couple with a young child and who know nothing about what happened. It was too good an opportunity to pass up, and it allowed us some cash from the profit after paying off the loan.*

We are thinking of moving far away, maybe Robert leaving first under some purposeful guise. We may even change our name and have Jane pose as Robert's widowed sister, and therefore my sister-in-law. It would explain why we live together. As for where, there are three towns that we're thinking about. If we do this, I will write to you under our new name in such a coded way that you know who I am and where I am. So please be sure to destroy this letter.

There had been no signature, and it was the last one from Dolly in the pile. Lucy walked out to the waste fire smoldering in the backyard and slowly fed into it not only that letter, but also all the rest of them. She couldn't take them with her, and they were too personal to ever be seen by anyone else. At the same time, she felt like holding onto them for the memories they triggered. But she knew that those memories most important to her would always be treasured in her heart, as was her love for her dear friends.

Resolute, she watched the yellowed pages catch, crinkle and slowly dissolve into black ash. She poured a bucket of water onto the smoldering pile, followed by shovels of dirt and another bucket of water, making sure the embers were safely out. Only then was she ready to walk away, satisfied with her decision to let go of all the letters. It was time she made new memories.

Just before dawn two days later, Lucy stood on the back porch of the house that she had shared with those she had loved so dearly. She and Freda had said their farewells the night before, and her eyes were still a little red with weeping. They had parted in the past, but there had always been the possibility that they would meet again. This time was different. Freda had roots in Placerville and Lucy had no roots anywhere. Even when she might be once again settled, it was unlikely that Freda and her husband would uproot themselves at this stage of their lives.

Images flashed through her mind of all she and Freda had experienced together in the gold rush towns of California during the rush. A highlight for Lucy as a young girl had been experiencing the elegance of New York City in 1855, her return to California on a wagon train as a servant, and the reunion with Freda in Jamestown two years later.

And then there were all the years she and Jim had spent with Freda while raising Roger, especially after they had moved to Placerville. The time she didn't want to recall were the hours she had spent in Freda's arms weeping after accepting the reality that Jim was dead. But, of course, that memory did crowd in, and it was with a determined effort that she focused on the reality, and urgency, of the moment.

Lucy straightened her shoulders and donned a wide-brimmed man's hat before slipping on her favorite leather riding gloves. She had carefully chosen a split skirt that fell well below the tops of tall leather boots, with a white waist under a leather vest and a light wool jacket. No matter what time of the year it was, it was always cool at night in the mountains.

Lucy walked across the yard to the barn where her horse was saddled and ready for her. The strawberry roan gelding had been purchased for her by Jim not long before he had left town, and was now only twelve years old; a well-trained, sound trail horse. They were old friends, she and Diamond, and she trusted him to take care of her on the precipitous trails that lay ahead of them. She glanced at the detested side-saddle still on its stand, and said good-bye to it forever.

The saddlebags held various supplies along with a hoof pick and curry comb for Diamond, food stuffs in two burlap bags, and a bedroll and rain slicker tucked behind the saddle. She had packed into a cloth valise, now wrapped in oil cloth, a plain black skirt and two extra waists, one black and the other burgundy, as well as a light shawl and two silk scarves. For those times when she might find room at an inn, she also had a flannel nightgown. The tall boots she wore would have to suffice for all occasions.

Most importantly, she wore a money belt under her clothes, into which she had placed a good amount of cash, her few pieces of good jewelry, and a Wells Fargo money order for her savings. She smiled to herself as she thought of the small velvet pouch of gold nuggets wrapped in a man's cotton shirt, along with denim pants, tightly rolled up at the bottom of one of the saddlebags. A woman dressing as a man was illegal, although in earlier years it had more than once saved her life. Lastly, she felt the weight of her gun in a side pocket, and finally felt prepared for whatever might arise on the journey.

Nevertheless, underlying what to others appeared to be a courageous decision, hovered anxiety that she was working hard to dispel. Most of this was not, however, about the journey, but about Roger's reaction to her sudden appearance in his life. If, that is, he was still in Aurora by the time she got there.

As Lucy rode out of Placerville, she pulled up at the first rise on the road. She took a last look back, breathed in the pine scented air, and turned Diamond away from the place she had loved so dearly for so long. With a touch of pressure to his sides, the horse hastened forward.

Not long out on the Placerville Road, also known as the Carson Route, Lucy looked around her, reminding herself that she was on a slightly different road than the one Dolly and Robert had taken. With the approval of the Board of Wagon Commissioners created by the state legislature in 1858, John Johnson had in 1864 begun improvement of the grading on the north side of the river. But he had stopped work when Messrs. Pearson and McDonald had opened an improvement of their own. The toll collection system with which Lucy now had to contend wouldn't end until 1886, when El Dorado County would purchase the privately improved sections and make them public roads.

It wasn't the condition of the road that surprised Lucy, but rather the road traffic. It was so much lighter than it had been during the rush to the Comstock Lode, back when Dolly had described their journey. It was, however, still a busy route full of men, and very few women.

Lucy was not without way-stations where she could stop, and possibly work her way in to be served. Freighters had destinations to reach and teams of horses, mules or oxen to care for, and no time to waste on a strange woman. If she could wrangle a cup of coffee or a biscuit, she considered herself fortunate. When the crowd looked too rough, Lucy simply chose to eat a piece of jerky from her supplies and drink from her canteen.

Not long after leaving Placerville, she passed by Smith's Flat, as it was only three miles into her journey. At Sportsman's Hall she ate a good meal and retired for the night under a tree out of sight of the station and the road traffic. In the days that followed, she was able to reach Pacific House just as darkness settled; avoided Dirty Harry's and some of the older, less civilized stations; made her way to the stations of Moore's, McCanlia's, Yarnell's, Georgetown Junction and Berry's Flat being called *Strawberry* by some. At this last she smiled at the notoriously unsociable Mr. Berry and partook of his dubious hospitality. There was a fireplace there so large that logs five feet long burned in it during the winter.

As she traveled along the South Fork of the American River, she could hear it churning at the bottom of the road's steep drop-off. The blue sky was filled with only a few streaky clouds, making the view beautiful as well as comforting, as it indicated no summer storm approaching. She chose to think of it as an approval of what she had chosen as a new phase of her life. She let go of the past, and embracing the beauty of the moment, began to eagerly anticipate whatever adventures might lie ahead.

When the road evened out, Lucy allowed herself to look around at the view. Springs seeped from the rocky wall to her left, colorful plants hosting butterflies and bees lined the road edge, and yellow tanagers sang among the trees while the jays scolded those below. She inhaled the pungent scent of fir, balsam and pine mixed with the warm trail odors, and laughed at a covey of quail scurrying across the road, just missed by wagon wheels and hooves. These were rare moments and helped deflect her focus from an aching back and saddlesores.

The road climbed, reached its peak at Summit, and then began its downward descent toward Hope Valley. She had eaten a good meal at Phillip's before passing through Summit (7,260 feet in elevation), and was now glad that Osgood's Station was not only welcoming, but also respectful of a woman traveling alone. She had not always been met with such admirable behavior. She had been leered at, laughed at, pushed aside and sworn at more than once. One man had tried to take Diamond from her, but hesitated when he realized why she was reaching into her pocket. He had backed off further when other men had started in their direction, at which point Lucy had mounted and quickly blended into the traffic on the road.

Almost at the end of what she thought of as the first phase of her journey, Lucy had a passable meal at Myer's Ranch and stayed the night there. She passed Sierra House past Woodburn's Saw Mill and looked out over a landscape filled with scrub and a scattering of weathered trees. For the first time, Lucy realized she was exchanging the green high Sierra for a world of deserts and low hills, and comforted herself by spending a day at the Hot Springs Hotel south of the town of Genoa.

She luxuriated in a hot bath, ate a delicious meal, and delighted in a sound sleep on a good straw mattress. But she dared not linger. Something in the nature of an urgent hunch moved her forward, mostly made up of the fear that she would miss Roger if she didn't hurry. Aurora was no longer the boom town that had been described in Dolly's letters. Consequently, it might not be where a gambler would want to stay too long.

As Lucy saddled Diamond, she looked at the expanse of surrounding scrub and forced herself to accept that mountain climes were a part of her past. She experienced a strange sort of grief at the thought as she traveled through a 15 mile stretch of bleak, dry land broken occasionally by small ranches and truck farms. Lucy watered Diamond at the small town of Sheridan, then continued on to Genoa.

She had planned at the start of her trip to spend time resting in this small, well-established village with a fort to protect it. She had been correct in assuming that at this point she would be sore, tired and in need of rest. Diamond would no doubt be ready for some rest as well. It would not help her to be without a sound horse for the difficult last part of her trip, nor to be in poor health once she reached her errant son.

She secured Diamond at the Tingham Livery Stable after receiving assurance that they would care properly for him, and then checked into the Gilbert Hotel next door. The two-story frame building was inviting, and she was relieved to see that her room was clean and the window opened easily. She was soon seated at a table in the hotel's dining room, where she consumed a man-sized steak to the humorous amazement of those around her. When she realized she was being watched by two couples at the next table, she smiled in their direction. "I just finished a ride from Placerville." The men's expressions turned to one of begrudging respect, while the two women expressed dismay tinged with wistful contemplation.

Lucy enjoyed a piece of unidentifiable berry pie while thinking back to the first major leg of her *adventure* over the past week. That was the way she chose to think of her ordeal getting across the mountain. Many of the way-stations had been there in name only, having popped up during the rush to the Washoe mines at the peak of the Virginia City excitement, back in the early 1860's. Since that was over, and the country had recently experienced an intense recession, many of the smaller stations had closed down if they were close to larger ones offering more space for freighting teams.

Lucy smiled as she recalled the various looks cast in her direction by surprised or disbelieving men when realizing this was a lone woman in their midst. In the main, it had been the older men who had been the most accepting, possibly because they had seen so many odd things in their lives. The younger men had been less tolerant, still clinging to the assumption that women stayed home and found their purpose in life among domestic pursuits, never moving beyond wherever their husbands or fathers placed them.

During the war, Lucy had wondered if that too would be her fate, with never again the opportunity to feel the excitement of a new experience, as she had so often enjoyed in her youth. But that had been before Jim had left their home only months before the end of the war. She almost laughed out loud as she thought about how quixotic was the nature of life.

The next morning, the clerk at the hotel asked her if she would be leaving on the stage. This was an unexpectedly welcome idea, the stage taking a good road that passed through Wellington, Nevada, before heading to Aurora. The stage line agreed to let her tether Diamond to the back of the coach if she agreed to care for him whenever they stopped. She purchased a ticket and hurried to pack her things, changing into a long skirt instead of her riding outfit. While one man tossed her saddle and bridle onto the top of the coach, another put her valise, bedroll, and saddlebags into its boot before helping her inside. Lucy settled onto the narrow bench seat and sat back against the padded wall of the coach with a degree of gratitude that was almost overwhelming. No long, dusty trail ride after all, never knowing what was around the next curve of the road. She even had a relatively clean duster to wear over her clothes. Yes, she was one happy woman.

Past Wellington, at Sulphur Springs Station the driver took an extra lengthy time eating and visiting with the owner. It gave Lucy time to stretch her legs out back of the stone and wood station. Having placed Diamond in a corral with food and water, she stood beneath an old tree with spreading branches and looked out over a small, fenced pasture where cattle grazed the sparse grass. The last two days had held more excitement and trauma than she had anticipated, and she had to admit to still feeling a little rattled. Adventure was fine, but danger was another thing altogether.

Three masked hold-up artists, as the driver referred to them, had stopped the coach just before they had arrived at Wellington. The outlaws had found little of value among the five men traveling with her, but their main disappointment had been discovering that there was no strong box on board. And although most of the bandits had ignored her, one of them had let his eyes linger on her a bit too long. She had dared not reach for the gun in her pocket, but she had been glad that she had it in case the man had tried to take her with them. Thankfully, the man who was presumably the leader of the group had yelled a command, and they had all left quickly.

At Wellington, they had been treated to strong coffee and big pieces of apple pie while Lucy's fellow passengers quarreled among themselves about petty matters. Suddenly, one of them had lost his temper and had driven his fist into the face of another passenger who had called him an insulting name. Peace had been restored when the station proprietor stepped in between the two combatants while threatening them with various consequences if they didn't sit down and shut up. Back on the stage, the two men had glared at one another all the way to their present stop.

Lucy's attention was suddenly diverted to the screaming of Diamond in the corral. She turned and ran, joining everyone exiting the station just as a large rattlesnake rose up and struck out at Diamond. Lucy, who prided herself in not being a screaming type of woman, nevertheless found her voice in that moment. The stage driver pulled out his shot gun and blasted the retreating snake into several pieces. Lucy ran to her horse, now up against the far fence, quivering and holding his front leg cocked and barely touching the ground. While Lucy spoke soothingly to Diamond, the station owner bent down to examine the wound.

"Hold him," he commanded. He brought out a jackknife and made a small cut over the bite, letting the blood flow freely. Diamond squealed and pulled back, but not so much that Lucy couldn't hold him.

"Is he going to die?" Lucy choked out.

"Depends on how much venom the snake gave him. Sometimes they don't even let go of any. Sometimes they inject a load of it." He then washed the cut with the lather of lye soap and wrapped it lightly so it could drain.

The stage driver pulled Lucy aside. "The thing is, ma'am, he isn't going to be able to run behind the stage now, and we'll be leaving shortly."

Mr. Wiley, the station keeper, came up to them. "You can stay here until the next stage to Aurora comes along, but that won't be for three days. Or you can leave the horse and I'll keep him for myself if he lives. If you get back here fairly soon, he'll be yours again, of course."

"If I do that, I'll be sure to pay you for his feed."

"That's very decent of you. And if he did get a load of venom, I'll see he gets a quick end and doesn't suffer."

Both men left her alone then. She stroked the white diamond in the center of the horse's forehead and fought back the urge to weep. She knew there was only one practical decision she could make. When Mr. Wiley approached, she told him where she was going, her and Roger's name, and that a message left at "will call" at the post office would get to her. She climbed into the stage, holding tightly to her emotions and barely noticing that it was the previously quarreling men who attended to her. One helped her inside, while the other adjusted the leather window shade next to her place so she could see Diamond as they pulled out.

The stage passed through the sprawling outer reaches of Aurora, past the cemetery, a scattering of homes of various sizes, then warehouses, stables, and finally a jail that looked none too secure. Lucy's stage finally reached the town's compact core of businesses, hotels and saloons. The stage stopped on Pine, still the main street through the somewhat worn and faded town. Its appearance wasn't helped by the fact that everything was covered in a fine dust that shifted from one building to another with the rise and fall of each breath of wind.

Wearing her black skirt, burgundy waist and black wool jacket, Lucy stood on the old wooden sidewalk with her cloth satchel at her feet, along with her saddlebags, rain slicker and bedroll. She had given her saddle and bridle to Mr. Wiley at the station for his generosity in caring for Diamond.

Having carried her things as far as the Levy Brothers General Merchandise store, her aching arms demanded relief. None too gracefully, she sat down on a wooden bench and leaned back against the front of the brick building. Looking out at the low, desolate hills with huge brick mills on two of them, she ignored the curious stares of those passing. The street in front of her was lined with sturdy buildings mostly of brick, but overall everything presented to Lucy a town past its prime. Two of the wooden buildings slumped a little to the north, and Lucy wondered if they were feeling defeated, or were just tired. That, she could well understand.

Her next thought was, "Well, if this is Aurora, I can't say much for it." This was most definitely not the town that Dolly had described. Aurora then had been full of freshly whitewashed buildings, new construction expanding the town, and streets without weeds along the edges. There had also been many more people on the sidewalks.

Looking down the slope of the street, she saw that many of the buildings were boarded up, even while telegraph poles every few yards carried cable out into the desert. Other than that, it looked like a lot of other western mining towns that had seen a boom and was currently dealing with the bust that inevitably followed. Even the wooden sidewalks had changed somewhat, now only in front of occupied buildings grouped together, and missing from the open spaces between. The line of roofs was also inconsistent, some buildings false-fronted, some peaked, and some even flat if covering a brick building.

Some buildings had the back half running down a steep slope, and others were cut into the banks of a deep gulch. But whatever the construction, the whole presented the worn image of a once exciting femme fatale who had not aged well, who sagged in all the obvious places, and who could benefit from a little makeup. But no matter any effort now, she would still be just a faded reminder of a fabulous youth.

Next to Lucy was the Fleischman & Kaufman merchandise store, and beyond that the Howard & Sanchez Bank. Into this last she carried her things, approaching the young clerk at the counter with a tentative smile as she dumped everything at her feet.

"Excuse me, sir, but would you happen to know a young man by the name of Roger Murphy?"

The clerk's brows raised in surprise, and he answered cautiously. "I might. Would you be having business with him?"

Lucy couldn't help but laugh. "No. I'm his mother come to visit him."

"Oh! How nice." He then hesitated again. "Um, do you know what he does here?"

"Probably the same thing he's done since a child. Something with cards, no doubt, although I don't profess to know what game he might be profiting from at the moment. And I assume he's fairly well liked, especially by unmarried ladies."

The man laughed. "That's all true. Although you can count the number of marriageable ladies in the town on one hand." His tone of regret made Lucy fight back a chuckle. "You'll find Roger at the saloon right across the street. Would you like to leave your things here with me? I'll put them in the back and no one will bother them."

Noting that the clerk carried a side arm in a worn leather holster, where it was readily seen, she didn't doubt his word. "Thank you. That's very kind of you."

Lucy hesitated at the edge of the rough, plank sidewalk. Her heart beating hard, she again wondered how Roger would react to her showing up like this. But first she had to get across the mud of the wide, rutted street without ruining the bottom four inches of her skirt, or alternatively holding it up so high that she would cause a scandal. There were a few boards laid out as an inviting bridge across, but there was considerable mud even on those. She set her jaw and put out a foot in preparation of sinking into unknown depths of filth.

At that moment of resolution, she felt herself being lifted off her feet by strong, muscular arms. A deep voice reached her through the thick brush of a copious beard. "Let me help you, ma'am." And across the boards she was borne before being set down in front of the saloon. As she sputtered her thanks and adjusted her small bonnet that had been knocked askew, the man tipped his hat and moved down the sidewalk.

Laughter and loud voices coming from inside the saloon through an open, narrow door recalled her to the moment, and she stepped inside. Before her was a dozen or so men, some standing at the bar along the righthand wall and others seated at three tables near the bar. One of the tables was covered in green felt and piled with chips. It was surrounded by three miners in denim pants and flannel shirts, as well as two men in rumpled suits. They all had piles of chips in front of them, and were glaring at the one empty chair at their table. Miner, shopkeeper, deputy, banker or mining superintendent; it didn't matter. While gathered around such a table, only the purity of the whiskey and the turn of the cards held importance.

Lucy ignored the surprised looks cast in her direction, the men unsure what to do about a woman who seemed unfazed by the smells and sights that greeted her. But there were no hoots or ribald comments, for she was after all dressed in modest fashion, and carried herself with a self-assurance that disallowed anything but respect. Maybe she was a good woman who was lost, rather than a lost woman who was looking for good business.

Behind her, Lucy heard a surprised masculine voice. "Mom?"

Braced for his reaction, Lucy turned around. "Hello, Roger."

She looked at the tall, handsome man before her with blue eyes like his father's. Those eyes were now showing startled surprise. But he did not look angry. She also noted that he sported a man's thin mustache, and wore a tailored suit with a shiny gray vest, a fresh white shirt and a black string tie. She barely recognized this matured man, obviously a gambler of status. But when a grin split his face as he stepped forward, it was the boy she remembered who wrapped her in his arms and kissed her cheek. Lucy was flooded with immense relief.

"What the hell are you doing here, Mom?" He immediately colored, realizing that his language was a bit strong, used as he was to the society in which he worked.

Lucy grinned too as she stepped back and declared, "You're the hell that I'm doing here."

He laughed, as did a couple of the curious men nearest them. "Sorry about only leaving a note." It was not possible for him to have looked more sheepish.

"I guess I understand. But you could have discussed it with me."

"Mom..."

"I know, I know. I would have tried to talk you out of going."

Eager to change the subject, Roger looked down at the floor. "Where's your luggage? How did you get here from Placerville?"

"My adventures getting here are for telling at another time, but my luggage is at the bank. The nice clerk is looking after everything for me."

"That must be Harold, a friend of mine. In fact, I room with him and his mother."

They were interrupted by a deep voice hollering in their direction. "Hey, Murphy! The game isn't over, you know."

"Hold your water!" Roger yelled back. He then turned to his mother. "Say, why don't you take my place while I go get your things? Then I'll take you to the best boarding house in town. Unlike when Dolly and Robert were here, it won't be difficult finding you a room."

Roger led her to the table where he had been playing. "Fellas, this is my mother. She's going to fill in for me for a few hands." He pulled out a chair for her while the flabbergasted men at the table tried to find an unobjectionable way to object. Roger walked away before they could find it.

Lucy turned to them and asked, "What are we playing?" She picked up the deck of cards and proceeded to shuffle them with a dexterity and speed that raised more than one masculine brow.

"We're playing stud poker," one of the men told her. "Nothing wild. Is that okay with you, ma'am?"

"Oh, yes, that's just fine." Smiling, she swung her gaze around the table. "Just call me Lucy."

During the time that Roger was gone, Lucy won two of the four hands played. One of the more observant men, the foreman at one of the big mills above the town, suspicioned that she might have won the other two hands if she had tried harder. But just like Roger, he noted that she accepted defeat with the same grace as she accepted winning pots, and therefore had gained respect from everyone at the table. As the foreman thought about it later, he realized that the two pots Lucy had won had easily been larger than the ones she had so tactfully lost. A few curious glances were cast in his direction as he laughed loudly while walking down the sidewalk.

What those observers were not aware of, however, was the man pondering whether or not the handsome lady was married. On the other hand, he considered, a clever woman like that might be more of a challenge than he'd want to live with day in and day out. He shook his head, shrugged, and made his way to the local brothel.

The boarding house to which Roger brought Lucy was run by a nice older lady who welcomed Lucy with enthusiasm. Mrs. Donnally was a stout lady with gray hair that frizzed out from under a white stuff cap that hid the fact of just how thin her hair had become. After her husband had left suddenly, Mrs. Donnally realized she had nowhere else she wanted to be, and with the house paid for, had decided to stay put. She loved to cook, but felt her efforts were unappreciated by the three miners who boarded with her. With a lady of quality around, Mrs. Donnally looked forward to planning real meals again, and maybe the lady would even pitch in sometimes. But mainly she was eager to have another woman with whom she could visit, and maybe gain information about life beyond Aurora.

Two mornings later, loud pounding on the front door of the house of Harold's mother brought Roger awake. While pulling on a shirt over pants barely buttoned, he opened the door to find Mrs. Donnally before him, wringing her hands along with the hem of her apron.

"Oh, Mr. Murphy! You must come quickly. Your mother is in her room and she's taking on something awful."

Struggling into his coat, Roger hurried down the street with the excited landlady trailing behind him. "Is she ill?"

"I don't think so. She received a letter and hurried to her room to open it."

Roger didn't bother to knock, opening the door to his mother's room and promptly closing it. Mrs. Donnally almost bumped her nose on the wood of it, but reluctantly returned to the kitchen.

"Mother, what's wrong?"

Lucy looked up from the chair by the window, ran a handkerchief over her face and swallowed hard. "Freda's dead! And so is Randy."

"No!" Roger kneeled by Lucy's side and took her in his arms while choking back his own emotions. "How?"

"It was an accident. A run-away rig. It went into a ravine and landed on top of them both. I can't imagine her not being in my life, even from a distance. I just wrote her yesterday."

"I know, Mom, I know. Who wrote you the news?"

"Zelda Jones. Before I left Placerville, I told her she could write me here in care of general delivery."

"Yeah, I used to play with Joe Junior when I was a kid. His mother thought he was in line for sainthood. Boy, could I have told her stories that would have changed her mind about that!"

That brought the beginning of a smile to Lucy's face. "No doubt that's true. But she was a good friend to me and Freda. Oh, and I also got a letter in the same mail from Miss Hershel, Randy's sister. But it was written just before the accident. She's married to a wealthy business man. When we're settled somewhere I'm convinced is permanent, she said she'd freight to me those things that I put in storage with her before leaving Placerville." Lucy took a deep, shuttering breath. "I know at least that Freda was happy with her life. She was in good health even though in her sixties, and she'd had a good life. The last day we were together before I left, she told me she had made out a Will where she stipulated some things to come to me, like the photo of her sister. That was just to tease me, I think, because her sister hadn't been overly fond of me."

Roger left his mother then, knowing that she would spend some while recalling the times she and Freda had shared. He wouldn't admit it openly, but he too needed time to process this news. Freda had been his "other mother" as far back as he could remember; teacher, disciplinarian, and comforter. A long walk brought him into the privacy of the cemetery north of town, and there he sat on a bench for an hour.

Late in October of 1875, word reached Aurora that there was a huge fire rampaging through Virginia City. A number of men quickly organized themselves and headed to the fire, bringing with them not only tools, but also their understanding of how devastating fire was to a town built mostly of wood. Roger ran from saloon to saloon, passing the hat. When the men got underway, they had with them a generous sum for the relief effort. However, they returned only a week later, having arrived just in time to help clean up debris from the fire already out. They claimed they would have stayed longer, but they had work of their own awaiting their return. Besides, they had run into an early snowfall on their way to the fire, and they didn't know if a bigger storm was on the way.

As it turned out, they were right to worry. The winter of 1875/76 in Aurora was a tough one for everyone. Lucy, who was used to living with light snow only occasionally falling, had always been able to get into town. She now found that was often not possible for weeks at a time, so Roger had to fetch things for her personal use.

Mrs. Donnally seemed always able to get the miners she boarded to bring her food supplies and chop wood for the stove, since they benefited by doing both. Lucy read the few books in the house twice over. She also wrote letters that couldn't be mailed until the stages could get through the passes. She finally allowed Mrs. Donnally to teach her how to crochet, and she in turn taught her landlady how to play a number of card games. Spring came as a welcome event for everyone in the town.

With much of the snow melted and hints of green out among the brush, Lucy wrapped her shawl around her shoulders and stood on the front porch of the boarding house just as the sun went down. Her skirts swaying in the evening breeze, she watched a subdued sun sink behind a hill. Someone in a nearby house was pressing out a gentle refrain on a squeeze box, and a coyote called to its mate in the distance. Lucy inhaled the smells of suppers being prepared, mixed with the spicey scent of wet sagebrush after a rare shower that morning. There was little noise from the few saloons still operating, no sound of a fist fight in an alley, and because of the direction of the wind, no loud clanging from the mills on the hill. Then again, these were mills with barely enough ore to process, and sometimes they shut down at night.

The peacefulness of the moment was soothing, but she couldn't escape the dread of confronting Roger about a decision that had to be made. And she considered it a decision for both of them. But for now, tired from a long day, she went up to bed, knowing that Roger would go home to his bed only when the last of the men in the saloons left for theirs. How he could play so well, even when she knew he was tired, she would never figure out.

The saloons must have cleared out fairly early, because Roger was up and at her boarding house not long after dawn the next day. He was just in time for breakfast with Lucy, the house's tenants having left for their jobs. Mother and son sat silently but comfortably together at the well-scrubbed, wooden table in the middle of the kitchen. There was barely enough room to move around it while preparing meals, but it served as a handy work surface, especially when rolling out dough.

Roger chomped down on his butter and jam-slathered bread with a thoughtful concentration that was mirrored by Lucy. When she realized this, she asked him, "You didn't ask why I prepared this morning's meal instead of Mrs. Donnally."

Snapping out of his reverie, Roger blinked a few times. "I guess I should have noticed, huh? She's an admirable landlady, after all."

"Yes, she is. But she has a bad cold, so I told her to stay in bed and I'd take over for the day."

Mrs. Donnally, that most admirable of landladies, had in the beginning doubted that such a fine lady as Lucy could handle the rowdy miners to whom she rented. Or even that Lucy could cook. But one morning soon after Lucy's arrival, Mrs. Donnally had awakened to the smell of frying bacon and heard Lucy beating flapjack batter in the big crockery bowl. Therefore, on this morning, she had relaxed and gone back to sleep after hearing Lucy in the kitchen.

The food consumed and coffee cups refilled, Lucy looked across the table at Roger. "You know, I could do this."

"It's not exactly the first time you've cooked breakfast."

"No, you silly goose, I mean run a boarding house. At least a small one."

"Here in Aurora?" His surprise was obvious.

"Well, no." She looked down at her hands wrapped around the cup. "I had in mind somewhere else."

After a moment's hesitation, Roger surprised his mother. "Thank God! Because I don't want to stay here any longer."

After they locked eyes, neither of them held back their laughter. "Shh," Lucy whispered. "I don't want to wake Mrs. Donnally. But, oh, I'm so relieved to hear you say that."

She wasted no time with questions about why Roger wanted to move on, but simply began making plans. First off, she needed to obtain a suitcase for recent purchases. Maybe she could swap her saddlebags for one. No word about Diamond had reached Aurora, and she forced herself to face the fact that she would probably never know his fate. The one thing that she knew for sure was that she needed to be ready when the stage arrived in two days, taking them on to their next adventure.

CHAPTER 8

1876

Relieved that Roger too had been thinking about leaving Aurora, Lucy asked him, "Where shall we go?"

"I thought we might try Bodie."

Lucy wasn't sure Bodie was much of an improvement in their circumstances. "Really?"

"I have a friend there and he says things are right on the edge of picking up. Billy O'Hara used to run the dining room of the Exchange Hotel here back in '63. He swears the Bodie hills are full of gold. He's been saying that for years, and now there's some evidence that he's right. He was hired in '65 by the Empire Gold and Silver Mining Company to run their boarding house. Others have come and gone from Bodie, but not him. He loaned money to some men who wanted to start digging, and when they up and left while owing him, he took over their property."

And so, as Roger suggested, he and Lucy "tried Bodie". Only they quickly discovered that it was more like Bodie was trying them, and finding them wanting. At least Lucy knew that to be true of herself. Roger displayed his prowess in the few saloons, two gambling halls and the new dance house with a back room, all located at the north end of what would someday be a mile-long street.

Now, it was just a collection of buildings on either side of a strip of muddy dirt wide enough for freight wagons to pass each other. Some of the buildings had received a little white wash, but most were still raw wood, as though people were waiting to see if further expense was worthwhile.

Not being a high-toned town, Roger dressed less obviously than he had in Aurora. His white shirts were always clean, but he wore no shiny vests, and sometimes he just rolled up his sleeves and wore no jacket.

Those who lived and worked in Bodie were good for small-stake games that were mostly for entertainment, which suited Roger, as he quickly considered them friends. Most of the serious gamblers with whom Roger played were passing through on their way to Aurora, or passing through Bodie on their way from Aurora to anyplace better. The latter group seldom had as much money as the former, but were eager to improve their circumstances by winning a big hand at cards. Roger enjoyed giving them a life lesson about that.

Since it quickly spread through town that Roger Murphy was an honest or "square" dealer, the locals usually left the table with *almost* the same amount in their pockets as when they had arrived. He sometimes let the down-and-outs win, but he still did well for himself. The bartenders ignored his youth and what they thought of as his unnecessary generosity. They just smiled to themselves, happy to have this amiable young man practice his profession in their establishment. Which is a polite way of saying they welcomed the increase in drinks and bar food they were selling.

Lucy, on the other hand, spent a great deal of time in the boarding house. Each day she read a few pages of some book or newspaper brought in from Aurora or towns north, wrote letters to friends in Placerville and Jamestown, and then consumed a light luncheon at the single nearby café that was part of the merchandise store. She then went for a long walk, often stopping to visit with Elizabeth Kernohan, who was living alone with Helen Anne. She was no longer the child Dolly had written about, but a lovely young lady, and a great help to her mother. Someone said her father had gone to Washington state on business, and had just not returned. Lucy also sometimes visited with Elizabeth's sister Marietta Horner, married to Roger Horner and the mother of Daniel, the first child born in Bodie.

After two weeks of the same daily routine, however, Lucy had reached the point of wondering how she could stand much more of Bodie. Desperate for anything different, she left the boarding house and went for a walk that took her closer to the bluff than she usually ventured. On the edge of town, she stopped at the foot of a dirt path that led to a miner's small, two-room cabin, watching with curiosity as a man came toward her carrying two old suitcases. She vaguely remembered having met him, but couldn't recall where or when.

Looking at his cases with hope in her heart, she asked, "Are you leaving town?"

"You're goddamn right I am! I'm on to Virginia City."

"Who owns the cabin?"

"I built it, so I guess I do. But the mice can have it and everything in it. I hope they freeze to death this winter. I almost did in the one just past."

And with that he walked with purpose toward town to await the stage's arrival. He did, however, suddenly remember having met this woman and looked back just in time to see the lady walk into the cabin. What he didn't see was Lucy picking up the broom left behind, her eyes alight with excitement while vigorously sweeping the bare wooden floor. Not long after that, when a young man walked by on his way into town, she gave him two bits to go to the boarding house and leave a note that she wrote out for Roger.

When two hours later Roger showed up at the door of the cabin, Lucy had prepared a list of things they would need in order to settle comfortably into their new home. Roger looked around with obvious skepticism. "Are you sure you want to live here? There's not even a rug on the floor."

"It's on the list." Ignoring his frown as he read the long list, she continued talking, more to herself than to him. "There's a surprising amount of bedding for the two beds, one here in the main room in the corner that can double as a sofa, and one in the back room that acts as a storage room. The kitchen area over there is remarkably well stocked with pots and skillets, and even a good supply of flour, sugar, and such like. There's a pile of wood out back that needs to be cut smaller for the stove." Knowing her son well, she turned to him with a frown. "If you don't want to do that for me, then find someone in town who will, and send them 'round. I'll pay them to do it. Oh, and if you happen to see a cat that might like a good home, bring it, too."

"Okay, I accept the move, but it's a long list." He was wondering how he was going to carry it all.

Lucy just barely resisted rolling her eyes. "For heaven's sake, Roger, the merchandise man no doubt has a wagon and will deliver. Considering how much money we'll be spending with him, he probably won't even charge us for that. Now get along, and while he's delivering our order, you can stop at the bakery and fill this other list." She looked at him with mock severity. "I think you can manage to carry home what's on that list."

Roger said nothing as he left to do his mother's bidding, just beginning to feel some of her enthusiasm for putting down roots. But there were reservations underlying; thoughts that he wasn't yet willing to voice to Lucy. She was having too much fun, and it could wait.

With the cabin scrubbed, supplied and arranged, and now referred to as "the house" more out of tradition than acknowledgement of reality, Lucy went out each day to purchase fresh food when it was available. She quickly learned the sound of the freight wagons bringing supplies and would grab her hemp shopping bag. At the merchandise store, she would pick through whatever was delivered while it was still fresh. Of course, the few other women in town did this as well, but they all returned home with at least some fresh fruits and vegetables. Well, as fresh as anything could be that had been stuffed into sacks on a wagon traveling through sand and dust, sometimes for days. When at the butcher shop, Lucy made sure the tabby cat given her by Elizabeth was not forgotten.

Lucy and Elizabeth made a deal with a rancher from the Mono Lake region, so that whenever he came to Bodie with fish caught in the streams flowing into the lake, he would come to them first. Sometimes he even had gull eggs, ducks or quail. Lucy's ice box was small, and winter ice stored in sheds was sometimes difficult to obtain, but into it she would stuff whatever couldn't be used within a day.

Summer in Bodie was a time of preparation for the harsh winter that always followed. At over 8,000 feet in elevation, Bodie was usually buried under feet of snow for several months each year. Second story windows became the main entrance to two-story structures, one-story houses had slides dug down to their doors, and covered walkways turned into tunnels with the street side a wall of hardpacked snow. With this in mind, along with mounting anxiety, Lucy purchased as many fresh vegetables and fruits as she could and began drying or canning them. Roger's room began looking more like a storage room every day.

His only complaint was Lucy bringing in the cat each night. It had decided that the stillness of the dark house was the perfect time to hunt out any mouse so foolish as to still be in residence.

Roger repeated his major complaint one morning. "The bumps and thumps of his activity at night gives me the willies."

Lucy decided not to ignore him this time. "I notice you don't mind stepping over his little gifts lying in front of the door on your way out in the morning."

"Hey, he's your cat. And they're his gifts to you, not me."

Lucy's only thought, as she disposed of the morning's rodents, was that evidently chivalry only extended to single women and not to mothers. It also occurred to her that their bickering no longer had any degree of humor in it, as it once had done. With no ready reason for this coming to mind, her anxiety increased.

After a couple of weeks of cabin living, Lucy headed out for her afternoon walk. She passed among the two-dozen wooden and adobe buildings forming Main Street, some with a boardwalk out front and some not. As usual, she enjoyed the exchange of greetings with those she'd come to know, but she was preoccupied with thoughts she wasn't eager to share with Roger. She barely noticed the men in suits, men wearing denim jackets, and those fresh from the mines still wearing overalls and carrying lunch buckets. She did notice that there were only a few women out and about.

She was stopped by Elizabeth, recently married to Almond Huntoon who had businesses in Bridgeport and Bodie. She informed Lucy that a Mr. George Storey had arrived in town, having heard that a "rich find" had been discovered. He had approached Messrs. Essington and Lockbey, owners of the Bunker Hill claim, asking them to sell out to what he called "San Francisco capitalists" whom he represented. The rumor was that he would receive a $10,000 commission for this sale, with Essington and Lockbey each receiving $65,000.

It wouldn't be until September that Col. John F. Boyd would arrive to check on the status of the purchase on behalf of those San Francisco capitalists. They included brothers Seth and Dan Cook, along with William M. Lent and Col. Charles W. Tozer, among others. Mr. Lent and his partners had allowed this sight-unseen purchase, even while the memory remained of a diamond hoax four years earlier that had taken in some of San Francisco's most practiced speculators. Mr. Lent, president of the fiasco, and his fellow investor, John Boyd, especially remembered. They had bought in on the diamond deal before finding out that they had purchased 40 acres of desert liberally "salted" with worthless, South African rejected diamonds.

But the Bunker Hill claim turned out to have a rich ore body. Having incorporated as the Standard Mining Company, the fellow investors had immediately begun operations, which gave new life and hope to those who still believed in Bodie's future. With activity at the mines increasing along with everyone's expectations, building within the town also increased. It included more businesses along Main Street, as well as homes on short streets behind Main.

Up on the hill, shafts were being sunk, timbered and installed with steam hoisting machinery. A 20-stamp mill was under construction, due to begin actual work in July of the following year. In fact, a year after purchasing the mine, the Standard Co. would pay out its first dividend of $50,000, and would pay this out every month until March of 1880 when it would raise it to $75,000 per month for a short while.

Now, however, there was a different kind of excitement taking place. Two brothers, Ed and Warren Loose, who had worked the railroad's progress across the country, arrived in Bodie. Ed bore the common family frame, being six feet tall, strong of body, and projecting the determined attitude typical of those just arrived in a new mining area.

Ed soon located a claim on the southwestern line of the Bunker Hill claim, calling his mine The Bodie. Soon after this, following considerable exploration of the Bunker Hill by its new owners, the Standard Company decided that their mine's vein of rich gold-bearing quartz extended into Ed Loose's claim. They tried to convince Ed to give up his ground, but he didn't easily convince and soon there were veiled threats being made.

Ed took on his brother Warren as a partner, while at the same time sending to Utah a request that their other brother, Will Loose, join them. Will was known as a hard-drinking, athletic young man who could outride and outshoot most men. Hearing of this, the town prepared themselves for some good sport, since they had heard that William Lent was sending a crew of "bad men" to the town, headed by a man named Burkhardt. But the confrontation wouldn't take place until the following year.

Fast forward to May of '77 and Will's arrival. Ed and Warren would wisely keep their brother up at their mine, away from the temptations of booze and inciting taunts. They planned to continue keeping him 500 feet above the town and out of the way of those who wanted to see him take on the opposition. When the gun-toting Burkhardt would show up in town, he would be surprised to find himself unpopular with the townsmen, who he had thought might back him up. He would return to Mr. Lent to beg for more reinforcements, but Mr. Lent, not wanting to start an all-out war, would fire him on the spot.

It would take considerable threats and counter threats, the building of a fort-like structure over The Bodie, and an accident that would almost kill Warren, but eventually the Standard would agree to buy out the Loose brothers. In the end, the brothers would be satisfied and the Standard would proceed to develop their mine just as the town began to show real progress.

But even with just the Standard Company's Bunker Hill claim starting work in '76, Roger and Lucy could tell that the feeling in town was that prosperity was on the horizon. It was the kind of success that people of that era claimed as the ideal of the American spirit. After all, only *one-hundred years* had passed since San Francisco had commenced its rise to prominence with the founding of the Presidio. *Twenty-six years* had passed since California had been wrested from Mexico and had become a state. *Twelve years* had passed since Nevada had also become a state. The Civil War was *eleven years* in the past, even if not entirely laid to rest. *Seven years* earlier the country had witnessed the hammering in of the golden spike that had connected the east and west coasts with rail travel. And in *this year of 1876*, Colorado had been admitted as the 38th state. With all this progress celebrated during the country's centennial celebration in July of 1876, why wouldn't everyone be expecting Bodie to join the ranks of that progress?

And yet, even while believing in the confidence of those around her, Lucy was not happy. This was a man's town. Oh, yes, there were a few families here, but female society was scarce. She was accorded respect because she was a widow with a grown son. A single woman never having married, called a *spinster*, would have been considered "shopping for a man". A divorced woman would have been looked at with suspicion, everyone wondering what might be wrong with her. Lucy didn't care about any of that. She only wanted a few women with whom she could occasionally share moments of cordial conversation over a cup of tea.

But the only women she knew had families. They spent a good portion of each day just shopping and cooking food, and getting it on the table at a time convenient for their husband's work schedule. Two days a week they focused on the washing, ironing, and mending of laundry. The rest of their time was spent cleaning their home, with maybe some little time educating their young. They had little time left over for socializing.

Lucy, on the other hand, had daily chores that took up only a little time each morning. Of course, even with just her and Roger's laundry, it still took a day to wash and dry the clothes, and another to iron them. But then there were five other days. She had lost interest in canning, which was messy, hot work. After sweeping the floor each morning, she flicked a feather duster over the dust that never seemed to leave the small amount of furniture in the cabin. And she had read every book on the shelf while eating alone most meals. This was not her idea of how she wanted to spend her days.

For Roger, there were pickled eggs in jars on the bars at most saloons, and even chops and steaks at the chop stands in a few of them. Breakfast wasn't much of a problem, as mother and son were both happy with coffee and bread that Lucy cut thick and spread liberally with jam. She did try to have a decent mid-day meal for them, but seldom anything fancy. She occasionally volunteered to collect donations to assist injured miners, but there were no other pressing social causes to champion and take up time.

Having dragged a kitchen chair out into the shade of the front porch's small overhang, Lucy looked up from her book when the cat rubbed against her leg. As she lifted the purring bundle of fur onto her lap, she observed the construction of several new buildings going up on main street. With each fall of a hammer, faith in the town's growth was proclaimed. Unlike Aurora, Bodie would always be a mainly wooden town, with few buildings of brick known as "fire proofs".

Lucy wondered why it was that Roger seemed to be getting restless. He didn't work for any one gambling house, so he had no percentage to hand over. But the gambling public among the Bodie population had begun to realize that this young man was more talented than even the best of their egos could brag about. It was difficult to fill a table with players, and Roger didn't have the funds to finance a faro bank. He was good at billiards and could have done fairly well with that, but no one yet had a table.

That night, after hearing his mother vent a deep sigh while looking out the kitchen window as they ate, Roger studied her thoughtfully. For the first time, it occurred to him to wonder what his mother did during the afternoons and evenings while he was gone. He always had clean shirts and underwear, the cabin was always neat and clean, and she gave him meals that were hearty and tasty. She had seemed to enjoy canning food, but she wasn't doing that any more. It slowly occurred to him that there must be long periods when she had to entertain herself, and although she always seemed to be reading a book or writing letters, what else did she do? At this point, he began to think that maybe his listing of her activities was actually his own need to justify having taken her for granted for so long.

"Um, Mom, are you happy here?"

She looked at him with a raised brow. "Why are you asking me that?"

"It just occurred to me that there really isn't much here for you. In Placerville, you were always busy helping others, or attending the theater, or visiting friends, or doing projects around our big house. You can't do any of that here, and you don't have any close friends, either. You and Elizabeth Huntoon have spent some time together, but not very often lately."

"No, but I'm very fond of her."

There was a long moment of silence between them before he asked, "Do you think we could move on from here? Maybe head to Carson City, or even Virginia City?"

"I'd love that!" Considering how quickly and enthusiastically she had accepted his suggestion, Roger couldn't help but laugh. Lucy colored slightly and shrugged. "But only if that's what you really want to do."

Mother and son were soon packed, and had taken leave from their friends, with Elizabeth taking charge of the cat. They were ready to depart from Bodie two days later when the stage came through from Aurora, heading to Bridgeport. From there, another would take them to Genoa in Nevada by way of the California towns of Silver Mountain, Bulliona, Monitor, Markleeville, Woodford's, Fredericksburg, and Sheridan.

Lucy and Roger didn't know it, but they were leaving just before the boom. In 1877, a dozen mining companies would be formed. Mines with names such as the Standard, the Bodie North, the Bulwer, and the Noonday, would become legendary, with $1 million worth of bullion shipped out, and double that in '78, reaching $3 million in both '80 and '81. In '82 and '83 the mines would once again see only $1 million, and after that, declining fortunes would begin. But for seven years, the town would grow and flourish, even with a reputation for violence that would fuel stories that would live on as legends.

When the stage pulled up in Sheridan, not far south of Genoa, Lucy declared to Roger, "I'm hot, tired, hungry and stiff. And I would very much like to visit an outhouse. Why don't we spend the night here? When I passed through here before, I noticed that it has a decent inn."

Roger looked around him and spotted a saloon, noting that it seemed to be the only one. "Sure. Why not?"

After getting his mother settled into the small traveler's hotel, Roger took his time walking down the short street to the saloon. The town had been started as a way-station by Moses Job to assist emigrants arriving from the East, and was situated beneath a hill that was locally known as Job's Peak. It was an agricultural town of several hundred people living on nearby farms, and not much different from other towns that had started up along what was known as the Emigrant Trail. Van Sickle's Station was not far away, along with Wingfield's. Over in Jack's Valley, Ben Holliday, the creator of the Overland Stage to California during the 1849 gold rush, had also set up a station. Typical for roads that had to be maintained locally, those that connected through the area were all toll roads, with toll bridges over the Carson River and its creeks.

Sheridan was surrounded by fields of grain and acres of truck gardens, the produce eagerly purchased by western-bound emigrants with few supplies left after following the Humboldt River and then crossing the 40 Mile Desert. Even with the advent of cross-country train travel, wagon trains would continue to travel this route into the 1880's.

Fresh vegetables available in and around Genoa were therefore worth almost any price, such as turnips at $1 a bunch. Even more encouraging, if not surprising to the emigrants, was the fact that they were treated fairly in these towns along the foot of the Sierra. Still, because of their rarity, boots in the shops sold for $35, hats for $5, and tobacco $1.50 for a pound sack. For those anticipating the arduous crossing of the Sierra, they dug into their waning coffers and paid up.

In 1854 alone, during the California gold rush, 213 wagons and 7,528 head of cattle, 7,150 sheep, and several thousand people with only carts or backpacks, had been marked down as passing through the area. It was only a fraction of the total number that had passed through by the time Lucy and Roger arrived there. Unfortunately, by the mid-1850's the ravines and creeks over on the west side of the Sierra had been pretty thoroughly prospected out. The incoming travelers discovered that "easy gold" rumored to be lying in the streams was a thing of the past; if ever really true. The concept had always been scoffed at by those who had done the difficult and dangerous work of finding it. Those early disappointed souls who had refused to turn around and return home upon being faced with this reality, had found other ways to make their living. Some even made their fortune and their mark on history.

With Sheridan's flags and streamers packed away after the centennial celebration, Roger looked around at a calm little town. Standing outside the Barnett & Turke general store, he could hear music and laughter coming from the dancehall above. The village also had a blacksmith, a small but busy saloon, and a rarity in any town, a watchmaker. Just three miles south of Genoa, Sheridan was an example of a changing era. It's location had transitioned from being in Millard County in *Utah Territory*, to being in Carson County in *Nevada Territory*, and it now resided in Douglas County in the *State* of Nevada. It would continue as a trading and supply center for the valley until its devastation in a 1910 fire.

Having spent a restful night, Lucy was refreshed and eager to get started again, only to discover that the stage would be arriving later in the morning. Roger, having obtained this knowledge the night before while raking in his pile of chips, slept soundly until well past sun-up.

After enjoying a satisfying breakfast at the hotel, it was Lucy's turn to walk the town. She found it a short walk. Heading north, she passed men emerging from a meeting of some kind from the hall above the general merchandise store. The men smiled at her with a tip of their hats as they watched her trim figure saunter past and continue to the watchmaker's shop.

The owner turned out to be a dour but accommodating man who cleaned the brooch style timepiece that she wore pinned to her dress. He showed her several lovely pieces of jewelry, but she chose a simple ring of silver pounded thin.

After that, the blacksmith pretended not to notice the lady watching him shoe one of Ben Palmer's prize horses, but he did flex the muscles of his bare arms a little more than needed. When the end of the boardwalk was reached, Lucy wandered on, enjoying the view of the scrub-covered hills from which the Sierra rose up into its majesty. She was serenaded by the chortle of birds among the cottonwoods just beginning to show a few yellow leaves, as well as the deep-throated, rhythmic croaking of a bullfrog sitting on the edge of an irrigation pond.

"If I was an eagle," she thought, "I could soar up and fly over the crest of the mountain to return home." But then she corrected herself, not for the first time. Placerville was no longer *home*. In fact, she had no home now. How long that would last, she had no idea, and found it an uncomfortable thought.

Lucy was feeling something akin to what many a weary traveler in that spot had felt over the last two dozen years. Whether by wagon, stagecoach, horseback, or more recently by train, thousands of people had uprooted their lives and headed west in search of a dream fulfilled. They had stood right where Lucy was standing on the Emigrant Trail, their old lives behind them, and the rugged peaks of the intimidating Sierra before them. The only thing they had possessed in abundance had been their faith in their ability to survive and create for themselves the life for which they yearned. This was true even for those running away from something or someone, and there were always plenty of those. Lucy thought of Dolly, Robert and Jane, and knew that to be only too true.

Lucy wondered how many of the emigrants who had passed this way had really felt brave and fearless, as had so often been portrayed in books, not to mention by men leaning on saloon bars in full bragging mode. Instead, had they quivered inside with anxiety? Lucy was rested, but she knew that for many early travelers, the exhaustion of the moment had overcome the optimism that had carried them across the country. Those were the families that had decided to settle on the eastern side of the mountain. It had remained for the most determined of the pioneers to make the arduous trek over the mountain. In the process, they had discovered passes and carved out roads that had benefitted the thousands who followed.

Lucy pulled herself out of such reverie and returned to the hotel, finding Roger in the dining room where she joined him for coffee. When they heard the stage pull up out front, Roger took a last bite of a much-reduced pile of flapjacks, downed the rest of his coffee, and tossed coins onto the table. "I've carried our bags down already, so we can get on the stage straight away. That way, you can get next to a window and have control of the shade."

Roger rolled up the leather flap over the window and tied it loosely with the strips hanging on either side, so it would be easy for her to adjust. Doing these little things for his mother helped abate the lingering guilt he harbored for having left home so abruptly that it had prompted her to leave behind her beloved home. It would take a few years, but he would eventually realize that it was one of the best decisions he had ever made.

Just as they were comfortably seated in the coach, three men in dusty suits joined them. There was little conversation as they continued the next leg of their journey to Genoa. The stagecoach of the Haines & Company Stage Line soon approached the outskirts of Genoa, passing large trees surrounding a pond in which several locally popular swans glided side-by-side. Two of them dunked their heads beneath the water, pulling them out with a joyous honk as the water dripped off their faces. Everyone on the stage smiled at a moment so unexpected that more than one would record it in letters and journals.

Lucy caught sight of some wary sage grouse, two feet long and fat, hurrying to hide beneath the sagebrush. One of the more curious of the grouse lagged behind, exposing his black throat patch and belly as he stretched up for a look at the noisy intrusion into his territory. Three ravens sat on a telegraph pole's cross-beam, silent and glaring, while several deer ran from the road edge where they had been grazing. Lucy felt as though the stage was being welcomed, blushing at such a silly thought until she glanced at Roger across from her. He was fighting a smile, but whether from similar thoughts or at her because he knew her so well, she couldn't tell.

The minute Lucy stepped out of the stage in Genoa, she was entranced. It shouldn't have been that way, given that it was just a simple, small town of wood, brick and stone, but she wasn't the first to feel the pull of its charm. It would never lose its welcoming nature, felt by travelers passing through, whether in 1876 or 150 years later. Many people, when tired of a big city's insistent haste and the impersonal detachment attending it, would remember their time in Genoa, and sigh with wishful longing.

Lucy filled her lungs with the cool air scented with pine, fir, and Pinon Juniper. She looked up at the birch and willow trees along the edge of a stream leading down the Sierra, soon to be ablaze in the yellow and orange of autumn. Lucy felt as though she was just a little too early to catch the curtain going up on one of Nature's most brilliant performances. Turning to the east, the view was far different, being that of Carson Valley agriculture cut through by the blue ribbon of the Carson River. Beyond that was the sagebrush steppe that gave way to Nevada's deserts. In that moment, Lucy was determined that they would not hurry to leave Genoa, instead taking time to rest and think carefully about their next move.

Roger was happy to stay longer. There were several saloons and plenty of people who didn't know his skill. When those in the town would

eventually catch on, he knew there would be those men traveling through
to and from Carson City, Virginia City, and even the mill towns along the
Carson River.

Standing by the stage, Lucy realized that this Genoa was not the one
that Dolly had visited over a decade earlier. Many of the buildings Dolly
had seen were still there, but now with additions, and with a greater
number of them lining the few streets that made up the town. Main Street
cut through the middle, south to north, before heading out toward Carson
City. And Main Street was cut across by Carson, Mill, Nixon and Fifth
Streets. That was pretty much it, except for "The Square" with its tall flag
pole right where Nixon crossed Main; although because of the curve in
Main Street, it was actually more of a triangle.

Genoa would never be considered a large town. This was good for those
living there, a population of hardy pioneers turned farmer, shopkeeper, or
cattle rancher, and who didn't have to burden themselves with the expense
of owning a riding horse. However, the farmers and ranchers who lived
outside of town inevitably owned a wagon, and if the horse wasn't being
used for work on the land, it could be hitched up for a trip into town.

Lucy felt a sense of odd enchantment as she stood on the boardwalk
and looked around her. Most of the houses were of wood, with only a few
of brick, or at least partially so. As from the beginning, central to the town
was the stockade that some called "the fort". This was more of a traditional
classification than a necessary need, as so-called Indian troubles were well
past, and white marauders knew that there was nothing in Genoa worth
their effort. Besides that, the citizens were reputed to be fierce defenders
of their town. A jailed thief once described his capture like that of a bag of
cats let loose on an invading rat.

The most contentious subject in the area was water rights. Water came
from springs and melted snowpack that lingered well past winter. Some
homes, originally built by the Mormons who first settled the town, had
piped water. Those more recent settlers had only rights to irrigation water,
and therefore had to dig wells for domestic use. Most of the larger ranches
had above ground tanks or clay-lined reservoirs to collect rain water.

Whatever it took, considering one's circumstances and property needs,
they found a way to provide themselves with the precious liquid. Roger
had been informed by the man next to him on the stage that the tradition
in the area had become, "Steal a man's cattle or his wife, and there may

be harsh words exchanged. Steal a man's water, and arms will soon be in evidence." The man had uttered a dry laugh and had returned his gaze out the window.

While Lucy made a few purchases at the dry goods store, Roger chatted with the stage driver. He discovered that there were five saloons in town, down from ten in the early 1860's. As they talked, three men from the Washo Indian tribe walked down the dusty street, avoiding the sidewalk. They wore denim pants, a dark cotton shirt, and a cow hide vest that went partly around their torsos, the gap across the front closed by four rows of string ties. More interesting to Roger were the symbols painted on the men's faces with blue and red dyes consisting of vertical lines on the chin, and other markings on the forehead.

"What do the marks on their faces mean?" Roger asked the driver.

"No one knows but them, and they're not tellin'. Maybe some kind of protection against one of their demons." The driver shrugged. "I just don't know."

"Do you know those men?"

"Yeah. The one in front is Henry Jack, and the one in back is Smokey. Don't know the other one."

"Do they live around here?"

"Some do, but most Washo live up in the Pine Nut Range and come here for supplies a couple times a year. They've petitioned the Indian Agent for some land of their own, like the Piutes and Shoshones have, but nothing has been done yet."

In fact, it wouldn't be until the 1940's that they would be given some decent land near Dresslerville, and at the upper end of the Carson Valley.

Lucy and Roger settled into the Raycraft Hotel on the corner of Main and Mill Streets, south of the public square. They considered the Central Hotel and the Nevada House, being across from the stockade. These establishments were right in the heart of town, near the shops and saloons, so Roger preferred them. But Lucy wanted to avoid the noise of such a busy area.

Besides, at the Raycraft, there was a veranda off their room on the second floor front where she could sit and observe nearby businesses and the travelers on the road through town. She could also see across the street to the busy Johnson Store, the blacksmith, the hay yard and the

Douglas Market. She liked Ellen and Joe Raycraft, finding Ellen a friendly informant about the area, and who also made a wonderful pot of tea.

Roger was amenable to staying there, since it wasn't that far a distance to the saloons, and he enjoyed meeting the men of the town as he walked the street. It was an opportunity to let them know a new game was awaiting them at the saloons. He especially liked Hansen's Saloon, which had a comfortable, almost homey feel. Someone had papered the walls with floral wallpaper and nailed an array of photos and paintings on the wall above the mahogany bar. He also felt immediately comfortable with the barkeep, the diminutive Mr. Hansen with his old felt hat pushed back, and who was always ready to pour out a drink with a big smile. The saloon was only large enough for three small tables across from the bar, and entering for the first time Roger found these occupied, so he took up a place at the bar.

Overhearing several conversations gave him insight into the town. He felt himself relax as he stood among these friendly men who came in to appease their thirst while taking a break from their work at ranches, homesteads, businesses, or the new courthouse at the north end of town. The locals still talked about how Mrs. Gilman, the owner of the boarding house two doors down, and known as a "volatile old body", had cut down a tree in front of the saloon when she had been angry with Mr. Hansen. At the same time, Roger observed firsthand that Mr. Hansen was not a man who hesitated to voice his opinions.

Talk turned to the grand ball that Genoa's Odd Fellows Lodge 15 had organized the previous November. Mr. Livingston, on the Committee of Arrangements and a resident since 1860, stood at the end of the bar and talked of how he was looking forward to another event just as grand. Room was made for Mr. Harris of the Harris Store, along with Recorder/Auditor Fred Furth, when they came in and joined Mr. Livingston.

Roger asked about the small Chinatown on the south end of town that they had passed. He was told they had been brought there by John Reese back in 1858 so they could dig a water trench down from the mountain to the Reese Grist Mill on the western edge of town.

One of the men present nodded his head and made the comment, "Them Coolies is damn good workers."

Another commented, "The Injuns ignore them as much as the whites do. They think they're an inferior type of Injun." No one offered a comment in reply, knowing that this information was offered for the newcomer's benefit. "It's rumored that when the Chinese first arrived, an Injun pushed one of 'em into the river. He couldn't swim, and drowned. The Injun who pushed 'em in told his tribe that the man wasn't an Injun or he would've known how to swim." This was met with a combination of low laughs, disgusted shakes of the head, and even one undecipherable angry grunt.

Roger was predictably curious. "What happened to the Indian?"

"Nothing that I know about," responded the teller of the tale. "But it sure taught the Coolies to stay away from any Injun."

Roger tactfully said nothing, but felt like saying a lot. Consequently, he learned that most of the Chinese who had lived there had moved on to work at the mills along the river north of Carson City, with only a few remaining in Genoa. He also got the impression that some of those around him had made friends in the Chinese community, while others were barely tolerant of their lingering presence. Having lived his whole life in both California and Nevada towns, he was only too aware of the poor treatment of not only the Chinese, but also other "foreigners". Over time, the Chinese had garnered at least a little respect for their ability to thrive in areas in which those who thought themselves superior declined to settle.

One of the men present stepped away from the bar. "I'm heading out to Wally's hot springs for a soak. Anyone want to go with me?"

Two men agreed it might be something they had a mind to do. When Roger inquired about this, the first man explained. "It was built back in the '60's. There's a small village there now, just off the road. There's a barn and stable 'cause it's aways to get there. The two-story hotel, with its bath house fed by the hot springs, is nice. And there's a good saloon there, too. I go whenever my rheumatism acts up. The doc says the minerals in the hot water is just what I need, and it sure does seem to help for some while. Ole Hank Monk goes there when he gets banged around too much by that stagecoach of his."

Roger startled the men by saying, "I think my mother stayed there after riding across the mountain from Placerville." He explained why she had made the trip and the men had a good laugh at Roger's expense. He grinned and laughed with them, and one of the men bought him a beer. Their comments about Lucy, however, were only those of respect, and maybe a little awe.

Roger was told that Walley's had forty rooms, good food with all kinds of "delicacies of the season" available, a grand ballroom, and the only swimming pool in the valley. David Walley and his wife Harriet had even added eleven bathrooms. That got *a lot* of comment.

"Too bad about David Walley dying last year. The place got sold recently, and the new owners are making what they advertise as improvements. Huh! It was always plenty good enough for us."

When the men's talk turned to local financial matters, Roger moved away from them. A table had become available when four men left to get back to work. Three travelers through town walked into the saloon and saw Roger, dressed in his best suit and vest, and they thought he might be a gambler. When they saw the way he shuffled the cards between sips of his beer, they were sure of it. Roger looked up and smiled at them. Realizing that he was a friendly young man, they assumed that he was inexperienced, and maybe over-confident in his ability. The men returned his smile, and while one of them went to the bar for their drinks, the others pulled up a chair. Two hours later the three men left, determined not to ever again make hasty assumptions about young people.

Three days later Roger suggested to Lucy that before they headed to Carson City, maybe they could visit Dayton.

"Why on earth now?" She immediately was sorry for her tone when it occurred to her why this might be important to her son. But she let him express it, which he did after a moment's thought as to how to put his feelings into words.

"I thought we might visit the cemetery there." He saw the look on his mother's face, and knew that he didn't need to say for whom he wanted to search. Jim Murphy had been working close to Dayton when he had disappeared, and was presumed dead.

Lucy nodded her head slowly. "Okay, let's pack up and get under way."

Since the two others on the stage were also heading to Dayton, the driver by-passed Carson City and took them along the Carson River, past the mills there, and straight on to Dayton. Back of that pioneer town, on the rise of a hill where visitors could look down on Dayton's few but nevertheless busy streets, they found the cemetery. Behind it, the emigrant road passed by, carved out over the last few decades by thousands of wagon wheels and livestock.

Roger ignored the more recent granite and marble memorials and walked quickly to the older headboards and crosses. Some had names and dates painted or carved on them, and some did not. There were even a few large rocks painted with names and dates. Whatever the construction, Roger was only interested in whatever might be a decade old.

Lucy watched him move from grave to grave, sadness clutching at her throat, not for herself but for the disappointment she knew that would follow for Roger. She had written to the town's sheriff years before, and he had written back his assurance that there was no one buried there by the name of Jim Murphy. But she kept tactfully quiet while Roger searched, because she knew her son needed to do this for himself. Just as she said nothing when he tried to assuage his guilt by doing little thoughtful things for her.

It didn't take him long to check every marked grave in the small cemetery, but he lingered on the far side of it so Lucy wouldn't see the stinging glisten of his eyes. She said nothing, pretending that she was unaware, but relieved that Roger didn't pose the idea that maybe his father was in an unmarked grave. Joining Lucy where she stood looking down at Old Virginy's grave, Roger tucked his mother's arm through his and led her from the cemetery.

Instead of going to Carson City, they opted for Gold Hill up-canyon from Dayton. It would be a short ride from Gold Hill to Virginia City by stage, but even quicker on the Virginia and Truckee Railroad that left from the depot at the north end of Gold Hill. For someone coming all the way from Carson City to Virginia City, the 21-mile route passed through six tunnels within several thousand degrees of turns. Its early name being that of the Virginia, Carson and Truckee River Railroad, local humorists declared it the Very Crooked and Terribly Rough Railroad. A few locals, therefore, expressed disappointment when the name was changed to the Virginia and Truckee Railroad, shortened even more to simply the V&T.

Lucy wanted to rest, and Roger wanted to test the local gambling talent, so they settled into the Vesey House, still known by some as the Old Stone Hotel. It now had a wooden extension to the south and a comfortable lobby that looked more like an inviting parlor. Filled with gratitude that two rooms had just been made available in such a crowded town, Lucy enjoyed the comfort the hotel offered. Roger enjoyed the small — really small — bar that faced the street. There was no gambling, there being no room for it, but he found the company pleasant and the beer good.

The town was not as populated as when Dolly had written about it, but there were still hundreds of people filling the sidewalks and roads. Mining activity was still active up on the hill to the west, with the downhill sweep of the town now filled with mills, warehouses, small homes, large boarding houses, and several saloons. The Methodists and the Catholics both had a church, and a small school offered education to the few children who showed up for it. The town even had an office of the Bank of California, the first commercial bank in the Western United States. As evidence of the richness of the mines, it was considered the second richest bank in the nation.

While Roger made his rounds of the saloons and gambling halls, Lucy read a copy of the Gold Hill News. She shared the lobby with a lady who introduced herself as Mrs. McCormack. She lived in a tiny house nearby, but preferred sitting in the lobby where she could visit with anyone who chose to happen by. James Lowery, the proprietor, was happy to allow this, as Mrs. McCormack gave the place a softening and welcoming atmosphere. Besides, she was a long-time resident of the area, and here, that counted for something.

Two sofas faced each other over a low table scattered with newspapers, magazines and public notices, with arm chairs on either end creating an enclosed conversation area. On this morning, Lucy's reading of the newspaper was accompanied by the clicking of Mrs. McCormack's knitting needles moving at a speed that made Lucy blink. She thought the woman would be the perfect model for an advertisement in a newspaper for a millinery shop that sold cozy, knitted items. The woman stopped to adjust her shawl and looked up to meet Lucy's gaze. Lucy had the impression that this was a woman who had experienced harsh realities in her life, adding wrinkles to a face barely past forty, and her hair pre-maturely gray.

James Lowery entered from the side door and walked through the room. "'Morning, ladies."

They responded in unison. "Good morning, Mr. Lowery."

Mrs. McCormack lowered her voice and leaned toward Lucy. "The day after Christmas back in '73, a man checking out decided to spend a bullet on Mr. Lowery instead of money on his bill. James ducked just in time and Tom Miller was arrested. Always had a bad temper, that man."

"It's a lovely hotel," Lucy returned. "Very comfortable."

"That it is. Of course, there's not the number of people here like back in the middle '60's when there was 15,000 people here and up in

Virginia City. But it's still a wild little town." She grinned with pride as she cheerfully added, "Back in the summer of '71 Jabez Spencer shot and killed James Murray just out front."

"You did say James *Murray*, not Murphy."

"Oh, my dear, you look so pale!"

"Are you sure of the name?" Lucy insisted.

"Oh, yes. I knew both men."

Lucy settled back on the sofa across from Mrs. McCormack, her heart beats returning to normal while she offered a brief explanation. She received the standard condolences, one widow understanding another.

"Also in that summer," Mrs. McCormack continued, "this hotel suffered quite a mishap with a steam engine. There's a framed copy of a newspaper article over there on the wall about it that you can read."

Lucy did just that, the article dated June 21, 1871. Entitled "Sixty Horsepower Sensation", it read:

"About 6 o'clock last evening a terrific crash resounded from the Vesey House, inducing everybody to rush wildly thither from all parts of town. The cause was as follows: a large, new engine of 60-horsepower for the Yellow Jacket south works, came into town loaded upon the 'back action' of a huge team, and passing up the steep cross-street to the works, had just made the turn up Telegraph Street when the chain attaching the back-action to the forward wagon broke.

"The back-action with its ponderous load started immediately downhill, stern foremost, and would have smashed directly into Odd Fellows Hall, had not a man caught hold of the tongue and directed the runaway wagon towards Main Street. It directly got such strong sternway on, however, that he could not control it, and in another instant, it pointed itself full tilt toward the Vesey House, which it struck with ponderous force about the center of its broadside, crashing directly into the dining room.

"The boarders were all at supper, the tables being filled, but seeing through the windows this rampant engine charging upon the institution, they jumped lively and got out of the way just as the thing crashed through, carrying a goodly portion of the side of the building with it. Nobody was hurt, but some dishes got broken, and grub, pickles, sauces, etc., were distributed about the floor reckless of cost.

"Neither wagon nor engine were injured in the least by this forcible 'housing', and shortly afterward the team hitched to the tongue, snaked the

formidable intruder out, and left a good job for a carpenter to repair damage.
It was a right lively sensation while it last, and it was very lucky that no one
was hurt."

Lucy sat down and arranged her skirts. "Wasn't it later that year that
the prisoner's broke out of the Nevada State Prison?"

"Yes, it was. There was a whole lot of excitement about that!"

"I had a friend living in Carson City at the time. She had a friend,
Mrs. Ganby, who suddenly disappeared right around then."

"Oh, I remember that. I knew Mrs. Ganby slightly. Few knew her
well, I guess. It was thought by some that her husband wasn't dead, but
was one of the escaped prisoners who was never recaptured."

"My friend had hinted the same thing."

"No one could be sure, of course. She was such a nice woman, although
very shy. I think it was because she was black, you see, and didn't feel that
she fit in well in the town."

Lucy smiled to herself. Dolly had never mentioned Mrs. Ganby's
color, because it wouldn't have mattered to her. Lucy felt a stab of aching
nostalgia as she thought of her dear friend no longer in her life.

Mrs. McCormack asked Lucy several questions about Placerville,
having traveled through on her way from San Francisco to Carson City
back in 1862. She had been accompanied by her husband and young
daughter, on their way to the mines in Gold Canyon.

At the mention of 1862, Lucy flinched. It was not missed by Mrs.
McCormack, although she said nothing. Lucy smiled in appreciation of
the woman's tact. "Were you by any chance in Placerville during the trial
that caused so much excitement?"

"We arrived just after."

"My friends were directly involved, and because of all that happened
that summer, they left the town that fall. They ended up in Carson City."

"It was them that knew Mrs. Ganby?"

"Well, one of them did."

Mrs. McCormack nodded her head. "Life can be hard. I could have
moved on up to Virginia City after my husband passed. He's buried there,
but we lived here, and this is where my memories are."

"May I ask how your husband died?"

Mrs. McCormack hesitated a moment before asking a question of her
own. "Have you ever been down in a mine?"

"No. I've heard men talk about it, and I've even seen drawings in magazines. And I saw a photograph of some men who were posing on an open cage platform before being let down."

"Those may give you an idea of what's there, but it can't convey the closeness of the air, or the ever-present knowledge that you're hundreds of feet beneath the earth and the freshness of the open air. And then there are the smells of the different layers of earth, the wet timbers holding up all that earth, and the tallow candles in iron spikes jabbed into the walls. You were a married woman, so I need not describe to you the underlying smell of a sweating man. Multiply that by a hundred. It gets so hot down there that they work shirtless and regularly douse themselves with water from barrels. There are, of course, air vents that feed into shafts to carry air down to them, but the vents never carry quite enough to overcome the sense of being buried alive."

"You sound like someone who has been down in a mine."

"Once. Just once, and then only on the first level. But it was quite enough, and of course, my husband John would describe it to me when he would wake suddenly in the night. He especially dreaded his next day of work after being assigned to a lower depth. The Crown-Point Mine here, which is where he worked, had gotten down to the 1,000-foot level."

"Did he work all that way down?"

"No, he worked at the 800-foot level. This was back in '69. The men accepted the danger, of course. The pay was good. But accidents were a regular occurrence, more in some mines than in others. The foreman where John worked was a good man, and he was very careful, especially when it came to the handling of black powder."

"Did your husband die in an explosion?"

"No. That would have been a more merciful occurrence." A veil of determination passed over her face as she strove to hide her emotions. "There are many things to fear when mining underground." Mrs. McCormack suddenly stopped and looked down at her knitting, which now lay limp on her lap. Lucy looked at her with concern and started to reach out a hand, but Mrs. McCormack only smiled. "It's all right. I've adapted to what happened."

"What was that?"

"You don't know about the fire at the Crown-Point? Oh, my, I thought everyone had heard about it."

Lucy only stared back at her new friend in horror. "Fire! Oh, dear God, not down in a mine."

CHAPTER 9

1876 – 1877

Reading correctly Lucy's reaction, Mrs. McCormack simply nodded her head. "Yes. Back in '69 we had a fire that affected three of the mines here in Gold Hill. You must remember that below ground there are miles of tunnels and all are lined with square sets of massive timbers, posts holding up floors of heavy planks, and all of this on multiple levels. Where earth has crumbled between the timbers, men put in wedges and braces, and wood stairs lead from level to level. And there are dozens of wooden chutes lined with planks leading from level to level."

"That's a whole forest of wood!"

"Yes. And when wood gets wet, it rots and must be replaced. If it isn't, a cave-in results. We had weathered a few of those."

It was not a good time to be a tree in a California or Nevada forest. By 1860, deep shafts had been necessary to reach the rich ore discovered below the shallow depths thus far worked. The leads were over forty feet wide, and promised a degree of wealth that could not be ignored. But the posts and rock pillars used at first could not support the weight of a deep mine. A young mining engineer, Philipp Deidesheimer, after a month of studying the problem, came up with a system of timbering composed of square sets. They could be adapted to any size mining operation and even added on as tunnels extended further. Each timber was 18" by 18" square, and stood six to seven feet tall, with horizontal braces up to five feet long. The ends were cut so the beams could be locked together, allowing for an unprecedented degree of safety for the miners. It became a system used across the country for decades.

Mrs. McCormack shook her head. "No matter how many safety precautions were taken, there was always the threat of accidents, or worse. On April 7 of '69, my husband went to work on the early morning day shift. Not long after, the bells began to sound throughout the town. The disaster bells, I call them. Fire truck bells, mill whistles, bronze fire bells on the street outside businesses. The air was filled with their clamor. The townspeople, especially the women whose husbands were at work in the mines, ran in the same direction as the fire trucks. I'll never forget the scream of one of the big horses pulling a truck, because it was what I wanted to do, but couldn't.

"At the mine, we were kept away by barriers of rope and a line of men who kept us well back. But men's voices reached us, such as 'too much smoke', and 'gases at the 1,000 foot level'."

As Mrs. McCormack wiped at her eyes, Lucy told her, "If you don't want to continue, we can change the subject."

"No. If you're going to spend much time around here, you should know what has gone before."

At that moment, a petite woman with blonde hair came and sat in the chair near Mrs. McCormack. She put her shopping bag on the floor at her feet and removed her gloves. "I heard you telling this lady about the fire, Effie. Would you like me to tell her this next part?"

"Thank you, Mrs. Allen. That might be best."

"How do you do? I'm Lucy Murphy. I hope my inquiry hasn't stirred up too much unpleasantness."

"Oh, my dear Mrs. Murphy, we live with this all the time. But no one around here allows us to talk about it, thinking it will upset us." She pursed her lips. "How much more upset can we be just living with the memory?"

"Please call me Lucy.""

"And I'm Penelope. Are you settling here?"

"My son and I are going on to Virginia City soon." Lucy motioned to Mr. Lowrey as he passed through and, while handing him several coins, asked if they might have a service of coffee and cake. He was happy to oblige and headed to the kitchen.

Penelope Allen picked up the thread of the conversation. "You see, it wasn't only the Crown Point that was involved." She sat back in her chair and smoothed her skirts with hands that had seen years of hard work. She looked at them and sighed, as though accepting that rose water can only do so much. She then focused her green eyes on Lucy. "Over at the Kentuck Mine, the shaft cleared of smoke enough at nine in the morning that men were able to go down and bring up two bodies. The rescuers told us what we might expect, and some of the women began to weep."

"Where I was," Effie McCormack said, "we heard about some of the men that had been in the cage, which after all was just an open platform with low sides. It seems that the men on it were so weak from lack of air that they fell back against the wall of the shaft. They were crushed by the very vehicle that was lifting them to safety."

"At the Yellow Jacket," Penelope said, "around noon some firemen working with the miners went down to the 800-foot level and recovered four bodies, all of them having passed out from the bad air down there."

Mr. Lowrey approached with a tray of coffee pot and cups, along with three plates of pound cake topped with dollops of jam. Hearing what they were talking about, he left quickly with no comment. But Lucy had seen the lift of his brows, and wondered if he was just surprised, or expressing disapproval.

As Lucy handed out the refreshment, Effie McCormack took a cup of coffee but shook her head at the serving of cake. "I continued to hope, along with the other women around me, because my husband wasn't among those. All available men were helping. My young daughter was clutching my skirt, tears silently running down her cheeks. We all hoped our men might have found a pocket at the lower level where fresh air could find them. A lantern was sent down to the 1,000-foot level in the Crown-Point Mine, along with a note letting anyone there know that rescuers would try to reach them if it was known for sure that there were men alive down there. The lantern and note came back up untouched. We had to accept that they were all dead, either from fire or the gases. Weeping soon became almost as loud as the shouts of those helping."

Mrs. Allen took up the story. "Father Manogue, himself having once worked in the California goldfields, brought us his compassion and kind words. As did other religious men who passed among us."

Mrs. McCormack nodded. "Over the next hours, cages full of bodies were brought up. They were taken to an open area and laid out in rows so they could be identified by the women rushing toward them. The bodies were tagged, and wagons arrived to carry them away to a warehouse set up as a morgue. And men volunteering as gravediggers began to dig north of Virginia City at the new cemetery there."

Penelope poured more coffee into her cup. "Thick columns of horrible-smelling smoke and gases rose steadily from the Kentuck and Crown-Point shafts. It was a combination of pinewood and the hot ores burning below. It got so bad up at the mouth of the shafts, that those men near it were becoming ill. Still, people waiting behind the ropes continued to hold out hope."

Mrs. McCormack sighed deeply. "But the men were realists, and it was finally agreed that anyone remaining below had to be dead, and also couldn't be retrieved. It was more important that the fire be put out. At first, they thought they might close up the shafts and pour water down through the ventilation flues. But they realized that doing that would for sure kill anyone who might possibly be alive down there. Which I suppose shows even they still held onto a little hope.

"The Yellow Jacket mine was not as bad, so firemen went down with long hoses fed down to them from a hydrant above. They went all the way down to the 800-foot level with miners who unblocked cave-ins and shored up weak timbers. The walls were so hot, even after watered, that they could feel the searing heat from them. Soon the water they were standing in was at the boiling point. Because the steam was combining with sulphur fumes and gases from the hot mineralized ores, the air was so bad that they sunk an air-pipe down from the main blower above. The workers were besieged with sudden flare-ups and poisonous gases. They finally realized that as long as the shaft was open, they could escape, but if something happened to block it, they too would die down there."

Mrs. Allen shook her head. "My current husband was a fireman back then, and to this day he has periods of melancholy that I know relate back to what he experienced that day. It was these rescuers who later told of the men who had died down there. The smoke and gases had hit the miners so quickly that even the swiftest among them had still only been able to reach the bottom of ladders before overcome. The first cages going up were so crowded that the weight of the men caused the lift operator to fear some would fall off. But those were the ones who escaped, although their lungs were compromised for weeks or months. My husband still coughs in a strange way sometimes."

"A friend of my husband's," Mrs. McCormack said, "crawled toward the shaft that led up, but also down from his level. It was totally dark down there, what with candles and lanterns having been extinguished one way or another. He was afraid of stepping into the empty shaft and falling down it to his death, so he crawled toward it, reaching his hands out before him. He had just reached the opening when some men ran past him, and as he had feared, fell straight down. Right after that, the cage came down and he scrambled onto it and was brought up with those already on it."

The women silently sipped their coffee, each with their own thoughts. Then Mrs. McCormack spoke softly. "When my husband left that morning, I made sure he had on a clean blue shirt. I had repaired his suspenders on one side, and as he looked down at my neat stitching, he told me what a gem of a wife I was. He kissed me on the cheek, took his hat from the hook on the wall and plunked it on his head like he always did. He gave me a wink before opening the door and walking out, whistling as he went as a way of teasing me since he knew it irritated me. I'd give anything to be so irritated again."

By this time, the horror of what she was picturing in her mind as she listened to these women made Lucy want to stop them from continuing. But she could tell they didn't want to stop. Reminding herself that she only had to listen, while they had to live with the reality of it, she kept still.

Mrs. McCormack rearranged her shawl as she squared her shoulders with a determined lift of her head. "All day long a stream of water was kept going at the 800-foot level, but it wasn't enough and by nine that night a second stream was put on at the 700-foot level. At two o'clock the next morning, thirteen bodies were recovered at the bottom, while others were found on the level above that. All afternoon, more bodies continued to be found, and over the next two days as well. Finally, on the 10th, the inevitable decision was reached that the fire had not diminished, and at eleven that night all the shafts were covered with planks and soaked blankets, and then earth piled on top of that. After that, steam was forced into the Yellow Jacket shaft through an air pipe down to the lower levels, allowing it to spread from there through the tunnels."

Mrs. Allen nodded. "Some of the last bodies to be removed had been so hot below that they had to be wrapped in canvas coated with tar. Relatives were not allowed to view them. But my best friend begged so much that they allowed her to see the top of her husband's head, and I went with her. I had experienced my shock three days before, and I knew she would need a friend. She held the hand of her little daughter as she stroked her man's hair, saying, 'Good-bye, my husband.' As they walked away, the little girl asked if she could see her daddy. I caught hold of my friend as she fainted, and other women rushed over to help." Mrs. Allen fumbled for a hanky in her pocket, finally overcome with the telling.

Lucy insisted on ordering them all a brandy, which they added to their coffee. After the women had collected themselves, they finished the story for Lucy, explaining that on April 14, the steam had been shut off and some exploration attempted. Fires were put out as the men reached them, and this continued for days. Many times, the workers had to be rushed to the surface when they were starved for air. By April 28, six more bodies had been discovered, and although there were four more known to be on the upper levels in the Kentuck, the gases were so bad the workers had to leave. By May 2, the situation below had gotten worse. The mine owners closed the drifts between the Yellow Jacket, Crown-Point and Kentuck mines. They then closed all the shafts on the Crown-Point and Kentuck, sealing them tightly, as it was surmised that the fresh air sent into the mines to aid the workers had given life to the lingering fires.

Still, the mines were opened on May 20 and a body was recovered from the Crown-Point. The fire then again resumed and everyone had to evacuate before the last three bodies could be found. The fire was at least confined to the 800-foot level of both mines, so they walled them up at that point to keep the fire from spreading again. It did, however, continue to burn for over a year.

Seeing Lucy's expression of shock, Effie nodded with confirmation. "Worse than that, three years later the walled portion was opened up, and the rocks along the walls glowed red hot. It was in this walled area that the bodies of the last three miners were discovered, only now there were only fragments of their bones to be found. Altogether, about fifty men died."

Lucy knew that she would never again take for granted the life of a hard rock miner. She also now felt a special closeness with these women.

Over time, it would develop into a lasting friendship, and many more cups of coffee shared.

The next day Roger found Lucy in the café near the Vesey House where she was just finishing an early breakfast. There was one pancake left on the plate she had pushed aside and he reached for it eagerly.

Lucy looked up in surprise, watching the last of her breakfast disappear into her son's mouth. "What are you doing here? I thought you were going to sleep late this morning."

"I changed my mind." He swallowed and poured a large dollop of cream into the hot coffee the waiter had set before him. He treated his mother to a half-formed, tentative smile. "Would you mind if we visit Carson City rather than go on immediately to Virginia City?"

Always open to a new adventure, Lucy readily agreed. "Just let me get my things together."

"There's a stage leaving in half an hour, with two seats available."

Lucy, in the process of gathering herself to stand up, turned to him while suppressing a grin. "You already purchased the tickets, didn't you?"

"Well, yeah. I was pretty sure you'd be up for the trip."

Lucy laughed and headed out of the café. Roger followed, taking his mother's arm to lead her safely along the busy street, keeping himself between her and the road. He kept an eye out for passing wagons that could splash mud, or anything at all that could harm her. It was a courtesy any man even with basic manners would automatically render.

Traveling downhill on the main road, the rapidly moving coach of Billy Wilson's stage line swayed like a ship on a rough sea. But the air was too thick with dust to successfully carry that analogy too far. The passengers clutched their dusters about them, making sure the cloth covered as much of their clothing as possible. The rattling of the iron-rimmed wheels over the gravel road added fresh noise to that of the busy stamps at the mines and mills as they passed through Silver City and American Flat. In other words, it was a typical trip out of Gold Hill by stage on that route.

Fortunately, no one was riding on the small drop-down seats on the sides, so there was sufficient room for their legs. They were grateful for this, as they shared the coach with two men in miner's garb who were badly in need of a bath, and two others in nice suits who carried side arms and never smiled. But it was the two large horse flies buzzing about the coach for the last half hour of the trip that held everyone's attention.

They stepped out from the stage onto the sidewalk in front of the St. Charles Hotel, where they obtained two of the forty-eight comfortable rooms. Upon returning to the street, the first thing Lucy and Roger noticed was the number of trees that had been lovingly planted along the streets. Window boxes of spent blooms fronted many of the shops, and a street sweeper walked past with his cart. It was evident that this was a town that cared about its appearance, and for some reason, that realization buoyed Lucy's spirits.

With Roger off to scout the saloons for a game, Lucy was torn between going for a long walk or retiring to the hotel's reading room to scan the newspapers there. Or maybe she could buy a periodical and bring it with her to the second-floor parlor where she could sit with a pot of tea. Having read about Carson City from Dolly's letters of ten years earlier, she decided to see how mature the town had become.

Carson City sprawled over a neat grid of streets, with three roads entering from the south and the Virginia and Truckee Railroad's engine house at the north end. Travelers arriving by train for the first time often pondered why Caroline, William, John, Sophia, Ann, and Henry might be so important that they had a street named after them near the terminal. Only Carson Street, the town's main thoroughfare, continued north into Storey County. But over the last fifteen years, it was the road heading east to the mills along the Carson River, and then on to Gold Canyon, that had carried most of the traffic.

Passing through a warren of streets crossing each other, Lucy found herself staring up at the bright dome of the town's crown jewel. Where once there had been only the open expanse of the plaza, now loomed the Nevada State Capital building topped by a neat pergola, and that topped with the American flag on a tall spire. She was tempted to enter the building, but instead walked until she reached the eastern edge of town and its other place of pride; a large oval race track where sporting events took place, as well as celebrations and concerts. Travelers passing through often went home to announce that, "Carson City is a delightfully progressive town."

Carson City was a hub of commerce, with its railroad coming in from the mills, and its infrastructure of several paved streets, piped water, and gas lighting. But the town was also surrounded by orchards and fields of produce on farms and truck gardens. This produce was sent out to

California towns on both sides of the Sierra, as well as Nevada mining towns. Lucy sampled a locally grown apple while sitting on a bench outside a grocery store, and then went in to buy two more.

Knowing that Roger would be busy acquainting himself with the town's various saloons and gambling parlors, Lucy continued her walk until she reached a green space where flowerbeds overflowed with late summer blooms. She took advantage of a bench in its midst where she could enjoy the fresh air and inviting views of Carson with church spires and tall flag poles cutting the skyline. It was a clean look, unlike what she would later see in Virginia City, where the far view would be industrial and filled with black smoke stacks, giant piles of cast-off tailings, and lines of low hills that rolled out into the desert.

Returning to the hotel, Lucy found a small table in the dining room where a courteous young waiter brought her a pot of tea. About the time she had been revived by her first cup, the young man brought the rest of her order; an apple cobbler in its own little bowl served with a pitcher of rich cream on the side. She took out a large spoonful from the middle, chewed it with enthusiasm, and then poured in the rich cream. She continued to eat outwards from there, finally sitting back with a contented sigh and relishing the small but exquisite moment. She looked forward to lording it over Roger when she saw him, assuming that all he was consuming was beer and bar food.

But Roger was almost equally content, being in the Ormsby House Saloon that was spacious and welcoming of his efforts to get up a game. The warmth of the pot-bellied stove in the middle of the room wasn't necessary, but it was evidently well-ventilated, as the tin ceiling above it was relatively clean. Rather than a big wooden backbar, there were three large paintings on the wall, all darkened by years of cigar smoke. Above them near the ceiling was a large clock in a dark wooden frame, and Roger occasionally glanced up at it to be sure he would be in time to take his mother to supper. He tended to lose track of the time if the cards were in the mood to favor him.

Lucy and Roger spent that one night in Carson City, and returned the next day to Gold Hill by train, walking downhill to the Vesey House from the small, barn-red depot. They spent what little was left of that day enjoying the local newspapers, and early the next morning got on a train that took them to Virginia City. While waiting to depart, Lucy admired the Virginia and Truckee's steam train. It was an imposing sight, with its dark green passenger cars, varicolored window tops, and bright red and gold engine with a large black funnel balanced on its nose. When it finished taking on water, a whistle blew and porters wearing black vests over starched white shirts helped the passengers into the cars.

After the crossing of the intimidating but sturdy Crown Point Trestle, followed by numerous sharp turns and narrow tunnels, they arrived in Virginia City. Roger hired a rig with a driver to take them into town, traveling up hill to "C" Street, and then south to a cheap little rooming house recommended to Roger by the clerk at the Ormsby House. As Roger pointed out to Lucy, his winnings from the night before had gotten them this far in comfort, but it wasn't quite enough to get them into a first-class hotel.

Roger went out in search of a few games that would put coin in his pocket, and Lucy wasted no time before setting out to find work of her own. The first women to arrive on the Comstock were not the prostitutes; they were those with needleworking skills. Whether sewing ore bags, tents, or making hats and clothing as more women and children arrived, they were kept busy contributing to the settling of the town. Some "went out by day" to the homes of those for whom they were sewing, receiving a meal as part of their wages.

The problem was that Lucy really didn't have skills needed in such a town. She was a fairly decent cook, but there were men who were better and had much more stamina. She could sew or mend basic garments, but she could never pass as a seamstress. Freda had always cut out their dress patterns, so she couldn't apply as a cutter. She certainly didn't have the required youthful age to be a chambermaid in a hotel. And hotels only hired men as clerks.

Thirst and hunger brought her to a small café with a sign out front that declared it served French pastries. In Virginia City, anything French, from food to "fancy women", was considered desirable. She came to rest at a table next to a window overlooking "C" Street.

The sidewalks were crowded, since there were thousands of people situated in a town that was only able to spread out for a mile in each direction. Part of that was up Mt. Davidson to the west, and the rest downslope as far as the mines east of town. The north edge met five miles of steep road down through Newton Canyon, with the Geiger Toll House at the bottom. The town had slowly merged south with Gold Hill, separated by a hill they called The Divide where ruffians liked to waylay traffic. Lucy recalled her enjoyment of the calmer atmosphere and flat layout of Carson, and immediately realized that living in Virginia City was going to offer unique challenges.

She looked up and down the street within her range of vision. Although much of the town had been lost in the big fire the previous year, she was surprised at how much of it had already been rebuilt, most buildings now of brick. But she was also surprised at how much of the southern half had not been touched by the flames.

It was obvious that the shops were doing a brisk business, and there were a lot of them. In fact, now that she was refreshed, she could observe the town with a greater degree of objectivity. She ignored the cluster of men across the street hovering around the bulletin board of a mining broker's office. Everyone knew that the buying and selling of mining shares went on day and night, but as yet that held no interest for her.

Two large, heavily loaded freight wagons that were hitched together and pulled by sixteen large horses momentarily blocked her view. As the wagon moved slowly down the street, young boys followed, skipping and shouting and prepared to stay with it all the way to its destination. It was knowledge they could brag about to those in their respective gangs. In that moment of gleeful excitement, they didn't care if they got home late or otherwise displeased fathers who were inclined to give them a "good larruping".

Lucy admired the many brick buildings along the planked sidewalks. Some buildings were even four stories, shoved together so they shared common side walls. No alleys taking up unusable space in this town! But this meant that the buildings only had windows at the front on "C" Street, and on "B" Street as well if they were large enough to have rear entrances there. Although the first floors of most buildings were taken up with businesses, the floors above were often rented out as apartments or offices. The builders compensated for the lack of windows by putting in large skylights over the top floor that radiated light down a central stairwell and through transoms at the tops of doors. In case of a fire, it was like having an open chimney down through the building, but the owners only cared about attracting tenants.

Beyond the typical merchandise stores, bakeries and meat markets of any boom town, there were more substantial examples of steadfast prosperity. There was a bank and a brokerage house where stocks were traded, a Wells Fargo Express Office, the telegraph office, several tailors, a jewelry store, and two newspaper offices. The Masons, the Knights of Pythias, the Fenian Brotherhood, and the Odd Fellows were also present. Of particular interest to everyone was the current construction of the third incarnation of the International Hotel, which ran between "C" and "B" Streets along Union.

The *big fire* in the fall of '75 had destroyed the hotel's second version, the one Dolly had admired. It was now almost ready for its last; five stories of elegance inside a "fire-resistant structure" that was 66 feet across the front, 106 feet deep, with 144 sleeping rooms, bathrooms on each floor, and built at a contract price of $115,000. The plan laid out several parlors, including one just for men and one just for women, both to be furnished with velvet sofas and chairs. Men would also have a smoking room richly paneled and scattered with leather easy chairs, and a well-stocked reading room would be available to everyone. A large dining room complete with the finest crystal and china place settings awaited diners, with even a separate dining room for families with children.

The newspapers reported that the whole building was to be heated with steam, and would have a water-powered elevator more powerful than those used in San Francisco. The boiler room was beneath the "B" Street front entrance, accessible through a door under the raised sidewalk.

Lucy had earlier watched as men painted the exterior, applying deep red paint that allowed the white marble caps and sills of the windows to show more prominently. Now, with the exterior completed, work on the interior was speeding up. Lucy practically itched with curiosity. Maybe there would be a grand opening that she and Roger could attend, and maybe she could even buy a ball gown. She spent several minutes fantasizing about that.

On her way to the café, Lucy had especially enjoyed walking past the many restaurants (some with French names and touted as the best west of New York), cafes (huge breakfasts), and chop houses (just inside the door of saloons and offering free breakfasts to miners). The advertisements, as well as the citizens, bragged that the town was stocked with just about anything a person could desire. Whether fresh oysters from San Francisco or prime rib from Carson Valley cattle, it could be washed down with beer, whiskey, wine or champagne.

Roger had informed his mother that far removed from the center of town were the three "red light districts", along with a number of dance halls and hurdy gurdy houses. She had refrained from asking him how he knew this. Of course, for more respectable entertainment, one could go up to "B" Street to Piper's Opera House. It was a popular destination for traveling entertainments that regularly filled the seats with eager patrons ready to toss coins on the stage to show appreciation.

While there, free entertainment could be had just by watching the painted ladies displaying themselves in the boxes at the sides of the stage. Of course, these "damsels of the pave", as those most elite of the profession were called by the papers, were not shy about parading through town dressed and made up in extravagant style. After all, it always pays to advertise.

Young boys often hung out near the entrance to Piper's Opera House in the evening, hoping the wealthy mine owner John Mackay would arrive. He was generous with coin or even tickets to the wonders taking place inside the theater. It was the one place in town where the boys were careful to behave, not wanting to give their benefactor a reason to withhold his largesse.

Ah, yes, it was a wonderful town, cosmopolitan for those of sophisticated tastes, and at the same time surrounded by humble neighborhoods of ethnic purity. There, shopkeepers and miners lived with their families not far from the commercial district or the new three-story school building. This latter was, however, near the roughest area of town often referred to as the Barbary Coast, named after that tough, crime ridden area in San Francisco. But now, with the Fourth Ward School opening, many said there needed to be more focus on cleaning up the "sin-soaked" areas nearby. For Virginia City was also a town with a hospital and orphanage run by the Daughters of Charity, as well as temperance groups, benevolent societies, and those citizens interested in clearing out whatever they deemed offensive.

But no matter where one might live, or what one's profession, the idea that the town was beginning a "downward turn" referred to by the Spanish word *borrasca,* was kept from conversation. It was easier to pretend that the *bonanza* of '73 was going to continue. Anyone of a more realistic turn of mind simply kept their mouth shut.

Lucy loved the brightly colored posters plastered to the sides of buildings, hawking everything from tobacco to tonics. The newest ones were promoting train travel to Virginia City and Dayton. Words like *easiest, fastest, closest, shortest, swiftest* prevailed. She was pretty sure she knew why *safest* was not mentioned.

Soon there would be trains steaming their way over the hills from Carson City to Reno with engine names like *Dayton, Inyo,* and *Empire No. 13*; all denoting towns and counties along the Eastern Sierra, and each having a number as well as a name, as in "*good ole No. 25*". They were still hiring gandy dancers to build rail lines, paying them a dollar a day, plus room and coal oil.

Lucy continued to sit at her small marble-topped table in the window of the little French café, looking out onto the busy flow of traffic on "C" Street. She was sipping tea almost without appreciation as she watched people walk by, taking special note of what the women were wearing. It was obvious that these Virginia City women cared a great deal about their appearance, and were dressed more fashionably than she had expected.

Lucy would learn that less than a third of the population was female. Still, the women managed to make a considerable impact on society in general, as well as the cultural modernization of the town. It was mainly because of their influence that there was the new Fourth Ward School, as well as the hospital east of town just off Union Street. Of course, it was talented men who drew up the blue prints and saw to the actual construction of the Italianate style buildings; so sturdy that many would last well into the twenty-first century.

Excluding any difference based on ethnicity, the men shared a mix of common attitudes that were typical in such a large, industrialized mining town. If they had the money, those men considered *coarse* drank at the same bar as a cultured gentleman from the East, at least if they were in a two-bit house. Miners and wage workers drank more often at the one-bit houses where a drink was twelve and a half cents, although change for a quarter was ten cents. It was the comfortable companionship and inviting nature of the saloon that made the difference to most customers.

Regardless of what would later be promulgated by works of fiction, events such as fist fights, gun fights, and general mayhem was not common to these establishments.   Such things were usually reserved for the streets where there was more room, and where a bigger audience could gather.

In Virginia City, a man who prided himself on being a loud jokester was tolerated by patient store owners, and the rebellious types were kept somewhat under control by their more law-abiding friends. The presence of a sheriff and a police department helped. The single man who could only afford to sleep on a cot in a row with others at a boarding house accepted as normal that there were men who lived in big houses; some of them flaunting their wealth derived from the mines, and others using it to help the less fortunate.

But while the men were accepting of this wide-ranging dichotomy between those who worked and those who paid out, the women were less satisfied. They were also more acutely aware of the different levels of society, for regardless of whatever strata of it in which they found themselves, they read the lady's magazines from the East. For those who could not afford a dressmaker to match the drawings, they had to make their own clothes or remake what had so often been seen.   But any astute woman could recognize an alteration to a seam, a dress shorter because a worn hem had been cut off, or a bonnet retrimmed. Consequently, a woman's wardrobe was a more reliable means of declaring her place in society than even the neighborhood in which she lived.

Because women were held to a stricter code of behavior than men, they were expected to conduct themselves according to their perceived place in the social hierarchy. Some men grumbled that before the women came to town, things had been more open and less attention given to class distinction. It wasn't true, but they tried hard to convince themselves that it was. Of course, before the women came and demanded more civilized conduct and quality of living, the men had been focused solely on finding gold and silver. With something so universally important in common among them, their lives had been narrowly defined by those who had found it, and those who had not.

Now, after fifteen years, the town had gone through discovery, bonanza, borrasca and recently another bonanza. Along with all of that had been severe winters, zephyr winds, and a few fires. Typical of any town that had been able to sustain itself through so much change, both good and bad, it had developed a civilized understanding of itself. Crucial to this was acceptance of where it had been, and tolerance of where it was.

If a woman wanted to break out of the accepted norms that were considered at the heart of a masculine society, she had to be clever and just a little manipulative. Of course, she would probably call it an understanding of human nature. Lucy was not long in Virginia City before she fully embraced this philosophy, becoming only one of a large group of women whose common bond was surviving in a male-dominated world. Of course, such a thing was never spoken about, and even in some cases not consciously realized. But that didn't mean it didn't influence the behavior of many women.

Even though the town was in many ways accepting of its diversity, most of those who comprised that diversity preferred to live together in areas inclusive of "their own kind". Men of various origins worked together down in the mines, shopped in the same stores, and ate in the same restaurants. But when it came to living together, and in some instances drinking together, they preferred to do so with those of their own nationality.

About one-hundred African-American families lived north and south of Sutton on "B" Street, with single men in "D" Street boarding houses. Half of the domestics in the town were Irish women working in restaurants, or as nurses, seamstresses, or laundry workers. Irish girls as young as twelve worked as maids in homes or hotels, while Irish men worked in a wide range of jobs, especially if they were above ground. Mexican men were respected as hard-working and knowledgeable miners, even if sometimes referred to as "beaners". Cornish miners, often referred to as "Cousin Jack", were valued for their knowledge of mining techniques brought to the states from the coal mines of Cornwall, England. Most of this last group chose to live in Gold Hill.

The Chinese had their own districts with shops, breweries, saloons and eateries. They lived at the north and south ends of "H" and "I" Streets, and were commonly visited by other nationalities looking for a unique gift or eating experience. They also had opium dens that were usually in dark basements. Despite what future myth-makers would claim, these dens were frequented not only by townsmen of all nationalities, but also by a surprising number of women who referred to the drug as "my secret friend". The Chinese women were often thought to be prostitutes even when not, and those that were, had usually been bought in China and sold to Chinese masters in the states as slaves.

The rest of the world was also represented, not only by miners, but by shopkeepers, lawyers, blacksmiths, engineers, and entertainers; Chileans, South and Central Americans, Italians, Scandinavians, French, Swiss, Poles, Greeks, Hungarians, Turks, Pacific Islanders, Moroccans, Portuguese, and Spaniards. Each nationality had at least one holiday they celebrated with a parade, and which everyone in town enjoyed, using it as an excuse to drink, cheer and generally make a lot of noise.

After years of all these nationalities and different cultures working together, resentments that had festered beneath the benign appearance of acceptance, came to the fore in the early 1870's when a recession hit hard. Called *anti-sentiment expression*, the Chinese suffered the most from it. In the hard times of the *borrasca* that had caused increased financial tension, it had been the Chinese and the Cornish who had been the first to leave. Both groups had much to offer a mining town that could afford their talents, and they were willing to move on in search of any place more accepting of them. It was the Irish that hung on in Virginia City the tightest, adapting to whatever was available. Of course, when the *bonanza* hit in 1873, many of those who had left returned to the city.

It would take time for Lucy to learn all of this, but there would be plenty of that because she immediately fell in love with the town, and longed to be part of its exciting rhythms. Its undefinable but captivating spirit made her feel that exciting opportunities were waiting somewhere within its complicated set-up, if one could only discover them. Whatever it was, she felt that it wasn't just about gold and silver, but rather something oddly tantalizing that was unique to Virginia City.

But Lucy was also a realist. Yes, the dozens of brick buildings were pushed together along the cramped main roads, and the noise of the stamps at the mills and whistles at the hoisting works was a constant background intrusion. And, yes, the exotic smells of the many restaurants had to compete with the strange musky breath of the underground brought up through the shafts. But there were enough cooking stoves that never ceased turning out food from the Chinese district, the Irish quarter, and the dozens of downtown cafes, saloons, and hotels, to win the day. And, of course, there was always the excitement of fist fights, stock cheats, court hearings, and even an occasional killing. Nevertheless, it all came together like a grand orchestra that was just a little out of tune, but not so much that the magnificent sweep of its music couldn't stir the imagination.

Lucy and Roger were eager to explore it all. But before they could do that, they had to find a more permanent place to live. They settled for a room at a brick lodging house on the south end of "C" Street, where no other women were housed, but at least there was one running it. Only later did they realize this was the *Barbary Coast* area. Roger managed to secure a room at the end of the hall on the second floor so that three of their walls were of wood, and there was a small window facing the street. This meant that the wall connecting them to the room next door was simply framing covered with cloth and wall paper. This, of course, allowed neighboring sounds to be easily heard. As basic as it was, it still cost them $11 a month.

The four men next to them worked two different shifts, one during the day and the other at night. Because of the efforts of the Miners' Union, they worked a typical eight-hour shift, where non-union workers often put in a twelve-hour day. Lucy and Roger remained unacquainted with these men, but made sure they were as quiet as possible when in their room so the men on the sleeping shift were not disturbed. The men joked that their neighbors were mice that whispered and knew how to open a door.

Roger found work dealing cards in a couple of modest one-bit houses barely able to fit in two tables at the end of a long bar. Located just off "C" Street, the owners were impressed by Roger's well-maintained black suit and colorful vests, which they felt lent an air of quality to their establishment. They were relieved that although his boots were polished and his hat brushed, he didn't come across as slick. They didn't, however, believe for a moment that he was as old as he claimed, even with his small mustache to mature his features. The legal gambling age was twenty-one, but the owners looked at Roger's deep blue eyes beneath thick black hair, and concluded that he projected passable maturity.

Roger was aware of their attitude, but also that because of his youth, the customers would think him too young to be very practiced with cards. Roger's new employers watched him play a few hands, and they knew better. They looked forward to selling a lot of drinks to those trying to prove they could beat this young man if they played *just one more hand*. Roger didn't care what anyone thought of him, because he was charged a reasonable rate for his use of the table for a few hours each evening. During the day, he simply wandered to those saloons large enough to have a table where he could get up a game.

After several days of job hunting, followed each night by half an hour soaking her sore feet, Lucy was able to convince a woman who owned a millinery shop that she knew how to sew embellishments onto bonnets, which would be finished by more experience hands. In a soft Russian accent, Mrs. Jackson explained that Lucy was only an apprentice and would be allowed to do only those things of the simplest degree of skill. If Lucy proved her worth, after approximately two years she could become a *maker*, fashioning hat shapes from foundations. The next level up was trimming the bonnets with silk flowers, extravagant feather arrangements, and whole bird wings when available.

Lucy was given a stack of unadorned hats and was shown how to sew on bits of lace. Only because Mrs. Jackson was short-handed was Lucy allowed, after the second week, to attach a feather at a point marked in pencil. Whereas an unadorned straw hat might sell for $1, a simple, trimmed bonnet could bring in as much as $3.

Lucy never did figure out how the woman computed the money she earned, but applying several feathers earned her more than applying a veil. If she did several of each type of bonnet every day, it paid for their room that night as well as a roll for breakfast. For more than that, Lucy left it to Roger to supply the necessary funds. Knowing her son, she wasn't worried that they would starve. Lucy did not take this fact for granted, however, having gained insight into how hard life must be for a woman who had no one else on which to rely.

Shortly after Roger left for the day, a man showed up at their door, knocking loudly until Lucy hurried to open it. The man's British accept was so thick that she could barely understand what he wanted. Eventually, she figured out that he had gambled with Roger the night before and had been told that for a small fee Lucy could help him "smooth out" his accent.

Without trying to imitate his speech here, as it was full of an alarming repurposing of vowels, he managed to convey to her what he had in mind. "It would help if I could get people to better understand me. Maybe I could fit in better with the chaps I work with. Your son said you'd charge fair to help me."

Although Lucy wished that she could right then have a sharp word with that son, she invited the man into the room. Once seated, she handed him a newspaper and asked him to read a paragraph. She had him do it again slower, and corrected his pronunciation as he read. By the end of an hour, the man was doing considerably better. She gave him several common sentences to practice, and after collecting fifty cents, sent him on his way with directions to return in three days. As she held the silver coin in her hand, she realized that hour had been easy work compared to the hat trimming that earned the same amount and left her fingers raw.

When the man returned in a couple of days, he brought with him a man from Mexico who could understand English fairly well, but had a problem speaking it. He too paid her half a dollar for an hour's tutelage, and left with a newspaper marked with pencil to use as a study aid. By the end of two weeks, she had a dozen students and the beginnings of a nice savings.

By the end of September, with both mother and son working hard at their respective pursuits, they had enough saved to rent a small two-bedroom house on south "D" Street near Washington. A family had just moved out, desiring a warmer place to spend the coming winter. The rent was a steep $12 a month, but Lucy had plans for how they could afford that. The house was on the edge of the Irish quarter, where she found the men extremely polite, but the women seldom around because they were at work in town. It was also just south of the "red light district", separated from it by the Methodist Church and several hoisting works.

Lucy took the smaller bedroom for herself, and Roger made up a bed in a corner of the parlor. By renting out the larger bedroom to two miners who worked on the same day shift, the monthly rent was easily covered. Lucy used the time that the lodgers were gone for her tutoring business, and for helping foreign miners with their letters and other paperwork. At the same time, she baked pies that she sold to two restaurants on "C" Street. And she resigned from millinery work.

Most evenings she spent an hour ironing their clothes while the pies baked, especially Roger's shirts which he demanded be fresh every two days. There was a Chinese laundry not too far from the house that charged reasonable rates for washing, but she didn't want to spend money to have them do the ironing. However, after a man paid her two dollars for two sessions in which she taught him how to comport himself in proper society, she began paying to have even the ironing done at the laundry. It was then that she learned the truth of the myth that Chinese laundrymen spat on clothes to dampen them. Actually, they had a glass device in their mouth that when blown through acted as an atomizer to spread starch from a nearby bowl.

By the time fall color had saturated the trees, Lucy had managed to make a few more friends. However, it was not through her own efforts. Other women simply wanted to satisfy their curiosity about this busy woman who lived with a handsome son they were told by their husbands was a clever, *square* gambler. Having a reputation for being honest was for a gambler a tremendous asset, and Roger was proud of it. It also kept his wins from being challenged by ready fists, or guns.

Only once did he come close to a dangerous confrontation. The man had been new to the town and had arrived with a chip on his shoulder about life in general, and gamblers in particular. Fortunately, the other men at the table had set the stranger straight before he could become a problem. After the man won a good hand from Roger, the now mollified new-comer accepted the suggestion that he might enjoy a good meal at a restaurant across the street.

One of the women down the road from Lucy's rented house, Helene Morris, brought with her a cake by way of introduction. Her husband, a hoist engineer, was responsible for lowering and raising men on a small platform referred to as a cage. Such engineers were considered to be worthy of great respect, as they held so many lives in their hands every day. It was, in fact, a punishable offense to talk to a hoist engineer when he was at work. If men rang the bell from below indicating something was amiss, he had to be ready to bring them up immediately.

Helene Morris was petite and dark haired, and always seemed to Lucy to be exceptionally cheery. She was also chatty. "It's so nice having a woman closer to my age to talk to. Around here, they seem to be much younger. Which means they have young children and don't have time to visit. With mine in their teens, it gives me free time, especially when they're in school."

"I've been too busy to do much socializing," Lucy freely admitted. "I need to put by money so I can purchase a house and not have to pay out for rent."

"No matter where you live, the water company will charge you a minimum of a dollar a week. That is, if you use their pipes."

"Yes, and if they discover that I rent out a room, it'll be more."

"You know, a man several years ago suggested bringing piped water from Lake Tahoe here over Mt. Morrison. They thought him insane and he lost face. Now, it's done, and allows for good water."

"Unless the company decides to cut the pipe to your house for some reason."

"Oh, yes. Be sure not to be late paying them." Changing the subject, Helene asked, "Would you buy here on 'D' Street?"

"Oh, I don't know."

"I know some people associate our street as the red-light district, but that's not true at the south end here. Of course, there are a few brothels and even cribs further north." She looked at Lucy with speculation. "You do know, don't you, that those tiny cabins are what they call cribs, where the common prostitutes carry on their trade?"

"Yes, dear. If it doesn't shock you to know such things, don't suppose it would me."

Helene smiled. "Oh, good. I don't think I could be friends with someone afraid to besmirch their tender ears with life's realities." Lucy laughed, and that was enough for Helene to continue. "At least it's very quiet when passing through that area."

"That's because you pass through during the day. It's mostly at night that it's active."

"I suppose so. But men work around the clock in the mines. We up above ground know its daylight, but down in the mines it's always dark. Just lamps and candles to give light."

Lucy gave a shudder. "I forget sometimes the miles of tunnels that fill the ground beneath us. I've even heard tell of sink holes that open up under houses and stores where a tunnel hasn't been maintained properly."

"It doesn't happen often, but it does happen. A whole building was lost down a huge hole a year or so ago. The mine owners were fined a considerable sum, and the store owner's law suit still hasn't been settled."

"No wonder men demand a minimum of four dollars a day."

"Compared to what the mine owners are worth after manipulating the stock in their mines the way they do, it's not nearly enough." Helene took a deep breath and brightened. "But that's a subject that we oh-so innocent women aren't supposed to know anything about. My father once said that there's no perfect place beyond greed. Well, here, we're right in the middle of it." Lucy didn't know how to respond to that, having only heard fragments of men's conversation about stock manipulation. Besides, Helene was continuing. "It's definitely a man's town. When my husband and I came here in '64, the stores didn't carry hair pins or face powder. I had to ask them to order things like that. But, of course, they did carry the essentials for housekeeping."

"I assume men did their own housekeeping, too, and needed those things."

"Humph! They didn't use them very often, from what I saw. But then, they worked long hours and didn't much care about a swept floor." Helene changed to yet another subject. "There also wasn't anything here in the way of entertainments for women. So we got together and shared books, our quilting, and our gardens. Of course, that last was pretty uncertain, the weather being what it is."

"I only have a few books, but I'd be happy to swap with you if you'd like."

"That would be fine. The Miners Union over on 'B' Street has a big library for its members. I hear tell there are really big lending libraries in the East. I come from a small town in Oregon, and we only had the back of a stationery store where we could check out used books."

"There was a small type of library in Placerville, over the engine company's fire house. But we had a wonderful old book store that sold books, newspapers, and magazines if they could get them sent out from the East."

Helene reached for the tea pot on the kitchen table in front of her while Lucy sat across and continued to mark paragraphs in a newspaper destined for one of her students. "How old are you, Lucy?"

"I'm thirty-nine, Helene." Thinking the question a bit bold, she decided to match her. "How old are you?"

"Oh, I don't like to say. How old do you think I am?"

"Are you trying to be coquettish with me? After outright asking me my age?"

Helene looked at Lucy and chuckled. "You're right. I'm thirty-eight. You don't hesitate to say what's on your mind, do you? I mean, you don't play the word games most other women play."

"The only games I like are card games. I don't have time or patience for insincerity."

Helene raised her brows at that. "You mean, you know how to play poker and such games? Like your son?"

"Yes. Do you find that unsuitable?"

Helene thought a moment as she sipped her tea. "I think it's terribly exciting." A smile lit her face from lips to sparkling eyes. "But you should be careful which woman you tell that to."

Lucy smiled. "I already know that. I used to deal in a saloon in Placerville after my husband died, to help make ends meet. I didn't flaunt it, and I was never criticized." Lucy smiled grimly and leaned back in her chair. "I don't sew very well, and I'm only a passable baker. In fact, I wish I could just deal cards. I'm good at that. I learned from my husband." Her shrug was eloquent. "I just don't know how I'd go about getting such a job."

"Women dealers were fairly common during the rush, in the gambling halls I mean." After a moment of silence, Helene put down her cup and sat forward. "You know what we should do? We should go ask one of the spiritual mediums over on south 'B' Street. Some of them are uncanny good."

Two hours later Lucy and Helene left a plain, respectable house on south "B" Street, both of them hungry and looking forward to lunch. Lucy had been hesitant to go with Helene to see such a person, not just because she didn't believe anyone could read the future, but because of the expense. However, what the medium had said had been encouraging and kind, even if bland and what might be applied to anyone. Lucy therefore chalked up the experience as just a fun but meaningless outing.

This form of entertainment, as Lucy thought of it, was not unknown to her. Many people in Virginia City, both men and women, sought out advice and comfort from such diviners. Although the majority of the practitioners were women, a few were men, usually of some swarthy appearance. In fact, such diviners had been part of most towns since the beginning of what was called the Spiritualist Movement, started in New York in the 1840's.

"I think we should go see my friend Minnie Hoffman now," Helene announced. "We're already near her house south of the Colombo Restaurant. We can have lunch there afterwards. She uses cards mostly. Oh, and she has a German accent. But she's still easy to understand."

Lucy's murmured, "Um, well...", seemed to spur Helene on. Lucy was tallying up the cost of this little adventure, along with lunch, and was finding it more than she wanted to spend.

Before she could find a tactful excuse to bow out, Helene said, "Of course, lunch and Minnie are my treat. No argument. Oh, there's also Madam Solama down the street from Minnie. She has a room at Mrs. Beebee's place at #24. She advertises as a Moorish Spiritual Medium, whatever that means. There seems to be some mystery attached to her."

"I find anyone with the name Minnie to be reassuring."

"Then let us be off to her house."

They had taken the walk up to "B" Street slowly, stopping several times to catch their breath. Lucy didn't want to go down the hill to a restaurant, just to climb back up again, so she readily accepted visiting Minnie right then. Just because women were adapted to the town's altitude, and the common effort of walking its stair-stepped streets, it did not mean that it was easy. Especially considering the layers of heavy clothing they wore, along with a restrictive corset.

Sitting with a small table of some dark wood between herself and the medium, Lucy looked closely at Minnie Hoffman. She was a woman in her mid-50's, her dark hair parted in the middle and pulled back into a bun. She had a round face with round eyes, and a mouth that would sometimes form a round moue of surprise when a card was turned over that she found unexpected. If Lucy had passed her on the street, she would have considered this modestly dressed woman as someone's maiden aunt.

"Ah!" Mrs. Hoffman glanced at Lucy's left hand and exclaimed, "I see that you are no longer married."

"I'm a widow." Lucy's voice was calm, having trained herself to make this statement without showing the jolt of emotion she always felt when saying it.

"Well, yes, I suppose so. But... Well, never mind that now." She removed a brightly colored taro card from the top of a deck to reveal another. "You have a child. A boy?"

Thinking that accuracy wasn't much of an issue with a 50/50 choice such as that, Lucy merely nodded.

Minnie turned over another card and then laughed. "He'll marry well. But she'll be a challenge to him and cause him consternation often, at least in the first few years of their marriage."

Lucy didn't know what to say to that, so she remained silent. But Helene couldn't withhold her impatience. "Tell Lucy about her future!"

Minnie frowned at her friend before turning to Lucy, asking her to shuffle the cards. Seeing the facility with which she did that, Minnie chuckled. "You should be dealing in one of the better gambling halls." She took the pack of cards from Lucy, and upon touching her hand, looked at her with an intentness that Lucy found uncomfortable. "Ah, yes. You don't have to worry about women judging you if you do that. They won't know unless you tell them."

"Well, the men I'd be gambling with would undoubtedly tell their wives."

Minnie smiled. "Don't be too sure about that. We all like our little secrets." Lucy and Helene exchanged glances, and then refocused on Mrs. Hoffman as she laid out the cards in two rows. Instead of turning them over one at a time, as she had been doing, she turned them all over. For several minutes, Minnie scanned them thoughtfully. Finally, she nodded slowly, as though having received some kind of reassurance of an earlier impression. "You, my dear, must take the long view. You will be happy again, beyond your imagination now. You will eventually have your wildest desires fulfilled."

Lucy's laugh could only be described as derisive. "The only way that could happen would be if my husband came back from the dead."

The medium was in the process of gathering the cards when she suddenly sat back and stared at them, frowning at one that had flipped over when caught by her sleeve. "There are ways that can happen."

Lucy, thinking the woman meant talking to the "spirit realm", prepared herself for a sales pitch for expensive hours with Minnie claiming to be in a trance talking to spirit guides. But nothing of the sort was offered, and in fact, Minnie seemed in a hurry to end the session. "I can tell you're hungry and wanting your luncheon."

"Did you divine that?" Helene asked eagerly.

"No. I heard your stomach rumble."

Amid shared laughter, Minnie managed to hustle Lucy and Helene through her front door. As soon as they were seated at the restaurant, Helene said, "I wish I knew how to read cards."

"So you could open your own business?"

"No. So I would know what she saw in that card that flipped over. It seems that whatever it was, it disturbed her."

"I thought so, too." But while Helene simply shrugged and buttered a roll, Lucy felt an uneasiness coupled with an impatience for whatever was going to happen. But Minnie Hoffman had indicated a need for patience. Lucy, only half believing what she had been told, resigned herself to wait for her future happiness "beyond imagination now".

CHAPTER 10

1876 - 1877

Once home from her psychic adventure and resting in one of the two over-stuffed chairs in front of the fireplace, Lucy's thoughts drifted to Dolly. It certainly wasn't an unusual thing for her to do, but she felt the pang of separation most severely when something out of the ordinary happened. Sharing it with Dolly would have made it a richer experience, something to be recalled in later years and enjoyed all over again. This brought to mind an unexpected letter received back in the summer of 1874. It had been one of the few letters from Dolly that she had immediately destroyed after reading. When she had first read it, Lucy had been grateful for the solitude of the house and that Roger had been somewhere else. He hated to see her distressed. She could still recall it almost word for word.

__July, 1874, Carson City__: As you can see, we have not yet moved on. Things seemed to have settled down into a nice routine for us and so we stayed. But now everything has changed, triggered by the very thing Robert has dreaded, although he was unaware of my presence.

I was coming back from the market when I saw Robert crossing Fourth Street ahead of me. A man unknown to me stepped off the sidewalk into the street and called to Robert.

"I know you," the man called out. "I saw you working the other side of the mountain. You think you're so damn fast, but I'm faster."

"I don't know who you think I am, but I'm just a blacksmith and handyman. And I carry no gun."

"You're handy alright. You're handy with a gun."

Robert took off his jacket, dropped it on the ground and turned all the way around so the man could clearly see that he was not carrying a gun on his body. Robert then picked up his jacket and prepared to continue on his way. The man would have none of it.

"Stop right there!" He pulled a gun from the back of his waist and walked slowly toward Robert, who now stood perfectly still. The man held out the butt of the gun so that Robert was forced to take hold of it. The length of it lay across both of his hands as he took the measure of its weight, while the sun glinted off its silver body, as though proclaiming its power. I clamped a hand over my mouth so as not to cry out. With a slow shake of his head, Robert hung his arm straight down, the gun pointing at the ground. It was obvious to everyone gathering on the sidewalk that Robert was not eager for what was to follow. In fact, I don't know when I've ever seen a man look so sad.

The challenger saw this too, and hesitated for a second, giving me a flash of hope. But he only stepped back further, his gun hand also hanging down while he carefully watched Robert. The two men stood facing one another, silent and seemingly relaxed as their eyes locked on their opponent. Then, at a slight tightening of the stranger's shoulder and neck muscles as his arm came up, Robert crouched down at the same time. There was a report from both guns, one slightly ahead of the other. All activity on the street became a frozen moment in time. But my eyes were on the stranger who sprawled in the dirt, bleeding and still. Robert straightened up and turned away, looking as though he wanted to throw up. Men ran up and carried the stranger to the doctor's office, but he was dead by the time they got him there.

Robert meanwhile had dropped the gun and it lay in the dirt, repulsed by the last to have touched it; and who never wanted to see it again. A man nearby picked it up and followed Robert as he headed to the sheriff's office. Several men slapped him on the back and offered to buy him drinks. Laughing, they said things like, "We didn't know you bent that way," and "We'll have to be careful not to rile you in the future." Robert said nothing while shaking them off.

I hurried home and poured myself a stiff drink, wondering if I would soon be bailing my husband out of jail, or just able to visit him while he was held for trial. However, the sheriff assured Robert he wouldn't be arrested, as he had seen what had happened. It was declared to be obvious self-defense.

Once home, Robert sat on the sofa looking out at the street, brooding and miserable. I approached hesitantly, but sat next to him and reached out to lay my hand on his as it rested on his knee.

"*I saw what happened.*" *He flinched as though I had caused him physical pain. He started to pull his hand away, but I held it fast, making sure he knew that we were in this together.*

"*I never wanted this,*" *he whispered, the words catching in his throat.* "*No one even knows who he is.*"

"*You had no choice. Anyone could tell he wasn't the type to die in bed.*"

"*One of the men who wanted to buy me a drink afterwards said I had style. That means he recognized that I've been a gunman. He'll put that around, and it'll carry expectations.*"

"*Well, so what? You don't have to explain yourself to anyone.*"

"*But I do!*" *It was a cry of anguish, not a brag.* "*I need to get it around that it was just a lucky draw. I need to get everyone to forget today. Otherwise, our life won't ever be the same.*"

I hated to admit it, but we both needed to face the reality of the situation. "*You know men won't forget it.*"

Robert slowly nodded his head. "*You're right, of course. I know more than most that you can't escape your destiny when you've lived by the gun. Even if it was a long time ago.*" *His fatalistic tone frightened me.* "*I'd begun to think that it had all happened to someone else. Because, to me, I was someone else back then.*"

"*Come eat some dinner. It's over and done with.*"

"*It's only over for now. Some new guy will show up and try the same thing, and it'll be him or me. It's just the way it is.*"

August 14: *I held back this letter, unsure whether or not I would send it to you. Now I can add to it. Robert was right. A man did show up, and one of them did end up in the dust of the street. And again, it was the other man. But in a way, it was also Robert. The spirit that was my husband has gone out of him. He is sullen and brooding, and works very little. I have had to take in sewing and the washing of light women's things so that we don't have to touch our savings. Jane has moved back in with us and helps out, too. I will write more when I can.*

The letter had been unsigned and crammed into an envelope, with the address barely legible. After that, it had been a bad time for Dolly and even Jane, because Robert suddenly disappeared. It got around Carson

City quickly that he had deserted his wife, with her now having to take in sewing in order to make ends meet. Jane was helping by tutoring students in their small rented house.

At the time that Dolly had sent Lucy that letter, there was in the town with Dolly and Jane a woman by the name of Hermoine, who had a close friend, Elsbeth. Hermoine was considered by *women in the know* as the dominant cat, and the mousey Elsbeth her tame plaything. It didn't help that Hermoine was a tall, robust woman who wore large bonnets in the hopeless assumption that it visually reduced her size, while Elsbeth was a diminutive woman whose entire wardrobe was in various shades of brown.

Hermoine looked at her friend and smiled. No one had the courage to tell her that her smiles were frighteningly similar to a mountain lion barring its teeth. But they also never told Elsbeth that she always involuntarily flinched when Hermoine smiled at her in this way. Or that this reaction made Hermoine's smile broaden. There was little gossip worth the name that these two women didn't cheerfully repeat. Dolly was very well aware of this. Nevertheless, she unburdened herself to Hermoine one day after accepting an invitation to lunch.

The day after Dolly submitted herself to this inquisitional repast, Hermoine sat on her front porch and rocked contentedly next to Elsbeth. She leaned a little closer to her cohort, causing Elsbeth to draw back as far as the chair would allow. "It must be true," Hermoine purred with satisfaction. "No woman in her right mind would say her husband deserted her if it wasn't true."

"The shame of it!" Elsbeth flung her hand to her throat in feigned shock. "She must be a great friend of yours, or she wouldn't have told you."

"Oh, yes." Hermoine sat up straight and arranged her shawl in what she assumed was an elegant drape around her broad shoulders. "I attract confidences. Women know they can trust me."

Elsbeth said nothing in response to that, keeping a silence that was yet profound in all it conveyed.

"Of course," Hermoine continued, "she was loath to say it, but her need to talk was great. She hinted that she was thinking of returning to Placerville, or maybe a town not far from there. And the poor thing being saddled with Mrs. Leon as she is, too. Some kind of relation, I believe. But Jane is, after all, a woman with a sad tale. Her fiancé killed the way he was, I mean." She shook her head, a half-smile flitting across her mouth.

"I think, my dear, that those two women are going to have a difficult time of it in this town now. I mean, in the society of good women."

"But they've done nothing wrong!" Elsbeth realized her words could be thought quarrelsome, and knew Hermoine wasn't going to like that. "Of course, such associations can't be comfortable for them."

"And we all know that where there's smoke, there's fire." She turned to her friend and barred her teeth. "As the saying goes."

Elsbeth put forth her most ingratiating smile. "And old sayings usually have some truth in them, don't they?"

That made an obvious hit with Hermoine, and Elsbeth hoped that her near defense of Dolly and Jane, two kind women she admired, would be forgotten.

Two months after Dolly's last letter, Lucy had received another, this one undated and hurriedly written. It was worded in a coded way, as though from someone not associated with Dolly and Jane. It was signed by *Mrs. Bob Anthony*, that last name being the give-away as to its source, as that was Dolly's maiden name. This one, Lucy had immediately burned after reading.

My dearest friend: There are many reasons why we are moving on. My husband has already preceded us by several weeks. Oh, by the way, the law is still looking for the person who killed that man, George Mull. When it became known that my friend Jane Leon was his fiancé, and that he was a married man, she was questioned again by the sheriff. He accepted the word of Mrs. Robbins, the woman with whom Mrs. Leon lived, who swore they had been together the night of the killing. But many of Mr. Mull's acquaintances are being questioned yet again, and we can't be sure we won't be among them. Ridiculous, I know, to think that we could have had anything to do with it, but the innocent are often thought to be guilty. If not by the law, then by society.

So, we are leaving, which we had planned to do eventually anyway. The wagon is packed, the horses hitched up, and before it is light out, we will be on the road. Mrs. Bob Anthony

Lucy didn't for a moment believe that Robert had deserted Dolly, but she knew others would be only too eager to accept it as fact. Lucy often wondered if the trio had gone to Lone Pine, in the southern portion of the Owens River Valley, situated between the Sierra and the Inyo Mountains.

She remembered Dolly speaking about that area as though it had intrigued her, and it was very far removed from the Carson Valley. Lucy sometimes wondered if she was so closely aligned with Dolly in thought that she could sense this from her. Then she would laugh at such an idea and find something to keep her busy so she wouldn't feel the pain of loss.

Unfortunately, Lucy had not heard again from Dolly by the time she had left Placerville in the summer of '75. And there being no way that Dolly could know that her best friend had left Placerville, Dolly was lost to her forever, neither knowing where the other was to be found. This thought, as it always did when it occurred to her, brought a lump to Lucy's throat. She had suffered many losses in her life, but only the loss of Jim was harder to bear.

Placerville had been a welcoming town filled with friends and enjoyable activities. The area had also been beautiful, with its big shade trees, surrounding forests and rushing creeks. Lucy had written to a number of her old friends after leaving, hoping to maintain contact, but although she had heard back from a few of them, the correspondence had not continued. Still, she couldn't help wondering what was happening on the other side of the mountain in the various gold rush towns in which she had spent the whole of her life. But Virginia City was her home now; where at least most of the time she felt that she fit in.

Lucy worked at that, making sure she joined where joining was possible, where women with status gathered, where women married to men of influence might let slip information that would help her get ahead. It was, after all, what men did without question, and she was a woman on her own. She had Roger, of course, but she wanted to be independent of him, for his sake as well as hers. Just because she had decided to make her home in Virginia City, she knew it didn't mean that Roger would be content to stay there.

The excitement surrounding the buying and selling of stocks was not something to which Lucy was immune. She had purchased several feet in a mine just before rumors spread that the owners had hit a major new lead of rich ore. Her stock had soared, along with every other shareholder. But one morning while out shopping, she overheard a woman complaining that her husband's crew had that morning been left down in the mine where he worked, and the men weren't being let out. Lucy immediately sold her shares in that mine, interpreting this as a sign that the new lead had failed to meet expectations, and the owners didn't want word of this to leak out before they could sell their shares.

She was correct, and two days later with the bad news known, the men were released. It was not uncommon for mine owners to do this, sending down bedding along with good food, water, and quality whiskey. Of course, when this happened, it could mean an opposite interpretation; that a new lead had been discovered and the owners wanted time to buy stock before the news got out. It was only one of several stock manipulations foisted on the public over the years, many ending up in court and some not even discovered. But in every instance, while a few of the townspeople increased their wealth, most did not. Nevertheless, people couldn't help notice that the mine owners and their superintendents always came out unscathed.

Although Lucy had made a considerable sum in this instance, she didn't like the uncertainty and unfairness of playing such a game. Especially since it meant that so many people who purchased stock in good faith were being mercilessly manipulated. As it turned out, Roger had been one of them. He grudgingly admitted that he had lost close to a hundred dollars, but Lucy was pretty sure that it had been more than that. Still, if he wasn't willing to be forthcoming with her about it, she forced herself to keep quiet any time the subject of stock swindles came up.

What Minnie Hoffman had said about Lucy working in a saloon had stuck with her, and the more she thought about it, the more it appealed to her. At the end of one evening's supper, she put her coffee cup on its saucer with a hard clink. It signaled to Roger something coming from his mother that was of importance.

After explaining what she had in mind, Roger's quick response startled her. "Hell, yes! That's a great idea."

"You wouldn't mind having a mother who deals cards in a saloon?"

"It's not all that uncommon, Mom. Besides, you're very good at it. And you'll be able to accumulate the money you want to buy a home of your own."

"A home of *our* own, my dear."

He found it difficult to hold her gaze. "Not really. I have for all practical purposes moved out on my own already. I work until after midnight, so I often stay with friends I work with, or, well, other friends." He fought back a smile, realizing the interpretation his mother would put on his words. She was wrong to do so, but he didn't set her straight.

Lucy was determined to ignore the implication. "Well, of course you do. I know that." But she didn't look like she was all that comfortable with what she was thinking and brought them back to the matter at hand. "Then you're okay with the idea of my dealing cards?"

"Yes, Mother, I'm fine with it." He couldn't keep the laughter out of his voice, as it surprised him that she cared so much about his opinion. For the first time, he felt their conversation to be that of two adults instead of mother and son. It gave him a burst of unexpected satisfaction. So much so that he almost told her about his "other friends", business associates whom she would consider sketchy. But he thought better of it. Broad-minded his mother might be, but there was no point in pushing the boundaries of it. "Do you want me to ask around to see which saloon or gambling hall might be willing to hire you?"

"That would make it so much easier. But it should be a reputable place." She then looked at him with her own smile. "You might start getting into the habit of calling me Lucy. I shouldn't be seen as a woman with a grown son. Not if I'm going to try and pass as thirty instead of forty."

"Oh, you can do that easily." He sat back, crossed one leg over the other and grinned at her. "If they're willing to buy the idea of me as 21, they should be willing to buy that you're 30."

"I was only joking. I'd have had to be nine when you were born!"

"Oh. Right."

"No, maybe I'd just better tell them I'm 36. It's not unusual for girls to marry and give birth at 15."

Roger looked at her more closely, cocking his head to the side. "Maybe you could wear just a little make-up. Then maybe the idea of age won't come up at all." As he stood up, he added, "But not so much make-up that you look, well..."

"Like a soiled dove?"

"Well, yeah." And together they laughed, two conspirators aligned in a prank to be played on a society that was far from ready to understand the term "modern woman". Lucy was only too aware that she had to be careful in choosing those with whom she discussed ideas anywhere close to the volatile subject of suffrage.

Roger decided to start his quest at the best saloon he knew, and approached the proprietor of the Crystal Bar, known as a posh two-bit saloon anchoring a 3-story, brick building called the Douglass Building.

Surprising Roger, if not himself, the proprietor decided to take Roger at his word. But Roger was unaware that he had a well-known and respected reputation among saloon owners. So when he said that he knew a woman who was remarkably good at dealing cards, whether monte, twenty-one (also known as blackjack or *vingt et un*), or any version of poker, his opinion was received with respect.

When the proprietor met Lucy for the first time, he was convinced his faith in Roger had been justified. He was more than willing to give this charismatic woman a chance, and the subject of age didn't come up. What he saw was an attractive woman, a little taller than most, with a trim but voluptuous figure, and a faint scar on her cheek that lent her mystery. She was dressed in a simple, green satin dress with a tight bodice, and a deep neckline. Thinking most women's fashions silly and over-blown, he was glad to see she wore no obnoxious hoops or crinolines that made movement awkward. He didn't, however, object to fashion dictating that her dress was sleeveless, as was acceptable for a fancy dress. Men could see a bare leg at a hurdy-hurdy house, but a bare arm on a good woman was a rare treat outside of a formal ball.

On her first night at work, Lucy made it clear by her comportment and her vocabulary that she would not tolerate bad manners or coarse behavior. The men's reward was to receive flirtatious friendliness that pleased them greatly, along with the request to, "Just call me Lucy."

The proprietor of the bar liked that his lady dealer wore her hair caught up in feminine curls with only a small cluster of silk flowers on the side, and wore no jewelry other than a small gold nugget on a silver chain. He was a man who recognized class when he saw it, and he was always pleased to have it in his high-class, richly appointed establishment. When he saw how skilled his new employee was when she played a hand, rather than simply dealing, he was even happier. At the end of the first night, as he counted his portion of her winnings, he was ecstatic.

Lucy loved working there. It was one of the nicest of the saloons in town, what with the exclusive Washoe Club being upstairs by way of a curved staircase that curled upwards at the back of the room between the bar and the dining area. The saloon was twenty-five feet across the front, wider than the usual eighteen feet of a one-bit saloon. This allowed for four sit-down tables across from the bar and a faro set-up at the back. People entered onto a narrow-plank wooden floor that was kept swept and polished. But it was the ornate, crystal chandeliers hanging from the beaten tin ceiling that gave the place its name.

The addition of a cigar room to the right as one entered, hidden from view by a heavy drape, attracted men who could afford a dollar cigar and the best of imported champagne and whiskey. Of course, upstairs in the Washoe Club, members could get the same quality, but not everyone could afford the $150 membership fee. So townsmen walking past the building looked with envy at the narrow and steep stairs in a vestibule on "C" Street, or the shorter steps out back on "B" Street, and tried to imagine what it was like in the hallowed realms of "the Millionaire's Club".

Lucy's greatest surprise was the few men who, after seating themselves at her table, would take out a derringer and lay it on the table. Most men, if they carried a gun, kept it in their coat pocket. One could see the bulge without having its presence act as an unspoken insult. When she asked Roger about this, he told her the men who most often publicly let it be known that they were *carrying*, were attorneys. With hundreds of mining claims disputed in the courts each week, the representing attorneys attracted a considerable amount of resentment and anger.

During her first week of working evenings and leaving in the dark of night, whenever Lucy came in contact with a woman in town, she braced for a berating or a cold shoulder. Or at least a veiled comment about a woman's proper place in society. But nothing of the kind occurred. She soon discovered that the men with whom she gambled didn't tell their wives about Lucy, the new dealer in the Crystal Bar.

Before leaving her table, many times a local man would give her a nice gratuity along with a tip of their hat and a wink. And each time Lucy remembered what Minnie Hoffman, the medium so well-versed in human nature, had said about people liking their little secrets. Minnie Hoffman's accuracy in this regard allowed Lucy to harbor a tiny bit of hope that Minnie had also been correct about someday finding happiness again.

"Of course," she told herself, "I'm not particularly unhappy." Nevertheless, underlying even the most enjoyable of experiences was a sense of it not being quite what it should be. Festivals were not quite as festive as might be expected; sad occasions were missing the solace of reassurance; and funny moments that might later have become an *inside joke*, fell a little flat. Full contentment was always just out of reach. But then, she reasoned, maybe it was supposed to be that way in life. Otherwise, why would people strive for more and better, as those in Virginia City were certainly doing. But that thought was nothing more than a handy tonic to assuage her pining for Jim and Dolly, and she knew it.

With her new-found income, Lucy more readily accepted invitations from women friends when they wanted to gather over lunch. Helene had developed a wide range of friends, and she was eager that Lucy be included whenever possible. Only sometimes did Helene regret having done so, soon realizing that Lucy didn't mix well with women who thought "modern ideas" unladylike or even vulgar.

At one such luncheon as the holidays approached, Helene dabbed at her lips with her napkin before announcing, "I saw Elley Bowers in town yesterday." She thought this a safe topic, as Mrs. Bowers had become a popular seeress, traveling with her glass peep-stone to towns in the area. Since Sandy's death in '68 and her daughter's passing in '74, Eilley's fortunes had fallen away. She was left with doing whatever she could to survive, so she lodged with various women friends, of whom she had many. From their homes, she kept appointments with people who were eager to see their questions answered in the clear expanses of her stone.

Mrs. Stewart, whose late husband had been an attorney, arched a brow as she turned to Helene. "Did you have a session with her?" Lucy listened for mockery in her tone, but realized the woman was seriously curious.

"No, but a friend of mine did and I went with her. Mrs. Bowers was quite put out that it has gotten about that she has predicted the destruction of San Francisco's Grand Hotel in an earthquake. Of course, she's denied doing so. It's an absurd idea, after all."

Mrs. Stewart nodded, not without sympathy. "The Local Matters section of the Enterprise helped her by putting in a notice saying it wasn't true."

"I saw that," Lucy commented. "It also said that she didn't predict an earthquake within the next six months and has never even thought of such a thing."

Mrs. Flick was a barber's wife, and known for her caustic tongue. Her southern drawl did nothing to soften her sharp criticisms and subtle jibes. She joined the conversation by shaking her head and thus drawing attention to herself. "It's not enough that the poor woman has to contend with her fall from grace in society, but now she has to deny something so impossible."

Lucy turned back to Mrs. Stewart, a woman known for her large wardrobe. "I've been admiring your dress. The sewing is very fine. Hand stitched, I presume."

"Thank you, yes. I still prefer it. Machine stitching puckers so easily."

"May I ask who made it?"

"Mrs. George Gray."

"Oh, yes, Mary Gray. She does such nice work."

"Her being right in town makes it convenient, as she does mostly pinned-to-form fashioning, so I'm always assured of a proper fit."

Mrs. Flick had been listening intently. "Isn't Mrs. Gray a black woman?" Her drawl was more pronounced than before, as it always was when she was perturbed.

Lucy nodded. "Yes, she is. Does that matter?"

"Oh, not really. I guess I just don't think of such delicate work as coming from one of them."

Lucy's jaw tightened and Helene braced for an outburst from her friend. Seeing this, Lucy merely asked, "You're from Mississippi, aren't you?"

"Yes, I am. Does that matter?"

"Oh, not really." Lucy took a sip of tea, and to Helene's relief, changed the subject to the damage done from the latest zephyr winds. The others joined in the new topic so quickly that Mrs. Flick was unable to continue her veiled innuendos. Helene's humorous stories and contagious laughter soon had the group relaxed and enjoying themselves.

Roger had been correct about Lucy's ability to save money by dealing cards. After he pointed out to her the one "tell" she had, that of fingering her gold nugget pendant when she was pleased with a hand, she corrected that and soon was raking in even more money. Although she was soon able to cease her other money-making pursuits, she still occasionally assisted a foreign gent, as she called them.

One young man of nineteen, besides speaking broken English with a heavy Italian accent, was unable to read or write English. Before coming to the West from Italy, he had stayed in New York for several months. It was there that he had met a pretty "older lady" of twenty-four, who when she saw the amount of his savings, had shared a passionate night with him and then suggested they marry. However, as soon as she realized that his money was to be spent traveling to the West, her ardor had cooled considerably. She suggested that she join him after he was settled in the West and had made his fortune.

With Lucy's help, he had been sending his lady-love a letter every two weeks for the last several months, emphasizing that he was working in a mine and saving his money so he could send for her. So far, he had heard nothing in reply. Consequently, when one morning he knocked on Lucy's door with an excited burst of energy, his black hair in disarray and waving a letter in his hand, Lucy smiled with relief. Inviting him in and leading him to the kitchen table, Lucy sat across from him and eagerly read the short note to herself.

I want you to know that I have married your friend Delbert. He's here and you're not. And his mother is dead and yours is not.   Lucinda

Lucy's mind reeled at the directness, if not meanness, of the letter. With an effort, she smiled at the eagerly grinning young man across from her. "Well, um, she says that as fond of you as she is, the distance between you is a big problem for her. And she has therefore decided to consider the attentions of another man, and thinks you should find a better marriage partner than she could ever make you."

He sat in stunned silence for several minutes. "That all she say?"

"Um, well, she does say to give your mother her best regards."

"Yes? Mama hate her and she know it." His sigh was deep, but resigned. "I guess Mama right. I can do better." He rose up, tipped his hat to Lucy, and silently left the house.

Looking down again at the hastily scribbled note, Lucy found herself agreeing with his mother. She was glad he had not asked to take the note with him, possibly asking someone else to read it to him. In case he changed his mind and returned for it, she quickly tossed it into the stove's firebox.

Helene Morris was the only woman who knew of Lucy's new source of income, and she thought it hilarious. Helene loved knowing such an independent woman. Her husband was a member of the Washoe Club, and therefore frequented the Chrystal Bar, so Helene knew he must have seen Lucy. She wondered at the fact that he had never mentioned it, but when Lucy explained about the men's protective attitude toward her, Helene decided she would not let on to him that she knew. She told Lucy it was a "two-way secret", and was storing it away like a squirrel gathering nuts for future use. She didn't see Lucy roll her eyes after turning away.

Helene was happy to keep a protective watch on Lucy's lodgers when her friend was at work. She convinced herself that she needed to make sure

the men didn't invite unacceptable people to Lucy's house. She needn't
have worried. The two men staying there were usually too tired at night
for anything beyond a quick meal and a drink on the way home to a good
night's sleep. And many times, they skipped the drink. Eight hours down
in a mine, with only as much fresh air as could be pumped down to them
through air shafts and steam-generated blowers, took the starch out of the
heartiest of men. It didn't matter what time of the year it was; it was always
hot down at the lower levels.

Roger came home after a day away, but didn't bother to explain where
he had been. He had left his mother a note saying he would be back in a
day or two, but that was all. So now he waited for Lucy to ask where he
had been. Instead, she moved around the kitchen, humming to herself.

"You look like you've just been told all your stocks went up."

"Not quite so good as that, but I do have something exciting to tell
you."

Roger made himself comfortable at the small kitchen table after getting
himself a mug of coffee and pouring in some cream.

Lucy shook her head. "Have a little coffee with your cream, why don't
you?"

"Yeah, yeah. What's happened?"

"Well! Have you been in the new Washoe Club?"

"No. I'm not willing to fork over the fee."

She sat down and took a sip of her coffee. "Well, I have. I'm probably
one of the few good women who has been in it."

"I doubt they bring the other kind of woman there."

"Maybe, maybe not. But that isn't the point."

Roger laughed. "I'm just teasing you. How did you manage to get in
there?"

"I was invited to deal a big game in one of the two private card rooms."

"Who was playing?"

"I promised to keep it confidential, but there were four of them and
let's just say they're often referred to as the Big Four."

Roger's brows raced to meet his hairline and he stared at his mother,
trying hard not to feel a little envious.

"Oh, Roger, the place is so beautiful! And the money that has been
spent to furnish it is hard to imagine. The windows are French plate glass
and the carpets thick Axminster with bright patterns. Tables for newspapers

and magazines in the reading room are black walnut inlaid with laurel. And the walls are lined with shelves full of books in leather covers that I longed to see. The chairs and sofas are upholstered in rich fabrics, the walls are papered, red velvet drapes are at the windows, and huge gilt-framed mirrors are hung on some of the walls."

"Ah, yes, so the famous and infamous can view their magnificent selves."

"Don't be snarky, dear. When I got there, I was asked to sign this large registry book that was almost a foot tall. There were two columns. The man who had invited me signed in, and I signed across from him. He led me through a pair of folding doors, which are between some of the rooms so they can be made larger when needed. Like between the reading room and the billiard parlor. Which, by the way, has two exquisitely carved Strahle tables. Those two rooms then become 22 by 60 feet. Because those rooms are at the front, they're lighted during the day by natural light, but it was night soon after I got there, so gas-fed, polished-steel chandeliers gave us light. In the corner of the billiard room is a marble wash stand, and deep arm chairs sit along the wall for those watching the play. The wine room is connected through an open archway from the billiard parlor, which I thought very thoughtful. But there are heavy drapes they can pull across if they want."

"Who gave you this grand tour?"

"It doesn't matter. He plays at my table rather often."

"Oh, yeah?"

Lucy ignored his question and continued with her tale. "What they call the wine room has a huge sideboard holding all kinds of liquor and cigars. The porters were just clearing the lunch table of silver chafing dishes and platters. They asked me if I wanted a glass of something, but I declined. The card rooms are smaller than I thought they would be, but ours served its purpose. The table was black walnut, the chips ivory, and the card backs beautifully colored. On the way to it, we passed a room with a telegraph and operator, so the men can get stock reports day or night. There were several men standing around it while I was there."

"How will you ever be content to deal down below in the bar again?"

"Oh, you! It was just a bit of fun. But the players seemed to be satisfied with my dealing. It was a novelty for them to have a woman doing it, and after they realized I knew what I was doing and wasn't going to be gabby, they seemed quite content."

"Gabby?"

"Oh, yes, that. They thought I didn't hear one of them make a snide comment about women unable to resist talking and therefore not being conducive to playing cards."

"Did you set him straight?" Roger was wishing he had been present in that moment to hear his mother's response.

"I said nothing!" Her tone was one of exaggerated dignity, which told Roger she had wished to say plenty. "Two of the men told him to mind his manners, and in words I won't repeat. At the end of the game, I received a very handsome tip from each of them. Well, all but one, not to say his name. But I don't think it was *fair* of him." She winked at Roger.

He laughed at his mother's subtle hint, but didn't press her further. "I hear they've asked the artist C. B. McClellan to create a series of paintings for the club. Views of Virginia City and the scenery around us."

"Oh, yes. The papers talked about it. The paintings should be very valuable someday."

"As compared to just pricey now?"

"They won't be for sale. They're to be on display in the club." After a moment, Lucy shrugged. "I thought you'd enjoy hearing about the place."

Roger stood up. "I'm sorry if I sound a bit sour. I just think it's a lot of opulence that cost a lot of money, when there are so many here making use of the soup kitchen."

"I'm not unaware of that. It's why I contribute to the kitchen as much as I do. Kathryn gives our leftover fruits and vegetables to an Indian woman who comes to the back door every week, too. So I refuse to feel guilty because I was able to spend time in luxury for a few hours."

"I didn't mean to imply that you should." He kissed her on the cheek. "And who the hell am I to talk? I just spent forty dollars on new clothes."

"Besides, you never know if it might pay off sometime, knowing such important men."

After Roger had gone, Lucy wandered into the parlor and stared out the front window. But she was not seeing the "D" Street traffic, or the back of the buildings just above that fronted on "C" Street. She was picturing the men who had been at her table that day in the Millionaire's Club with stacks of gold double eagle coins sitting in front of them as they leaned back in their plush chairs, wearing beautifully tailored suits. She was remembering the smell of expensive cigars, and the clink of crystal decanters on crystal goblets as the club porters refilled glasses with imported bourbon. The only constant sounds were the muffled voices from nearby rooms filled with mine owners and their superintendents, stockbrokers, lawyers, bankers, judges, and owners of hotels.

There had been little talk between the men at her table while playing. Only phrases said in subdued voices, such as "I'll take one", "Oh, hell, give me three", "I'm out", or "I'll call." And, of course, there had been chuckles attending winning hands, and disgusted sighs upon losing hands folded.

She had started dealing at sundown, and had returned home at noon the next day. A break of half an hour had been announced at midnight, and another at six in the morning. Two shorter breaks had been called, much appreciated by Lucy's various aching parts. Mr. Mackay had brought her a plate of finger sandwiches during the midnight break, and Mr. O'Brien had refilled her water glass several times, always asking if she wanted something stronger. Oh, yes, it had been an experience she would never forget, and she couldn't help but wonder if it might be repeated. Who was the game's big winner? Considering the lengths to which the players went to keep the game private, the wins and losses of the evening's play must be left to history.

As Lucy's bank account grew, so did her plans. But the bonanza of 1873 was slowing down. The town was experiencing the closure of small mines, and less ore being taken from even the larger ones, not to mention stock swindles being uncovered. Consequently, men were being laid off both in the mines and even in some of the supporting businesses. Nevertheless, men still found the time and money to gamble. So, although Roger and Lucy's tips were less than they had been, the two were far from destitute. Lucy did, however, take on a few clients needing her reading and writing services. And Roger took a part-time job doing the books for one of the larger general merchandise stores.

While visiting the Female Employment Office, Lucy hired a young Irish girl to come in every morning. Kathryn fixed breakfast for everyone, cleaned the kitchen, made the beds, ran a feather duster over whatever showed dust, and before leaving for most of the afternoon, made sure there was sufficient wood cut to fuel that night's supper. She returned faithfully at five o'clock to feed Lucy and Roger before their stints at the saloons.

Lucy made lists for Kathryn, who thoroughly enjoyed shopping for the best bargains she could find. She made sure Lucy was aware of the prices in the stores, and reported with pride that she had found beans at ten cents a pound, seven cents a pound for onions, and five cents for potatoes and apples. She complained that she couldn't find a roll of butter that pleased her, even at $1 a pound, until she found a market that rose to her standards. And she showed her outrage at peaches for ten cents each, although Lucy assured her that they were worth it.

Kathryn took pride in keeping the lodgers' room clean, even if the word "pigsty" was sometimes muttered beneath her breath. But she always gave detailed attention to Lucy's room, even weekly turning the mattress while Lucy was at work. And, without being asked, Kathryn made sure lime and ashes were regularly tossed into the privy out back. When Lucy learned of this last, she increased Kathryn's weekly wages by $2.

Not long after hiring Kathryn, Lucy chose to make a modest investment in the Female Employment Office. Begun in 1866, Susan Carroll and Mary Conway had been needleworkers who had seen a need as more women sought "respectable employment". They advertised that they would find women "accommodation to families in the way of obtaining female help". With the assistance of these two women, townswomen soon discovered that they could do more than nurse or wait tables. Census manuscripts reflected women who worked as merchant, cook, bookkeeper, book folder, house painter, hairdresser, upholsterer, florist, and even a dairy operator. In Virginia City of the 1870's, diversity of women's work became as evident as diversity of nationality had been from the town's beginning. As long as they comported themselves in a reasonably lady-like manner, the newspapers reported on it with casual notice, and no one seemed to object.

Now, with so many husbands and fathers out of work, more women were seeking reputable employment and the agency was unusually busy. One night at the Crystal Bar, a man tipped Lucy a handsome amount after winning three large pots. She took that money, along with a little more, and invested it in the employment agency. In return, she was to receive a small percentage of their profits over the next year.

After that, when Lucy felt unexpectedly "flush", she made similar deals with other businesses that she knew were in a financial bind. One of these was a group of women who owned a mine at the north end of "B" Street. They were not the original owners, but were carrying on a tradition that had begun at that location in 1871. The Territorial Enterprise had commented on that original group. *"We do not see any reason why women should not engage in mining as well as men. If they can rock a cradle, they can run a car; if they can wash and scrub, they can pick and shovel. Although some gentlemen friends of the ladies are attempting to persuade them from continuing work, they are determined, and we are pleased to see it."* Even so, women in mines remained a rare event.

When the milliner for whom Lucy had worked lost business due to taking time off during an illness, Lucy loaned her the money to purchase new inventory, and for a very low interest rate. When one of the livery stables wanted to stock more hay than they had the previous winter in order to care better for the horses and mules they boarded, Lucy loaned them the money to purchase it.

The only thing she demanded from these businesses was that the public not be aware of her "small investments". To the businesses, however, her generosity was anything but small in importance, and they were determined that she would never rue the day that she had helped them. That Christmas she received a gift of a lovely new bonnet, the offer of a light rig any time she wanted to use one, and a small quilt accented by appliqued tea cups from the ladies at the Employment Office.

Helene was always eager to hear stories of Lucy's work. So over coffee one morning, Lucy recounted to her friend something that had occurred the previous evening at work. "The play was continuing toward the end of an exciting session between five men where I was dealing. Those men standing around watching had been making side bets, some of which I didn't understand, but one was simply who they thought would win the most hands during the next hour. When the watchers finally settled their intricate side bets, there was some grumbling, but mostly joking and laughter. I found it interesting that there was not one man who accused another of not understanding what had been negotiated. It was quite admirable."

Helene merely responded with a sharp "Huh!" When Lucy looked at her in surprise, she elaborated. "These are the same men who can't remember the three items their wives asked them to purchase at the market on their way home from work." When Lucy laughed, Helene joined in, and two women who often felt somewhat lonely, were a little more closely bonded in friendship.

The holiday season was a festive one with dances, parties and the store fronts along "C" Street decorated with trees brought in from Lake Tahoe. There was employment for over 2,000 miners, and the daily output of ore was close to 2,000 tons with the monetary value for the year near $50,000,000. This meant that the famous, incomparable Comstock Lode that had attracted thousands of people from all over the world, had in only 17 years produced over $300,000,000 worth of gold and silver. With this repeatedly pointed out in the newspapers, the subject of unemployment rates and the rise in store prices held less interest. People were determined to get on with life and enjoy their holiday celebrations.

The first half of January 1877 was so dry that sprinkling carts had to keep down the dust on the streets. Only when light snow fell from the thirteenth through the eighteenth were they of no further use. On the nineteenth, the snow came down hard all day, accumulating to two feet. This cut off the mail stage, and then more snow brought down telegraph lines and blocked the rail cars. This was followed by a day of smokey fog the Indians called "pogonip". After a few clear days that allowed for the clearing of snow off roofs, sidewalks, and rails, another heavy snow hit at the end of the month.

Snow built up through the canyons and at times was deep enough to stop work at the mines. Sledding down the canyon became an exciting pastime for those with more courage than sense. The newspapers reveled in the story of two young men who pulled their sled to the top of The Divide one night and slid their way down the two and a half miles to the Devil's Gate Toll House. With snow shoes on the feet of horses, sleighs were pulled through the almost deserted streets in the afternoons, sleigh bells giving a tuneful accompaniment. Young people found any excuse to enjoy being outdoors, especially when this was followed by hot cider parties, where dancing and frisky socializing could ensue. Fortunately, February spawned a few weeks of clear and pleasant weather.

The town might have been feeling the hot breath of borrasca down its collective neck, but those who had not left town before winter set in were convinced that the bottom of the stock decline had been reached and upward recovery would soon ensue.

In the center of town, work was continuing on the interior of the eagerly awaited International Hotel, and rumors of its magnificence stimulated everyone's imagination. There were also rumors of its growing indebtedness and the contractor unable to finish the project. The owners, Mr. Hanak and his partners, advanced a sum of money that allowed work to resume, and the town breathed a sigh of relief.

Anyone new to Virginia City that spring found it difficult to accept the idea of a slump. The tall steeple at St. Mary in the Mountains Catholic Church now reflected a glistening, galvanized iron siding that some proclaimed was a blessing from God. St. Paul's Episcopal Church, built in the Carpenter Gothic style, had opened for services that February amid celebrations and an exuberant choir. At the same time, parents all over town were making clothes for their school-age children so they would look fine as they entered the new Fourth Ward School. And up on "B" Street, the ornamental gables had just been placed on the front of the new Italianate style Courthouse.

Lucy came to the conclusion that the grocer she liked best was located on the edge of the Barbary Coast area at the southern end of "C" Street. It had not been considered a prime location for building the most frequented businesses, as that area was on the uphill side of Mt. Davidson's slope. Lucy was not unaware that the name *Barbary Coast* derived from the infamously violent and crime-ridden area of San Francisco, but she liked Mr. Werrin and his well-supplied market. Besides, if she purchased too much to carry, he would have it all delivered to her home.

After the great fire of '75, with so many of the brothels along the lower part of town having been burned, the unscathed Barbary Coast area had accepted their trade into its midst. By 1877, however, with the town rebuilt, many of the girls had left to return to "D" Street, where it was declared legal to do business.

Lucy wasn't the only woman in town who liked the grocer's vegetables, honey, and fair prices, but she was one of the few who would shop there by herself. However, she did make sure she didn't cross into the most disreputable portion, having heard the tales of violence there. The newspapers made sure of that. The market's close proximity to two saloons that acted as a brothel was unfortunate, but Lucy chose to ignore that.

She couldn't, however, ignore what had led up to a recent town gathering that had attracted people from as far away as Carson City. In 1875, one of the Barbary Coast establishments had been owned by Peter Larkin, with a neighboring saloon owned by a woman friend of his by the name of Nellie Sayers. Both known for their fiery tempers, they were for a long time often seen in one another's saloon, attending dances together and accepted as lovers.

In the summer of that year, it became obvious to all that something had happened to change the two saloon owners' loving attitudes. Neither missed an opportunity to speak ill of the other, or to complain about the customers that regularly visited the other's saloon. The animosity seething between them lingered unabated until Nellie took up with Daniel Corcoran. Soon after that, Peter Larkin hired a young prostitute recently arrived from San Francisco calling herself Susie Brown.

Helene explained to Lucy that when Larkin had quarreled with young Susie, she ran to Nellie for comfort and was hired on by her as a serving wench. Her eyes alight with excitement, Helene continued the story. "One morning in August of '75, an angry Larkin approached Nellie's place, but was chased away by Nellie's boyfriend, Corcoran, now the place's bouncer. Within minutes of that confrontation, the report of a gun could be heard, and Corcoran was found with a fatal wound in his stomach. The police arrested Larkin, and a jury finally declared him guilty of murder. He appealed that, I believe, dragging things out."

Lucy had been present for his well-attended hanging on January 19. The hanging had been treated as a major event by people as far away as Carson City and Dayton. Women and children had arrived in a festive mood carrying picnic baskets and blankets. The hotels, lodging houses and homes of friends had been full for several days with the added visitation, and the restaurants had long lines of those waiting to be seated, even with the addition of tables. The clean-up afterwards had given the bottle collectors and rag pickers a considerable boost in their income. Now, each time Lucy approached the grocer, she tried unsuccessfully to put all of that out of her mind.

With the melting of snow, it became possible for the Virginia & Truckee Railroad cars to get through to deliver loads of carpets, furniture, and other goods for the completion of the International Hotel. It was revealed that the cost of all this was around $40,000. Considering the expense and the tight completion schedule, Mr. Hanak decided that he could trust no one better than himself, so he took charge of the International's management.

On Saturday, March 31, 1877, the nation's flag was run up the tall pole on the roof of the impressive hotel and the doors opened to admit a choice guest list of invitees. Gas-fed crystal chandeliers and wall sconces, along with tall white candles in silver candelabras, lit every public space of the hotel. The light shone out onto the surrounding streets, and even those who were of too low a status to attend the opening, found comfort in such an example of the town's prosperity and evident stability.

Mirrors that reached to the ceiling reflected the light onto the mahogany and velvet furniture where sat such notables as wealthy mine owner James Fair and his long-suffering wife Theresa (they would divorce in 1883), attorney Billy Wood, Judge Mesick, Bank of California titan William Sharon, and Rollin M. Daggett, founder of San Francisco's Golden Era publication. Attorney William Woodburn was there, too, although he drew a few surprised glances. It was said he had affiliations with the Irish group called Fenians. Many of the women gave the handsome Robert Graves, superintendent of the Empire Mine, a second look, but flirting was rampant throughout. And the next day forgotten. Nevertheless, both newspapers and ladies' groups rejoiced at new fuel for their reportage.

The main floor was reached by a flight of broad stairs leading up from the "C" Street entrance. Standing in the lobby located in the center of the building, those arriving could look up through a huge skylight and see that daylight was beginning to wane. Some of the ladies longed to cross over to the elevator and ride it up and back down, but dared not show interest in such a thing. It might show them as less sophisticated than they wished to appear.

Lucy, dressed in a gown of beige satin, was the guest of a handsome gentleman who was at the time a top-ranking member of the Washoe Club. Since it was situated on the floor above the Crystal Bar, the members were frequent participants at Lucy's table. But only Daniel (last name tactfully withheld) had summoned the courage to invite the lovely and popular lady dealer to the grand opening of the hotel.

They reached the dining room by a short flight of steps, the room opening up under a 20-foot ceiling that covered an area 42 by 42 feet. It was sparkling with dozens of candelabras, twinkling crystal glasses, and silver serving pieces on long buffet tables under the front windows. Near the entrance was a sideboard that was larger than any Lucy had ever seen, now covered in silver platters full of canapes and finger sandwiches. Waiters roamed among the guests with trays of glasses filled with champagne, accepted by those milling around trying to see and be seen.

Lucy was not least among those women preening and posing, taking advantage of the opportunity to show off the rich fabric and style of their dresses, their carefully coiffed hair, and their jewelry. Since women wore only simple brooches during the day and then only at the throat, evening attire gave them the opportunity to display all the best of what they owned. Bracelets, necklaces, pendant earrings, even a tiara, could be seen glittering beneath the hotel's artificial lights. The women stood out as colorful butterflies perched on the arms of men in black evening attire, or at least a carefully pressed, dark suit. Lucy found it an easy, and humorous, matter to identify those men who were proud of this rare opportunity for their woman to shine, and those men who found it disconcerting.

Feeling the pinch of new shoes, Lucy looked longingly at the tables covered in spotless white cloths, flowers artfully arranged in the center of each. Instead, she spent several minutes talking to Mrs. Fair, a kind and gracious woman who worked generously to help those less fortunate. Which was unlike her husband, who had a reputation as a mean-spirited and self-serving mine owner, unless you were one of the chosen few who managed his affairs. His nickname uttered behind his back was *Slippery Jim*. On the other hand, he paid closer attention to safety issues in his mines than some owners, and the men respected that.

Lucy wandered between small groups of acquaintances while her companion greeted men who were eager for his patronage in their business schemes. He turned no one away, always eager for whatever turn of advantage he might gain.

Roger was there as well, with a lady on his arm that Lucy had not met. She didn't miss the woman's artful application of makeup, the gown's neckline lower than any other in the room, or that she was obviously a few years older than Roger. That son, however, completely ignored his mother, passing her with a nod and a curt, "Lucy."

Lucy in return simply nodded and turned back to her companion. Since he was talking to two men she didn't know, and whom Daniel didn't seem disposed to introduce to her, she moved over to the banquet table. As she filled her plate with delicious delicacies prepared by the hotel's esteemed French chef, she could overhear a trio of men nearby.

A tall, lean man with a neatly cropped beard was speaking. "My wife seems to think I should appreciate her more. I like a clean house like any man, but I'll be damned if I'll apologize because I forgot to wipe my feet before coming into my own house."

One of the two men, near the end of his thirties and sporting a luxurious mustache, nodded his head. "My wife sews for several ladies when they need to get their brats fitted out for school. She says it's hard work, and sometimes she declares she's too tired to make my supper. I then have to eat a sandwich or fixed myself a couple of eggs. I didn't bargain for that when I got married."

The third man, who had thus far remained silent, was clean-shaven and younger than the others. He now spoke somewhat hesitantly. "I dare say women do work hard to bring in extra money. My wife..."

"Oh, sure," the lean man who had started the discussion cut in, "but what a man does lasts. If I toss a barrel aside, the wood may rot away, but the iron stave hammered into shape by a man will last for decades. A dress sewn together by some woman will fall apart within a year. The candles she dips will burn up or even melt if not kept properly. And women's fancy bonnets come apart if not mended frequently."

The young man seemed confused. "Are you saying that what men create is of more importance because of its permanence?"

"Well, don't you think the gold and silver coins made from the mines here will last longer than anything you can name that a woman puts her hand to?"

"I guess so." However, the young man wasn't giving up so easily. "Might not a woman claim that her raising children, who will become the next generation, is a contribution to the future? Is that not a form of permanency?"

Neither of the other men offered a rebuttal to that until the lean man rocked back on his heels and declared, "The future. Oh, yes. But I'm talking about now and today."

The young man frowned, choosing not to comment on the fact that he thought the subject was about that which lasted into the future. Instead, he said, "We all know that the ore will someday be gone. But I guess the mines themselves might last far into the future, even a hundred years from now."

The older man, whose wife sewed clothes for the children of the future, stroked the draped length of his mustache as he nodded. "I hadn't thought of that, but I guess you're right. It'd be almost impossible to fill in the hundreds of miles of tunnels and shafts under the town."

Having eaten all that her tight corset would allow, Lucy put her empty plate onto the table off to the side provided for this purpose. She had decided to leave, having lost patience with being ignored so long by Daniel. She was also tired of the evening-long effort to hold back much of what she had wanted to say during various conversations. Consequently, the three men were surprised at her sudden appearance in their midst.

"Excuse me, gentlemen. I couldn't help overhearing you discussing things that don't last. One thing that doesn't last for long is a woman's patience. Especially with a husband who lingers in the saloons until after midnight, and comes home smelling of beer." Looking at the first man to have spoken, she added, "Or of some other woman's perfume."

Not waiting for a comment, she turned away from them and sailed from the room in a manner she hoped displayed dignified poise. Roger had been standing nearby, and his lady friend wondered why he was suddenly holding back laughter. The men of the conversation were blinking in surprise while trying to formulate a clever rejoinder to this insolent woman who was familiar, although they couldn't quite place her. In any case, she was already leaving the cloak room with a heavy cape draped over her shoulders.

"Give it up, Bob," the young man chuckled. "You have to admit she's right."

The lean man, now known as Bob, shrugged nonchalantly, although his high color showed his embarrassment at having been caught out. "Yes, well, I was about to head home anyway."

The woman with Roger slipped her arm through his and lowered her voice. "I've had enough of all this. Let's go back to my room. My landlady is gone for the night."

Having been out with Susan several times, but not in any way on an intimate basis, he was more than willing to give in to what she was suggesting. She was a partner for hire at a dance house, sometimes referred to as a hurdy-gurdy dance hall. The girls were paid to dance with men, sit and talk to them over watered-down drinks, and sometimes present small staged entertainments. But that was all. If the girls did more than that, it was on their own time. Susan had a good reputation, at least as far as Roger knew, and he found it easy to talk to her. She had worked on the other side of the mountain and was familiar with Placerville, which for him was an added bonus.

He had enjoyed a fumbling encounter with sex when he was sixteen, and had since then several times been allowed to feel a soft thigh beneath a skirt. He was thus only too aware of his lack of experience. He knew Lucy assumed he was more practiced, and he let her think so because the whole subject was uncomfortable for him.

Susan's room was on Howard Street above the town, and although the distant thud of the stamps could be heard, the noise from the center of town was absent. With only two candles alight on the dresser, the room felt cozy and inviting, and Roger felt very much at home. The sheets were cool on his skin, his head still a little muddled from so much champagne, and Susan was a tantalizing combination of perfume and warm skin. After sharing a series of progressively passionate kisses, she lay back on the pillows so that the silk of her nightgown slipped off her shoulders.

Roger touched the smoothness of her throat with wonder, acutely aware that he had never felt even velvet as supple. He nuzzled her neck and smelled the sweetness of rosewater, mixed with what was pure Susan. Hands that had hundreds of times held cards with tender reverence, now felt the sharpness of her collarbone and the thinness of her sheer gown. He drew this down over her body, revealing breasts that perfectly fit his cupped hands. Tossing the gown onto the floor, his heart raced as he slowly explored the curves of her body, gasping as she found that part of his that was most ready for what was to follow. An hour later, his desires and his energy gloriously spent, he felt himself drift into sleep with the scent of her pressed against his side.

When Roger awoke just before dawn, Susan was gone. He immediately looked for his money clip and found it just where he had left it. Feeling ashamed of himself for having doubted her, he dressed and walked through the town just as it was coming to life. He could hear lively music coming from the dance hall, and realized that Susan was at work, with other men holding her close. He comforted himself by the thought that they didn't know her as he did. Then, as he proceeded down the sidewalk, he remembered her having said to him, albeit playfully, "You're a natural." And Roger began to doubt that Susan was as innocent as her reputation seemed to imply, although he wasn't sure he really cared. He wasn't looking for the permanency of commitment, and he conveniently assumed Susan felt the same.

CHAPTER II

1877 - 1878

With Kathryn out shopping, Lucy was picking up around the house after seeing her lodgers leave for work, but she was thinking about the grand opening party the night before. So much wonderful food, so many beautifully dressed ladies, and such a lot of champagne flowing. Of that last she was feeling the effects, but not so much that she wasn't determined to get on with the day. Rachel Beck and Mary Mathews were collecting for the poor and she had told them she would canvass her neighborhood for donations. Mrs. Beck's husband owned a general merchandise store, and Mrs. Mathews was a public-spirited widow from the East with a somewhat sickly young son.

A soft, tentative knock on the front door interrupted her thoughts. She opened it to find Daniel standing there, hat in hand.

"I tend to forget my manners when I over-indulge in drink. I should have been available to see you home. I did look for you, but someone said you'd already gone."

"Come in. I have coffee on the stove still hot." She led the way to the kitchen and put a cup of the black liquid on the small kitchen table, motioning for him to sit. "Help yourself to the cream in the pitcher, and the sugar." As she seated herself across from him, she smiled warmly. "Thank you for the courtesy of an apology. But I was quite capable of seeing myself home only a few blocks. Thankfully, all downhill." They shared a chuckle while nodding, more than once having thought of mountain goats as they climbed from one street to another. "It was a lovely party, and I'm grateful for your invitation."

"I would like to take you to dinner tomorrow night, if you're free."

"I don't think so, Daniel. But again, thank you for the invite."

He looked disgruntled, and it was clear that he wanted to say something. He took a big swallow of coffee. "Should I consider not playing at your table in the future?"

Lucy laughed. "Of course you should, if you want to. I consider you one of the many dear friends I have here."

Daniel relaxed then, but looked at her quite seriously. "I have the best of intentions, you know. You could marry worse than me. I make a good living, I've invested well, and you'd have a solid place in society."

"You are indeed a very good catch, but I'm just not interested in remarrying, something you've indicated you want. Why should I waste your time and money on me if nothing will come of it for you? It wouldn't be fair play of me. I respect you too much to do that."

Mollified by her explanation, he still couldn't hide his disapproval. It was beyond his grasp to understand why a respectable widow of her age would not be looking to remarry. "I think you're very foolish, but I accept that you mean what you say." He stood up and retrieved his hat from the coat rack by the door. "Good day, my dear."

Watching him walking down the path from her door to the street, Lucy could no longer hold back a mumbled response. "Patronizing ass!"

Daniel wasn't the only man to think Lucy a candidate for romance and possible marriage, if they could just talk her into it. She did enjoy several men's company for a short while, but always made it clear that such enjoyment would only continue if they were content with their relationship being one of friendship. Then there were those men who were already married, and were only interested in a clandestine romance. Those received an immediate refusal, and a lecture on the meaning of commitment.

After it got around that Lucy Murphy wasn't looking for a husband, she still would occasionally accept an invitation from a single man whom she considered intelligent and interesting. It was usually for dinner, but several times it was to one of the many town dances where she enjoyed taking a few turns around the floor. Lucy was a good dancer, and enjoyed a partner who didn't trod on her toes.

Unfortunately, more often than not, after what the man considered an appropriate length of time, he would begin to suggest a more permanent or at least exclusive relationship. Whether it was to enter into marriage or to live together, which was more common in mining towns than later generations might think, Lucy would inform the eager suiter that she was not interested. Even the idea of exclusive dating was not something to which she would agree. She resigned herself to the fact that she would seldom see these men again in a social capacity.

One such spurned gentleman stood at a popular two-bit saloon one evening, well-saturated in whiskey and complaining of "these damn independent women". After several more drinks, he went so far as to declare Lucy Murphy a "cock tease". He promptly received a punch on the nose from one of Lucy's admirers, while another held him up to receive a hit to the chin. While holding a bar towel to his bleeding nose, the foul-mouthed man was told by the bartender never to return.

Eventually, Lucy was simply considered a nice widow lady who preferred to not marry again, but who was an enjoyable dinner companion or dancing partner. As long as nothing more was expected. Opinion was divided between those who wondered if her deceased husband had been so wonderful, or so horrible, as to constitute such a stand to not remarry.

After the arrest of saloonkeeper Peter Larken in 1875 for murder, and even after his hanging the previous January, Nellie Sayers had continued her activities as a supplier of prostitutes. However, in the summer of 1877, the police received a number of complaints from the public reminding them that a school was now close to the Barbary Coast area. And some of those children had to pass through that area in order to get to the school. After a couple of raids on her place, Nellie was arrested for running "a disorderly house", the accepted term in polite company for a brothel.

The newspapers gleefully declared that her arrest meant the area was being cleaned up. Nevertheless, when released on bond, Nellie changed nothing about her behavior or her place of business. She had been able to buy her way out of every disruption to her business for years, and saw no reason why that should change. With the public's focus on them, however, the police decided they could no longer look the other way. Nor did they want to when they discovered that Nellie had pimped out a girl of thirteen who had been drugged and raped.

Immediately, Nellie and her type were eliminated from the area. Soon, new buildings and store fronts were under construction, a sure sign to many that capitalism had usurped debauchery, although some would debate that conclusion. In due course, a stockbroker opened an office fronting on "C" Street, along with a milliner and a fancy-goods store. A furniture store ended up in the building previously occupied by Nellie's place. And business increased sharply at Lucy's favorite grocery store.

Happy to be inside out of the summer heat, Roger reached for another biscuit and hungrily sopped up the last bit of his mother's stew. It was one of his favorite meals, and Lucy made it only when the vegetables available in the markets were fresh. Fully sated, he sat back and sipped the coffee Lucy had poured into his cup. He resisted adding cream, having recently decided to start drinking it black like the older men did.

Lucy said nothing about this, focusing instead on the bulge in the pocket of her son's coat. "I wish you didn't carry a gun."

"Given the manner of my employment, and the fact that many men have one somewhere on them, I really have no choice."

"Oh, I know, but..."

"Are you saying that your gun isn't near you when you're dealing?"

"Well, yes. It's in my handbag down at my feet or in the hidden pocket of my skirt."

"Don't most women's skirts have hidden pockets on the side?"

"Yes."

"Okay, so don't worry about it. It'll be okay."

"I love the way men so often say something will be okay, when they really have no idea if that's true."

Roger smirked at his mother. "I think it's because we just don't want to fuss over some things."

"It's called mental laziness. Just remember that saying that something will be okay, won't make it be okay."

He had noticed when he arrived that she was wearing what he called her "I-want-to-say-something" look. He decided this would be a good side-track to the current uncomfortable topic. "So, Mom, tell me what's really on your mind."

She wasted no more time with preambles. "I joined a...club, this afternoon."

"Why did you hesitate just now? Is it a club or not?"

"It's really just a group of women who have gathered together to promote a certain agenda."

"That being?"

"It's called The Wife-Beater's Pillory Club. We're trying to call attention to how often it comes to light that some woman has been beaten by her husband. Sometimes it's by a brother or father. The Chronicle is running an article about it for us in tomorrow's paper."

And indeed, the next day the Virginia Chronicle ran the following article:

THE WIFE BEATER'S PILLORY

The women-beater's post, which now stands grim and inexorable at the corner of the county jail, is an object of interest to scores who visit it daily. It is about 8" sq., made of pine, with two round pegs, about an inch in diameter, run through it at a point about 5' from the ground. The arms of the victim will be run through these pegs and tied behind. No one passes the post without stopping to inspect and make some remarks. A woman who passed it yesterday passed by it for a moment and ejaculated, "Thank God!" The post has several inscriptions scribbled upon it in pencil, some of which read as follows: Stewart's bill; The Widder; a household treasure; no family should be without it.

Lucy and her fellow club members didn't for a moment think this would completely rid society of those men who took their frustrations out on women in violent ways, but it certainly got people talking about the issue. And such debate was for them a first step in warning men that their actions had at least some degree of consequence; if not from the law, then at least from society, which could sometimes be more severe in its judgements.

A week later Lucy seated herself at the beginning of what the ladies called a club meeting. This day, it was more in line with a round-table visit over lunch, since they spent only a few minutes discussing the pillory. Lucy didn't know them all well, but she was eager to make more friends with those of diverse backgrounds. As a way to emphasize that their group was not to be influenced by men's rules, while together they had agreed not to use the title *Mrs.* followed by their married name. So unusual was this that only after they had agreed upon it did some of them learn the first name of several of their friends.

Lucy, along with an elderly lady called Eileen, and a young woman from the Cornish region of England, Harriet, were white. Alicia and Maria were Mexican, and Sally was African-American referred to as *black*. Marlene's origin was uncertain. She had light bronze skin and dark eyes, and a slight accent that no one could identify but were too polite to question. These were a few of the ladies who had decided to bond over a common cause, which at the moment was simply that of being served luncheon in their favorite French cafe.

After they had ordered, Alicia commented, "I brought a parcel of shirts to St. Vincent's School for Boys the other day. My boy outgrew them some time ago, but well, I'm just now able to let go of them. He's growing so fast!"

Harriet nodded. "My daughter refused to wear two dresses she had. They were too tight under the arms. So I donated them to St. Mary's Asylum for Girls."

Marlene, who seldom contributed to whatever was being discussed, now spoke up. "Mrs. Mackay donates generously to both of those, I believe."

Everyone already aware of this, no one said anything. It was clear from her expression that Marlene regretted having made the effort to join in.

Lucy tried to come to her rescue. "They're certainly deserving institutions. But I must say that I find it interesting that the boys have a *school*, whereas the girls have an *asylum*."

Eileen turned to her. "I'm sure the word asylum is meant only from the perspective that girls need protection."

"Rather than education?" Lucy had made a great effort to keep any suggestion of challenge from her voice, and hoped it had been enough.

"Well," Eileen shrugged, "boys are going to have to earn a living at some point." Lucy looked into blue eyes offset by frizzy gray hair sticking out from beneath a simple bonnet. Eileen always reminded Lucy of a delicate porcelain doll handed down through generations, and somewhat neglected by the last of them. Pink fluff from her old shawl clung to ever-present pearls that she claimed had once hugged the neck of her grandmother.

There was so much Lucy wanted to say, and they all realized it. But she merely sighed and took a sip of her tea. Unspoken, but understood by them all, was the fact that sometimes women were forced by circumstances to also need employment. But after growing up in a society that didn't come close to preparing them for such a harsh reality, the experience could be a painful one. "Equal pay for equal work" would be a difficult discussion over a hundred years later, but in the 1870's it was a completely unknown concept, aside from a few of the more enthusiastic suffrage champions.

Eileen, eager to change the subject, mustered her courage and asked Lucy how long she had been a widow. Upon finding out that it had been over a dozen years, all of those present showed a sharpened interest.

Maria leaned forward, gently asking, "Is there some reason you have not remarried?"

Lucy started to shrug, about to make a light comment to deflect attention from herself. Then she changed her mind. These women dealt with serious facts of a woman's life, and she felt it would be disrespectful to be anything less than honest.

"When a child of eleven, I roamed the streets of San Francisco, before it even had that name. I observed the behavior of many different men from various walks of life, and I decided then on the kind of man I would settle for if I ever gave in to the restrictions of marriage. I decided it would be a man who I could respect, and one who loved me for who I am, and not who he thought I should be. Having discovered that I liked learning new things, I wanted a man who wouldn't be intimidated if I happened to show intelligence. I was determined to never be any man's property, or someone drifting along behind in his shadow. At the same time, I didn't want to be in competition with him. I wanted to be in harness with him."

Sally nodded. She was a middle-aged widow who had recently remarried, and was admired for the work she did to bring relief to the poor. Her voice always sounded a little tentative when she spoke, possibly because she was always careful about expressing herself. Even among such nice white women as these, it didn't pay to forget that you were always looked at as different. And, therefore, expressing yourself held the potential of your words being held against you. But at least today, Sally felt safe in the present company.

"We all had such high-toned ideas when we were girls." All the women nodded at Sally's words. "We fantasized that our husbands would be akin to some prince charming, but we all eventually accepted the reality. And so, we're now married."

"But not to prince charming!" Alicia said, thinking of how loudly her husband had belched after that morning's breakfast. Laughing at the truth of the statement, each for their own reason, they were all glad that it was Alicia who had put into words what they were all thinking. She was a dear woman and much respected. More than once, when some of them had brought supplies to a family in need, they had discovered that Alicia had already begun helping the family. She just never talked about it.

Lucy spoke softly, trying hard not to let her next words catch in her throat. "But I did have all that once. I won't settle for less now."

The women looked down at their plates, finding it difficult to accept what Lucy had said as possibly true. But they were also somewhat in awe of a woman whose marriage had contained enough of what she had always wanted so that she still remembered it as ideal. For a long, quiet moment, the women simply chewed, sipped, and dabbed at their mouths with their napkins. Anything to avoid meeting Lucy's gaze. They all thought such ideas of what could be expected in a marriage unrealistic, especially for a woman as independent as Lucy. To cover their discomfort, two of the ladies started a new discussion at the same time, and the conversation continued at a leisurely pace about local events.

But while the other women were focused on these subjects, Lucy was recalling that she had recently made much the same speech to a gentleman upon the occasion of their fourth outing together. They had attended a lecture at the Opera House, followed by a late supper at a nearby restaurant. Upon returning to her house, he had made romantic overtures.

After delivering to him a more generalized version of the speech just given to her lady friends, Lucy had waited for her date's reaction. She had been hopeful that the man would understand and want to continue to ask for her company, as she liked him very much, having met him when she had been in her teens. They had been on a wagon train out of Missouri headed to Oregon, but she had left the train suddenly, without realizing that Percy had been attracted to her.

He was pleasant to look at, being tall, broad-shouldered, and clean-shaven, which was somewhat uncommon. But even more than agreeable in appearance, he had always been very agreeable in personality, and they enjoyed discussing world affairs and the events they attended. She liked that she had never heard him say anything mean about anyone, and was always fair in his assessments. Maybe that was why he was an attorney with good prospects of becoming a judge.

His first reaction to her declaration to not marry was only a brief moment of hesitation. "And you don't think I'm that kind of man?"

"Not entirely, Percy." Since he had been so direct, Lucy had decided to be the same. "You have money, ambition and humor, and a fine character. And I certainly admire your kindness and generosity to others. You also have a wonderful ability to view situations with a balanced fairness to both sides."

"You sound as though you admire me."

"I do. Very much." He had glowed with satisfaction at her compliments, figuring he had made the necessary inroads to her heart that might lead to the permanent situation he desired. But she hadn't finished speaking. She moved to his side on the sofa. "I've also seen how you blush and try to pull me away from a conversation when I'm expressing an opinion, something I realize only too well that women aren't supposed to do in mixed company. That tells me everything I need to know about you as a long-term partner in life."

"And here I thought I was being so subtle that you'd not notice." His smile had been so charming that Lucy almost hadn't responded.

"I know I'm a little more outspoken than most men can comfortably deal with. But I don't care, you see. You do. And that's what matters, doesn't it?"

Her hand resting lightly on his arm, he put his hand over it and gave it a squeeze. "You're right. It makes us good friends, but not marriage material. Just always remember that if you ever need me, you have only to ask."

"You're so imminently suitable for the many women who are always trying to catch your eye. You won't be alone for long once it's known that we're no longer seeing one another. With your ambitions, you need a supportive wife who can enhance your approach to the bench."

"Well, my dear," he had said as he rose up and took hat in hand, "I've enjoyed our time together. But I think I'll take your advice and shift my attentions to a woman more suitable to that of a judge." He had hesitated at the door, looking at her with regret mingled with longing. "It would have been so fine."

Now, as she listened to the women talking about their families, Lucy had to smile. People's reactions to the realization that Lucy Murphy was not a "willing widow" were certainly mixed. However, the response she had received just the week before had been far from amusing. She had tried to be gentle in her refusal of the man's suggestion that they could at least share "intimacies of the boudoir". But it was still a rejection, and his pride didn't allow for a gracious acceptance.

"I suppose you think I should thank you for your honesty." His words had been snapped out while his face turned a deep red. "But I won't do that. I think you don't have the womanly qualities that would make you a good companion. So, if you'll excuse me, I'll take my leave of you." And giving action to his words, he had picked up his hat and walked out of the house without another word or a backward glance.

As Lucy had stood staring at the door, biting her lip in consternation, a male voice behind her had startled her. "He wasn't good enough for you."

"Roger! I didn't know you were here."

"I know. I didn't trust the old windbag, so when I heard you setting him straight, I decided to stay in the other room."

Lucy had smirked. "And if the evening had proceeded to intimacies?"

"Oh, I didn't for a moment think that would happen." He didn't even try to hide a smirk. "I knew you wouldn't think him suitable. I also knew he wouldn't take it well. I've played poker with him several times."

She had longed to ask Roger what kind of woman he thought was suitable for *him*, but she didn't dare. Considering the company he kept, she assumed he had several times experienced the pleasures of the bed. But she also knew that only when he was seriously interested in a woman, would he bring up the subject of romance.

Lucy was brought back to the moment when Harriet commented, "Did you see in the *Enterprise* where they reminded us that they've been in business for the last eighteen years?"

"Yes," Lucy joined in, "saying that it has, and I quote, 'daily given greeting to the men of Nevada'."

Maria leaned back in her chair and grinned. "Oh, boy, I bet I know where you're going with this."

"Well, after all, don't they think women ever read their newspaper? Couldn't they have said the *people* of Nevada? I know it's subtle, but as long as women are so casually dismissed from inclusion, it becomes acceptable to ignore our ideas and opinions."

"We aren't outright dismissed," Alicia posed. "We're just not always recognized."

Lucy fought back a sigh of frustration. "It amounts to the same thing. To not listen to us is to perpetuate the myth that we're not intelligent or capable of sound logic."

Marlene nodded. "It does seem like they could have been more inclusive in their comment. I'm actually glad you pointed that out, Lucy." She laughed and looked at Lucy with great fondness. "I must admit I don't always appreciate your perspective on things, but maybe I should pay more attention."

Lucy felt herself blush, something she rarely did. The unexpected graciousness of it charmed the ladies, and their laughter and smiles expressed their approval.

"Well," Lucy added, "the article did refer to its readers as 'splendid people who have been most generously appreciated'. That was certainly inclusive, so maybe I'm just being picky."

"Oh, hey, don't go soft on us now!" Maria grinned at Lucy and the others chuckled.

Alicia spoke up. "That reminds me. Did you read in the paper about the raid of one of the opium dens over in Chinatown?"

"So?" Maria asked. "That happens all the time."

"Yes, but they arrested four young men and a girl. And they were all Americans!"

"Oh, their poor families. How shameful!"

"I know. The paper said that the sight of these young persons in court ought to prove a warning to all."

Sally shook her head. "Yes, but it won't stop young people from being curious about such things. Often to their detriment."

The young man who had been serving them walked up to the table. "What a delight to see ladies having such a good time together. Can I refresh the coffee pot?" Although some of them had been on the verge of leaving, they agreed that they were enjoying themselves. Not wanting such a congenial get-together to end, they stayed to enjoy one more cup of coffee.

Lucy was the first to leave the pillory ladies' luncheon, and those remaining wasted no time with their comments.

"Didn't Lucy used to teach foreign miners and help immigrants with paperwork and such?" Eileen asked.

Harriet spoke up, her English accent forcing the others to listen carefully in order to understand her. "She's a kind and elegant lady, and even though her house is rented, she's decorated it very nicely."

"It's hard to believe now, isn't it?" Eileen received no response to her question. "I mean, she's not the first lower class to rise to middle class by their own efforts."

Harriet felt as though Lucy needed defending. "At least she doesn't put on airs. After all, she takes in lodgers."

"Many people do that," Maria reminded them, having wished she had an extra room just for that purpose. "I hear she serves them very good breakfasts. As lodgers instead of boarders, they have to eat the rest of their meals out."

"Most of what she serves is made by that Irish girl she hired." Eileen uttered a suppressed cluck of her tongue and started to add something more.

Wanting to avoid the Irish topic, Alicia quickly asked, "Her son is a gambler, isn't he?"

"Yes," Marlene spoke up, "but my husband says he's honest. And they're both generous with what they give to charities. I've even seen Lucy collect for the Daughters of Charity orphanage, even though she's not Catholic."

"The sisters take in children of all religions," Sally reminded them. "They don't care about anything but a person's need."

Eileen seemed to soften visibly. "I must say the sisters were very kind to a friend of mine when she was ill. They brought her soup and little savories to keep her spirits up."

"That reminds me," Alicia began, "did you hear that Mrs. Babcock had a baby girl?"

They all nodded, but it was Harriet that spoke first. "She was surprised when she found herself expecting. They'd been married ten years and it had never happened."

Eileen lowered her voice. "She's rather intellectual, you know. Used to be a school teacher. And many doctors say that when a woman develops her brain overmuch, her reproductive organs shrivel."

Harriet laughed outright. "I've heard the same thing said. Lucy would say that's just something men say to keep women from getting the vote or sitting on juries."

The other women looked at Harriet with less surprise than she had expected, and a couple even appeared to be seriously considering her words. Harriet tucked the moment away at the back of her mind until she could tell Lucy all about it.

"Before we leave," Marlene asked, "do you all think we should have another concert?"

Eileen shrugged. "You mean like the one in '75 that the Benevolent Association gave at Piper's?"

"Yes. That one was so successful that it raised a lot of money."

"I wasn't here then. What was it like?"

"Oh, so grand." They all murmured their agreement. "Most of those participating were women."

"That would make Lucy happy," Alicia mumbled.

Marlene ignored her and continued. "Mrs. Moore played a sailor's hornpipe and Felicia Genesey dressed up like an Indian maiden and recited the poem *Hiawatha*."

"Don't forget the Beck girl," Maria said. "She sang *Good Night My Sweet*. Such a nice voice."

"When was it held?" Sally inquired.

"January. And the money was spent for relief for the poor and destitute during that winter."

"Well," Eileen summarized as she stood up, "I think it's something we should think about. But speaking of entertainment, you're all still coming to my card party tomorrow night, aren't you?"

They all acquiesced, having talked their husbands into it with little effort. It was, after all, a party that included cards.

The "meeting" over, each woman felt they had some new things to think about while involved in their daily routines of cooking, cleaning, laundry, and sewing. And doing the shopping to support all those activities. And, of course, living according to the rules set by husbands they considered to have much more interesting and eventful lives.

But at least in Virginia City, both men and women had available to them clubs, organizations and charitable interests in which they could participate. There were also many regular social functions by way of dances, parties and theatrical events. But only the men had the freedom to express their views in the local newspapers, in mixed company, or at the ballot box. While the men saw nothing unusual in this, every woman was acutely aware of this difference, whether agreeing with it or not.

As summer progressed, Lucy spent some of her time looking for a permanent residence for herself, and possibly Roger. Leaving the Piper Opera House after attending an afternoon lecture, Lucy decided to wander further up "B" Street. She passed an organ grinder on his way to the main business area on "C" Street where he could expect a few coins tossed in his direction. He struggled with the weight of the colorfully painted, wooden box with its single support leg, but at least he was headed downhill.

Lucy had admired the houses along "B" Street for some time. However, when one had come up for sale, it had been much too grand and expensive. They were owned by business owners, mining superintendents, attorneys, and civil servants with status. Of course, now that the town was in a bit of a slump, with many people leaving town, she wondered if asking prices might be lower.

Just past Sutton Street, a man was posting a *For Sale* sign in front of a two-story, east-facing house that was in urgent need of repair. The picket fence was missing paint and pickets, the rose bush climbing on it was in desperate need of pruning, and the tiny front yard was full of weeds and forsaken flowerbeds. Unusual for Virginia City, the house was wide across the front even while extending back. It had also not been painted since receiving smoke damage from the big fire of '75 that had barely missed its north side. Lucy suspicioned that the interior needed a lot of work as well. Consequently, she quickly approached the man and asked to see inside. After assessing the quality of her clothing and the obvious expense of her bonnet, he was only too glad to accommodate her.

She had been right. The small entry was no larger than a closet, with hooks on one wall for coats. But passing through this, she was surprised to find herself in a good-sized room that served multiple uses. There was a large window on the wall to her left fronting the street, and a dining area to her right with a door beyond that was open to the kitchen. A quick peak into that spacious workroom showed that it had a bay window at the front, where sat a small table. Although it was in need of a good cleaning, Lucy admired the kitchen's surprising number of spacious shelves and cupboards, two ice boxes, and a fairly new stove. The linoleum covering the floor was new, even if evidently seldom mopped.

It was at this point that she realized the house was actually a backward L shape. The stairs on the far side of the room, between the parlor and the dining area, rose steeply to a second floor. There Lucy discovered four small bedrooms, two to the left of the hallway and two to the right. This portion of the house created a void beneath the upstairs rooms, which was used as a storage area accessed from outside.

Throughout the house, some walls needed replastering, and all walls needed painting or papering. The dark wood of the plank floors, doors and frames, simply needed cleaning and polishing. But all the rugs and runners had seen better days, and most of the sconces were missing their glass globes. The house had obviously been well-used for a considerable length of time.

Although Lucy had a somewhat limited budget, she had a large amount of imagination, and she saw nothing but exciting possibilities. For instance, the house sat up against the property line on the northern edge, and she wondered if she could build an addition on the south side in the crook of the backward "L". And maybe that could be a bedroom suite for herself, accessed by a door from the southwest corner of the parlor.

More ideas raced through her mind along with fabrics for drapes, bedspreads, chairs and a sofa. For Lucy saw this as not only her home, but also a lodging house for three boarders and a spare room for Roger or guests; all upstairs and away from her private realm downstairs. To encourage this, there was just enough room at the far end of the upstairs hall, in front of a window, for a small table between two chairs.

After discussion with Roger, they pooled their savings, obtained a small loan, and purchased the house for a surprisingly low "as is" price. Fortunately, the owner was desperate to leave town as soon as possible.

It took them considerable effort, but they were determined to have everything Lucy had envisioned. While starting first on the outside, they slept on cots in the dining area. Thankfully, the kitchen needed nothing more than a good cleaning. Kathryn tackled this with enthusiasm, while also taking over in the garden.

The street soon had a white house with green trim, along with a neat front garden surrounded by a freshly painted, white picket fence. The gravel path from the gate to the front steps was trimmed by new boards, and the steps themselves were sanded and oiled. Roger balked at some requests for his help, but the rose bush next to the gate got his attention after it snagged his jacket a couple of times. It immediately began to thrive from the pruning.

Once construction on the inside began, Lucy sent to Placerville for everything she had put in storage, which included those things left her by Freda. Three weeks later the new rugs had just been put down when two freight wagons arrived. Only when she placed her beloved rocking chair with its petti point roses in her bedroom, did she allow herself to feel entirely satisfied with her new home.

After the freighters had been paid, Roger left his mother to herself. He knew she would take her time unpacking the crates and barrels and burlap wrapped packages, deciding where each item should go. He also knew that among the many moments of joy, there would also be a few spent tearfully recalling events that had been shared with those loved ones who were now gone from her life.

As Roger had predicted, Lucy laughed aloud when she discovered an old whalebone corset packed around some tea cups. But she fought tears when she unwrapped the picture taken on her and Jim's wedding day. She set it on the dressing table in her new bedroom where she could see it every day. She smiled through tears when she draped a long string of buttons over the corner of a painting, having with Freda's help collected them during the California gold rush when a young girl. On their wedding night, Jim had cut a button from his shirt and added it to the end of the string, bringing the good luck custom to a close.

Consternation set in when Lucy lifted out the ambrotype photograph of Freda's sister Maud, taken by the great Civil War photographer Mathew Brady in his New York studio. Should she display the old... She stopped herself. Yes, the woman with whom she and Freda had lived when they had been in New York had been severe and bigoted. However, she had generously allowed teenaged Lucy to remain with Freda in Maud's large house, even if it had been more as a servant than a guest.

Lucy polished the photograph covered with a blister of glass. She decided to hang it on the wall near the small parlor stove, near the wall end of the sofa, which was Lucy's favorite place to sit while reading. The photo was, therefore, out of the line of sight of those sitting on the sofa as it extended out into the room. The door to her bedroom was on the same wall and also behind the sofa. While seated there, Lucy could look past the dining area's long table, and into the kitchen. In fact, that's where she took a break from unpacking, watching Kathryn as she prepared lunch while sweetly humming and practicing her artistry with food. Lucy luxuriated in the awareness that for the first time in her life, everything around her had been arranged to suit just her.

Roger came bursting through the front door and headed for the cabinet with the coffee cups, giving Kathryn a big smile. In response, she turned a lovely shade of pink, barely keeping herself from emitting an unseemly giggle.

Roger hollered from the kitchen, "What's this old felt hat doing on the counter? You have a man upstairs?"

Kathryn did giggle at that, then gasped at herself in surprise. She placed a platter of sandwiches on the table, then grabbed a feather duster before hurrying upstairs.

Lucy walked to Roger's side and looked down on the hat. "It was found by the man repairing the wall between two of the upstairs bedrooms."

"It was in the wall?"

"Surprising, I know, but yes. Kathryn tells me that it might be some kind of tradition, supposed to bring good luck from the one who put it there for all those who might ever live here."

"Does that mean we've created bad luck by removing it?"

Lucy looked at him in surprise. "I hadn't thought of that. The hole is still in the wall. Why don't you go up and put it back in, maybe higher up so the man doing the repair doesn't see it."

Roger grinned, grabbed the hat, and bounded up the stairs. When he returned, he merely winked at his mother who was now seated at the kitchen table. Carrying his coffee mug to the table, he sprawled in the chair across from Lucy and looked around him. "Is that a water filter?"

He had gestured at a two-foot high terracotta vessel, impressed with scrolls and grape leaves, with a brass spout near the base. "Yes. I got it at Mr. Beck's store."

"But we have piped water from Lake Tahoe now."

"I know, but better safe than sorry. Truth be told, Dolly had one like it that she described in one of her letters."

"Yeah, but back in the '60's, it was necessary in order to have decent water to drink."

Lucy said nothing, and it occurred to Roger that it might have more to do with sharing something with Dolly than it did about the water.

The next day, while busy with the decorating of the upstairs rooms, Lucy hurried down to answer persistent knocking at the front door. She found an upright piano sitting on her front walk, two young men resting their elbows on it. There was also a man with a long, drooping mustache standing on the porch, hat in hand and a big grin on his face.

"You were so kind to my family when my wife was ill, and now that we're leaving town, I want you to have our piano for your beautiful new house. My wife insists."

Lucy couldn't object after that speech, so she let him and his sons into the house. There was just enough room for the piano on the south wall.

When Roger entered the parlor later that day and saw the piano, he laughed long and hard. "I could easily come up with a joke about your starting your own bawdy house, but maybe you wouldn't appreciate that."

Ignoring him, Lucy looked at the piano with skepticism. "Neither of us know how to play, but I suppose that at some point someone staying here will. I'd better get it tuned."

"There are several piano teachers here in town. You could learn."

"Yes, well, maybe. Your father was very accomplished. He was employed as 'the professor' in the parlor house where I was the cook. He played for the customers at the start of some evenings."

"Yes, I know. In Nevada City in the 1850's." He had heard the story many times before. "But that's about all I've heard about those days. I'm still waiting for more."

"You'll have to continue to wait." Lucy's smile turned suddenly wistful. "But maybe someday."

Thinking her answer nebulous in the extreme, he had no choice but to accept it. He always did. Also as always, he remained curious about just how his mother had gotten that scar on her cheek. It was very faint now, and barely visible to others. Whenever the California gold rush town of Nevada City was mentioned, her hand moved to the scar, if she didn't stop the gesture first.

But right then, Roger was more concerned about whether or not he was going to be able to work that night. Or keep from falling on his face.

He felt awful, but he didn't want Lucy to worry, so he turned toward the front door. That was a mistake. The room began to spin and he groped for the arm of the sofa.

"Roger!"

The voice was his mother's, he was sure of that, but it seemed to be coming from very far away. But then her strong arms led him to the sofa, where he willingly collapsed onto it. Feeling a cool hand on his forehead, and hearing her announce that he didn't seem to have a fever, he began to relax.

"Kathryn!"

Hearing panic in Mrs. Murphy's voice for the first time ever, she rushed down the stairs. "What's wrong?"

"Go for the doctor, the one I told you about that Mrs. Beck recommended to me. She said he's got more common sense than most of them."

"Yes, Ma'am." With a quick glance at a very pale Roger, the source of more than one of Kathryn's nighttime fantasies, she fled from the house.

At that point, Roger ceased to fight for consciousness and simply allowed himself to sink into oblivion. His last thought was that he didn't understand what was happening, because generally he felt perfectly fine. When the doctor arrived and examined his patient, he said about the same thing.

"Has he been over-exerting himself?"

"I don't think so. But he does work every day late into the night."

"Really? What does he do?"

"He's a professional gambler." Lucy was quick to add, "And a square one!"

The doctor's long beard quivered as he chuckled. "I thought I recognized him from somewhere. Well, Mrs. Murphy, it's my opinion that he's just plain exhausted. Between work, and maybe too much after work recreation, he needs a couple of days of rest and some decent food. And he might also be a little dehydrated. These young men think they can live on excitement and beer, but it catches up with them eventually." He handed her his card. "Send for me if there's any sudden change for the worse."

"Thank you. Mrs. Beck was right when she said you were a good, common-sense doctor."

He didn't comment, but he knew what she meant. Some of those calling themselves *doctor* had never seen the inside of a classroom, much less a medical school. Following her own common sense, Lucy put cold compresses on Roger's forehead and whenever he came to the surface for a few minutes, made him drink some water fortified with lemon syrup. That night he stayed awake long enough to eat a little chicken soup, and a little brandy in his water. He slept soundly after that, and well into the following day. He then sat up and announced that he was enormously hungry.

The weeks Lucy spent unpacking and decorating were the most enjoyable she had spent in a long time. Even Roger, after he had regained his strength, seemed to enjoy helping. As did some of his friends when he commandeered them into helping bring furniture up the stairs. That Lucy and Kathryn fed them well might have contributed to their enthusiasm.

That is, until one afternoon when Roger found his mother standing in the middle of the parlor looking around her with a puzzled frown.

"What's wrong?"

"I'm sure I had displayed that little cranberry glass vase on the sideboard there. But it's not there now. Freda gave it to me for my birthday the year you were born."

Roger made a noise at the back of his throat and barked out, "Son of a bitch!"

This was the most common profanity used by men, but seldom by Roger, and Lucy was startled. But not as much as she was when Roger stormed out of the house mumbling even more seldom used oaths. An hour later he returned, the vase clutched in a hand that showed abrasions across the knuckles.

"Roger, what happened?"

"You got your vase back. And I lost someone I thought was a friend."

"Oh, Roger, I..."

"I don't want to talk about it!" And they never did.

Roger insisted on being there to help Hugh Muckle, the stone cutter, when he delivered the new wash stands. Mr. Muckle was a jovial man who spent much of his time creating beautiful headstones for delivery to the cemeteries. He also made stone benches, one of which sat in Lucy's new garden out front.

Lucy had him create wash stand tops for each of the bedrooms, each one a flat marble slab with an upright, 24-inch backsplash. The one for her room had at both upper corners a carved corbel topped with a small piece of marble large enough for a soap dish. It was placed upon an ornately carved Eastlake dresser that had been purchased with the house, as had much of the furniture. The wash stands in the upstairs sleeping rooms were small and simple, and each rested atop a pine two-drawer dresser Lucy had purchased in town. There was just enough room for a bowl and pitcher in the blue and white, flow-blue style, which Lucy had purchased in bulk at Mr. Beck's store.

While Lucy's room had long drapes, the rooms upstairs had curtains of cotton for ease of washing and ironing, and were a sunny yellow and white check. When winter would arrive, she planned to cover the windows in heavily lined broadcloth in a dark blue that would still compliment the yellow walls. She quickly discovered that people leaving town didn't always want to take all their quilts with them, and she was able to accumulate a sizeable number, stacking them in each rental room on a small wooden chair in the corner. Miscellaneous local art decorated the walls in those rooms, along with a simple kerosene lamp on the nightstand, beneath which was an enclosed space containing a new thunder mug.

Finally, every room was complete, along with two miners sharing a room, a recently divorced mining engineer in another, and the third occupied by a newly arrived older couple. Their son owned a shop in town, as well as a nice home on "A" Street, where he was taking his time adding on a room for his parents.

Lucy awoke each day more contented than she had been since leaving Placerville. Kathryn was not as unhappy as she might have been, considering so much extra work, because Lucy had hired a daily girl to clean the bedrooms. She also had the baked goods delivered every other day from a "C" Street bakery. Thanks to Kathryn, the house was always clean and the household efficiently organized. And Lucy was surprised to find herself bored.

Also, after such a long time spent working on the house and its related expenditures, Lucy realized that her savings were much reduced. Having chosen to spend all her time at home for the last month, she decided to return to work. She was welcomed back to the Crystal Bar with enthusiasm by the owner as well as the men who had often played at her table. Word spread quickly that *Lucy* was dealing once again, and she worked each night until after midnight.

That fall, word came to those in Virginia City that investments in Aurora had been renewed, and a deep shaft was being planned. Those who had kept faith with the town were convinced that the rock at the 100-foot depth was actually a cap over rich ore. Mr. H. M. Yerrington of the Virginia & Truckee Railroad organized the New Real del Monte Company to prove that this was true, and the company opened with a $5,000,000 capital fund. Ironically, the site chosen was on the appropriately named Last Chance Hill.

Although only a few men in Virginia City were willing to invest, Roger decided to risk some money in the venture. He therefore watched closely as the work began that December of '77. It was under the supervision of George Daly, who was always explaining that he was no relation to the hanged outlaw. With two shafts, one for hoisting and one for a pump, the first underground platform was set up at the 300-foot level where a quartz vein looked promising. Consequently, men were hired to work around the clock. The town's population and economy picked up, and hope ran rampant. And the work dragged on through winter. In fact, it was taking so long that Roger, more willing to face reality than his fellow investors, found an eager buyer for his stock. He took a small loss on the deal, but he slept much better at night. It was at this point that he came to the conclusion that he was better at accepting the uncertain deal of the cards than he was at coping with the quixotic nature of stock prices.

No one knew it at the time, but it would take until 1881 for Aurora's new shaft to reach 800 feet down, at which point the water filling up the shaft would pour in ahead of the huge pump's ability to keep it out. The water level would eventually stabilize at 300 feet, but it would be too late for those who had for so long hoped that Aurora would not fall victim to the fate of so many western mining towns. In 1883, Hawthorne, Nevada, a stable town on the Carson & Colorado Railroad line, would become the new County Seat of Esmeralda County. That the railroad was also a project of Mr. Yerrington. would not be missed by investors.

In 1888, Aurora's Masonic Lodge, often one of the first organizations to establish itself in a new town, would close down. The officer's jewels, set in Aurora silver, would be sold to a new lodge in Lovelock, Nevada. There would remain a few dozen stubborn hopefuls who would refuse to leave Aurora, mainly because they didn't know where else to go. But in 1897, when the post office would close, they would figure it out.

Although eventually it would become one of many western ghost towns, it would remain one with a rich history and numerous legends of the kind that never quite die away. Oh, it would flame to life for ten years at the start of the next century when a new consortium set out to mine the tailings left behind, but after that, it would be well and truly over for Aurora. The only thing of value it would have left would be the bricks of the buildings, and eventually those would be hauled away by human scavengers.

January of 1878 had days of snow followed by breaks where the snow turned to slush, then froze, and then melted again just in time for another snow. February was much the same. On a day that saw no falling snow, Lucy eagerly accepted an invitation from Helene to join her and some other women at a birthday luncheon for Helene. Lucy had met two of the three women, but not the third. They were all dressed in fashions fairly current, but Mrs. Hewes was particularly well-dressed, with fur trimming her coat. The lace on her waste was more finely woven, the velvet on her hat showed less wear, and the leather shoes wrapping her ankles were obviously new. After removing her gloves, her hands also showed that she did less work around the house than those of her friends, which meant that she had a full-time servant rather than just a daily girl who lived out.

After enjoying their lunch topped off by bread pudding, conversation continued at a leisurely pace. The porcelain coffee pot painted with pink roses was lifted a final time and Mrs. Hewes turned to Lucy. "You have an Irish girl, I hear."

"If you mean a young woman who acts as housekeeper and directs the daily girl, yes, I do. I've recently hired an older Chinese gentleman to come in and bake three times a week. It's actually less expensive than buying from the bakeries. Why do you ask?" She was trying hard not to sound defensive, but she had sensed a degree of criticism underlying the question.

"Only that you have to be careful with such as they are. You simply can't just trust the Irish. And everyone knows about the Chinese."

Lucy forced herself to remain calm. "Neither can you *just* trust anyone. Until you get to know them well, that is."

"Well, of course."

The two friends of Mrs. Hewes averted their eyes from their imperious friend. They also knew Lucy fairly well, and were well acquainted with how outspoken she could be. Although they secretly admired Lucy for it, they didn't think Mrs. Hewes would be as accepting. Still, they were immensely pleased that they were not going to miss this match-up between the two women.

Lucy put down her cup and cocked her head to the side. "I find it interesting how so often when people comment on the behavior of a foreign-born person, they connect it to their place of origin. Whether Irish, Chinese, or even someone from England, for that matter. It's especially true if they do something that's disapproved of. Why do people immediately bring up where the person is from? How does that equate to their behavior? And God forbid they happen to be brown, black, or Piute."

Mrs. Hewes leaned forward. "Why do you find that interesting, as you put it?"

"Because when a white, American-born man does the same thing, no one says, 'And he's a white man born in this country, you know.' If anything, he should know the rules better than someone born elsewhere. But instead, he's given less condemnation and his being white never enters into the discussion."

Lucy was used to having people look at her with surprise, but that day pretty well took the prize. Even Helene looked a bit disconcerted. Lucy tried to elevate the moment by adding, "But then, what do I know? That's only an argument I overheard some man making the other day when talking about the San Francisco riots."

Of course, it was a lie, but it brought about instant relaxation of the group, for now they could attribute her words to some unknown man with unorthodox views. But, being a man, that wasn't really so terrible. Society made allowances for that from men. But only those women present who read newspapers, whether their husbands approved or not, knew about the riots in San Francisco that had resulted in the death of four people and the destruction of over $100,000 worth of property.

Chinese immigrants in mining camps and big cities had always been resented for their ability to work hard and save what they earned. They did this even though paid less than other nationalities. As a logical response to being shunned, they built their own communities and spent most of their money there. Being exotic and different also worked against them in a society that had strict opinions about what was acceptable.

At the same time, some of their businesses, such as laundries and markets, attracted customers away from white businesses. Disgruntled people looking for somewhere to place blame for their lack of success, claimed that the Chinese willingness to work for lower wages was interfering with the national labor market. No one mentioned, of course, that thousands of them had been brought to America to work on the Transcontinental Railroad, and then left to survive on their own when it was completed.

When the 1873 economic downturn hit the country, later referred to as *The Long Depression*, approximately 150,000 people from Eastern cities came to California over the two following years alone. They were still thinking of California as the land of golden prosperity, so most headed for San Francisco, the largest center of commerce. However, with so many people adding to its population, San Francisco's unemployment rate climbed alarmingly.

With the Chinese community working for lower wages than other workers, it fueled a discontentment in San Francisco that seethed into rage that needed an outlet. Following a rally of the so-called Workingmen's Party in July of '77, where the speakers refused to address the Chinese "problem", those attendees angry at this exclusion of topic set fire to Chinese laundries and stormed toward the Chinese district. After two nights of firefights and rioting, an uneasy peace was reestablished by hundreds of police wielding billy clubs, 1,200 deployed state militia, and a citizen's vigilance committee armed with hickory pickaxe handles from a nearby factory.

The *Daily Alta* newspaper wrote that, *"There are more sore heads in San Francisco today than can get well in a week."* The riots may have ended, but it sparked the development of the Workingmen's Trade and Labor Union of San Francisco, with the slogan "The Chinamen Must Go!". They changed their name to the Workingmen's Party of California, with their president Denis Kearney, an immigrant from Ireland. Anti-Chinese sentiment continued to spread throughout the United States, settling down somewhat with the passage of the Chinese Exclusion Act in 1882.

The conversation at Helene's birthday gathering turned to fashions, and Lucy turned silent. At that point, she was wise enough to realize that no one really wanted to hear any more of her ideas about anything, especially if it was about social issues that didn't directly affect the women's carefully cultivated lives. Men, and therefore society in general, had given them a role to play; and whether or not these particular ladies had ever been discontented with those roles, they had by now accepted them.

CHAPTER 12

1878 - 1879

After the luncheon broke up, all the women went off in various directions. Lucy went to a nearby merchandise store and began looking through the fabrics in an effort to calm her lingering irritation. She knew it was irrational, knowing as she did that her way of thinking was out of the ordinary. She also realized that her real dissatisfaction was not having another woman as independent in spirit as herself with whom she could share ideas. The closest she ever came to finding some such woman was when visiting those running The Female Employment Agency. But they were busy maintaining both a business and a home, and no empathetic connection with these women had developed for her. So, Lucy philosophically shrugged and got on with her shopping.

She picked up a bolt of cheap *cotton domestic* for possible use as dish towels. Summoning her sense of humor, she reminded herself that she was not Joan of Arc on a mission, but rather just a modern woman with errands to run. After all, there were plenty of women in the country pushing suffrage issues. Recalling the looks she had received from her friends at the luncheon just past, she thought, "Good luck with that, ladies."

While waiting for lengths to be cut from the bolt of fabric, her friend Mildred Conway rushed up to her in an obviously harried state. Her bonnet was askew and her shawl was falling off her shoulders. Lucy reached out and adjusted it for her.

"Oh, Lucy, I'm so glad to see you. I need a great favor."

"Of course. How can I help?"

"I promised Mrs. Mathews that I'd bring several loaves of bread to the soup kitchen and work a short shift. I'm due there in about ten minutes, and you know how she hates anyone to be late. I don't want to endure one of her lectures again. But I need to fetch my Johnny from school."

"Mildred, would you like me to get Johnny and bring him to my house until you can come for him?"

"Oh, could you? I'd be ever so grateful."

"Think nothing of it. Now, you go do what you need to do. And give my best to Mrs. Mathews."

Mildred made a funny face by crossing her eyes at Lucy while rushing out the door, knowing Lucy was teasing her. The very straight-laced Mary Mathews would someday publish a book detailing her time in Virginia City, filled not only with details of her daily life, but also infused throughout with narrow, sometimes poorly informed opinions. They were ones, however, not uncommon in that era.

After paying for her purchases, Lucy walked the three blocks to the Fourth Ward School, avoiding the mounds of shoveled snow along the way. She stopped briefly out front of the new building, looking up at the Mansard roofline that lent it such a distinctive appearance and creating a wide ledge. It was from this ledge that two boys were crawling through a window to get back inside. Lucy shook her head and climbed the flight of steps up to the lobby.

Standing at the foot of the stairs, she heard a yelp of boyish glee behind her. Turning around, she looked up to see a boy of about ten facing forward while riding down the railing, arms out to keep his balance while tightly gripping the wall below with the heels of his shoes. By the look of the streaky marks on the wall's paneling, he wasn't the first to have done this. Approaching the end, the boy jumped off and started to run past Lucy.

Grabbing his arm, she held fast to him. "Whoa, Johnny. Do you remember me?"

He stood up straight and looked at her face carefully. "Oh, yeah, you're Mrs. Murphy. My mom thinks you're bold, but she likes you."

Lucy looked down at him and tried hard not to laugh. "Well, she has an errand to run and asked me to bring you to my house until she can come for you."

"Okay." They walked out into the crisp but sunny day, Lucy taking her time descending the school's steep flight of steps. "You don't have kids, do you?"

"I have a son, but he's grown now."

Realizing that Johnny was preparing himself to be bored, an active boy's idea of hell, Lucy took pity on him. "I hope you don't mind if we stop at the candy store on the way home. I'm out of my favorites. And I hear they've also stocked some of the Penny Dreadfuls imported from England. Would your mother object to my buying you one?"

His face alight with excitement. "Oh no, ma'am, she'd be fine with it!"

Lucy doubted it, but she didn't feel that the magazines were any more of a bad influence on young boys than simply living in a mining town. And evidently Mildred already thought her *bold*.

With great pride, Johnny informed her, "I've already read the penny part-story about Varney the Vampire. Do you know what a vampire is?"

"Yes, dear. Just remember that they're a character of fiction."

Johnny wasn't ready to let go of such a tantalizing concept. "Yeah, well, maybe. The last dreadful I read was called *The String of Pearls* about a barber who kills his customers while they're in his chair." He looked a little uncomfortable. "Mom thought me odd for not wanting to get my hair cut right after I read that one."

"I think the barber only killed those who were getting a shave. Because he had the razor in his hand and the men's necks exposed."

"Oh, yeah, right. Well, that's better. But I think I'll grow a beard like my dad's." He ran ahead of her the rest of the way to the candy store, and the periodical display.

Although Johnny had proclaimed his mother okay with his reading such material, when he heard her at the front door of Lucy's home, he quickly folded the thin sheets and hid them beneath his coat. He also carefully wiped his mouth and ran his tongue over his teeth. Lucy said nothing, earning a grateful if somewhat sly smile from Johnny as he left with his mother. Lucy answered with a wink that earned her a grin, and respect from Johnny's gang when he relayed to them his afternoon excursion, with only a few embellishments.

But Johnny's smile was nothing compared to that of Roger's when he came bursting into the parlor of the house later that afternoon. He only occasionally stayed in the guest room, but he never knocked, as he considered the house partly his. Those boarding there were divided over whether or not his behavior was appropriate. Lucy and Roger thought their interest amusing, and beyond that, paid no attention to them.

Lucy, sitting in the parlor at a tiny writing desk between the door to her room and the warmth of the parlor stove, looked up and smiled. She was always happy to see him, no matter his mood or his reason for coming to see her. "You're fortunate the lodgers are out or you'd get a dirty look for such an entrance."

He kissed her on the cheek. "I have a surprise for you."

"Oh?"

"A late birthday present."

"For my last birthday you took me out to a wonderful, and I might say expensive, dinner. That was more than enough."

"Okay, okay. Then let's say it's a Christmas present. Just come with me."

"It's not in your pocket?"

He pulled her up by her arm and started toward the front door. "Just come with me."

She barely had time to grab her heavy shawl. Once outside, he led her to a single-horse black rig tied to the post by the gate. "Is it so far away that we can't walk?"

He helped his mother up onto the seat before running around to climb in the other side. "There's still icy patches around from the last storm."

After a jog down "B" Street over to Taylor and then down several blocks, they stopped in front of the livery stable in which Lucy was invested. "We're returning the rig already?"

Roger said nothing, simply helping her down and leading her into the barn. Mrs. Beck and Helene were standing by a stall, both grinning and their gloved hands quietly clapping at her entrance.

At the same time that Lucy asked her friends, "What are you doing here?", she glanced into the stall next to her friends. The horse standing there tossed his head and nickered.

"Diamond!"

Roger opened the stall door and Lucy rushed in, throwing her arms around the horse's neck while her tears wet its fur. She let go only long enough to take Roger's offered handkerchief and blow her nose. She looked at her son with wonder. "How?"

"He was put up in a poker game in place of money." He reached out and rubbed one of the horse's ears. "I wasn't about to accept such a bet until the guy mentioned that he worked at a stage station on the route to Aurora, and the horse had been left behind by a woman traveling through. I took a chance and accepted the bet. I won, and here we are."

"Oh, I'm so glad you grew up loving games of chance!" She turned back to her horse, whose soft nose was now being rubbed by Helene. Lucy picked up a brush and began slowly running it over Diamond's side. He responded by swinging his head around to nibble at the sleeve of her dress. At this point, her friends informed her they were going to a nearby café for pie, and that if she wanted, she could join them.

Mrs. Beck chuckled. "I don't think she'll be leaving here any time soon." The women left together, Helene dabbing at her eyes with a gloved hand.

Roger watched his mother, reveling in the fact that he could do something to make her so happy, as he had often watched her scanning the horses on the streets. Roger was of the opinion that his mother led too solitary a life. Oh, she participated in a number of social causes and the groups that supported them, and she regularly visited her investments. But beyond luncheons with lady friends, she now seldom accepted an invitation from a gentleman. Considering how much the town loved dances and organized them every month, she had plenty of opportunities to enjoy herself if she chose.

Any time Roger tried to discuss this with her, she set him straight. "I'd much rather be home reading a good book than having my toes stepped on by some sweaty oaf with shreds of tobacco in his beard. Believe me, if ever I'm introduced to a man I'm attracted to, I know how to make my interest known."

Roger had as yet not found a good rejoinder to that, and had finally decided to let the subject rest. When he had told one of his lady friends of that conversation, he was surprised at how exuberantly she had laughed. "Oh, Roger, all women from the time they're fifteen know how to make their interest in a man known to him. Just let your mother lead her own life."

Although he had been very young when his father had left home to do his part in the war effort, Roger remembered many of the times they had spent together. As he had grown up, Lucy, Freda and his father's Placerville friends, had regaled Roger with stories of his father's kindness, courage and generosity. And several women had told him how handsome they had thought Jim Murphy. Consequently, Roger figured that if his mother was waiting to find someone to match his father's qualities, she would remain single for the rest of her life.

Roger and his friends were planning to attend the grand opening celebration of Mr. Sutro's tunnel near Dayton as soon as it was completed, and it was rumored that it could happen as soon as the snow melted. For a town where people got around mainly by walking, ice and snow was a challenge they tired of quickly. The spring thaw, and the many activities in the warmth of summer, was something they looked forward to with enthusiasm.

As Roger rode down the canyon to Sutro City on Diamond in September of 1878, his thought focused on the day's celebration and the incredible perseverance of Adolpho Sutro. The final connection of the Sutro Tunnel with the Comstock mines had been made the night before, and fortunately, most of the foul air had been disbursed through air shafts. No one wanted a repeat of July's fatality when a worker died from what the coroner called heat exhaustion, but which had been exacerbated by bad air. Roger found the tunnel entrance enhanced by an American flag flying on a tall pole, and dozens of people waiting near it for the appearance of Mr. Sutro. The crowd's excited murmur of expectation competed with the screech of a hawk soaring overhead and the occasional whinny of a horse. Dust rose and settled as people arrived by buggy and on horseback, and Roger surprised himself by finding the excitement somewhat contagious.

Mr. Sutro and his two sons had entered the tunnel through the Savage shaft that morning, and had shaken hands with the crew and visitors waiting for him. By way of the tunnel, he was now walking to the little town being called Sutro City. It was rumored that he was going to give all of his employees the day off after the speeches and back-slapping were over. First, however, they were to enjoy several kegs of lager that were being set up on long planks resting on saw-horses off to the side of the tunnel entrance.

Work had begun on October 18, 1869, although Mr. Sutro had talked about his idea for a drainage tunnel as far back as 1860. Initial ridicule had slowly evolved into mere skepticism, but in 1865 he had finally gained approval from the state and federal legislations. The search for investors had been his next step, and it had required months of perseverance and negotiation.

The poor ventilation and water accumulation at the lower depths in the mines had been a concern from the beginning of deep excavation. If access to the gold and silver was to continue, it was commonly acknowledged that something had to be done to make work safer in the lower depths. The Sutro tunnel was four miles long, at a grade of one and one-half per cent between the tunnel entrance near Dayton, leading uphill to the Virginia City mines that were working at the 1,640 foot level. This meant that most of the mines on the two and a half miles of side tunnels would be properly drained, which would avoid the need for bigger and more expensive pumps to get out the water. It would also make for easier transport of ore, supplies and men via the rails that ran along the floor of the four-mile main Sutro tunnel.

By 1866, Mr. Sutro had formed the Sutro Tunnel Company in order to sell stock in his project. Most of his initial investments came from miners eager to see improvement in working conditions, especially after the 1869 Yellow Jacket disaster. It was at this point that the Miners Union had pledged $50,000, enabling Sutro to begin work on the tunnel. He even obtained capital from European investors. Twenty-three of the leading companies on the Lode had by the tunnel's completion also contracted with Sutro, agreeing to pay a fee of $2 per ton of ore extracted through the tunnel. Additional services were available at twenty-five cents per person traveling through the tunnel. So innovative and effective was the engineering on the project, that it would eventually be used in Colorado mining operations at Idaho Springs, Cripple Creek, and Leadville.

To everyone's amazement except that of Mr. Sutro, whose faith in the project had never wavered, immediately upon completion of the tunnel it began draining four million gallons of water each day. This water would not go to waste, being used to irrigate farm plots around Sutro City that would grow fresh produce sold in Virginia City and Dayton.

Roger tied Diamond to a long rail set-up for horses next to the area quickly filling with buggies and wagons. He looked beyond the crowd to the simple wood and brick tunnel opening and saw that Mr. Sutro had not yet arrived. In Roger's opinion, referring to the site as a city was a gross exaggeration. However, there were a number of barn-like maintenance sheds, along with a market, a boarding house, two small saloons, a cafe, and a number of cabins for those working in the small village. Someone had even optimistically planted trees between the buildings.

Standing off to the side of the crush of people, Roger spotted Oliver Steel emerging from the crowd. He was the proprietor of the Yosemite Saloon on "C" Street, a successful businessman well-liked and respected. Roger had started his career in Virginia City working at the Sacramento on the corner of Union and "D" Street. Although seemingly outside the business district on "C" Street, the Sacramento was located in the Frederick House that fronted on "C" Street, across from the International Hotel. However, Roger had not been long at the Sacramento, as Mr. Steel had lured him away to work exclusively at the Yosemite.

Although a one-bit saloon, it was a nice one on the uphill side of "C" Street, with sufficient room for two tables at which men could gamble in the evenings. Roger's reputation had grown quickly, and after several months there, he had realized that he no longer needed anyone's backing. He had then gone out on his own to work at some of the better two-bit saloons, and under obligation to no one. Roger had run into Mr. Steel a few days prior, and during their conversation had mentioned coming to the opening, even though none of his other friends were going to take the time for it.

Mr. Steel walked up to Roger, shook his hand, and smiled broadly. "A grand day, is it not? Wonderful what Sutro has accomplished."

Roger managed a somewhat inane response. "And a wonderful benefit for all the miners."

"Yes, sir. It certainly is." But it was obvious that Mr. Steel was preoccupied, scanning the crowd with a raised hand blocking the sun from his eyes. "There's a man here I'd like you to meet."

"Oh?"

"John Wagner. Lives in Bodie now. A great champion of that town's prospects." A grin split his face. "Ah, there he is. Hey, John, over here."

They were approached by a slender man of medium height, clean-shaven and wearing a white Stetson. After introductions had been made all around, supplemented by enthusiastic comments on the glories of the weather, the men turned to the tunnel opening, applause alerting them that something important was happening. Mr. Sutro emerged at the front of a small group of people, his hand raised in acknowledgement of the enthusiastic greeting that had met his arrival.

Roger had never met the man of the hour, and was surprised to find him a portly gentleman with a receding hairline, modest mutton-chop side whiskers and a nicely trimmed mustache. His long, sloping nose and broad chin gave him the appearance of a sharp thinker, and possibly communicator. When the obligatory applause and cheering died down, Mr. Sutro made a short speech. As soon as it ended, men made their way to the tables of beer provided by the great man.

The mines supplied men with money, but it was where this money was spent that interested Mr. Wagner. Pointedly ignoring the crowd, he turned to Roger. "I hear good things about you."

"Oh, yes?" When Mr. Steel moved a few steps away, it occurred to Roger that there was something of significance about this introduction to John Wagner.

Mr. Wagner gave the crowd a brief, uninterested glance before turning back to Roger. "Are you returning to town soon?"

Roger refused to show that he was startled by the direct question. "I was just about to do that very thing."

"Good. I'm hungry. Be my guest at the International Hotel. Meet you there." Not having asked a question, he didn't wait for a reply. "Come on, Steel."

While Roger untied Diamond, he watched Mr. Wagner and Mr. Steel approach a light buggy with its shiny black body and large side wheels. Mr. Steel took up the long reins and guided the two black horses neatly through those standing nearby. Now certain that this meeting had been planned, speculation of all kinds raced through Roger's mind. When Diamond sensed his nervousness and acted in kind, Roger quickly mounted and hurried back to Virginia City.

Seated in a quiet corner of the elegant dining room of the International Hotel, the waiter arrived with their drinks and menus in hand. Mr. Wagner waved away the menus and placed an order for steaks all around, as well as one side and a basket of bread. Picking up his glass of boozy lemonade popular in the town, he took a long, satisfying swallow. Roger sipped his beer as he watched Mr. Steel pour essence of ginger into a glass of ale. Gingered ale was a popular drink with some, but Roger found it triggered his gag reflex.

He turned to Mr. Wagner. "This is very enjoyable, Mr. Wagner. Thank you."

"Oh, please, Roger, let's skip the formalities. I'm John."

"Fine with me."

John immediately came to the point. "Have you heard about Bodie lately?"

"What part of it?" Roger asked. "Its rapid growth, its reputation for violence, or the rich discoveries in the mines?"

"It's all true, some of it more and some of it less than you've probably heard. The mines are producing, so the town is growing rapidly. Men are pouring in, and we all know where they want to spend their evenings. I understand you're a square dealer."

"Yes, I am. And I intend to stay that way." If he was correct about what was coming next, Roger wanted to be sure John Wagner knew where he stood. However, thinking that he might have come across on the defensive, he added, "Where I've worked here, that's been respected."

"As it should be!" John barked. Several people looked in their direction, but immediately looked away when they saw Roger's smile and realized it was a friendly group of men. "Wagner's Saloon has a good reputation, and I want to keep it that way."

"What does that have to do with me?"

"I want you to come work for me. Steel here says you're very fond of Faro, but there isn't that much call for it here. They love it in Bodie."

Roger felt his heart beating in his chest. "You're offering me a job at your saloon in Bodie?"

"Have you seen it?"

"No. The last time I was in Bodie was back in '76. I lived there for a couple of months."

"Ah, that was before the boom. You'd hardly recognize the town now, there's been so much building." John took another swallow of his drink before fixing his eyes on Roger. "I'm offering you a very good deal." He proceeded to lay out the terms he had in mind, and Roger kept his poker face well enough in place that even the great saloon empresario couldn't tell how he felt.

Rather than comment on what John had offered, which was indeed generous, Roger simply asked, "When would you want me to start?"

"As soon as you can get there."

"Let me be clear on one thing." Roger took a swallow of his beer and leaned back in his chair. "I won't work with a gaffed deck, only an honest shoe. Every punter at my table needs to know there's no cheating going on. That goes for them, as well. If I see anyone moving their bets or find a copper with a horsehair on it, I need to know you'll back me if I kick them out of the game."

"No problem. You'll be in charge of your bank. Now, what do you say? I picked up a nice painting of a tiger here in town and I'm eager to put it up in the window of my place in Bodie."

Roger smiled at the reference to playing Faro as *bucking the tiger*, playing cards often having a picture of a tiger on the back. "Can I meet you for breakfast at the café by the Yosemite Saloon? Say, eight o'clock? I'll give you my answer then."

John, having thought Roger would immediately jump at the offer, nevertheless agreed. Their steaks and sides arrived, and the hungry men cut into the tender meat and savored the creamy mashed potatoes saturated with butter. Conversation was general and minimal for several minutes.

As their plates were removed, Oliver Steel said, "Someone reminded me that Crazy Horse, the Oglala Sioux Chief was killed a year ago this month."

"Bayoneted by a Fort Robinson soldier," John mumbled, "when he was resisting confinement."

"That's in Nebraska, right?" Roger asked.

"Yeah," Oliver answered, noting that John was choosing to remain silent. "Doesn't seem right, somehow."

"What doesn't?" John's cheeks were a little flushed. "Death or being put in prison?"

"Both." Oliver looked a little embarrassed, but was determined to express what to many men might be considered an unpopular sentiment.

Roger looked out the window at the bright sunlight and the clear blue sky, thinking how naturally he could choose to go outside any time he wanted. "Maybe they're the same to someone so used to being free."

The two older men looked at Roger in surprise, as though not expecting such empathy from someone so young. But they both nodded in agreement, relieved that they all shared the same attitude. And a little surprised that they did.

"I hope you gentlemen will excuse me," Roger told them. "I need to change my clothes before going to work." He shook their hands and told Mr. Wagner, "I look forward to seeing you in the morning."

As soon as Roger left them, John turned to his friend. "I don't understand, Oliver. What's to think about?"

"He has a mother here in town. But don't worry. Lucy Murphy is a dealer herself, and a very independent woman. She'll no doubt encourage him to take the job."

"A dealer? Really? Is she comely?"

"Very. But if you're thinking of hiring her too, you can forget it."

"No, I don't suppose Roger would like that."

"Oh, that isn't it. She's just very rooted to this place, and from what my wife told me, not a great fan of Bodie as a place to live. Certainly not compared to Virginia City."

"As long as her son doesn't feel that way."

"I don't think you need worry about that. Roger likes excitement."

"How old is he, by the way?"

"Um. Not really sure, but definitely over twenty-one. I think about twenty-four."

"That's okay, then."

Oliver put his lips onto his coffee cup in an effort to hide his smile. He had standards, besides knowing the law, but Roger was very good at what he did and deserved every break coming his way. Besides, he owed John a big favor, and he now considered it repaid.

Oliver sipped his drink before leaning forward. "Have you been over to see the Shooting Gallery next to Flowery Street where it narrows near 'C'?"

"That's the saloon that has a shooting gallery in it, right? Owned by two Irishmen?"

"Yeah, that's the one. Hard to imagine drinking and shooting going together, but so far, I haven't heard of any accidents."

"I went by it, I think. In a three-story, clapboard-sided building? Its doors open onto South 'C', right?"

"That's the one. They have lodging rooms upstairs, with a few being used as offices."

From this topic the men began a general discussion of Virginia City's saloons, which were a varied collection of types. Beyond the fact of some being one-bit and some being two-bit establishments, and whether called a saloon or a bar, there were those that were narrow but deep with no room for tables, and those that were spacious enough for gambling and even a billiard table. Among other attractions in some of the saloons was a bowling alley, and another with a shuffle board court. More than one offered barbering services, and many provided newspapers. Food could be meager to sumptuous, with most beer served in bottles. A few, while calling themselves a brewery, offered beer on tap. Although most excluded loose women, a few allowed dancing girls to flirt with customers before going off to the dancehalls for work. But out of the 100 saloons, only a couple allowed backroom sexual commerce.

The one thing they all had in common, however, were their entry doors. If there were any with bat-wing half doors, such as would someday be portrayed in movies, they were encountered only beyond the standard double doors on the street. Tall, narrow, and with panes of glass in the top half, the doors used in Virginia City allowed customers to enter and exit without incurring another coming the other way. More importantly, they kept out the dust of summer and the cold of winter, which the bat-wing style would not have done.

Still sated from the rich meal, Roger went immediately to *Lucy's Lodgings*. There was no sign out front with this name on it, but her white house with the green trim was now being called that by many townspeople. Lucy referred to it as a *lodging house* because she gave those staying there only breakfast. If she gave them supper as well, it would be called a boarding house. The expense and hassle of serving an evening meal was something Lucy had decided to avoid.

This bright afternoon, Roger found his mother at the small kitchen table in the bay window. She was sipping coffee from a delicate cup and saucer, the tall porcelain pot on a warming plate in the middle of the table. She carefully closed the ledger of household accounts and laid it aside.

Having seen her son coming up the front walkway, and the intensity of his expression, when the door closed Lucy called out to him. "I'm in here, dear. The coffee's hot. Get a cup off the shelf and join me."

Only when he was sitting across from her, gripping the heavy mug with the large handle that he preferred, did Lucy fix her eyes on her son. At the same time, her neck muscles tensed. "You look like you have something on your mind. What's happened?"

"I went out to the Sutro opening today."

"How was it?" Nothing alarming about that, she thought, relaxing a little.

"Interesting. Lots of people, lots of congratulations, lots of beer provided by Sutro."

"That's nice." She was still waiting for what was to come, and was surprised at the sudden anxiety she was feeling.

"I met someone from Bodie while there. John Wagner of Wagner's Saloon. Nice guy. I could barely detect his German accent. He's got a big place in Bodie, with its own chop stand, and an area for Faro at the back of the main room. It's becoming very popular. I've heard a lot of talk about it."

Lucy smiled, relieved that nothing terrible had happened, and pretty sure what was to follow. "Is it a good offer?"

Ignoring the sudden lump in his throat, Roger looked at his mother and grinned. "Why do you always make things easy for me?"

"Because I'm your mother and I'm quite fond of you." She loved the way he grinned when he was overcome with emotions that were difficult for him to express. "When do you leave?"

"He wants me there as soon as possible. I'm to give him my answer at breakfast in the morning."

"How will Mr. Steel and the other places where you work take the news?"

With a shrug, Roger gave her the details of his meeting with Mr. Wagner that had included Mr. Steel. He was obviously too enthusiastic about this new turn of fortune to care over much about those in Virginia City, even those who had given him so many opportunities. Lucy mentally flinched at this display of callousness, but had to admit that the whole town was fundamentally based on grabbing the main chance.

She put aside her feelings, and all she wished to say as a mother who preferred to think of her son as a caring individual. "Was the steak good?"

Roger laughed. "Very. Are you okay with my going?"

"It's not like Bodie is so far away that I'll never see you. With the railroad from here to Carson City and good stages after that, it isn't that difficult a trip. Do you want to take Diamond with you?"

"I wouldn't dream of taking him from you. You go riding every week, and I know how much you enjoy him." He laughed outright as her face relaxed. "Look how relieved you are! It was a kind offer, but you're glad I refused."

"Well, yes."

"I'm going to my rooms to see what I should pack and what I can give away. I may just go to Bodie with Mr. Wagner. I'll need to find a place to stay once I'm there."

His mind was obviously racing to what came next in his life. Lucy was suddenly very quiet. She watched him rise up, grab the hat he had tossed onto the kitchen counter, and smiled at the quick kiss on her cheek. When the door slammed behind him, she felt the sudden silence as a weight on her chest.

The flurry of his arrival and departure seemed to have lasted only a matter of moments, and Lucy was reacting to the startling abruptness of it. She surprised herself by the sudden welling up of tears and the almost over-whelming desire to give into them. Instead, she slipped a pinafore apron over her head and washed the few dishes in the sink, followed by a thorough mopping of a kitchen floor that didn't need it.

When Kathryn arrived to find her kitchen chores already completed, she sensed Lucy's distress and got herself out of the way by going upstairs with a bucket and clean rags. Lucy grabbed her hemp shopping basket, dropped in a few over-ripe apples and headed to the stable to visit Diamond. By the time she returned to the house, Kathryn had finished upstairs and was making a big pot of tea.

With a steaming cup in front of them, Lucy told Kathryn of Roger's planned departure, her tone brittle with underlying emotion. Kathryn, having always harbored a slight crush on the master of the house, realized that any possibility of fulfilling her hopes had come to an end. When her beloved Mrs. Murphy retreated to her bedroom, Kathryn quietly left the house.

Three soaked hankies later, Lucy took a deep breath and decided to stop feeling sorry for herself. She went to the kitchen to eat whatever Kathryn had left her for supper, after which she changed her clothes, powdered her nose, and made her way to the Crystal Bar. Only her regulars thought her a little less sparkling than usual, but they were soon focused on the game and thought nothing more about it.

The next afternoon Lucy sat down at her dressing table, looked at the picture of her and Jim in its silver frame, and forced herself to accept the new arrangement of her life. Roger was gone, the awkward moment of saying good-bye endured. Oh, the infamous *awkward farewell*, experienced throughout history by so many; the desperation choking the throat, the mind frantically racing for a way to stop the seconds flying past, and finally the reluctant acceptance of what must be.

The fact that such partings had been experienced by thousands of people over thousands of years made no difference to any one individual, and certainly not to Lucy. She had been the one staying behind, while Roger had been seething with eagerness and excitement. So, for his sake, she had stood by the stage, smiling and waving and keeping her eyes dry. She had accomplished this only by refusing to allow herself the memory of her last parting from Jim during the war.

The rest of the summer of 1878 was the same as the ones before it; hot, dusty, and windy. It was also filled with an almost constant whirl of activities. With over a dozen different nationalities present in the town, and each one celebrating something related to their heritage at least once a year, parades were a popular and almost weekly occurrence. Immediately following most of these was a dance where food and drink was plentiful for a minimal donation. There was, as an example of a few such parade sponsors, the British Benevolent Assn., the Helvetia Society, the Italian Benevolent Society, the Welsh Club, the Friends of Poland group, and the Scandinavian Society.

It was at one of these events that Lucy became friends with Amanda Payne, a thirty-seven year old woman who owned a boarding house on North "C" Street, as well as a restaurant and saloon. Although she was a single woman, she was referred to out of respect as "Mrs.", as was the custom of the day for women who owned businesses. She was also a supporter of the Methodist Episcopal Church on "F" Street that her fellow African-Americans attended. The two women had another thing in common. Besides both running lodging houses, they both worked as a dealer. When they were able to visit one another, they joked between them that they never seemed to run out of conversational topics. Amanda had been in Virginia City several years longer than Lucy, and delighted in recounting stories about the early years.

Amanda told Lucy, "You said you left Placerville in '75. That March, about the time you were packing up, we had a bit of excitement when human remains were found in the old shaft of the East Comstock Mining Company. At the inquest, they said the remains were of a man unknown to anyone. So the whole thing just fizzled out, and nothing more was said about it. Oh, there was a lot of speculation, but nothing for sure."

"Couldn't they tell if he had been shot or stabbed?"

"No. Maybe hit on the head, but any damage of that type could have been from the fall down the shaft." Amanda looked at a troubled Lucy. "Hey, hon, that type of thing happens from time to time. Don't let it bother you. Worse things than that happened in the early days here, before we became so civilized."

Lucy had resisted asking for more details or, having read that morning's newspapers, debating whether or not "civilized" was all that accurate.

For Lucy, that summer produced some wonderful memories. She attended many of the town dances, sometimes on the arm of a gentleman and sometimes with several ladies. Either way, she wore down the soles of her dancing slippers while finding an excuse to have two new dresses made.

"Ho, for Treadway's!" That was what the billboard announced to one and all, and in front of which Lucy and Helene stopped as they left their favorite French café.

"Oh, Lucy, this is the big annual picnic! It's so much fun!"

"I've heard of it, but I've never been."

"Then we must do it! You'll love it!"

Lucy agreed that anything different would be welcome, especially if it took them out of town for the day. And as usual when Helene suggested something new, Lucy was eager to join in if she could think of it as an adventure.

Treadway's was the farm in Carson City used as a park when the Miner's Union or the public school district organized the popular picnic. It was the highlight of the year for many adults, but it was especially so for children. The boys were always intent on playing games when they weren't stealing green apples from Mr. Treadway's trees. They ignored the plums, pears and peaches, and if the apples were a little too green, the repercussions of their consumption wouldn't follow until that night. At that point, it would e their mother's problem.

Little girls saw it as an opportunity to dress up, as well as consume an alarming number of sweets. Teenage girls would try to match the refined comportment of the ladies they saw promenading along the streets, when they weren't practicing their flirting skills. Teenage boys would flex their muscles at the many games available, while trying to come up with ways in which they could spend a little time with those flirty girls.

Of course, not everyone could afford the admission price of $2.50 when going by train, or $1.00 if arriving on one's own. Each year, the week leading up to the picnic was the best time for businesses to hire extra help, as there were so many men and boys eager to earn extra spending money.

So it was that at 8 AM on a Saturday, Helene and Lucy climbed onto one of the railroad's twenty flatcars now set up with rows of benches, with the edges fenced to protect kids that refused to stay seated. Each car held up to 150 passengers, and it required two engines to pull it all.

As the two women looked around the rapidly filling flatcar for a place where they could sit together, Lucy admired the little girls in their colorful cotton dresses and hair ribbons flying in the breeze from carefully curled tresses. She then spotted movement beneath several of the benches. Looking down at the one in front of her, the familiar head of a small boy peeked out.

"Johnny!"

"Shh. Please don't give me away. My dad said I had to earn the money for today and I only have $2.00, and that has to pay for the eats."

"Am I correct in seeing a few of your friends also here?"

"Yeah."

Behind her, a conductor asked Helene to show her ticket. Lucy quickly seated herself on top of Johnny's hiding place, spreading out her skirts so that he was completely hidden. She held out her ticket and smiled up at the conductor. He smiled back and moved on. Having seen Lucy's action, Helene had done the same for a lad across the aisle, and now the two women smiled at one another with conspiratorial glee.

Once under way and the conductor having moved on to the other flatcars, Johnny wiggled out from under the bench and plopped down beside Lucy. "Why did you do that?"

"Why not? It's a day for fun, isn't it?"

Johnny looked at Lucy as though he had never seen an adult before. Then, remembering the magazine she had bought him, he mumbled that maybe adults weren't all the same after all.

"Besides," Lucy said, "if you get caught, I want to be able to tell your mother that at least I made sure you were safe."

Johnny nodded his head in the manner of a wise sage. "Yeah, mothers worry a lot."

"You have to remember that it's still on everyone's mind what happened to that boy who tried to jump from the platform to a moving train."

He shut his eyes and swallowed hard. "Yeah, that was awful. Everyone in my gang swore an oath that we'd never dare each other to do something that dangerous."

Lucy didn't expect that oath to hold, but she didn't argue the point. The train's whistle pierced the air, and a frisson of excitement and expectation ran through the crowd. The train crept through the town and the "E" Street tunnel to the accompaniment of cheers from the passengers, while smoke and cinders from the engine filled the air around them. No one complained, and soon they were picking up speed and the created breeze blew it all away. In and out of tunnels they went, the courting couples taking advantage of the brief moments of darkness. They passed through sage flats, past old abandoned mine shafts, along the edges of ravines, and then through the last tunnel that passed under old Fort Homestead and brought them into Gold Hill.

More passengers were picked up at the depot, including on this trip Mrs. Sandy Bowers, now known as the down-on-her-luck Washoe seeress. She had been telling anyone who would listen that the latest rumor about her was wrong. She emphatically denied that she had prophesied the collapse of Gold Hill's Crown Point Trestle. To prove her point, she got on the very train that would be crossing it that day. Nevertheless, as the train crossed the 350-foot span that loomed 90 feet above the deep ravine, most people on board held their breath. On the other hand, they usually did.

At Silver City, just before American Flat and the longest tunnel on the line, more excited picnic-bound passengers were picked up. Passing through the 600-foot tunnel was always a thrill, and the exhilaration of the experience lingered long enough to quell impatience while more people got on board at Belcher, Scales, Mound House and Empire.

Finally, the train reached the boundary of the ranch on its north side, stopping at the entry gate where "Farmer" Treadway, now in his sixties, met them with a big smile and waved them all in. They recognized him by his deep-set eyes, wide mouth and distinctive, short gray beard. A native of Connecticut, he was a product of the Mexican War, the California gold rush, and the rush to Washoe. He had chosen to settle in Carson City where he developed a 10-acre farm, and had served in the Nevada Territorial Legislature. Over time he owned 300 acres of timber land about three miles west of Carson, as well as 110 acres east of it. It was he, in fact, who had been the first to ship fresh produce to Virginia City via railroad. His potatoes and beets fresh from his farm had been very welcome. Therefore, everyone felt that he was a friend, and greeted him as such.

Johnny and his pals immediately disappeared into the orchards to feast on apples, as well as across the lawn to watch the foot races, target shooting, and archery contests. The last of these was one in which ladies were welcome to participate. The young courting couples wandered toward the grape arbors and the small forest of shade trees. Many of the adults headed for town to do a little shopping, or take a tour of some other public building.

Lucy and Helene spread a blanket they had brought with them under a shade tree, watching the hustle and bustle of the crowds from afar. After walking around to see the sights, they stopped at the lunch tent before returning to their blanket. They then dozed off while leaning against the tree. They therefore felt somewhat rested by the time the train left at 4:30 in the afternoon. That was not the case for most of those with them. The little girls' dresses were limp and stained, and most of their ribbons were missing. Grime and stickiness clung to the rumpled clothing of grinning boys like badges of honor.

Lucy looked around for Johnny, but didn't see him. She had to settle for assuming that he was okay, and somewhere on one of the flatcars. Fortunately, it was known that the conductors spent little time checking the tickets of those returning. They too had exerted themselves overmuch during the long day, but they still had to stay alert during the three hours it took to return on the uphill, twisting route. The train, now with three engines pulling, strained all the way, even as more and more people disembarked. Once back in Virginia City, there was just enough daylight left to see everyone home.

That summer saw excitement mounting regarding several of the mines north of town that had worked down to the 2,100-feet level. Stocks soared higher than they had been for months in the Mexican, the Lady Bryan, the Alta, and the Wells Fargo. On the night of August 28, people even gathered in the evening along "C" Street to share the celebratory atmosphere that attended anticipation of a new bonanza. Some investors were invited to the Sierra Nevada mine, the Ophir, and the Julia, to take samples of likely rich ore. Men buying and selling stocks filled the sidewalks in front of stock dealers' offices, and the Enterprise newspaper declared, "It is beginning again to look like old times."

By the approach of fall, Lucy had put aside both memories of that summer and the suddenness of her son's departure. She put on her favorite day dress, and walked into town to enjoy watching one of the town's many colorful parades as it moved down "C" Street. The bands were of course playing loudly, and although it wasn't clear to Lucy who was sponsoring this particular parade, people of all ethnicities were cheering around her. All was joy and fun and lack of care, and Lucy realized that she was feeling a great degree of contentment. She no longer missed Placerville, she was glad to know that her son was happy, and she was finally able to recall the good times with Jim without immediately switching over to the ache of loss. Yes, she thought, "My life is one of settled satisfaction. At last."

That fall, Lucy made two trips to Gold Hill to visit her friends Effie and Penelope. Lucy loved riding the train, which allowed her to visit her friends more often than she might have if stages were the only choice. There was something wonderful about the heavy clang of the brass bell bouncing off the nearby buildings; the flat-cars piled with lumber; wooden box-cars with their heavy sliding doors hiding treasures, and maybe a few hobos, from public view. As she sat in the First Class passenger car, leaning back against soft velvet upholstery, she could hear the iron wheels grinding on the metal tracks, the grit of the roadbed heard crunching when the giant rolled slowly through the tunnels. And, oh, the thrill of the whistle as the big engine puffed out billows of steam as it left the stations, giving a smaller toot when it approached a tunnel or a sharp turn. Lucy loved it all.

Although she did make a trip of four days to Carson City and a shorter one to Dayton, she was mostly content to stay in Virginia City. There, she had frequent visits with her friends, meetings with various charitable groups, fundraising bazaars, and dances almost every week. Besides, working at the Crystal Bar most nights, the turnover of her lodgers, and the up-keep of the house and garden, kept her too busy to be away for very long.

The start of that winter of 1878 found Virginia City citizens greeting the first of the season's snow flurries. More interesting to many, of course, was that there were mining successes that caused the stock prices to rise, along with mining failures that sent stock prices down. The worst of that winter was when everyone realized that their summer hopes of a new bonanza were not to be realized.

Certainly, no one was now being invited to enter the mines and take samples. Only the stock manipulators were happy, having collected fees for all the deals that had taken place at their behest. Even the San Francisco big wigs lost money, blaming those in Virginia City for spreading rumors of strikes that bore no real promise of developing. Eager to move on, many people in Virginia City waited eagerly for the spring weather of '79, their only decision being whether to go north down the Geiger Grade and on to Reno, or out the other way to Carson City.

That winter there were several mining accidents. Some miners survived, and other miners were followed by funeral processions to the cemetery north of town. There were weeks when deep snows blocked the passes and freighters with supplies couldn't get through. But at the first bit of improvement to the roads, there was a rush of the wagons coming in on slushy roads with special gripping shoes on the mules and horses. The railroad cars may have been blocked by snow and the tracks iced over, but the old freighters and their wagons still managed to get supplies through to the town. Whether or not history would consider these stalwart freighters heroes, those living in mountainous towns certainly did.

Overall, people had done a good job preparing their businesses and homes for the winter, and they therefore got by well. Some, of course, had to rely on others for assistance, but there was never a lack of that. By the time Christmas was over, everyone was filled with eager anticipation of the year to follow. Consequently, the New Year's Day celebrations were as raucous as they ever had been.

At the start of the new year, on January 25, 1879, Lucy attended a celebration put on by the Scottish citizens commemorating Robert Burns, poet laureate of Ireland. It was a magnificent supper party, with many toasts to "Bobby Burns". There was also a reading of his poetry, and much eating and drinking. Overseen by a Highland piper in full uniform, bagpipes and all, it was a sentimental and yet exuberant occasion. It was one of Lucy's favorite evenings out.

Helene arrived at Lucy's on a February day that was unusually clear. Lucy opened the door just as the rig of Helene's husband moved on down the street toward the Masonic Hall. Lucy was thrilled to see her friend and greeted her warmly.

"I hope it isn't an inconvenient time for you, Lucy."

"Not at all! It's a delightful surprise. Come into the kitchen and I'll make us a pot of tea. It's Kathryn's day off, and I made cookies this morning. They're actually pretty good."

"I was just so tired of being cooped up in the house."

"I know what you mean. At least today there's no snow falling or wind blowing."

As they chatted while enjoying their refreshments, Helene kept an eye on Lucy in a judicious manner that was unusual. "Lucy, should I not bring up what happened the other night at the Sawdust Saloon?"

Lucy put her half-eaten cookie on the tea cup's saucer. "I have to talk about it sometime, I suppose." She looked out the window and up at the clouds sure to soon form into a storm. "I was dealing poker at the next table. I saw Charley Fosgard playing Faro along with several other men. He looked frazzled, and with each hand that he lost, more so. I'd played with him in the past, and he'd never acted that way."

"He's been an engineer at the C&C Shaft. That means he makes more than the miners, but I think he's always gambled more than he could afford."

"Maybe that's why it happened. He just reached into his pocket and took out a Colt Navy revolver. I immediately feared for the dealer, as it seemed to be pointed in his direction. But before anyone could react, Charles put it to his head and pulled the trigger."

"Oh, Lucy! Even reading about it in the paper was horrible. I can't imagine what it must have been like to have seen it."

"It was awful. He flopped over the table, blood going everywhere, and other stuff I don't want to think about. One of the men took off his coat and flung it over Charley's head, and someone else ran out the door for the Sheriff. I threw my cloak over my shoulders and hurried out just as some reporters showed up. I didn't want them to see me there and mention my name."

"How are you coping with it?"

Lucy looked at her friend and sighed. "Helene, it isn't the first time I've seen a dead man, or bloodshed by violence. It was a long time ago, of course. Mainly, I just feel a deep sadness for anyone who feels there's no other solution."

Helene nodded and changed the subject. With all its modern inventions and seeming sophistication, Virginia City was still mainly just a mining camp. And every camp since the gold rush had seen its share of those who had, for reasons of their own, lost faith in the value of life. Sometimes that life belonged to another, and sometimes it was their own. Either way, the taking always left a wake of sadness behind.

CHAPTER 13

1879 - 1880

As in all new years at the beginning, people were filled with optimism at the start of 1879. In Virginia City, they were also expecting better times. Nearby California was celebrating having its Constitution ratified, which was a significant sign of progress for the whole area. The greatest news for the whole country was that the Specie Resumption Act had passed. This meant that for the first time since the Civil War, paper money known as Greenbacks were valued the same as gold. No longer would only coin be accepted by businesses, or the Greenbacks be valued less than their face value.

Lucy for one was very glad to hear this. She had more than once purchased Greenbacks from those in dire need, paying them more than the banks or businesses were willing to pay, although still less than their face value. She took what bills she had and used some of them to hire a team of out-of-work men to build on a two-tub bath house at the back of the house. This left the older and smaller building free to be used only for laundry. Piping and drains were added, although it increased what she paid the water company each month. After purchasing a small stove and large iron kettle for the bath house, she still had a few Greenbacks left over to be deposited in the California Bank. It was a testament to how many of them she had purchased in her effort to help others. No one would ever know that some of those whom she had helped had been soiled doves down on their luck.

One of the things that created interest among men in the changing rooms of the mines, as well as those leaning on bar railings, was the news that there was a prisoner in the Bridgeport jail. There had been another, but the previous month on December 12, the Chinese prisoner had been hanged for murder. The white man left in the jail was awaiting his trial, also on murder charges. The local opinion in Bridgeport about the outcome of his trial prompted those who had built the scaffold for Chow Yew to leave it standing.

Then, in the snowy cold of January, the man escaped amid Bridgeport's celebration of James Sinnamon marrying Martha Oberchain. News of this escape missed the town's newspapers, but it managed to percolate through men's discussions into that of some women's groups in Virginia City. That the escaped prisoner's last name was Murphy created a number of discrete jokes among the women, but their dedication to the rules of polite behavior kept them from teasing their friend Lucy Murphy. In any case, Lucy was not aware of the rumors. As things turned out, months later she would have to decide whether or not her friends' restraint had been a blessing or a curse.

April of 1879 found Mother Nature having a difficult time of deciding whether to drag out winter, or blow into spring. It settled for cold mornings, and pleasant but windy afternoons. As Lucy dressed in her dark purple dress reserved for funerals and affixed her mourning brooch to it, she decided not to wear any of her other mourning jewelry pieces. She was thinking of the burden of grief among so many of her friends, whether it was for the loss of a loved one or that of a cherished business.

It was a gray day, which fit everyone's state of mind perfectly. It wasn't a mining accident that had taken out Mr. Williams, although it had taken place in a mine. He had just fallen down dead. He had been dealing with a persistent cough for some time, and his wife had insisted that it was because of the bad air down at the thousand-foot level where he worked much of the time. But no one had been willing to listen to her. The air was always bad down in the mines, and men were always coughing, but they didn't just drop dead. This debate was laid aside during the necessity of burying him, but it would be a contentious issue as long as the mines continued.

In the early years of the town, people had been buried in Six Mile Canyon on either side of the wide ravine running through it. Julia Bulette, one of the common prostitutes to inhabit the town in its early years, had met a violent end back in January of 1867. She had been one of the last to be buried at the old Mount Pleasant Cemetery on the south slope of the canyon, amid the others of the town who had died in those earlier years. Later, after the establishment of new cemeteries nearby, it would be surmised that she had not been allowed her final rest among her fellow citizens. However, this was simply a misinterpretation of that early cemetery's location.

Mr. Williams was being buried in the Masonic Section of the Silver Terrace Cemetery, near the split path that outlined the Masonic symbol of a trowel. Typical of the Victorian era, much was being made of his passing. The black horses were wearing tall, black feather plumes on their heads while pulling the highly polished black hearse through town, its glass sides displaying the coffin within. A procession of those nearest and dearest followed this all the way to the cemetery, where those not so near and dear awaited their arrival.

Mrs. Williams was pleased with the chosen coffin. It had a small glass window over the face portion, and she was pleased that everyone would have a last lingering view of her dear husband. She was unaware that such coffins were actually designed to assure the gravediggers that the deceased was truly dead before putting them in the ground, making sure there was no moisture on the underside of the glass.

After the tapered coffin was lowered into the ground on ropes, the reverend said a short and hopefully comforting prayer. Everyone then quickly and silently left the area, leaving behind the family to be consoled by the reverend while two men lost no time shoveling dirt into the hole. Being one of the last to leave, Lucy heard the first clods of dirt hit the wooden coffin with a hard finality. She fought the urge to shudder. Although many of the mourners accompanied the widow to a nearby restaurant for cakes and ale, Lucy returned home.

Kathryn greeted her in the parlor with a crystal glass half full of Lucy's favorite bourbon. Overcome with gratitude, Lucy gave Kathryn the afternoon off. She then put the bourbon aside and cut herself a very large piece of coconut cake that she took to her bedroom, along with a large mug of coffee. After removing her corset and slipping into a robe, she sat down at her writing desk and ate the entire piece of cake. Smirking with satisfaction, she unpinned her long hair and picked up the silver-backed brush.

After several minutes of brushing her hair while deep in thought, she turned from the mirror and looked around her bedroom. The four-poster spring-bed was neatly made with quilts and fluffy pillows, and the two-globe, cranberry glass lamp on the nightstand was the best available. The art work on the walls was pleasant, and the rugs were thickly padded. The crystal wall sconces on either side of the bed's headboard were waiting to be lit, and there was a fresh blotter on the little writing desk below one of them. It was the room she had dreamed of the whole of her life; luxurious, perfectly appointed and clean. Why then was she not fully satisfied with it?

Only when she forced herself to look beyond the room's appointments did she find the answer. The decorating had included fine new fabrics, rugs and furniture, and she was proud of the over-all effect. But other than a few objects like her string of buttons and the wedding photo, it was still just a bedroom with no special shared memories associated with it.

Eager to retreat from that sad realization, she took up a recent letter from Roger and lay down on the bed to read it while there was still light from the windows on either side of the bed.

Mom,   *Summer 1879*

I continue to like it here. The winter was pretty brutal, but it meant that even more men spent time whiling away time gambling and drinking. So work remained steady. And, yes, it is a bit wild here, and the town struggles to establish law and order, but it means that each day is exciting. The streets are full of traffic day and night, stages rush in with people and then out again carrying bullion from the mines.

Mr. Wagner's saloon is one of the largest in the town, being thirty feet across the front and a hundred long. It's on the northwest corner of Main and King Streets, near the Chinese district and the fair but frail ladies on Bonanza Street just behind. We call it 'Maiden Lane'. The saloon, no matter what time of day or night, is always filled with miners, shopkeepers, and men in suits. There's less of a social hierarchy here than in Washoe, which I like.

With so much room, there is a bar to the left as you walk in and to the right the Capitol Chop Stand that serves surprisingly good food like fried steaks and pork chops, and fresh bread with lots of butter. The prices range from two bits to two dollars. Still, I usually eat at the Can-Can Restaurant down the street. I like Mr. Callahan and he sometimes joins me at my table, bringing free coffee and dessert with him.

The center of the room at Wagner's is filled with tables for eating or gambling, but it is at the back of the room where I work dealing Faro. There are usually stacks of silver and gold coins on my table, so I carry a gun at all times. And, of course, there's the guard on a rise to my right who always has a shot gun across his lap.

I didn't realize that Mr. Wagner had once been a Senator until I was on my way here with him. He lives with his wife, a doctor who administers mostly to the poor and needy. They have quarters at the rear of the saloon, with its own private entrance. John has mentioned a couple of times that he might be retiring next year, but I'm not sure he really means it. Because at the same time, he's planning to take over the Gem Eating House, just three doors south of the Standard Mine's offices. He wants to rename it the Bon Ton Eating House.

You wouldn't recognize the town now, with all its growth. We have two markets, Miletich and Company's San Francisco Market and Mr. Jeritch's Miners Market. They always seem to have plenty of fruits and vegetables of good quality. I recently tried what Mr. Kilgore calls Bologne sausage at his meat market. Pretty tasty. He gets a lot of his meat from the cattle raised in Mono County by Rickey and Company, and the ladies here always get as much of it as they can when it first arrives. After the freshness passes off, the meat often gets wiped with vinegar, which smell is a dead give-away. The slaughterhouse is outside of town to the north. It's quite a place, surrounded by large corrals, pens, stables, and tanks holding water.

Harvey Boone has a nice store, too. He came here two years ago and in fact is keeping the brick yard busy as he builds on a brick warehouse behind his store. He's also in the process of building a big barn with corrals on both ends of it, and is bringing in a huge amount of firewood stacked near it. He's a great guy and I know no one who says anything against him.

This April the ladies of Bodie put on a "grand ball" at the Miners' Union Hall. The music was okay, but it was the food that was grand.

Mr. Boone and Mr. Wagner joined with some other men and have formed the Bodie Water Company to bring water to a reservoir out by the Mono mine in case of fire. They're selling stock to raise money for the project. Ten-inch pipe will be laid down hill 700 feet to the town with a fall of 175 feet to Main Street. The pipe is being made at the Gilson & Barber store, and they have brought in a riveting machine that's huge. It was brought in on a wagon pulled by over a dozen horses and was quite an event.

I have a room at the Standard Boarding House, just opposite the Standard works. I pay $8 a week, and the food is pretty good. I'm comfortable, and I enjoy my work. I've even made a few friends who are good company. I'll let you know when there is a time I think would be good for you to visit.

Your loving son

Laying the letter aside, Lucy reached for a book. It wasn't long before her eyes grew heavy, and she drifted into a deep sleep. Finally, her dreams of Jim and the life they had shared brought her the comfort for which she had longed, so that even upon awakening she was content to leave the dream and return to reality.

Helene arrived at Lucy's for lunch that summer, looking a little wilted from the heat. Sitting at the kitchen table with the last of the light meal before them, Lucy refilled their coffee cups. "I must say, Helene, I admire how easily you walk up through the rise of streets."

"Just because I'm thin doesn't mean I haven't developed good muscles in my legs after all these years. You'd do the same if you didn't live in the heart of town."

Lucy didn't say so to Helene, but she was grateful for her location every time she set out to do shopping on "C" Street, only one steep slope down to the main business district. The children with sleds might have been happy for the steepness of Sutton and Taylor Streets when snowed over, but few adults felt the same.

Helene put down her coffee cup and cleared her throat. "Lucy, I have a great idea about what we can do tomorrow."

"Oh, yes?" She tried to sound enthusiastic rather than cautious, but wasn't sure she succeeded.

"Have you ever hiked up Mt. Davidson?"

"No. Isn't it rather dangerous, what with so many old coyote-hole mines from the early years?"

"It can be, but not if you stay on the main worn path. It's the one the men use to get up to the big flag pole on holidays."

Lucy rolled her eyes, while Helene sighed and nodded her head in silent agreement, both knowing what the other was thinking about. That flag pole had been a major source of both pride and consternation since the previous winter when it had blown over in a strong storm. The Eagle Engine Company No. 3 had considered it their duty to raise the flag each Fourth of July, and they had pledged to raise enough money for a new flagpole. They even declared that there would never be another good strike on the Comstock until the flag was at the masthead "on top of our guardian mountain". Lucy was surprised at the amount of faith that was put in this superstitious declaration. Even with this thought to be true, the collection of the money needed took a long time. Finally, pieces of the old pole were sold as souvenirs. Eventually, on June 21, a cast-iron flagpole, 84 feet in length with an 18-pound globe at the top, had been pulled into place by the strength of six horses and a sturdy freight wagon. But it hadn't been until July 2 that it had been put in place, just in time for the Fourth of July celebration.

Among those who had hiked up to the top to see it raised was Lincoln White, a sketch artist who produced a drawing of the flag as it was lifted to the top. The pole had been a gift from James Fair, although some of the ladies claimed it had been at the suggestion of his wife. Just as the flag had reached the top and unfurled in the wind, the California Mining Company cannon had blasted out a salute. The cheering had been appropriately loud, and had been carried by the warm breeze all the way into town.

Two days later the sight of the flag upon the mountain brought a smile to many a citizen as they had turned out to watch the annual Fourth of July parade. Milk wagons full of ice to refresh the participants had lined up, and the parade started. It had traveled the traditional route, first along "B" Street to the junction with south "C" Street on the Divide, then down "C" Street to Carson where it headed back up to "B" Street and over to Piper's Opera House.

Behind the brass bands had traveled the decorated wagons. One of the most popular had been the one carrying a girl dressed as the Goddess of Liberty, surrounded by young girls in crisp white dresses who giggled while waving to the crowd. Following that came the fancy uniforms of the Emmett Guard in bright green, the Washingtons in red, the Nationals in blue, and the Masons dripping with gold braid. Next, there were men pulling cannons and others with rifles on their shoulders, following in precise formations.

The crowd had applauded sedately at the approach of a long line of Piutes with colorfully painted faces and a scarcity of clothing, later commented upon by the newspapers. Although stoic in their demeanor, every one of them had become a little less so once they spotted the tables of refreshments meant for the participants. In the past they had been led by Captain Bob on a mule so small that he had to bend his legs so his feet didn't scrape on the ground. But he had died in February from pneumonia, some Piutes saying it was because he had chosen to live in a white man's wooden shack instead of a more typical Piute wikiup.

At the very end of the parade had walked Mr. Gilrooney, one of the town scavengers. He was accompanied by his popular, exotically dressed dogs. Some people later claimed that he, or maybe his dogs, had received the loudest of the crowd's cheers.

Helene brought Lucy's focus back to the subject of hiking up the mountain. "I hear there's an incredible view of the town and beyond from up there, after you get up above the homes on the lower reaches of it. You have sturdy boots with flat heels, don't you?"

"Yes. I also have a split riding skirt that would be good for such activity."

"Me, too. The shorter length will make hiking much easier. Let's plan on starting out tomorrow morning about seven while it's still cool."

The climb was less arduous than Lucy had anticipated, having developed more stamina than she had realized since moving to Virginia City. They chose a route that avoided the reservoirs constructed after the big fire of '75, with its system of mains and hydrants that now protected the town, and filled each winter from the deep snows and rains. During the summer, water could be piped from Lake Tahoe.

After passing several spur paths to old abandoned coyote mines, they chased several of the free-roaming goats off their path, and kept a wary eye on two hogs that were rooting around under some brush. This domestic wildlife was common around the town, even though that April an ordinance had been passed prohibiting "hogs and goats from running at large". Dogs were also supposed to be licensed and tagged, although many were allowed to roam free. However, they were summarily killed if they became a nuisance to horses.

The view was indeed wonderful, even though they had not gone but half way up. While catching their breath, the two women arranged themselves to take it in. They looked out over the buildings and lines of streets, capable now of seeing it all within the broader scope of the town. Along with the movement of people, wagons, and the train pulling out of the depot, they could see major buildings such as the hospital, the Fourth Ward School, and the tall spire of St. Mary in the Mountains church.

Past the huge waste dumps and piles of tailings brought up from the mines, they could see the famous Six Mile Canyon and the young trees that Nature was bringing forth to fill the barrenness after years of wood harvesting. The canyon traveled down from the base of Mt. Davidson, which the old timers still called Sun Mountain, passed Dayton, and ended up at the Carson River. Lucy reminded herself that it had been near this canyon that gold had first been discovered back in 1859, with the miners working their way from there to where now Virginia City held court.

Looking down at the Ophir Mine that had reigned supreme for so long, Lucy tried to imagine that summer of 1859 when two Irish placer miners, O'Riley and McLaughlin, had dug down several feet and found a mass of dark blue, decomposed silver ore. Not knowing what it was, they had washed it in the hopes of finding what gold it might contain. What they found beneath was a thick deposit of gold dust. They washed pans of it until it was too dark to see what they were doing.

Soon after that, cagey and greedy "Old Pancake" Comstock had come across the site, and seeing the men's gold dust, had immediately claimed that they were on his property and using his water. Having his whopping lie received well by the two men, Comstock played magnanimous and demanded only part of the claim for himself and his partners. The men agreed in order to avoid trouble, not only with this belligerent man and his partners, but what passed as the law. Besides, they had been making only about $2 a day in gold dust, and now were taking out $1,000 a day. O'Riley, McLaughlin, Comstock, E. Penrod and J. A. "Kentuck" Osborne agreed to split the 1,400 feet of ground on the lead, with Comstock and Penrod taking an additional 100 feet as a fee for water access to "their stream". Those 100 feet became known as the Spanish Mine; the area becoming known as Spanish Ravine. And eventually Comstock's sixth interest, which he sold early for a pittance, became the great Ophir Mine.

Around that time, James "Ole Virginy" Finney, actually a young man, lived and drank in the camp. After killing a man in California, he had changed his name from Fennimore to Finney, stuffed a gun in one pocket and a bottle in another, and fled to Washoe to make his fortune. One day he dropped and broke his bottle of whisky, and always good for a joke, he declared to those around him, "I baptize this ground Virginia." Those in the rough mining camp of shacks, tents, muddy streets, and basic stone arrastras had fallen in with the irony of calling itself the grand name of Virginia *City*.

Lucy smiled, recalling how none of those men had known the identity of the sticky blue sand. It was all about the gold for them. In time, they learned that the gold was mixed in with a rich type of silver sulfide that would yield thousands of dollars in gold and silver per ton. Those who joined them on the mountain would discover that the lode of silver ore continued about three miles long and a hundred feet wide at its broadest point, running north and south beneath the base of Mt. Davidson. Virginia City would develop at the northern end and Gold Hill at the southern end. It wasn't long before the little camps of Virginia City, Gold Hill, Silver City and American Flat merged into what was referred to as "the Comstock".

Although Lucy and Helene weren't all the way to the top of the 1,570-foot mountain, they were high enough above the town to give them a thought-provoking perspective. Helene broke the silence, more solemn than Lucy had ever seen her. "Do you think this is the way God looks down on the whole world?"

Lucy took her question seriously. "I don't know. I do know this is our world, and I'm a little humbled by all that has happened here since '59."

"And there's not only what we can see, but all that's underground that we can't see."

"Yes, a whole other world of shafts, tunnels, and machinery with hundreds of men at work among it all."

"My husband says the underground even has its own weather. He says that once the men are up and in the changing room getting ready to go home, as soon as they're in clean clothes with their faces washed and the dirt dug from under their nails, it's as though they've also changed into another part of themselves."

"From underground moles to men once again in touch with their human selves?"

Lucy turned around, slowly and carefully making her way back to the chaotic civilization that was now her home. She was eager to write to Roger and tell him of her day's adventure. At the same time, she tried not to wonder why she had seldom heard from him, and then only short notes.

Regardless of what Roger had said in his last letter, in one of her letters to him she had made a vague suggestion that she could come for a visit. A short note was the quickest response she had ever received from him. In it, Roger explained that the town was too chaotic right then with its rapid growth, over-crowding, and level of violence, not to mention a virulent form of pneumonia plaguing the town. He also told her that stages were being robbed with alarming regularity, and therefore travel was dangerous. He didn't mention that only the bullion boxes were ever taken, and passengers seldom bothered. But Lucy got the point and didn't mention a visit again in any of her future letters to him.

Lucy already knew most of what Roger had described, as Bodie happenings were reported regularly in all the newspapers. It was a town bursting at the seams with new vitality and much accompanying rowdiness. Although Lucy was somewhat disappointed, she didn't allow herself to take his words personally. As mothers are so good at doing, she rationalized her son's actions. She told herself that he was learning new things in a new and wild town, and that there was probably a lot for him to deal with at present. Although she was correct, it would be a few more months before she would know the actual reason why Roger didn't want his mother to join him in Bodie.

Early summer of 1880 arrived in Virginia City with wild flowers coloring hillsides and the planning of parties underway. But the winter had been a severe one in Bodie and there were still piles of slushy snow outside the window of Roger's hotel in Bodie. At the end of January, the temperature had gotten down to 26 degrees below zero, and wood reserves at some of the mines had been depleted so that they had to shut down. Only now, with the roads to the wood reserves open, was wood arriving in any quantity.

Roger wasn't expected at work until late afternoon, so he was spending the morning in his room at the Standard Lodging House, reading newspapers and drinking copious amounts of coffee. He had delivered breakfast to the man in the room next to his, where the man was recovering from a long illness. The man had come close to death a year ago when he had arrived in town during an outbreak of various forms of pneumonia. He had slowly recovered only because of Roger's assistance and willingness to pay for a good doctor. But as fond as he was of the man, Roger recognized that they both needed time on their own, especially now that the man was almost fully recovered.

Roger tossed aside the last of the newspapers and picked up one of his mother's letters, sent almost a year earlier. He had saved all her letters, as they made him feel connected to her. He had never anticipated being separated from her for so long, or that he would miss her as much as he did. Reading her letters, he could hear her voice in his mind, and it brought him comfort. His life had taken some dramatic and unexpected turns since his arrival in Bodie, much of it exceedingly difficult, but he could share none of it with Lucy. Only the fact that he could eventually do so kept any guilt at bay. He focused on the letter in his hands, the paper beginning to yellow, and worn along the creases as testament to how often he had read it.

My dearest Roger,   *Summer, 1879*

My thoughts often return to the hike up Mt. Davidson with Helene. As I stood there, I found myself in a contemplative mood. The breeze was cool on the dampness of my face, the smell of sage not overly pungent, and I was surprised at how pleasant was the moment. I was especially grateful for the quiet that Helene was also enjoying, so there was no talking between us to disturb our thoughts. Oh, we could still hear the thump of the stamps, but it was wonderfully less than usual.

Men have been trying from the beginning to force themselves upon this region; this land of alkaline dust, rocky outcroppings, and acres of sagebrush. No matter from what country they originated, those searching for gold brought with them their religious beliefs, their food, and their customs. And for a time, as they all quested after rich strikes back in 1859, they fit together well, each supporting the other. But then, with enough time having passed for businesses to get established as families arrived, their focus shifted away from mere survival.

It's as though they remembered they were social animals and must therefore arrange themselves according to those who have, and those who work for those who have. In this process they began making a distinction between "foreign" and "American born", and "white" from "others". This reminded me of those who came from England to America to form the original colonies. They wanted freedom from prejudices they perceived as set against them. But once settled in what is now our East, they themselves eventually became bogged down in their prejudices about those among them who thought differently. Over a century later, when they came West, they were still clinging to those "us and them" attitudes. Not to mention their opinions of who was deserving of basic rights, and who was not.

What could have been a unique experiment in cooperative co-existence in this special town, became just another city bound by prejudices handed down from parent to child for generations. It will probably take another hundred years for such attitudes to have changed.

At the same time that all this was passing through my mind, I could see church spires within the town that reach up to heaven in celebration of a God who those churches declare loves all his children. We could also see a parade marching through town, some group celebrating an event in their culture that is special to them. And, as always, it was being enjoyed by everyone in town; for a few minutes no one caring about anything other than an excuse to enjoy the moment, any food offered, and the opportunity to make a lot of noise.

Meanwhile, beyond the downtown with its dramas of cultural clashes and joyful celebrations, lay man's greatest imprint of his power; the spread of buildings composing mills, hoisting works, pump houses, warehouses, changing rooms, and offices. And, out of sight, the even greater evidence of man's power; miles of underground shafts and tunnels on multiple levels exposing riches to hard-working miners so that wealthy owners can become even richer.

Looking to the mines occupying the valley just beyond the town to the east, I could see steam rising from dozens of tall black smokestacks that fill the view, proclaiming the never-ceasing efforts of those working below. And between the mounds of tailings and ponds of waste water, lay piles of timber cut at Lake Tahoe. It stands ready as replacement for the rotting square-sets below ground that keep the tunnels from caving in on themselves, and which are right under our feet as we go about our daily business.

Lifting my eyes from the town's crowded streets and mines toward the far view, my whole sense changed. Acting as a calming to all the over-heated vibrancy of the town's busy industry, rises lines of misty blue and green mountain ranges standing one behind the other as a reminder of other canyons and ravines that can also be explored. Of course, some of them have been, but I wonder if there are not still undiscovered riches somewhere in these alluring ranges.

As Helene and I returned to town, the wind came up, although not so strong that it caused a problem for us. Mother Nature has remained silent too long, and any day now she will sigh with disdain in a breath so powerful that we call it a zephyr wind. But Nature presses back in other ways that we cannot ignore. Her hot breath reaches down into the mines and combines with the activity there to create heat so intense that the miners do much of their work practically naked, having to douse themselves with water every half hour in order to survive. Of course, the heat above isn't much better in the middle of summer, depleting quickly the past winter's ice cut from the frozen rivers and packed in sawdust in ice-houses. Then, just to prove that Mother Nature has a sense of humor, she turns a cold shoulder to the town and buries us in snow so deep that passes are blocked.

This is the conflict that continually confronts those who think they can, without consequences, steal the mineral wealth that has lain dormant for millions of years within Mother Nature's bosom. People think of the gold and silver as inexhaustible, and available to them for as long as they have the willingness to sacrifice themselves and the earth's resources. But Nature, and many a miner with gray in his hair, knows otherwise.

We are seeing families leaving town, jobs the men thought secure having been lost from those mines that are slowing production. The money they had been spending at businesses and saloons is also reduced, so some of the smaller *of these are closing. Other businesses are cutting back in various ways, but are at least staying open. We are an economy with one single industry, and that is mining. But we on the Comstock have seen borrasca before, and it is always followed by bonanza. One of these mines will hit a lead, and the economy will be back with a flourish. We must not forget that in the fall of '77, the Ophir miners discovered a small but rich vein at the 1,000-foot level. It has yielded 20,000 tons valued at $66 each ton.*

Through all the ups and downs of the Comstock, and even considering its productive contribution to the country during the war, I sometimes think we are forgetting the devastation of this success on the Washo and Piute people. When gold was discovered in Six Mile Canyon back in '59, in that moment began a massive change to their way of life. And yet, they have not lost their perspective of life, one Piute man responding to hearing me complain about the wind with, "It was here thousands of years before any of us." I felt humbled by the meaning back of his words. It would be a safe bet that not one man coming to this area back in '59 or after spent a single second thinking about those they were displacing, or at least impacting.

Denial or justification of the issue has become so common that if I raise the subject, I get little more than a shake of the head in mock regret. Worse yet is when someone makes a comment about how much better off the Indians across the nation are when on a reservation, ignoring completely how offended they would be if told they could not live where their family had been established for generations. But always the topic is dismissed as quickly as possible. And, in order not to ostracize myself from society, I shamefully say nothing more.

The other day, while at tea in a friend's house, one of the women present stumbled onto the subject when she commented that her son came home with two arrow points made from broken bottle glass. This brought up the acknowledgement that the Washo and Piute people have adapted to the changes to their ancestral grounds caused by the area's development. For instance, they wear a combination of white people's clothing along with rabbit skin vests and beads. Or they may wear a white man's hat, but their faces are still painted. Many people say it is a testament to how flexible they are, and have always had to be in order to survive. This may be true, but I also think that their appearance of adapting is mixed with a rebellious defiance by not completely accepting the invaders' way of life.

If I am in an oddly philosophical mood, attribute it to a lingering consequence of the hike up the mountain. It has allowed me to see many things more objectively than I have in the past, including the overall pattern of my life. And for some reason I cannot explain, I feel encouraged about the future.

I look forward to hearing from you soon.

Your loving mother

Even though Roger understood why, he still regretted not having written more often. He usually included a description of an event, details of Bodie's growing wealth, or an anecdote about some prominent individual. He especially made sure to reassure her about his health, considering the reports in the newspapers about the spread of various diseases in Bodie, especially a pernicious form of pneumonia.

He picked up a letter received from Lucy during the late summer of '79. It always made him smile when he read it, acting as a tonic to his occasional dark moods. Sometimes, his life in Bodie left him feeling a little overwhelmed. He would have loved talking to Lucy about it, but that just wasn't possible right then. Still, he had her news-filled letters that always left him feeling better, and he treasured every one of them.

My dearest son,   *June, 1879*

When Helene told me that a circus was coming to town, I got all excited. Last year's circus was such great fun. This one wasn't quite as good, but it had its moments.

They located the tents at the far east end of Washington Street in the flattest part of the field there. The circus train stopped at the old depot near the Gould and Curry Works and unloaded the big wagons, hauling them to the field from there.

The Great Arabian Circus had some animals, but not as many as last year's circus, brought here by Adam Forepaugh. But there were some fine horses that did tricks, and they sent up a big balloon. It was filled near the Obiston shaft, with many men volunteering to help with it. Lots of young boys tried to get ahold of the ropes, so they could brag about it to others, and the roustabouts had a hard time keeping them away. The balloonist wore shiny blue tights that glittered in the sun, and he swung from a trapeze hanging from the balloon as it rose up. It didn't stay up for long, coming down near the Mint Mine. Very exciting, and sales of tickets to the main event sold quickly after that. Unfortunately, after the circus moved on to Carson City, the trapeze broke during a performance, and the artist plummeted to his death.

Always, your loving mother

CHAPTER 14

1879 – 1880

At the end of September, Roger wrote to his mother, pressed by emotions he was finding difficult to confront, much less express.

Hello Mother,   *September, 1879*

I hope this finds you in good health, and not too bothered by the heat of summer. I can't believe I've been here a year, but not sure if it seems longer or shorter. There is always a lot happening in Bodie, but one thing that has taken place is haunting me. By the time you get this letter you may have heard something about it. and are feeling your own reaction.

You once told me about your time as a young girl in the California gold rush, when you and Freda lived in Placerville at its very beginning. Unlike the Placerville in which we lived when I was a child, it was at its beginning just a mining camp of log cabins, tents, and muddy paths between. Freda told me once about how you and she shared a small cabin with a pretty French woman called Eleanor Dumont, who dealt cards at a gambling hall.

From what I have been told, years later she was a decent gambler and only sometimes had to resort to selling her favors. She came here to Bodie just before I did, and dealt cards. But she also gambled her own money. When I realized that the woman people were calling Madame Moustache was the same woman Freda had described to me, I introduced myself to her. She was delighted to meet me, and asked about you and Freda. Her beauty was considerably faded, but I could tell that at one time she must have been quite lovely. Her stories of her time during the rush, like yours, captivated me. I bought her dinner, and we promised to meet again soon. But we didn't.

Earlier this month she showed up at my faro table, greeting me with a smile and a wink. She quickly worked her way through $300 worth of coin, winning a little of it back, but then losing it all. I could do or say nothing as her luck turned against her. When all her money was gone, she simply walked out into the night. The next morning, she was found on the road to Bridgeport by a sheepherder grazing his flock in one of the small meadows along the road. She had swallowed a bottle of morphine and was dead.

I feel that I should have gone after her. Maybe I could have helped her in some way. But I was in the middle of a game, with piles of coin on the table, and I just couldn't leave right then. I hope this news, if you are not already aware of it, does not overly disturb you.

Lucy had in fact read about it in the newspaper, and it had brought on the sadness of memories long buried and not particularly welcome. Freda had been closer in age to Eleanor, and had formed a special bond with her. But Lucy had been fond of the outgoing French woman, and was sorry to hear of her unfortunate fate.

Roger had gone on to write about other events in Bodie that he thought Lucy would find interesting. Also, in an effort to keep her from coming to visit him, he began writing more often than he had previously. In the winter of '79, just before the roads closed, he had sent her a long letter with lots of stories about Bodie. He had even included clippings from newspapers. He ended each letter by assuring her that he was doing well, and that he still loved his job, proclaiming Mr. Wagner the best of employers. The receipt of these letters had only increased Lucy's desire to be in communication with her son, so she too wrote often. He picked up one of those letters, received in March of '80 when the mail could get through once again.

Dearest Roger,   *December, 1879*

I rode Diamond over the Divide down to Gold Hill last month. I wanted to see my friend Margaret. She runs the Comstock Hotel on Main Street, as I'm sure you remember. I've been in better kept hotels, but she is a charming woman and has suffered much criticism from those who judge her harshly for divorcing her good-for-nothing husband. Some women think she should have left the area to avoid the shame of it. Instead, she has stayed to run the family hotel all by herself. She doesn't serve food at her hotel, so we had a delightful lunch at the Vesey Hotel, where the food is always good. We chatted like gossipy school girls throughout. Several of Margaret's friends joined us for tea late afternoon. I rejected her invite to spend the night and rode home, reaching the stable just before dark.

As I walked up Taylor on my way home, I passed a man standing on the corner of "E" and Taylor Streets. He wore a white drape over his head with holes cut out for the eyes, so that I couldn't see any part of his head. I looked further up the hill and saw another just like him on the corner of "D" Street and Taylor. They both had shotguns raised up across their bodies, and stood as still as statues. I knew from experience that there would be other men posted on other corners of the block.

As I paused near the first of these men to catch my breath, I felt the man's eyes watching me through the eye holes in the mask. I boldly asked, using the common code words, "Someone get a ticket to leave?"

The man only grunted before saying, "Just keep going, ma'am."

I nodded and picked up my pace until well past the next corner, where the similarly dressed man with a similar shot gun silently watched me pass. But then a door opened behind him and a man with a long gray beard peeked out. Immediately, the masked man barked at him. "If you open that door again, I'll blow your damn head off!" The door slammed shut, and I heard a low chuckle from behind the mask.

It was useless to think that there would be an explanation in the newspapers the next day, as the work of "the committee" always remains unknown. They haven't been seen for several years, so I'm told, so whoever had incurred their wrath must have done something they felt the law would not punish. Just as I reached the house, I heard the boom of a small cannon, and knew that the masked men would disappear within minutes. And I knew, too, that in the morning the town would have one less man among us. Whether he had been banished, would be found hanging with a rope around his neck, or was dead at the bottom of an abandoned shaft, would probably never be known. But one thing I do know. They should either wear gloves or remove their rings, because I recognized the first man from a time when he had been holding cards at my table.

The fruit trees in the backyard are resting now after producing a wonderful crop for us this year. The apples were especially nice, and are stored away for enjoyment throughout the winter. Kathryn and I planted some tulip bulbs along the fence out front and look forward to seeing them in the spring. That was the same day that she and I decided to go out to the baseball field near the gas works to watch a game between our Bonanza team and the Gold Hill Actives. We won 9 to 7.

Kathryn and I decided to expand the chicken coop. Don't ever tell me a woman can't smack a few nails with a hammer! It did take both of us to do the job, and most of the day at that, but we got it done and now have four more laying hens comfortably at home and producing well. Our coop isn't as large as many of the others around town, but it serves our purposes.

I attended an incredible dance party this summer. The owners of the New York Mine in Gold Hill decided to hold a party underground in their mine, in a large chamber of it. There were tables of food and drink, and a small band. There were 100 of us individually invited, and as we arrived at the hoist works, we were brought to a cage that has lowered hundreds of miners down to their jobs with a swiftness that has become legendary. We, however, were lowered at an unusually respectful speed. The women had been told not to wear hoops or crinolines under dresses, and we understood why once we were being lowered on the narrow platform.

We were led along a tunnel a short way, none of us speaking. The only sound was the crunch of gravel underfoot and the heavy breathing of the older party-goers. We passed some tools leaning against the wall where they had been left at the end of a shift; a long piece of metal with a flattened tip called a spoon that the miners use to scoop out debris from a drilled hole, and several very long sticks used as tamping rods to push the dynamite charges deeper into those drilled holes. A couple of lidded lunch buckets were with the tools, and the thought occurred to me that their owners would be wanting them in the morning.

All the while I was down there, it was difficult not to think about the many yards of rock and dirt and timbering above the ceiling of our tunnel. The only light was from the lanterns carried by our chaperones and candles in iron holders embedded in the walls. These depths were never intended for man or beast, and yet here we were not only intruding into it, but planning on dancing within it. The mineral gods must have been laughing as the music echoed off the walls, flattening the sound of it somewhat. It only reminded us that we were underground, although I doubt anyone needed such a reminder.

We ate, drank and danced until well after midnight, and then were taken back up a few at a time. I bet the hoist engineer slept well after that night, and I hope someone brought him some of the food we enjoyed as a reward for his efforts. I must admit that I was very grateful to be once again above ground, but it had been an unusual and memorable evening.

I met an interesting woman the other day. I had heard her name mentioned by some women at a nearby table while at breakfast at a café. So when the opportunity arose, I introduced myself to her. You may have heard of her yourself. Her name is Cad Thompson.

Roger, when first reading the letter, had at this point been smoking a cigar, and had choked rather badly for several moments. Would his mother ever cease amazing him? He had turned to the next page of her letter with his breathing erratic. Lucy would have loved his reaction, knowing that there would certainly be one.

Yes, dear, I know what she does. She owns The Brick, a lovely two-story brick house on the corner of "D" Street and Sutton. Her girls live in the basement rooms, but they freely use the parlor (which has a piano and lace curtains), with the five upstairs bedrooms used for business. It's probably the most prestigious brothel in town, although she considers herself partially retired. We fell into conversation, and after I mentioned that I had for a short time been a cook in a good parlor house in Nevada City during the rush, she relaxed considerably. At that point, I could detect the Irish accent that she has tried so hard to overcome.

She has been in Virginia City since the mid-1860's, probably arriving around the same time as Dolly and Robert in Carson. She's a striking woman. Lots of red hair and beautiful clothes. I enjoyed listening to her description of what it had been like during the big fire in '75, and how she had rebuilt her house after that. Most of the more respectable "houses" on "D" Street that had been destroyed moved their business to the Barbary Coast area while rebuilding commenced, but then moved back to "D" Street as soon as they could. They didn't want to become associated with that "low-class area", as Cad called it. There is evidently a very strong sense of hierarchy among the fair but frail.

What Lucy did not relate to Roger was the conversation that she had overheard in the café, wherein Cad Thompson had been mentioned. The trio of ladies at the next table, in keeping with what was always of great importance to the women of Virginia City, had been attired in fashionable dresses and bonnets of the latest style. However, it had not been the women's appearance that had attracted Lucy's attention, but rather their conversation as they lingered at their table.

Cad Thompson's name came up, although Lucy missed the context in which it had. Lucy was surprised to hear one of the women boldly state, "My husband was one of the men who put out the hay fire at her place." There had been expected understanding imbued into her words "the fire", and indeed all the women had nodded in acknowledgement of what was meant. This is what had attracted Lucy's attention to them, as it was not the big fire of '75 that was meant.

"Oh, I remember that," one of the women had exclaimed. "It was back in the fall of '66. Some men were upset because she was acquitted of battery against one of her girls. So they set fire to some straw bales in front of her place. The men didn't mean for it to happen, but the fire spread to the house, and a fire engine came to put it out. They say it made a mess, what with all the water they pumped inside." She lowered her voice. "I thought it a bit unfair, since the accusation that had originally angered everyone was never proved."

Another of the women snorted, although in a very lady-like manner. "If they thought they were going to wash out the evil there, it didn't work. She not only rebuilt The Brick, she built two more such places."

Shaking her head to the disruption of her large bonnet, another woman had changed the direction of the conversation. "The Thompson woman is a madam. That's worse than that Julia Bulette loose woman that got herself murdered back in '67. She was just one of many on her own, even if talked about now."

"Oh, she wasn't so much." It was a casual comment by one of the women who seldom spoke. "Just another trollop popular with one of the engine companies, especially Captain Peasley who got himself killed the year before her."

"She did nurse some of the men when they were ill, and she gave money to some of the charities. But, of course, such women as they are all do that when they're flush."

"Until she was killed so brutally by a man who robbed her, she was just one of a dozen of her profession. Like so many of them, she died in debt and unwell."

"She lived longer than some of them, being 28 when she was killed."

"Did you read in the paper what they inventoried in her cabin? She didn't have much jewelry, but a policeman said she had lots of dresses. Oddly, though, only one pair of shoes and one pair of slippers."

"I'm told she had some lovely furniture pieces in her cabin." This had been uttered with breathy awe by the youngest among them, and it brought all eyes to stare at her.

"It's called a crib, dear, and it was rented. Didn't even have a kitchen, although it had two rooms, which is larger than some of them." She had looked around at her friends who were trying to hold back a smile. "Or so I'm told."

"Well, her mahogany bedstead was one thing that I'd love to have." The women had looked askance at the speaker who dared mention a bed belonging to a prostitute. Seeing this, she had quickly added, "Although I'd rather have the carved black-walnut set that was in her parlor. Besides the sofa, there were two rocking chairs that would do on my porch." Lucy noted that the women appeared to find that acceptable.

"Well, a lot has been made about her since then."

"Probably because some people still aren't sure that John Millian was her killer."

"I met him once. He worked out at Hall's Pioneer Laundry north of town, the big steam plant that washes the linens for hotels and restaurants. He seemed a rather bland fellow."

"I thought him quite personable. A few of my friends and I brought him cookies while he was in jail. He said there were other men involved, and that he wasn't the one who actually did the killing."

"Maybe, but he was the only one they had for their revenge. His hanging certainly drew a big crowd."

"Hangings always do."

On that note of macabre finality, the women had left the restaurant. And Lucy had been left to ponder the oddity of human nature.

Lucy hosted Cad in her home twice. Her new friend, realizing why Lucy might not want to be seen entering The Brick, didn't offer to reciprocate.

Lucy told Cad about her time in Nevada City while still in her teens, and Cad told Lucy about her friendship with Rosa May, one of her girls of whom she was particularly fond. She also talked about her twenty-two year old son, Henry, who had committed suicide the previous year. Maybe it was because Lucy had a son about the same age that Cad opened up to her, because she certainly didn't talk about it to many others.

After each visit, Lucy felt a good degree of conflict within herself. She liked the woman, and admired her business acumen and sense of humor, but in principle she was against the exploitation of vulnerable women. On the other hand, such work was sometimes the only recourse for women who didn't know any other way to survive. Cad's place never saw the suicide of any of her girls, and The Brick was known for its lack of violent confrontations.

The only exception was the time a police officer had to shoot Cad's lover, John Dalton. He had his gun pointed at Cad and was threatening her, so the officer had no choice. This was, however, something Lucy did not hear about from Cad, but rather from Helene. Cad was tough yet compassionate, strict yet reasonable, and donated freely to many charities that helped the needy survive the harsh winters. Feeling a little disloyal, Lucy nevertheless kept her friendship with Cad to herself, and didn't burden Roger or Helene with the details of it.

On a particularly windy day, Lucy walked home from the post office after receiving a message that there was a letter for her at *will call*. She held in her hands a plain envelope, with the cancellation so smudged that she couldn't tell where it had originated. Once home, she slit open the envelope and pulled out a letter, the handwriting immediately recognized. Lucy was not the swooning type, but that moment almost brought her to that point.

Dear Lucy,

So much time has passed, with my letter sent to you in Placerville in '75 being returned after several months. I now know where you are only because Jane was told about you by a new acquaintance who recently came to our town from Virginia City. What caught Jane's attention was this husband of a friend talking about a young gambler named Roger that he claimed the men of Virginia City were missing now that he has gone to Bodie. The man said that the gambler's mother had stayed in town and continues to deal cards. When Jane inquired, and was told that the man only knew the woman dealer by the name Lucy, she was sure we had discovered your whereabouts.

Remembering back to the fall of '62, when we left Placerville, it seems like several lifetimes ago. We felt then that we had no choice about leaving, after all that had happened that summer. I'm sure Placerville was not sorry to see us go. And, frankly, we were not sorry to leave behind most of the people there. But that does not mean we did it without tears.

Jane and I tried not to show our sadness when we left, as Robert was having enough to deal with just getting us out onto the Placerville Road. I never expected such crowds on the road and at the stations along the way. When you left in '75, I doubt you saw anything near what surrounded us all the way until we cut off south to Markleeville. Because of my letters, you know what occurred in the years that followed.

Since leaving Carson City, we have been living in the Owens River Valley, in a small town called Lone Pine near the Owens Lake. Robert has found work at a smelting facility back of the lake near Swansea, coming home to us only every other week for three days. It would be for longer at a time if it didn't take most of a day to get here through the deep sand and over the rickety bridge spanning the river where it flows into the lake. And then most of a day to get back, because he uses our wagon so he can take back supplies for the men. Otherwise, he could ride the sixteen miles here on his horse in much less time.

Before that, back in '76, he helped build kilns for Colonel Stevens in a sandy wash on the edge of the Owens Lake. They first had to make the 8" by 24" adobe bricks for the bee-hive shaped kilns that are 20 by 20 feet. The kilns are used to make charcoal for use at the Coso and Darwin District mines that are coming to life now that the Cerro Gordo mines are played out.

Lone Pine is rebuilt, and much nicer, after the devastating effects of the March 26, 1872, earthquake. From the main road north of town, one can see in several places a giant scar where the top half of a large hill has been set back from the lower half. There are several of these places. The earthquake fault cuts across the southwest corner of Mr. Harvey's ranch, and right past where the town buried over a dozen of those killed that night. Mr. Harvey gave the town a small plot of land up on a hill for the burials, now called Harvey Hill, and he is now talking about giving several acres east of it to the town for a cemetery to be run by the Knights of Pythias group.

As you can tell, I am very proud of where we are. There is some mining still going on, although the last coach out of Cerro Gordo was in April of '78. But now there is a lot of agriculture around the town, herds of cattle, dairies, grape vines, and bee hives; all supporting a proudly self-sufficient community. Much of what we have is sent to Los Angeles, and even points north as far as Bodie and Aurora.

I have made some wonderful friends here, especially a French lady, Mrs. Maysan, whose family owns a merchandise store. And Mrs. Edwards, who has a store and a nice home just off the plaza at the north end of town. And I have been taught much about planting a vegetable garden by Anne Kennedy, who owns a lovely boarding house at the south end of town. She had a young lady boarding with her, but she has married and moved to Bodie. I think her name was Emily.

Through all the years since last we were together, I have learned many important lessons. I now realize that we're not always going to get what we desire in this life. But we <u>can</u> make the most of whatever we <u>are</u> given, and that is our choice. We can, however, be sure that our choices will start us down the path to another adventure. Because that's what life is; a series of adventures, some small and some big. I also now realize that we develop great strength of character from both, if we're paying attention, and are willing to learn.

It is my hope that this letter will find its way to you, even though the best I can do is to address it to "general delivery". If you are well-known enough, hopefully someone will let you know you have a letter waiting. If I cannot have your hand to hold, maybe I can yet have your words to read.

Your loving friend,
Dolly

Noting the return address at the bottom of the letter, Lucy immediately seated herself at her writing table, spending the remaining daylight hours filling pages with the details of her life after leaving Placerville. It was what she knew Dolly would want. She only stopped once to blow her nose, as emotions of relief and joy overcame her.

Lucy could hardly wait to write Roger with the news of Dolly. Yet that took up only part of the next letter to him. Being in one of her philosophical moods, she decided to tell Roger of having met Edward Lovejoy. Arriving in Virginia City only two years before, he had been a newspaper editor and a judge in Trinity County, California. He was also known for writing editorials defending the rights of Chinese immigrants and African Americans.

He is the son of the famous Elijah Lovejoy who was killed in 1837 while trying to stop the destruction of his abolitionist newspaper in Illinois. I remember reading that President John Quincy Adams called him the first martyr to the freedom of the press. His son, our Edward, along with his wife Julia, came to California in 1856, and they now reside with us in the anonymity that we so ably provide. They call us the pro-Union West, and thus Edward could take advantage of his famous heritage if he chose, but he does not. Nevertheless, he does write editorials that champion the common man and the decency to which we can all aspire.

I've been thinking about your father a lot lately. Not in any maudlin way, but rather recalling some of the wonderful times we had together. It has brought me great comfort.

> *With love,*
> *Lucy*

The sky was just suggesting sun-up in the summer of 1880, but Lucy couldn't sleep and was walking down "C" Street, waiting for a café to open its doors. The hollow thud of her shoes on the boards of the sidewalk and the rustle of her silk dress were the only sounds, usually lost amid the noisy crowds on the street or the wind rocking signs outside saloons and stores. Of course, although fewer mines were active now, there was still the sound of the stamps. But that was so normal as to go unnoticed by those who had lived there for some while.

Lucy's attention was suddenly diverted to a man across the street as he tripped on a board. She chuckled to herself as she recalled a lawsuit once brought by a man injured when tripping on an uneven board outside a business. The judge ruled on the man's behalf, even though the business owner had pointed out that the man had been drunk. The judge declared that a drunk deserved the use of safe sidewalks as much as anyone else, and needed them even more.

But such peace never lasts long in a mining town, and the streets came to life with a burst of energy. The doors of businesses and saloons were folded back, heavy keys banged against the iron of the bank doors, wooden shutters covering windows were removed, people walked out onto upstairs verandas, and watering wagons passed down side streets. Soon children were making their way to school, and when the shift whistle blasted from the east, miners in heavy boots and carrying lunch buckets hurried to and from work.

Lucy looked around at the town she had grown to love, having recently felt its heartbeat change from the exuberance of prolific output to that of a combination of desperation and faith. For herself, she wasn't worried. There would always be men wanting to gamble, and as long as she could maintain her looks, or at least her ability to charm and amuse, she would be able to deal cards. But she did feel concern for those barely able to put food on the table. And thus the reason why she regularly collected unsellable vegetables from the markets and brought them to those in need or to the soup kitchen, along with her homegrown apples.

Two Italian men known as scavengers passed by with their sacks of bottles and pieces of metal. Not far behind them came a Chinese ragpicker with his sack of cloth pieces, both found and donated. They were no doubt headed to Henry Robinson's junkyard on South "I" Street, a friend to the gangs of boys who brought him their finds. They ignored his breath that always smelled of whiskey and onions, because they liked his stories.

Henry was in his mid-fifties, and as was common in Virginia City, he was an immigrant from a country an ocean away; in his case, Austria. He was one of many who served an important part in the economy, as he made available a place where those at the bottom rung of society's ladder could get a financial reward for their scavenging efforts. This also allowed the town the appearance of cleanliness that otherwise would have been a trash-filled, distasteful reminder of the carelessness of those considered their betters.

Lucy offered the men a friendly smile as she passed, commenting, "Lovely morning today." Expecting no reply, she received no more than a quick nod of agreement.

In Bodie, feeling the warmth of the rising sun, Roger was finishing his morning coffee. Still having extra time before going to work, he read again Lucy's most recent letter.

Dearest Roger,   *June, 1880*

I believe I neglected to tell you about seeing former President Grant here in our town last October. He was here with his wife, son and daughter-in-law. The town was decorated with red, white and blue banners strung across the streets, streamers wrapped around posts, bunting hanging from windows, and flags of all sizes fluttering in the breeze anywhere someone could stick one. Little children clutched tiny flags in their hands and many received a smile from the Grant family. Mr. Grant made a short speech at a banquet given in his honor, but was kept moving on a tight schedule, those accompanying him trailing behind.

After touring the Consolidated Virginia and the California mines, Mr. Sutro received the visiting dignitaries at his new house out in Sutro City. They returned to Virginia City through his tunnel, which I think surprised a few people. But they were certainly game for anything presented to them, and they left much good feeling behind. However, someone said that when Mr. Grant emerged from one of the deep mines, his words gave away his true opinion. "That's as close to hell as I ever want to get."

After they left, and thinking about the speeches given by our town's dignitaries, I realized that what these amounted to was bragging about the town's past glories. Even the tour of the mines was about the incredible wealth they had produced in the past. Yes, we are very proud of the Comstock's heritage and contribution to the nation, but what will we become? The mines are playing out, taking out fewer and fewer thousands of tons of valuable ore.

Every week we see the stages leaving with men and women holding one-way tickets, most of them in their late teens and early twenties. Many of these men are heading to your town. It feels like watching our future disappear, leaving behind only the dust kicked up by the stages taking it away. Your newspapers make fun of our decline as Bodie soars to life, but we have lasted 20 years and we are many times larger. Where will Bodie be in 20 years as it enters a new century? Of course, one might well ask, how will both our towns be faring as they enter the century after that? In 120 years, a mining town must surely have grown or be dead, unless some other reason for its existence was found. But what on earth could that be?

Nevertheless, I refuse to believe that Virginia City is just another mining town that will someday be only a name on an old map, with foundations covered by sagebrush and the only sound the howling of coyotes wandering through its deserted streets.

This winter there was much talk about the Virginia and Truckee Railroad ceasing the run to Silver City. They have been tearing up the track used on that spur, the salvage being used for the Carson and Colorado Narrow Gauge. One of the sure signs of our failing economy is that Gold Hill's last two-bit saloon has decided to lower its prices and become a one-bit shebang.

But mining does continue, even processing low-grade ores that at one time would have been considered of no account. Considering the huge dumps to the east of town, this can continue for quite some time. Some say that we should back off the $4 a day wage, but that idea is met with hot refusal by the Miner's Union. And after all, such a good wage has been a point of pride for the town for years, and is what Bodie pays now. Meanwhile, mine owners search for new ways of reaching the trapped ore bodies, insisting that the next big discovery is just around the corner.

Whether that happens or not, I am content to remain right here. I am not waiting for "the next big" ... whatever. I am too busy enjoying the delights of right now. Yet, even as I say that, I have the strangest feeling that something exciting will happen soon.

My thought goes back to what Minnie, the fortune teller, said about taking the long view. Whatever has been leading up to this point in my life, I'm ready for it to reveal itself. Which reminds me that in your last letter, you teased that you were sending my way a great surprise. I eagerly await whatever it is.

> *Much love always,*
> *Lucy*

Roger put his coffee cup on the room's small table and walked to the window where he could look north in the general direction of Virginia City. He missed having the company of the man next door. Nevertheless, he grinned, knowing that by now his surprise had reached his mother, and that she finally had her greatest wish come true. Maybe running away from home five years earlier hadn't been such a bad thing after all.

WHAT'S THERE NOW?

AURORA, NV

4-wheel drive can get you to what is left, which is only a few foundations, the gulches, some rusted bits of equipment, and a rag-tag cemetery.

BODIE, CA (State Historic Park) (Entrance fee)

A good portion of the town is still there, in what is called "arrested decay". The Miner's Union Hall is now the museum, with a book store and tours available in the summer. Entrance fee, good parking with a restroom next to it, but no water or food available in the town. The last three miles up the hill are not paved (so you can get a feel for the way it was), and can be challenging after a rain; but four-wheel drive is not necessary.

BOWERS MANSION, WASHOE, NV (Regional Park)

Tours of the house in the summer (fee charge), but the grounds are open and public events are held there.

BRIDGEPORT, CA

A sweet little town, with awesome views, an historic courthouse and other buildings, and a wonderful drive through pastures up to the twin lakes amid tall timber. The Leavitt House (now the Bridgeport Inn) is a holdover from the early years. Provides good meals and limited lodging. Great museum on the east side of town.

DAYTON, NV

Charm and history all in one small town. Get the history driving tour map and go back in time. Be sure to visit the museum, and see where they kept the camels. Above the town at the back is the cemetery. Just above that, one can still see remnants of the emigrant wagon road through the area, and off to the east, where the original Lincoln Highway once ended.

DEVIL'S GATE

Not far up Gold Canyon, it's the only place where the road cuts between natural, high rock walls. Just south of it, there's a wide spot on one side where one can park and have a look back down toward the Carson River where the mills used to process the gold and silver. Just north as you pass through, and just before arriving at American Flat, was a dangerous point on the road known for its holdups.

DOGTOWN, CA

All gone except for some old ore dumps (mounds of dirt) seen from Hwy. 395, across from the road up to Bodie. Nowhere good to park, and not much left to see if you do. But you can get an idea of the austerity of the area.

EMPIRE CITY, NV

The only thing left is the cemetery. This can be found five miles east of Carson City. Off Highway 50, take Deer Run Road to the first right on Sheep Road. Cemetery is behind the industrial park and the Waste Management Facility where they park the trucks. Look uphill to your left to see the entrance.

Rebecca sold the last of the Ambrose Ranch lands to her son Charles "Ab" Ambrose in 1894. The town lasted into the 1900's, being shown on the 1956 USGS Dayton Quadrangle in 1956.

In 2008 the two-story home of Evan Williams, superintendent of the Mexican Mill, was still standing. It was being used as the offices of a computer company. It was torn down for a modern office building.

Nicholaus Ambrose died at 55 in 1880, and Rebecca at 77 in 1912. At the time of her death, she still lived in Empire City. Both are buried at the cemetery on the hill above the town's location. Their son Charles, born in 1866, lived with his mother on the Ambrose Ranch until her death. He died in 1929, leaving a wife, five sons and three daughters, and is also buried in the Empire Cemetery.

FORT CHURCHILL, NV (State Historic Park) (small entrance fee)

Remnants of the buildings, visitor center with history panoramas and artifacts, restrooms, picnic area, and cemetery.

GOLD HILL, NV

The Vesey House is now the Gold Hill Hotel. A great place to stay, with a wonderful dining room -- and the tiny saloon is still serving. As you drive through town, look UP to the hills that back it, and you'll see that there is still some evidence of when it was a thriving mining boom town. The train depot is visited as part of the Virginia City train tour.

MARKLEEVILLE, CA

An interesting tiny town. A rest stop with food in a beautiful setting. Camping nearby. Monitor Pass between Hwy. 395 and Markleeville is a scenic drive, but make sure your brakes are good.

MONO LAKE, CA (Tufa State National Reserve/State Park)

(North of Lee Vining, site of the Vining Rancho)

A stop well worth the time, with an extensive book store (with maps, t-shirts, souvenirs, etc.), Paiute/Shoshone artifacts and history, a theater showing films of the area's history, wild flower gardens, and incredible views of the lake. Good restrooms and drinking fountains.

Lee Vining, south edge of the lake, has several fun shops and a gas station, decent motels, a good bistro, a bakery that does great sandwiches, and an old-fashioned diner that opens early for breakfast. Museum in the old school house on the backside of town. Don't miss the upside-down house next to it.

MONOVILLE, CA

All gone. In the fall, one can see from Hwy. 395 a blaze of color in what few trees remain in the gulches.

SILVER CITY, NV

Neighbor of Gold Hill, it merges into it. The grave of one of the Groesch brothers is there.

VIRGINIA CITY, NV

Virginia City is for most people just a tourist destination, but a considerable number of people still call it home. It is well worth a visit, especially if you appreciate Victorian architecture, great old churches, lots of museums, views of the old mills and mining equipment, steam train rides, semi-authentic saloons, and walking on wooden sidewalks. With just a little imagination, you can get the feel of the way it was "back then". Look down at the base of some of the front columns on the buildings, and you will see imprints of the foundries that made them, and original building dates. See the Visitor's Center for driving maps, walking maps, lists of food venues, and places to stay.

WOODFORD, CA (rest stop & café on Hwy. 88 near the Hwy. 89 turn off down to Markleeville)

PLEASE NOTE

If you would like to follow the saga of Lucy, Jim and Roger Murphy in the order of the events in their lives, the books by Kathleen Haun featuring these characters should be read in the following order. However, each book stands on its own as a complete story.

The overall arc of time is from 1848 through 1885.

Chasing the Dream
Digging Deeper
Not Enough Forever
No Trees for Shade
Declining Fortunes